PENGUIN B

SAXOPHONE DREAMS

Nicholas Royle was born in Sale in Cheshire in 1963. He has published more than eighty short stories in magazines and anthologies such as *Sunk Island Review*, *aBeSea*, *Technopagan*, *The Science of Sadness*, *Shadows over Innsmouth* and *The Third Alternative*. He edited the award-winning anthologies *Darklands* and *Darklands 2*, and is currently editing two more: *Book of Dreams*, a collection of writers' dreams, and *A Book of Two Halves*, twenty-two original short stories about football. Nicholas Royle lives and works in London. His first novel, *Counterparts*, is also published by Penguin.

Praise for *Counterparts*:

'A really disturbing piece of powerful fiction . . . Royle keeps the pages turning' – Lois Rathbone in *The Times*

'Complex and thrilling right to the very last page' – Maaike Molhuysen in *Strictly*

'The final twist is as deadly as the bitter route it takes to get there. *Counterparts*, Royle's first novel, is a dazzling début' – Jo Knowsley in *Maxim*

'As original a work as anything to be found in the far reaches of the experimental or the post-modern, but without sacrificing lucidity . . . We can only wait to see how his singular talents evolve from here. Who can guess what his second novel will be like? Only one thing is certain: it will be far from ordinary' – Roger Keen in *Critical Wave*

NICHOLAS ROYLE

Saxophone Dreams

PENGUIN BOOKS

PENGUIN BOOKS

Published by the Penguin Group
Penguin Books Ltd, 27 Wrights Lane, London w8 5tz, England
Penguin Books USA Inc., 375 Hudson Street, New York, New York 10014, USA
Penguin Books Australia Ltd, Ringwood, Victoria, Australia
Penguin Books Canada Ltd, 10 Alcorn Avenue, Toronto, Ontario, Canada m4v 3b2
Penguin Books (NZ) Ltd, 182–190 Wairau Road, Auckland 10, New Zealand

Penguin Books Ltd, Registered Offices: Harmondsworth, Middlesex, England

First published 1996
1 3 5 7 9 10 8 6 4 2

Set in 10/12pt Times Monotype
Typeset, from data supplied, by Datix International Limited, Bungay, Suffolk
Printed in England by Clays Ltd, St Ives plc

To the memory of Russell Royle

Acknowledgements

This novel was inspired by the work of Paul Delvaux (1897–1994).

Thanks and acknowledgements are due to the following: the John Richardson Trio and guests, including Alan Barnes, Philip Caramazza, Theo Travis and Eddie Dove, for further inspiration; Kate and Dell for hospital procedure and lots more; Chris Reed and Skipp & Spector for publishing 'De Panne' and 'Saxophone'; Wilma Johnson for arctic images; John Burke, Geraldine and John McCaughrean, Fraser, John and Zoran for locations; the Czech Embassy, David Lillington and Eileen Cadman; friends, chisellers and miserablists; Chris, Clarissa and Fanny; Mum, Dad, Julie, Jo and Simon for everything; and the people of Prishtinë for making me so welcome – Shqiperia!

Contents

PART I

Forbidden Fruit

'I dream reality more than I paint it.'
— Paul Delvaux

The Last Supper

The police around Wenceslas Square appeared to be at a loss as to what to do as more and more people joined the crowd. Jiří Hašek's stomach felt as if it were filled with iron and salt water. The members of the Jazz Group looked around at each other, silently agreeing that this was the place. They reached down and opened their cases. The first three notes from Hašek's alto saxophone, opening the Group's version of 'The Pearls', had the effect of detonating tiny charges behind the policemen's lines. They exchanged nervous glances, tightened grips on truncheons and stood their ground.

As the Jazz Group played 'The Pearls', dissident playwright Václav Havel, at his end of the square, threw down a gauntlet of flowers on the pavement in front of the former carpet shop, now a travel agency advertising holidays to a wide range of destinations from the Low Tatras to the High Tatras. From the far end of the square, where the streets became a maze of alleyways leading into the Old Town, a wave began to rumble and gather momentum. Protesters had begun chanting 'Freedom, freedom, freedom' and 'Palach lives'. Doves were released, flags unfurled to the breeze, placards thrust above heads. At the outer limits of the crowd, normally timid people taunted policemen, who became increasingly agitated, each apparently waiting for orders from no apparent source.

The Jelly Roll Morton tune, disfigured and parodied in its characteristic manner by the Jazz Group, could be heard even over the cries of protest at the Old Town end thanks to the acoustics of the square.

For what followed, the nervous police were as much a catalyst as the musicians of the Jazz Group, and the protesters in the crowd.

*

A day earlier Hašek stood in the hotel bedroom lifting aside the thick brown curtain and looked down into the street. It was a habitual gesture; the possibility of them having been followed to the hotel existed, but it was small. He and the other Group members had all left Prague the previous afternoon for various scattered locations. They had then returned late in the evening and booked into the Ametyst Hotel independently of each other. Their homes had been under surveillance since Christmas and this elaborate exercise was necessary in order to shake off their tails.

Hašek stepped back from the window, having replaced the curtain, and opened his case, which was lying on the bed. Squashed in around the alto saxophone were the few items he had considered essential when he packed to leave his comfortable apartment in the Michle area of the city; he carried his hand towel and toothbrush over to the washbasin. Above the bowl was a small cabinet with mirrored doors. He tugged on the light cord and studied his face in the glass.

His thick, dark hair reached down to his shoulders. Day-old stubble shaded his chin and throat: he had decided not to shave. His deep-set mahogany eyes asked questions his mind didn't know how to answer. He *was* convinced he still wanted to go through with it, but now that the time was drawing nearer, he began to question his motives.

Hašek objected strongly to the harsh, regressive new laws introduced by the government over the past few years. Now all he wanted was an escape route. For too long he had wanted the freedom to play in public the music he chose. As for his own music, he had recorded it on cassette tapes, sending them illegally to Ankers in Norway. It was a difficult music, impenetrable to many ears, which heard only an unmelodious, formless noise.

In the government's view most jazz was insidious. It had been one of Bilak's personal initiatives to ban public performance and sales of records of music less than fifty years old. As a sop to the unintelligent, the government even *encouraged* people to listen to American jazz of the twenties and thirties. This, they said, was the golden era of jazz and what came after was mere corruption.

The fifty-years law came on to the books in the early eighties and the Jazz Group invited trouble by playing tunes by Monk,

Mingus and Parker. 'Trouble' meant police harassment, confiscation of instruments, hefty fines and, later, imprisonment.

Hašek had started writing his own pieces and the Group played them at one concert in Bratislava. The *Rudé Pravo* music critic, despite the fact he was spotted that very night at a Mozart performance 300 kilometres away in Prague, wrote of the Group's new direction: 'Finally realizing the folly of exhuming the fruiting bodies of possibly the most questionable period of American music, the Jazz Group have now embarked on a new, equally senseless path: playing their own material. In this respect they would appear to be walking the plank. The "music" – hardly deserving of the term – contains neither melody nor harmony. Long, bland notes are played in apparent counterpoint to each other, and no destination is ever reached. If this is a joke, it has surely backfired. It cannot be long before they fall off the plank.'

Hašek was quite pleased with the commentary; he still carried the clipping in his wallet. The rest of the Group took a less enlightened view. Consequently, they did not perform live any more of Hašek's pieces. Encouraged by smuggled bootleg recordings of contemporary European jazz figures, Hašek was convinced his music had some relevance to international developments, and he continued to work at it on his own.

An invitation arrived for Hašek to participate in the Hamburg and Northern Europe Jazz Festival. Taking this as proof that he was on the right track, he wrote back to accept in principle. The Germans got a campaign going, saying he should be allowed to attend, even before Hašek had begun the tedious process of seeking official permission. When the government came to consider the matter, the campaign was so far advanced that to refuse permission would have seriously damaged their international reputation. In those days they still had a ghost of one to maintain.

Hašek played at the festival in Hamburg. He performed his own music. The press at home derided him. The internationals were less sure about his music than they had been about his right to appear. However, a few Scandinavian and, strangely, Greek papers gave him very good notices, and Ankers the Norwegian wouldn't let him go back to Prague without promising to send him a tape of his music.

To the surprise of those who had expected him to defect, including his own government, Hašek did return home. His main reason for doing so, although he didn't tell anyone, least of all her, was Hella. They had split up for the fourth or fifth time not long before the Hamburg festival, but he hoped as always that they would get back together.

With the Group he played his part in their next project: they took the authorities at their word and played classic jazz from the twenties and thirties. But they did so with wildly exaggerated musical gestures and a profound sense of irony. The Group's followers judged this hilariously successful and numbers swelled at concerts. Police presence grew accordingly at the same time, for it had not escaped the government's attention – though it might have done were it not for the *Rudé Pravo* critic pointing it out – that the Jazz Group were taking the piss.

The police caused random obstructions at concerts and harassed punters for no good reason. On one occasion truncheons were used and concert-goers fought back. Arrests were made immediately and became front-page news the next day. The Jazz Group were, all of a sudden, a dangerous, rebellious influence on law-abiding citizens; attendance at their concerts, until such could be declared illegal, which seemed inevitable as the Group slipped 'further into depravity', was actively discouraged by the press and by police violence.

Hašek and the other Group members were named as anti-communist provocateurs, which by and large pleased them. To be ostracized by such an intransigent establishment, while not particularly difficult to achieve, certainly carried some kind of honour.

For a while after that they played along with the authorities, and concerts went ahead unopposed. They felt sure a close eye was being kept on them, and they knew for certain when they played Benny Goodman's little-known tune 'Be the Angel You Are' at a concert in Brno. The next day they were arrested in Prague on the charge of performing proscribed music in public.

A court case ensued in which the Group's defence was that 'Be the Angel You Are' was written in 1938, and that under the fifty-years law they were now perfectly entitled to perform it. The state prosecutor produced evidence to show that the tune was not written until 1939. Subsequent investigations on both sides eventually threw up the fact that the date of composition of this particular tune had long been disputed in jazz circles. Benny Goodman experts had not reached a consensus of opinion on the matter.

Only quite late in the day – after a week and a half – did the authorities finally twig that the Jazz Group had chosen the Goodman number to perform precisely because they knew of the dispute over the date and sought to exploit it to ridicule the government.

They realized too late: the Jazz Group case had become an international joke, at the expense of the authorities. Even such countries as East Germany and the Soviet Union had attacked the Czechs, saying they were 'behind the times'. Nicolae Ceauşescu of Romania displayed his unique disingenuousness by accusing Prague of abusing human rights. Undaunted by the widespread protests of the international community, the state prosecutor sentenced the members of the Group to twelve months' imprisonment.

It was in gaol that Hašek's dreams first came. He and the other Group members had been placed under the observation of a penal psychiatrist, who encouraged Hašek to talk about the dreams, which, out of boredom, he did.

The Jazz Group members were released after serving three months, just in time for Christmas. As a salvage operation for Prague's reputation it failed miserably. Hašek and his friends went home to heavily bugged apartments. Plain-clothes men loitered nonchalantly outside their doors and windows, caring little to disguise their intent.

Hašek had already taken the precaution of organizing a post office box in a false name, and so was able to receive communications from Ankers without the police's knowledge. (Though this remained dependent on him giving his tail the slip long enough to access his box.) He was intrigued by Ankers's descriptions of the visions he saw – of naked women sleepwalking through strange anachronistic landscapes – when he played along to the tapes. Although he had become infected with the other man's itch to get to the bottom of the mystery, he didn't for a moment believe that the somnambulists actually existed outside of a Norwegian mind that had perhaps inhaled too much northern sea air.

7

Hašek and the other Group members celebrated the New Year in traditional fashion by getting blind drunk in a string of bars in the Old Town, then descending on the Clock Tower in the Old Town Square. The police were never more than a few metres away, but on this night the Group were doing nothing the entire population of the city was not also doing. As the clock struck twelve, a trumpet fanfare from inside the top of the tower greeted the New Year and the townspeople who were gathered in the square hurled their bottles and glasses at the base of the tower. The policeman barring entry to the tower steps braced his machine-gun across his chest but, as broken glass showered around him, gamely did not call a halt to the traditional good-natured gesture.

A couple of weeks later Hašek went to Brno and the other Group members departed for random destinations, having first, they hoped, given their tails the slip. They came back at staggered times on the same day and booked into the Ametyst. As far as Hašek could tell the ruse had worked. The police would be expecting trouble on the 16th of January, the twentieth anniversary of Jan Palach's self-immolation; they would be intensifying their watch on the Group, to put an early stop to any plans they might have to join the demonstration that was bound to take place. Hašek wondered if the police knew they were watching empty flats and houses. But, in fact, not all the homes were empty: both Gustav and Bedrich were married and Vlastimil's girlfriend had agreed to stay over to make his flat look inhabited. It was only in Hašek's flat that the lights burned for no one but the police. Hella by now was living in East Berlin.

Every year since Palach's supreme self-sacrifice in Wenceslas Square in 1969, there had been some kind of demonstration to mark the event. The young student had intended to shake people out of the apathy into which they had fallen after the Soviet invasion that crushed the Prague Spring. His grand, selfless gesture had certainly done that and the flame was kept alight both by dissidents and 'ordinary law-abiding citizens' every year in Wenceslas Square.

Hašek had no doubt that this year the police would behave in much the same way. They would be wary, as ever, of someone repeating Palach's gesture. He hoped that bloodshed could be avoided, but that was not in his hands.

He looked outside at the street again, then let the curtain fall back into place and left the room to visit the toilet. The corridors and stairways of the hotel, where they were not lined with full-length mirror glass, were decorated in garish greens and mustard brushed-nylon wallpaper.

Coming out of the toilet, Hašek noticed a payphone on the next landing. He dug in his pocket and sifted through a handful of coins.

'Hella,' he said.

'Jiří,' a distant voice answered. 'Where are you? You aren't –'

'Yes, I am. Tomorrow.'

He paused. Hella said nothing, clearly waiting for him to continue.

'Won't you come?' he asked, knowing the answer would be the same as every previous time he had posed the question.

'Jiří. No. You know . . . Where are you now?'

'In a hotel. I'm out of sight.'

'I imagine you need to be.'

He wished she were there with him instead of on the other end of a crackly line. He hated talking to her on the phone. Dialogue had always been just a small part of the way they communicated. Her eyes divulged far more than her words; his touch carried more meaning than a lengthy explanation. The telephone was such a terrible reduction, a constriction of rather than an aid to communication.

'What?' he said, not hearing properly.

'I said: I wish you'd change your mind. Had you better not go now? Someone might be listening.'

What facial expression might have accompanied her plea for him to abandon his plan? Did she really care? And how much, if at all? Was she concerned because she had once loved him or because she still did, and just refused to let it control her life?

'Why won't you come?'

'Jiří, I want to be free and alone.'

'You can't be free there,' he said, believing it.

'Alone then.'

'But you're not alone. Come with me. You will be free.'

She fell silent again. He knew her contention that she would not attain any greater freedom if she went with him. It was a state of mind, not a question of politics.

'I must keep you apart from my changes,' she said.

He always wanted to pick holes in her argument, in so far as she had one; to find chinks in her armour.

'We've been apart for months now. Is it so great?' He heard that fateful petulance creeping into his voice. He heard himself as he knew she heard him and knew that he was digging the grave even deeper. How did she always manage to make him feel seventeen in these discussions? Just by being reasonable? 'You know how I feel about you,' he said. It wasn't meant to be blackmail, but he knew it sounded like it.

'Goodbye, Jiří. I'm always here if you need me. You know that.'

Yes, he knew that. But the dividing line between 'want' and 'need' was not always so clear.

She said goodbye again and hung up.

He stood holding the useless lump of plastic and feeling stupid. Behind him someone coughed. Automatically he moved out of the way and a man in a striped jacket occupied the booth, still looking for the number he wanted to dial.

He sneaked out of the hotel, putting at risk the plan he and the rest of the Group had worked hard to implement. The bizarre interior decoration of the hotel had not helped his depression; nor had the unsatisfying talk with Hella provided any relief. He had to get out.

The air was biting. He tugged his collar higher and marched up Lublanska towards the metro at IP Pavlova. The platforms were clean and grey.

Few other people were there to board the aluminium train when it rolled in after a few minutes. He watched the unchanging platform surface through the open doors as he waited for them to close and the train to move off. He would have welcomed some litter to break the monotony: a styrofoam take-away sausage tray or a crumpled cigarette packet.

From the loudspeakers in the carriage came the recorded

message: 'Ukončete výstup a nástup. Dveře se zavírají. Příští stanice: Gottwaldova'.

Her voice had not changed in fifteen years; still the same blonde-haired young woman wearing a Russian fur hat and broadcasting from a warm room in a distant snowbound city. Hašek had grown used to her voice and message, which changed from station to station only to name the next one, prefaced by the same 'Příští stanice'. He'd never taken to the new recordings made for the stations opened on lines which had been extended. The new tapes gave the impression of being recorded by an older woman, her grey-brown hair drawn into a tight bun, sitting stiffly on a swivel chair in the austere surroundings of a poorly heated government department.

Hašek recognized that the germs of romanticism were still multiplying within him.

'Příští stanice: Pražského povstání. Příští stanice: Mládežnická. Příští stanice: Budějovická.'

He got off.

Michle had never been a pretty part of Prague and just lately it had been going downhill. The patches of wasteground between the motorway intersections, also the open spaces between one high-rise and the next, had been allowed to go to seed. Although the soil appeared too thin and contaminated to support life, a few unpleasant weeds sprouted here and there like rusty bicycle spokes.

The people who had left the metro with Hašek dispersed. Not one apart from him crossed the main road and headed down Vyskočilova. Both to protect his face against the cold and to conceal his identity, he pulled the sides of his woollen hat down and tied the cord under his chin. The peak cast a shadow over his face which the streetlamps were too tall to illuminate. If he could be revealed by his shoes, then that was the risk he ran.

The expressway swept over his head and he cut down through the little passageway towards U Pomníku. Pulling up his collar and holding it around his chin, Hašek stepped into his road. His shoes scrunched on the frost. He peered between the streetlamps for a glimpse of his redundant guards, but could see no one. Slowly at first, then at normal pace when he realized that the sight of a hunched figure creeping towards his apartment building was a dozen times more likely to arouse suspicion, he walked along the right-hand side of the road. His building, the tallest in the street, poked above the lamps and spiky trees. His apartment was on the second floor; he was not yet close enough to see whether his lights were still on. Inside his cocoon of hat and coat it grew hot and damp with his breath.

On the other side of the narrow street, in the shadow between two lamp-posts, a policeman suddenly stopped blowing warmth into his cupped hands. Hašek was looking up at the windows of his apartment. They were dimly lit, as he had left them. He wondered if the shadows thrown against the blinds of his living room were too obviously only those of a television.

Then he caught sight of the clasped hands across the street.

His own breath caught in his throat as the policeman's froze on the air in a little cloud. Hašek walked on in a straight line, head down, heart thumping. Aware of the other man's head turning to watch, he raised his gaze to buildings on the opposite side of the street from his apartment. They were grey and featureless as his own: why *shouldn't* he find them just as interesting?

As soon as he got to the end of the street and turned out of the policeman's line of sight, he began, softly, to run.

All he'd wanted was a last look at his old home.

He surfaced at Můstek and walked up the length of Wenceslas Square.

It was quiet – largely because there were few people about, and most of them were police, in and out of uniform. Again, Hašek had to mask his face and keep his head down. He saw bundles of crash barriers as yet unstacked. They would not be needed until the following day. He felt a surge of excitement in anticipation of the demonstration. Skirting the statue of St Wenceslas, he turned right in front of the great museum.

He bought a hot sausage from a street vendor and pushed the dollop of mustard around the little tray. He would miss Czech sausage.

By the time he reached the hotel it had started to rain.

It was still raining when Hašek looked outside the next morning. It was also likely to continue for some time: the sky was slate-grey.

Hašek went back to bed and dreamed half-invented nonsense involving Ankers's sleepwalkers. Wearing only fur hats, dozens of semi-conscious women congregated in Wenceslas Square and repeated over and over again the recorded message from the metro: 'Ukončete výstup a nástup. Dveře se zavírají.'

He dozed fitfully through the morning and struggled out of bed, though with a fuzzy head, at lunchtime. The image in the mirror over the washbasin distressed him; he cleaned its teeth. Downstairs, seeing no sign of his friends, he ate a dyspeptic lunch. Feeling weak, he gave up trying to walk upstairs when he'd reached only the first floor and waited for the lift.

Gustav, Bedrich and Vlastimil were in the lift.

They had been concerned, they said, and were glad to see him. He brightened and, since the lift was otherwise empty, invited them back to his room.

As they trooped in, Hašek went straight to his saxophone case. He extracted a bottle of Stolichnaya from the bell of his instrument. The other men applauded quietly but enthusiastically and the bottle was passed around. For the first time in forty-eight hours, Hašek began to relax.

When the bottle was empty, the Group collected their things together and checked out of the hotel, one by one.

They met up on the other side of the river in the shadow of the Castle. Hašek thought of Franz Kafka every time the spires and toy building blocks of Hradčany Castle lost themselves in mist, as they did on that cold January afternoon. Kafka had shown how the real significance of the Castle was what lay hidden, beneath layers of mist and behind the walls within walls. Having enjoyed a brief period of official tolerance in the mid-eighties, Kafka's books were now banned again. Copies changed hands among the dissident and student communities, sometimes at a cost measured not in Czechoslovak crowns, but in years of imprisonment or persecution and human lives.

The wisdom of having booked a table became clear when they got to U Kolovratu. The tiny restaurant was packed with diners. Two couples ate their meals sitting at the bar. The proprietor welcomed them with a smile and led the way to a table at the back.

After relaying their order, Hašek fell silent, as his friends raised their glasses, filled from the wine bottles already placed on the table, and toasted Jan Palach.

The proprietor produced a basket of bread and Bedrich broke crispy brown rolls which he passed round.

They ate well and drank a number of bottles of Bulgarian red wine. Hašek stayed off the alcohol but put away as much rich beef and dumplings as the other men. He fought against sentimentality as morbid thoughts crossed his mind. Even if this didn't turn out to be his last supper, it would be a long time before he sat around a table again with these friends. The Group had been together for more than ten years and the persecution they had suffered had made them close.

Food kept coming and the Jazz Group kept eating it. More bottles of wine were opened. With a glance at his watch, Hašek nodded to the proprietor. The latter looked apologetic as he handed over the bill. When he looked at the amount, Hašek could see why. But he had enough cash to cover it. The others pulled out their wallets but Hašek insisted. If he couldn't afford it, he said, he would not have let them eat so much. Whether or not the evening turned out to be a success, he added ironically, he owed them more than a decent meal for the risk involved.

When they'd walked down the hill, crossed the river and the Old Town Square, a massive crowd had already assembled in Wenceslas Square. Although the numbers were great, they were not densely packed and the Group were able to move up the length of the square until they were in the thick of the crowd some two hundred metres from the St Wenceslas statue.

Policemen ringed the square at twenty-metre intervals. None, at least not in uniform, had got in among the crowd. Consequently, the Group were able to get their cases and gear to the top of the square largely unnoticed. Most people had some kind of prop, be it a white dove (many made do with pigeons), a Czechoslovak flag or merely a placard bearing Jan Palach's name, lest it be forgotten.

Václav Havel, like the Jazz Group also recently released from gaol, stood with other leading members of the banned Charter 77 human-rights organization outside the former carpet shop, where in 1969 Jan Palach had doused himself with petrol and set fire to his clothing. He had dashed across the square to a delicatessen on the other side. A transport inspector saw what was happening and ran forward to drape his overcoat around Palach, but was too late to prevent the creation of a martyr. Palach had already suffered second- and third-degree burns over more than 80 per cent of his body; he died a few days later in hospital.

A short note was found in his pocket pleading for an end to censorship and to the distribution of pro-Soviet propaganda. His note warned of further such self-immolations in five days' time if his demands were not met. Signing the note 'Torch Number One', he explained that he was committing suicide 'because our peoples find themselves on the brink of hopelessness and we decided to wake them up'. He wrote that he had had the honour to be the first name pulled out of the hat.

The group to which he alluded was unknown to all who read the note and investigations unearthed no trace of it. There was no Torch Number Two, but the authorities prepared themselves for copycat suicides on subsequent anniversaries. On significant dates dissident groups circulated rumours that there would be a repeat of Palach's gesture and the police became especially jumpy. This year, ominously, there had been no rumour; on the twentieth anniversary this was treated as highly suspicious. The great irony by early 1989 was that the Soviet Union and Czechoslovakia had taken such great strides in opposite directions, that there were now liberal Soviet magazines and newspapers banned in Prague, which dissidents demanded the right to read.

The Jazz Group began to play and the police became nervous. Demonstrators shouted 'Freedom, freedom, freedom' and 'Palach lives'. The familiar paraphernalia of street protest appeared: placards, flags and doves. People turned their anger on the police.

Here and there policemen broke ranks and hit out at protesters who jeered too close to the bone. Furious, buoyant protesters struck back. Small pockets of violence affected the mood of the crowd. In their thin lines the police came under greater threat from the mass than they seemed to pose themselves. Placards and poles were made into weapons. Younger, less experienced policemen began to fall and those still standing looked constantly over their shoulders into the shadows of the side streets which led off from the square.

The music continued to function as an absurd soundtrack to what could obviously develop into a full-scale riot; the tune, meanwhile, had changed to 'Doctor Jazz'.

Then, clearly, an order was given. From side streets on both sides of the square, armoured vehicles and tanks emerged. The effect on the crowd was to stoke its ardour. More policemen fell when the protesters saw they had been tricked and lashed out more in fear than in anger. In front of the vehicles came waves of paramilitary reinforcements armed with heavy batons and clubs. They laid into the crowd with vigour and impunity.

The crowd frayed at its edges as the fringe tried desperately to escape through the thickening cordon of police and paramilitaries. At the same time the uniformed tourniquet was tightening steadily, pressing the crowd in towards its centre. It seemed that the police and army wanted to do more than simply round up the troublemakers and arrest them; punishment on a massive scale was being meted out on the spot.

It was then that a preternatural hush fell over the square, police and protesters alike. They either heard and instantly recognized the whoosh of ignition or their eyes were immediately drawn to the bright flash of orange-blue flame at the south-east end of the square.

It took a moment for the reality to sink in.

The protesters were the first to find their voice. Each man and each woman was awed by the sacrifice. Each was shocked and impressed that one person had found the determination and conviction to repeat Palach's gesture. Each was immensely relieved that the responsibility had been lifted from their shoulders for another five years. Slowly, as they watched the human shape engulfed by fire, they began to murmur, 'Palach lives, Palach lives.'

Some of those at the south-east end, who had been listening to the music just before the self-immolation, had been puzzled by the sudden disappearance of the clear alto sax melody in 'Grandpa's Spells'.

The murmur became a chant taken up by 5,000 people. The security forces snapped into action, charging into the crowd on foot, swinging batons and clubs. From the armoured vehicles at the edge of the square, several water cannon were turned on the crush. The guy in the shadow of St Wenceslas continued to burn like a human candle, but instead of directing the water cannon at him, the high-pressure jets were pointed at the thickest knots of protesters.

The cloying smell of burning clothing was soon eradicated by the acrid stench of tear gas. Soldiers threw dozens of canisters into the middle of the crowd. Large numbers of people were immediately overcome by fumes. They and those only weakened were crushed and trampled by others fleeing. But flight was impossible. More soldiers entered the square from the side streets. Even at the south-east end, where before the major eruption the police cordon had been thinnest and was not backed up by troops, escape was now impossible. Police without gasmasks ran from the sides of the square to cover the north end, while the paramilitaries, the soldiers and, behind them, the tanks moved in.

When the first artillery shells were being fired, killing up to fifty people at a time, Czech television news, broadcasting to millions of homes, was showing film of party leader Bílak opening a brand-new Škoda factory in the far north of the country. 'Five thousand new jobs are created here today,' he announced proudly into the microphone.

The carnage in Wenceslas Square would go on for at least another hour, until the death toll neared 5,000. The sky darkened steadily. The original sacrificial victim still smouldered. Shortly before midnight, a soldier prodded and turned the charred remains with the barrel of his machine-gun and grimaced behind his gasmask, seeing nothing recognizably human.

Arctic Waist

Ankers turned the key in the lock, withdrew the small package from the box and left the post office. Shielding his eyes from the sun, he slid in behind the wheel of an ageing blue Ford Taunus. He pulled away up the hill, wrestling Hašek's tape out of its packaging and easing it into the cassette player. As it clicked into place, Ankers twisted the volume control, then relieved the Ford's gearbox by changing up into second.

Hašek's first note drifted out of the speakers just as the Taunus breasted the hill and the pines across the valley came into view. Ankers shifted out of gear and allowed the car to coast.

The notes sounded less like the product of a saxophone than the voice of an alto chorister divested of his church. Ankers shook his head, smiling his disbelief, as the music defied all unwritten theory in its progress from start to finish. It was like getting from one side of a lake to the other without either swimming across it or walking around the edge. 'Somehow,' Ankers had told a Danish music journalist at the Hamburg festival, 'Hašek has discovered new ways of getting from A to B, and there is never any question that B is not exactly the right place to be once he gets there.'

Listening on the stereo, Ankers could enjoy the music, but to experience its true nature he had to wait until he got home, which wouldn't be until his old car had climbed up the other side of the valley and turned down the unmetalled road to the promontory. The wooden house he shared with Inger overlooked the sea. A local proverb had it that on a clear day from this part of Norway you could see the Faeroes. Ankers had found an atlas in the attic of the house which showed that the islands were on the same line of latitude as this stretch of coastline, but he never discovered whether or not the birth of cartography preceded the origin of the saying.

*

When he got back he went to look for Inger before tuning his saxophone. He called her name as he passed from room to room and up two flights, even though he knew where she would be if she was in the house. When he reached the front bedroom on the top floor – not the one they used, but where Inger was often to be found as it offered the best, most expansive view of the sea – he approached the high-backed chair facing the window.

'Hello, Edvard,' she said, as he bent over the back of the chair. She placed her hand over his and pressed very lightly. He looked out of the window. 'I was just watching the sea,' she explained. 'You've got another tape.'

She knew he waited for the tapes and played with them when they arrived, although she had appeared to lose interest when he tried to describe the visions they conjured up for him when he did play along. They were like dreams, he explained, except that he remained awake. Inger, however, had turned back to the window, focusing on infinity.

He left her staring out to sea and went downstairs to his 'studio'. He had converted one of the rooms on the first floor into a passable recording studio. He had electric keyboards, two guitars, a drum kit, string bass and a tenor saxophone. There was also a six-track mixing desk and recording system. A publishing deal, struck several years before on the strength of some pop songs and jingles, had financed the cost of buying the house and building the studio.

Hašek's music was written both to stand alone and be complemented by another instrument to form a duet. Ankers slid the tape into the stereo and played tenor to Hašek's alto. The vision came almost immediately.

He was following tramlines. On either side the landscape was vague. As he walked, the sketchy definitions of trees, grassy banks and dunes were gently smudged and erased by dusk. He could barely hear the saxophone music in the background, as if this were a film and that the soundtrack. New, surprising notes threaded themselves in and he heard his own instrument answering them with counterparts; the music had suddenly become far more complex. Beneath his feet the tramlines had been joined by others merging from both sides. He tripped over points and studied the pattern of rails in order to discern his route out of the junction.

He followed one set of parallel rails that curved out from the ever-widening morass of tracks and headed into the dunes.

The knot of tonal confusion untied itself – slipped away, in fact, like a magician's knot which had never been there – and long mellow notes followed, sliding over each other: an F from the alto joined by the tenor's G sharp and then a D.

Sand blew over the tracks, shifting occasionally to reveal the gleaming steel beneath, but eventually burying them, so that he walked into the dunes without a guide.

The apparent source of the music changed. One minute it was the moan of a black-headed gull, the next the sea breeze fluting across the mouth of an effluent pipe. Making his own contributions involuntarily, he passed between dunehills anchored by spikes of marram, aiming now for the colonnades and pavilions he could see rising out of the sand in the distance. The three-quarter moon painted the buildings a ghostly grey.

When he got closer he could make out the women. As on every previous occasion they wore few clothes and appeared to be asleep as they walked, eyes wide open yet unseeing, passing each other in groups and sometimes singly. The strange, anachronistic buildings gathered around a square, over which the women crossed back and forth. With their hands they gesticulated and often seemed deep in silent conversation with their companions.

The music now emanated from between the columns of the displaced ruins and monuments.

He approached the edge of the square. On the far side beyond the buildings the sea beat against the shore. As he watched, the waves came in closer and were soon lapping around the crumbling stone pillars that barely held up the roof of an ancient Roman arcade. The women walked on and around unaware.

Trailing behind two women, in long dresses decorated with huge bows like mutant butterflies, was the old man. Ankers had glimpsed the old man on earlier visits and only sensed his significance.

Two women walked to the perimeter of the square, just a few metres from the incoming tide, which was now causing the arcade to tremble as it thrashed its supports. The women knew nothing of the danger. The old man's bespectacled face furrowed in concern as he looked towards them; he could see the women and the sea behind them. Was he too worried by the sea?

Ankers wanted to run into the square and warn the sleepwalkers, even though he knew they wouldn't see or hear him. Duetting with Hašek's previous cassettes, he'd seen the sea gradually advancing, its threat growing each time. This was the first time it had shaken the buildings. He looked around for the old man and just caught sight of him passing behind a dune 150 metres inland of the square. Despite the danger to the women, he knew he should follow the old man and so broke into a run.

There was an urgency in the old man's step which allowed him to walk more quickly than Ankers could run. The younger man was less accustomed to the sand; it sucked and dragged at his feet, slowing him down. In the distance a small railway station came into view, partially obscured in its own shadows cast by the moon. The old man climbed into the last carriage of a train which then began to move off, taking the music with it in its siren.

He was painfully aware of the notes fading to near-silence as he strove to run, like treading water, in the direction of the station. The landscape of the vision would vanish as soon as the music finished. He didn't want to leave empty-handed again and not be any closer to answering any of his questions or saving the sleepwalkers from drowning.

The final whispered note floated out into the pallid night as Ankers blinked at the sign which identified the station as De Panne.

He had always been convinced of it; now he knew.

The women were almost always seen in the vicinity of ancient Roman buildings. In the background were often dunes; occasionally there reared craggy, snow-capped mountains. Railways and tramlines sometimes cut through the perspectives and the sea could always be heard and smelt if not seen.

Although the disparate elements of the landscape recalled no place he had ever visited, Ankers was sure the world of the sleepwalkers existed somewhere.

He ran upstairs and found De Panne in the atlas. It was a

small resort on the Belgian coast. He had never heard of the place before, never so much as glanced at a map of the country. De Panne existed. The Roman ruins may have been the imagined remains of some phantom city, but De Panne existed, independently of his fantasy.

In the night Ankers awoke in a sweat. If he'd been dreaming he had no recollection. De Panne came to the front of his mind – the name on the station sign – but brought only a small tremor of excitement.

Then he realized what was wrong. He twisted round but Inger's side of the bed was empty. Sweat ran into his eyes and he rubbed his arm across his forehead. He sighed and lay across the bed. On the sheets he could still smell the salty warmth of Inger's body. Maybe her getting out had woken him. Ankers's throat swelled with emotion. He briefly pressed his face into the depression she'd left in the pillow, then turned over and lay on his back looking up at the shadows suspended from the ceiling.

He'd met Inger in the far frozen north of the country, on an icy spring day when his car had broken down. He'd been tempted up north by the early thaw, slung his saxophone case on to the back seat of the Taunus and drove. Hašek had recently sent the first of his tapes and Ankers thought it would sound good on the open road.

The days were still short, but they were warmer. Lapwings flew over the moors above Mosjoen, and, sitting in his car one night parked off the road half inside the Tysfjorden pine forest, he was watched by a snowy owl perched motionless on a low branch.

Late in the afternoon of the next day the chill returned with an almost audible snap. He'd ventured further north in the morning and so the freeze-up was that much more solid than had he stayed below the tundra line. As if it were a sentient machine with a keen sense of irony, his car overheated. The water in the radiator froze and burst a pipe. When it melted the radiator ran dry and the engine practically blew up, having warned him, if he'd cared to notice, with a faint smell of burning oil.

He was on a narrow road separated from the sea by a craggy, sloping cliff. He belted his coat and lifted the bonnet of the car and looked despairingly at the bubbles of oil sizzling on the cylinder-head casing. He dropped the bonnet again and walked to the edge of the slope, wondering what on earth he could do.

The sea rolled thick and grey like a blanket on to the rocky shore. It rushed into narrow gullies and splashed into shallow pools on the higher rocks. There were seals bobbing like buoys between ten and twenty metres out. Further out, the sea was exposed to a wind that snapped off the tops of the waves. Ankers realized with a start that there was someone down by the waterline.

She turned from the sea and looked up at him in surprise. Moving away from the water's edge, she took two steps towards him. Despite the bitter cold, her sleeves were pushed up to above the elbow and her left arm glistened with water caught in the small hairs. He looked at the seals; they were still drifting backwards and forwards a little way out. The woman brushed her wet arm against the light jacket she wore and looked back up at Ankers. 'My car broke down,' he said, pointing at the road. He wondered what he'd interrupted. The woman's cheeks were slightly flushed; she looked almost guilty. 'Do you know much about cars?'

She shook her head. Her blonde hair, straggly with salt from the spray, whipped her pale cheeks. 'But my father does,' she said.

Ankers shivered with the cold as the woman joined him and together they looked under his bonnet. The engine had cooled down quickly in the truly arctic conditions.

'I can risk driving it a couple of kilometres,' he guessed. She sat uneasily in the passenger seat and directed him towards the outskirts of Narvik, where her father had a small toolshop. He learnt her name but didn't like to ask too many other questions. After several days with only his saxophone for company, he liked her presence in the car. It was good to have the air warmed by another person's breath.

He drove slowly, with very little confidence in the engine holding out until they reached Inger's father's house. But his pessimism was unfounded. Inger's parents, burly, jolly people, came out to see who had arrived. Her mother poured him a generous pot of lager, while her father improvised on the Taunus with a reconditioned radiator from an old Saab. 'It will almost certainly be a successful transplant,' said the old man as he stamped into

23

the house and bolted the door to keep the draught out. 'But it's getting much colder outside. You mustn't continue tonight. I've put your car in the toolshop, where it shouldn't freeze up. You may stay the night here.'

Ankers looked at Inger's mother. She beamed and refilled his pot. Inger put clods of peat on the fire and looked out of the window at the sea. They fed him well. Several times he looked in Inger's direction, hoping she would smile or at least return his gaze. The more reticent she became, the more he was attracted to her. Aware of her parents at the other end of the table, he tried not to stare, but her eyes were so bright and blue with a tantalizing ring of yellow that he found it difficult to tear his gaze away.

Later, he helped to clear the dishes from the table. Inger's father was rebuilding the open fire. In the kitchen Inger's mother suddenly grasped his arm and looked searchingly into his eyes. 'Are you a good man?' she asked. Ankers was too shocked to reply. Transfixed, he stared back at the old woman until she appeared to be satisfied and released his arm.

He slept downstairs on the couch in the glow from the smouldering fire. Something woke him. He opened his eyes and looked around without moving. All he could see were the faint embers in the grate. Slowly he grew accustomed to the gloom and found that the dying fire cast a thin sheet of light over many objects in the room, turning them a dull orange. He got up from the couch and walked to the window. She was about fifty metres from the house, walking slowly towards the narrow beach, naked. The moon washed all colour out of the sand and out of her body, so that when she reached the beach she became almost invisible. A rogue wave splashed spray into the corona of her hair and jolted Ankers out of his trance. He ran through the kitchen to the back door and out into the night. She was just a few metres from the sea when he caught up with her. Drops of spray spangled on her shoulders. He drew alongside her and was shocked to see her eyes wide and staring. She gave no indication of being aware of his presence. Even when he put his hands lightly to her waist to stop her walking into the sea, she simply acquiesced. He stepped in front of her and waved a hand before her face. Her eyelids didn't move. The turquoise irises looked as unreal as glass. He shivered, seeing for the first time that he too was naked.

Distraction had blocked any natural reaction to the subzero temperature. Vulnerable now, he shuddered and his teeth chattered.

He looked at Inger. She did not even have goose-pimples. All that moved was her hair in the sea breeze. She looked completely untroubled and, if it were possible, both wide awake and in a deep sleep at the same time. He noticed the skin around her nipples was constricted: she was feeling the cold after all. He flushed as he realized he was appraising her body. Feeling guilty, he didn't want to wake her in case she reacted badly. But he had to get back inside – out here they would both suffer exposure.

He put a trembling arm around her shoulders and guided her back towards the house. She walked slowly and he couldn't tell if she'd woken up or not. When they were inside she collapsed. He caught her and lay her down on the couch. He covered her with the quilt he had been sleeping under and hugged her tightly when she started shivering in delayed reaction to the cold. Presently he succumbed to exhaustion. When he woke later, she was asleep but had at some point put her arms around him. Uncovered by the quilt, he was cold. The fire had died out. The only light was a ghostly incandescence from the window shed by the moon. The house was silent. He saw no harm in lifting the quilt and lying next to Inger. Her body had stolen the fire from the grate. He fell asleep with his hand on her breast, half a smile on his face.

In the morning Inger's mother grilled bacon. The smell woke them both and there was none of the awkwardness he would have expected. They drank coffee made with boiled milk and Inger's mother brought down two bathrobes so they could get up. Ankers found the irony amusing but appreciated the need for modesty.

It was not long before Inger agreed to join Ankers 1,000 kilometres south in his wooden house outside Floro.

That was a year ago. Then, when he responded to Hašek's suggestion that he improvise duet lines for the tapes he was sending from Prague, the visions began.

He only ever needed one take. The vision came when he began playing. Sometimes it was a series of still images – a ruined palace with black windows and a broken statue cast out on to the road; a cobbled town square dwarfed by a disproportionately large naked woman; a cortège of women in lace moving towards a series of large arches; a woman in a long dress looking at her naked reflection in a mirror; women wearing large knotted bows in a rock-strewn square surrounded by derelict ancient buildings and cracked hills; a woman embracing the statue of a male double amputee in the foreground, and in the background an old man with a paintbrush and palette walking towards a line of dunes, beyond which lies the sea.

More often they were moving pictures – a naked woman kisses a well-dressed man in a bare room, while outside in the tropical vegetation another woman plays a pipe. The woman leaves the room and joins a procession of women, all as naked and moon-bleached as she, and they enter a forest of gnarled trees and sprouting plantains which grow taller than the trees before their very eyes. They leave the forest and proceed down a crazy-paved boulevard towards a town composed of ancient classical build-ings crammed together in giddy perspectives, arriving just as dawn lightens the sky.

Ankers wrote constantly to Hašek, describing the visions and asking for more tapes. Once he had played along with one tape and seen the vision, there was no way he could do it again differ-ently. The improvisation he produced in the first take became the definitive accompaniment to the piece. Nor could he rerun the same vision by playing the same music again, suggesting that the generation of the images was a function of the creation of the music.

Gradually, Ankers became involved in the possible fate of the women as they walked in their sleep through more and more bizarre landscapes. The sea was now a constant presence and at times vaguely threatening. Ankers reasoned that if these women were merely a product of his imagination, then he should be able to control their destinies and so protect them from any such threat. If, however, he had no control over them, as soon ap-peared to be the case, then they must exist somewhere in the real world.

He didn't know now if Inger was still sleepwalking or not. She often left their bed and went to the upstairs room where she sat in the chair and watched the sea. Sometimes when he knew she'd

26

gone he went straight back to sleep; other times he got up and went to find her, then brought her back to bed.

He sat up and swung his legs out of bed. He pulled on a bathrobe and crossed the room. His feet fell softly on the polished boards. Wearily he climbed the stairs. He'd never bothered to furnish the upstairs room and all Inger had done was carry the high-backed chair up from the ground floor and plant it in front of the window. He leant over the back of the chair and suddenly flushed hot and cold as if burnt by ice: the chair was empty.

He looked out of the window.

It was happening again.

She was halfway down the promontory, at the end of which there was a steep drop.

Second-hand Tatra

Hašek ran for his life. Not knowing if any of the police he had dodged were in pursuit, he just kept running, clutching his saxophone case, changing tack sporadically and keeping his head low.

When he reached Mírů Square, instead of hugging the buildings round the edge, he launched himself into the gardens in the centre. The Christmas tree was still standing but its lights had been taken down. He crouched behind it and gasped for breath as he scanned the roads that led into the top of the square. Had he been followed? It seemed not.

According to the plan, a car would be waiting in Sázavská, on the other side of Mírů Square. Vlastimil's brother had undertaken to make available a get-away car, acquired from his own used-car business. Not for the first time, Hašek hoped the brother would have better resources and more imagination than to provide him with a Škoda.

Whatever the car turned out to be, Hašek was indebted to the other members of the Group, and indeed their relatives, for helping to arrange his escape. Gustav, baritone saxophonist in the Group since its inception, had obtained the dummy from the stockroom of the department store on Na příkopě where he worked as a clerk.

Eight bars into 'Grandpa's Spells', after Václav Havel had laid flowers on behalf of Charter 77 outside the former carpet shop, and while the police cordon at the south-east end of the square was still thin, Hašek stowed his saxophone and poured paraffin over the dummy's clothing, which he then set alight. Immediately upon dropping the match, he disappeared into the crowd and wormed his way to the edge. In a ridiculous piece of theatre, he fell out of the crowd as if he'd been jostled. Standing up with exaggerated difficulty, he eyed the nearest police officers – they were distracted by the fire. His heart thumping, he limped away from the crowd and broke into a sprint after a few strides.

He had seen the armoured vehicles and tanks approaching the square before he set fire to the dummy, and believed their sole function to be a show of force, as on previous demonstrations. He was confident the security forces wouldn't use anything heavier than water cannon.

Hašek crossed over into Wilhelma Piecka and turned into the second road on the right. Two of the streetlamps were out here and he had to squint to see anything at all. It had been agreed that to aid identification in the event of there being several parked cars in the street, Hašek's car would have both its indicators flashing.

Hašek saw an orange glow reflected intermittently on the shiny wing of a Škoda further down the street. He walked briskly towards it. Across the street from the Škoda, its bonnet just emerging from a narrow arched passageway, was Hašek's car. He noted with relief the absence of the too familiar Škoda emblem. There was a badge attached to the rounded front end, but Hašek didn't recognize it and there was too little light by which to scrutinize it. He sized up the car as best he could in its cramped improvised garage. Although its old-fashioned shape was vaguely familiar, he couldn't name it.

Behind him in the street he heard footsteps. He turned swiftly and startled only an elderly man returning home.

Once inside the car he gave scant thought to its make as he located the keys in the glove compartment and gunned the engine into life. He eased its length out of the passageway, gently turning to the right.

The car, he saw from identification marks on the dash, was a Tatra.

He accelerated to the end of the street, slowed down for any crossing traffic, then swung into a right turn.

The car lurched spectacularly at the rear left side, almost scraping the road surface. Hašek fought to regain balance, swore and pulled into the left, visualizing a flat or a blow-out.

He switched off the engine and jumped out. Stepping to the back of the car, he looked for the offending rear left tyre and got a shock when he saw that there simply wasn't one. The Tatra was one of the early, three-wheel models. So early, in fact, that the third wheel was situated not at the front but at the back. Hašek cursed Vlastimil's brother and asked God why the second-hand car salesman couldn't have given him a 1978 Škoda with 70,000 kilometres on the clock, like any normal person would have done.

In the distance there was a loud crack and a muffled bang. Hašek was too distracted by the car and its lack of a wheel to distinguish between possible sources of the noise, but he appreciated the urgency of which it was a symptom. Climbing back into the driving seat, he started the car for the second time and moved off.

His route to Palackého Bridge was by empty tramlines. All metro, bus and tram services had been cancelled for the evening to dissuade people from attending the demonstration. He half expected roadblocks but there were none. For a while he heard faint noises over the roar of the Tatra's powerful engine, but soon left them behind as the bridge drew closer.

On the other side of the river, Kafka's impenetrable castle disappearing behind nearer buildings, Hašek got straight on to the Plzeňská expressway and sped westwards out of the city. For a three-wheeler the Tatra could certainly eat up tarmac when pushed.

Soon the road was practically empty, which in one sense was reassuring – if he was being followed, his pursuers were still out of sight – but which could also be a problem if his isolation drew unwelcome attention from transport police. It would more than likely take him at least two hours to drive the 180 kilometres to Cheb. For most of that time he would be highly visible, driving a conspicuous anachronism of a motor car.

Exploring beneath the dash with his free hand, he found to his delight that someone had possessed the vision to fit a stereo. He took a tape from his inside pocket and slipped it into the mechanism. The near-full moon emerged from behind cloud as the first multi-layered notes of one of his recent compositions escaped from large functional loudspeakers cut into the rear shelf. He listened not out of narcissism but to criticize and find room for improvement. He'd sent a copy of this tape to Ankers. In recent weeks the Norwegian's pleas had become more and more urgent, strengthening Hašek's resolve. He had his own reasons for wanting to leave anyway, but Ankers gave him somewhere to aim for, without which he probably wouldn't know where to go once he got out.

Ankers figured somewhere on the sidelines of the contemporary European jazz scene. Hašek had met several people at the Hamburg festival, but Ankers had shown most interest in his work. And if going to the West to play with this man would give him visions to enjoy as fantastic as those Ankers had described, then Hašek had something to escape to as well as from.

The tape finished; he turned it over. On the other side were particular tunes from records featuring Charlie Parker and Lester Young, alongside whose solos Hašek had recorded harmonies of his own. Sometimes too tricksy, occasionally intrusive to a degree that became destructive, he still thought the experiment had validity. With easier access to bebop records in western Europe, maybe he would be able to take that idea further.

'They're just going up and down the scales and playing anything,' Hella had once said. It was a spring morning in Prague early in the decade, when the Group were still openly performing bebop and modern jazz.

'Didn't you enjoy the gig?' Hašek asked as he leaned out of bed to open the window, then sat back against the headboard.

'Yes,' she said unenthusiastically. He knew she hadn't. Pulling the sheet up to her shoulders, she said, 'But each one seems the same as the next. You all have your own solos and everyone in the audience claps after each one even though the song hasn't finished, then you play together at the end.'

'That's the tradition,' he said, disappointed that she chose to criticize a harmless and, he thought, entirely appropriate song construction. If she said it was too loud or inaccessible, he could accept those charges while not agreeing with them; but instead she attacked what he found most charming about the music. When she deconstructed it in the simple way she had, she made it seem arbitrary and worthless.

'I'm cold,' she said, glancing resentfully at the window.

He closed the window and made her a coffee which she didn't drink. He took his clothes and got dressed in the bathroom. On his return she still hadn't got up. He took his saxophone into the kitchen and stripped it down to clean it. He heard her moving

31

around in the bedroom, opening and closing drawers. He pressed a long-handled brush down the middle of the shaft and worked it up and down. Presently she came into the kitchen wearing her coat. Looking up from the table where parts of his instrument were spread out, he noticed a heavy bag on the floor of the hallway behind her.

'I'm going,' she said, 'to my mother's.'

She was wheezing with asthma presumably brought on by stress and her eyes were full of an expression he'd seen on previous occasions when she'd walked out, but which he couldn't name. He could see she was angry or bitter about something and knew from experience that she wouldn't divulge the nature of her concern.

'What's wrong, Hella?' He pushed his chair back.

She repeated, 'I'm going,' and within seconds had done so.

Not long after Cheb appeared on roadsigns he realized he was driving through its outskirts, built up at the beginning of the eighties to provide housing for assembly plant workers, who were later forced to move back to urban centres when the government closed down the plants, fearing that living so close to the border might give the residents itchy feet. Squat, ugly blocks of flats stood derelict. Walls above some windows were scorched black where disgruntled workers had set their useless homes alight.

Hašek needed petrol. There appeared to be only one petrol station in the town and in the freezing early hours of the morning that was firmly shut. He drove on as quietly as the old engine would allow.

He cut the lights and crawled along in second once he got through the town. The border was not far away. Two hundred metres ahead he saw a group of farm buildings. He turned into a dirt track and left the Tatra where it was concealed by a thick hedge. He began to creep round to the back of the buildings and stopped in his tracks when he heard the chug and rattle of an engine. Turning round and dropping to the ground, he saw a military Jeep pass along the road at the top of the track. Soldiers sat in the open rear section, laughing and pulling on cigarettes which glowed like fireflies.

Hašek grinned nervously to himself as he climbed to his feet.

He turned to face the other way and walked straight into someone who had been standing right behind him.

He recoiled and put up his fists to cover his face.

His attacker shook its head, snorted and retreated. Hašek shook his head in disbelief as he waited for his heart to slow down.

Beyond the hedge he saw several *more* cows quietly chewing grass.

At the back of the farm there was an old Škoda which looked as if it hadn't been moved in months. But it did have four wheels. If he could only get it to start. He knew he didn't have long: the fact that the cows were active suggested it must be nearly milking time. The sky over the horizon he'd fled was turning mauve.

The driver's door was unlocked. Hašek dislodged a panel under the steering column and groped about for the wires whose location Vlastimil's brother had tried to describe to him one evening when they had both put away several jugs of the dark, syrupy beer served at U Fleků. He tried several connections but got no response whatsoever. Through the grimy windscreen he could see that a light had come on in an upstairs window in the farmhouse. He climbed out of the car slowly and eased open the engine cover, to discover the reason for his lack of success: there was no engine. The gaping hole where it should have been instilled in him a sudden panic. Having got so far, he was going to be stuck here unable to escape from the country. Either the farmer would set dogs on him or he would get away from the farm and the sun would come up before he could approach the border.

Forcing himself to calm his nerves, he gently rocked the Škoda. Only an insignificant trickle of petrol rolled in the tank. Across the yard from the car was a shed. He walked without allowing his heels to touch the ground as another light came on upstairs. A cow bellowed. The eastern sky was tinged with pink. Hašek entered the shed and waited for his eyes to adjust. The place stank of oil and animal sweat. Hanging from vicious hooks attached to chains depending from the roof beams were sundry items of light machinery. From the shadows came a heavy rustling. At the back of the shed there was a shelf fixed high up on the wall. As Hašek's eyes moved along it they alighted on a petrol can.

In his haste he trod in something warm and yielding. He swore. Outside a cock crowed. The shelf was high. His fingers stretched, touched the can, pushed it further back. He found a foot-rest and reached high enough to grasp the handle of the can, but the foot-rest grunted and moved and Hašek took a tumble, dragging the full petrol can with him.

The pig slavered over his face, trailing thick strings of saliva. From the sudden stench Hašek gathered the animal was more frightened than he was. It pawed the straw-covered floor with its trotters and seemed to swing its bulk at Hašek as it tried to turn. The petrol can had become lodged between a barrel and the back of the shed. He tugged it free and ran around the confused pig to the door.

A voice was raised inside the farmhouse and a shadow passed behind a window. Hašek abandoned caution and raced across the yard. He reached the track where he'd left his car, when he heard a door opening at the back of the farm. In the twilight he first thought the Tatra had disappeared, but then its silhouette acquired definition against the hedge. There was a cold heavy dew in the air and he was sweating generously. As he emptied the contents of the petrol can into the tank as quietly as possible, his teeth started to chatter.

A large, dark shadow came around the side of the farmhouse towards the dirt track. This time it wasn't a cow or a pig. Hašek was in the driving seat now, having just got the engine to start. Abruptly he realized with absolute certainty that the manufacture of the three-wheel Tatra would have predated the introduction of the reverse gear. There was insufficient room to turn in a circle. And the man coming at him appeared to be holding a shotgun.

In blind desperation but with undoubted vision he rammed the gearstick into the traditional position for reverse. He throttled down, lifted the clutch and jerked backwards. Wavering crazily and almost coming adrift in the hedge, he managed to steer the car back on to the road. He was into first and lurching away at considerable speed before the bemused farmer had taken aim.

Not letting up for a moment on the acceleration he thanked God for the Tatra's previous owner, maybe even Vlastimil's brother, who had not only fitted a decent sound system, but also installed a reverse gear.

*

34

The way it happened was the result of circumstance, not choice.

He had thought he would search for a weak link in the electrified fences where there were neither soldiers nor watchtowers, and cut the wires before driving through, gambling his life on the random distribution of mines.

However, the flow of adrenalin occasioned by the hectic events at the farm didn't stop between his foot and the accelerator pedal. The speedometer needle climbed higher than it had on the expressway and kept on going. Trees and hedges flew past. Only last-minute twists on the wheel saved Hašek from being catapulted through the windscreen when tree trunks stepped into the road after sharp bends like willing suicides. The back end of the Tatra swerved like a child's bicycle, but Hašek had learnt how to compensate. The vegetation thinned out and the road lost some of its curve. Before he knew it Hašek was hurtling down a straight road towards the border post itself.

Several military trucks were parked in a group next to a low hut. Lights burned in the windows, accentuating the clinging penumbral quality of the dawn and the mist into which the dew was coalescing. A soldier stood in the doorway of the hut. A group of men had halted midway between the trucks and the hut. One of them had raised a cigarette halfway to his lips. Some fifty metres from the hut, tight by the wire fence was a watchtower. A woman's hand was in the process of opening a window. Already protruding through the gap was the muzzle of an automatic weapon.

Beyond the fence was a width of scrubland, then another fence. The mist obscured a group of buildings on the other side, so that they were just ill-defined shapes. A few dots of light flickered through the heavy curtains of moisture.

There were lights too away to the north-east where the mist was much less dense.

Where the road met the fence it was blocked by an orange and white barrier.

He was doing 120 kph and clearly was not well placed to carry out his original plan. His foot never left the accelerator, which itself never left the floor.

The soldier in the doorway disappeared inside and a handful of armed men emerged. The group of soldiers already outside split up: some ran to the hut, others back to the parked vehicles; one man stayed rooted to the spot, threw away his still-burning cigarette and extracted a pistol from his belt. The woman in the watchtower slid her window back and leaned out with the butt of an automatic rifle nestling against her shoulder.

On the other side of the fences vague activity took shape behind the veils of mist, which were suddenly torn apart by the bold swathe of a searchlight.

Hašek's Tatra bore down on the barrier. Most of the soldiers were either still running for their weapons or fumbling the safety catches. The markswoman in the tower fired over the car, pitting the tarmac several metres behind him. The rear passenger window was shattered by the lone pistol sniper, whose bullet ripped open the leather upholstery of the front passenger seat.

The barrier loomed in the windscreen. Still clutching the steering wheel and throttling hard, he dropped his head to his knees to protect his face from the impact and shattering glass.

Being an old car, the Tatra's windscreen occupied a relatively small surface area. The roof folded over to a greater degree than on most modern cars. The barrier hit what was effectively the roof and gave way itself since the car was going so fast. It buckled and twisted. Hašek was alert. He kept the car on the road and lost only a little speed, which he soon recovered.

The West Germans raised their barrier and the Tatra bounced over the uneven road surface within centimetres of it.

The Czechs were shooting after him and the West Germans were returning fire. But he couldn't get the blonde woman's voice out of his mind: Ukončete výstup a nástup. Dveře se zavírají. Příští stanice: Frankfurt.

Next stop Frankfurt.

Train de Nuit

'Ian,' she hissed. 'What are you doing? Come away from there.'

'Ssh.' Since his ear was pressed to the door he didn't need to turn his head to see her.

'Ian. Come away,' she repeated, beckoning him frantically.

He waved her back as he continued to listen at the door, to which was attached a plate bearing the name MR S. CLAYTON. Then the girl began to tug on his sleeve. The badge on her white coat identified her as Dr L. Bayley. Ian Cunningham knew her as Lucy. Her concern amused him.

'Come on,' he said, taking her arm. He'd heard enough. They walked quietly and swiftly to the end of the corridor.

'Are you busy?' he asked her. 'Let's go to the canteen.'

'You mustn't do that,' she said, referring to his eavesdropping.

'Clayton's breaking the rules, Lucy. I just need proof.'

'You can't stand there listening outside his door like that. What if he came out? What if someone other than me had caught you?'

Ian stopped and looked at her. 'You don't understand, do you?' he said. 'What he's doing is wrong. *Wrong.*'

She held his gaze but yielded nothing.

'Come on, let's go,' he said, resuming his stride. 'I've got a lot to do even if you haven't.' He said this in jest to rile her and it worked.

'You . . .' Lost for a suitable rejoinder, she ran to catch up with him. She stared at him from the side, trying to shame him into an apology. But he knew she'd taken the joke. As a house doctor she worked harder than anyone in the hospital and in proportionate terms was paid the lowest rate. Five days and two nights a week, plus alternate weekends; overtime paid at a third of the normal hourly rate. Though a nurse himself, Ian had campaigned alongside Lucy and her colleagues for better doctors' conditions.

They entered the canteen. Late in the day it was almost empty. Ian took a plate of spaghetti Bolognese and persuaded Lucy to get a cup of tea.

'I don't want this,' she said as she carried it, following Ian to a table well away from a group of porters and one or two doctors.

'Just pretend, then,' he said. 'I don't want this either. Look at it,' he added, as he set the plate down on the table. 'It's been sitting there since lunchtime.' Nevertheless, he sat down and forked a clump of spaghetti to his mouth. 'Listen,' he said, once she'd sat down. 'Clayton does a lot of transplant operations, right? And most of them are private. Wealthy patients.'

She interrupted him. 'I know your views on private medicine.'

'They're the same as yours. We've discussed it and we agreed. Right?' She nodded. 'Anyway, that's not the point. Sadly, private medicine is not only legal, it's encouraged. The government leads by example. But to get back to Clayton, I want to know where he gets all his organs from. Because I reckon he's doing it illegally.' Ian paused for breath.

Lucy scoffed. 'Why are you so suspicious? You just don't like him, that's all, either because he performs private operations or for whatever reason, I don't know. But if you want my advice, you're wasting your time. He's actually very nice. I don't know what you've got against him. He's just earning a crust like the rest of us.'

There were two high spots of colour on her cheeks. Ian could sense her annoyance. He didn't want the discussion to turn into a confrontation. He hated confrontations. But Clayton really pissed him off. And so did Lucy's sticking up for him.

'That's just it,' he said. 'He's not just earning a crust. He's taking home the whole fucking loaf. And I'm convinced at other people's expense. Maybe at the expense of their lives. This' – he grimaced at the spaghetti – 'is *seriously* unpleasant.'

'Are you jealous of Steve? Is that it?'

'Steve? *Sssteeeve*. Steve now, is it?'

'You *are* jealous.'

'Jealous? Why should I be jealous?'

'Because he bought me lunch that day.'

Ian laughed. 'Lucy, he can buy you a diamond ring for all I care. Don't you get it? I think he's breaking the law by the manner in which he obtains transplant organs. It's got nothing to do with him buying you lunch or being a member of the British National Party or whatever. You know, it's not a personal thing. He can do what he likes as long as it's within the law.'

'Ian, you've got a chip on your shoulder.'

'Oh, yeah, 'cause I'm black, right? So I've immediately got a downer on anyone who's white. Grow up, Lucy. Get real.'

'You wouldn't mind if he took me out to dinner?' she asked provocatively.

'Christ, Lucy, why do you have to turn this into an argument? You know I expect nothing of you or of anybody. If you want to go out to dinner with him, fine. Just don't bother me with the details because I don't want to know.'

He pushed his plate to one side and stared across the canteen, hurt and angry. The confrontation was giving him a headache and Lucy's attitude undermined his remaining confidence in the relationship they were supposedly having.

'Ian,' she said. 'Ian, don't get so cross. I don't want to go out with him, you know. I'm going out with you.'

He began drumming his fingers on his legs. A particular tune – 'Newk's Fadeaway' – had been in his head all day. He wondered where he'd heard it. A Sonny Rollins tune almost forty years old, it was unlikely he'd heard it on a transistor radio playing through an open window somewhere. He'd owned a record which featured the tune, but had sold it along with the rest of his collection two years ago when he'd decided to move to Brighton.

He nodded to confirm Lucy's last comment, which made her sound like a schoolgirl whose boyfriend has just found out she's kissed another boy in the park. He resisted the temptation to make some ironic remark and drummed away.

'Are you bored?' she asked.

'Jus' drummin',' came the reply.

'I don't know why you don't leave nursing,' she said, 'and join a band.'

'You know,' he said, sitting back and tapping out the fading final bars of 'Newk's Fadeaway' on the table top, 'I often wonder that myself. I think it must be you that keeps me here.'

She smirked and Ian wondered why he liked her. She seemed to enjoy making it difficult for him to like her at all.

'Do you like Brighton?' she asked out of the blue.

'Yeah,' he said enthusiastically. He thought for a moment about why she might have asked and about his answer. 'It's got a good atmosphere. Friendly and liberal. I like seeing so many gays in one place.'

She interrupted: 'You mean so there's fewer of them elsewhere?'

'God, you're incredible, Lucy.' He couldn't tell from her expression if she was joking.

She tutted and said 'God' herself. Joking, presumably.

'What about you?' he asked, determined to sustain a conversation. 'Do you like living here?'

'No, not really. I did. I'm bored of it, I s'pose.'

'You've got a very low threshold of boredom, Lucy.'

'I'm still going out with you, aren't I?'

'Here, eat this and die.' He pushed his plate across. 'I'm gonna get him. You'll see.'

Lucy shook her head and pushed the plate of spaghetti further down the table. Unfortunately for her the surface was greasy and the plate didn't stop until it tipped over the edge and crashed on to the floor.

'Gotta go. Bye, Lucy.' Ian sprang out of his chair and bounded to the exit. He looked back. Lucy stared after him, mouthing invective. A member of the canteen staff approached her from behind with a mop and an expression that would wither her when she turned round.

Ian sat with Alice after the doctor, one of Lucy's colleagues, had left to visit another ward. He held the hand of the frail old lady lying in the bed. There were purple shadows under her eyes; apart from these and two smudges of rouge like bruises on her cheekbones, her face was drained of colour. In her wrist Ian felt a pulse so weak he thought it might not have bothered. Alice's mouth hung open and she breathed unaided but shallowly.

'She will die tonight,' the doctor had said as he left Ian, who hoped the patient had not heard. The sky outside the window graduated through shades of blue towards evening and still the old lady breathed. Ian thought of different things as he sat there: ways in which he might expose Clayton, ways in which he and

Lucy had made love (which, when he thought about it, were merely ways in which they had had sex). Occasionally he spoke to the woman in the bed and tightened his grip slightly on her hand. 'You're OK,' he said, which he hoped was comforting rather than misleading. He meant that she was as comfortable as could be expected. The drugs shielded her from most of the pain. In any case, he didn't even know if she could hear him.

One night when they were arriving back at Ian's flat after seeing a film, *The Unbearable Lightness of Being*, he and Lucy had begun undressing each other as soon as the door closed behind them. They had fucked right there in the hall where the carpet was dirtiest, but they didn't care. They had thought they were in love, but now Ian thought it was probably the film that had generated their lust.

'Alice,' he said to the lady with the rouged cheeks. 'You're OK, Alice.' He tightened his hand on hers and her pulse faltered almost as if he'd squeezed the life out of her. It returned like a beat on a drum of softest skin. Like Buddy Rich in '2nd Avenue Blue'. He held on to her with his right hand and played a slow, high-hat cymbal with his left. His right foot hit the kick drum. *I'll get you, Clayton*, he thought. *I'll stop you, Steve. Sssssteeeeve! You'll never transplant organs in Brighton again.*

Alice didn't need a transplant; she needed a new body. The one she'd got was riddled with cancer. Flesh and marrow spiked with rogue cells, veins running with bad blood. But while she died slowly in a soulless ward abandoned by doctors with too many other patients to see, privileged customers took possession of organs by transplant from God knew where, courtesy of Steve Clayton. And he took home a healthy slice. Somewhere somebody died, or managed without a kidney.

Somewhere somebody died . . .

The beat was fading. No matter how good it was while it lasted, '2nd Avenue Blue' always did come to an end. Lost in the tune you thought it might go on for ever. The breathy flute, insubstantial at first but gaining confidence and body. Then the electric guitar: jaunty but still occasionally shy. The tenor sax took over with that natural ease and beauty of tone, a sense of oneness. The song was in its stride. Later the piano, which had been underlying the melody all along, came to the front, and out from underneath at the very end came the bass to lead the way out.

Somewhere somebody died . . .

At least she hadn't felt any pain. Ian hoped she'd heard the music as well. He withdrew his hand and folded her arm across the bed. He sat down again and looked shyly at the old lady's face. Her expression had not changed. But he felt uncomfortable watching her now, voyeuristically, so he looked away. He realized his foot had started again on '2nd Avenue Blue'. From the end of the ward he saw the sister gesturing in his direction. Her eyebrows arched in a question. He nodded to her, thinking to himself: *I'll get you, Clayton.*

He spent the evening in his bedsit, plotting ways in which he would get the evidence he needed. He could sort through Clayton's rubbish, hoping to find a box or wrapper of some kind. He could eavesdrop again, or tap his phone – too expensive to arrange. Intercept his mail – except anything incriminating would surely arrive by courier. Breaking and entering?

Occasionally he turned the pages of an art book which lay open on the floor. The artist was Paul Delvaux. At art college Ian had wanted to study Delvaux, but his teachers told him the Belgian surrealist wasn't suitable. It was that – the fact that he couldn't even study the painter of his choice – plus the fact that his own skill for painting never matched his enthusiasm for other people's work, that made him finally decide to leave art college and get into something useful.

He closed the book and switched off the television he hadn't even been watching and went to bed.

He dreamt of a tunnel under the sea. Of traffic moving through it. Of a train. He was aware of a persistent drumming from the tunnel walls, as if the tunnel hadn't been sunk in the earth and the sea was directly outside, and the tunnel walls were as flimsy as sausage skin. He shrank down in his seat and tried to block out the pulse but even the windows were rattling in their frames. He heard a wooshing noise coming from the aisle and leaned over. A stream of water was flowing up the aisle from the back of the train, rapidly gaining momentum. It sloshed up the sides of seats and splashed the windows.

Ian wrenched himself from his seat and slipped in the aisle. The water rushed towards him only half a carriage behind. Fear churning his insides to froth, he scrambled to his feet and fled. He dragged himself forward faster with his hands on the backs of the seats. But the water was quicker. The gap narrowed.

As the water lapped at his heels and shot tongues forward to grease the floor in front of him, he wondered why he seemed to be the only passenger on this phantasmic train. Where was everyone else?

As he asked himself this question he stumbled into another carriage which was full of people. Every seat was taken and all the passengers were staring at him. Immediately he felt embarrassed. The wave that had chased him had disappeared. But the floor and his trousers were still wet.

They all stared at him and his cheeks burned bright red.

Ian woke up in distress and realized he had wet the bed. He groaned and shifted position, but his sheets and duvet were sodden. Lifting his weight on one elbow, he raised himself off the bed. Gingerly he folded the duvet aside and eased himself out of the bed. He clicked the light switch and viewed the extent of his mishap. There was an enormous stain on the sheet. Ashamed and a little frightened, he switched the light off and slunk into the bathroom, where he showered quickly and towelled his body dry.

Back in his bedsitting room he ripped the sheet off the bed and tore the duvet from out of its cover. He took the sheet and duvet cover and flung them in the bath, turning on the hot tap and sprinkling washing powder. The mattress was damp but Ian wasn't going to sleep on the floor. He got two sheets from the cupboard and spread them out on the bed. Too tired to fit a fresh duvet cover, he just turned it the other way and tugged it up tight around his neck. He closed his eyes and was asleep again almost immediately.

This time he was in a waiting room. He recognized the scene from the Delvaux book. There was a counter on the left-hand side of the room and shelves on the wall behind it. In front of the shelves stood a dark-haired woman wearing a low-cut dress the same colour as the fronds of a palm which grew from a pot at the end of the counter.

Opposite the counter stood a naked woman. Her hair was fair and her skin pale. She was reflected at the far end of the room in a tall mirror, underneath which on a red upholstered bench seat lay another woman as naked as her counterpart. To the left of the bench seat an open doorway led out to the railway platform where the *train de nuit* of the painting's title stood waiting.

Ian felt nervous at first, then peaceful when neither the women nor the situation seemed to offer any threat. All three women appeared to have fallen asleep because, although they had their eyes open, their lines of sight did not intersect even at the most oblique angle. They had been frozen in mid-gesture like statues. Like painted figures, in fact.

Ian concluded that they were asleep and not petrified when he noticed that the train standing at the platform was puffing out smoke. If those little clouds could rise, then so could the women move.

Aware that his continued presence might wake them, Ian got to his feet and crossed the waiting room. The woman behind the bar, the one wearing the dress, had adopted a comfortable if unusual position in sleep: she was standing up straight, possibly leaning some weight against the bar. But the two naked women were awkwardly placed. One leaned forward on the balls of her feet, arms slightly forward; the other was in danger of sliding off the bench seat. Ian admired their forms but found their presentation in no way erotic.

He crossed the waiting room and stepped out on to the platform. The air was cool on his cheeks and wrists and he noticed for the first time that he was improperly dressed for the night. Instead of his green jacket he was wearing a white coat from the hospital, and it offered little protection. The platform was lit only by the moon, which that night was almost full. The carriages of the train he boarded were old-fashioned, relics of another time. Their lines were angular, the colours muted. When Ian had sat down, the train jerked from its standstill and moved slowly out of the station.

In the moonlight the landscape through which the train passed became monochrome. Pine trees stood starkly out from their lighter background, which looked as fine as sand. Soon the trees disappeared and the sand reared up in dunes. The train rattled on through a landscape suddenly more Rousseau than Delvaux, but in the distance a group of buildings took shape. Ian watched as the sketch was given more detail. What had seemed buildings were only ruins, classical ruins; a square lined with colonnades; porticoes and walkways; pillars, archways and circumflexes.

In the centre of the square a group of women walked to and fro like white mice in a cage. Bleached ghostly by the moon, they were as naked as the two women in the railway station waiting room. The train flew closer, then, when the square was almost within hailing distance, veered to the left. Ian was thrown across the carriage by the speed and suddenness of the bend. He landed across the aisle in another seat – they were all unoccupied – and a burst of acceleration pressed his cheek into the head-rest, which was as soft as a down-filled pillow.

The train plunged downwards as if the earth had collapsed – or the sands shifted – and darkness obliterated the view from the windows. But the rattle of the wheels on the rails continued. The thumping axles beat the same tattoo, but Ian couldn't even make out the seat in front of him.

After a time the interior lights came on. Ian blinked at the brightness, then blinked again at the carriage itself. It was different, more modern. Instead of duckboards the floor was smooth and level. The seats were new, the windows bigger. But there was nothing to see; only the black walls of a tunnel.

The dream was such that Ian knew he was dreaming and he tried to wake himself up but couldn't. He lifted his head from the cushioned head-rest and pressed his forehead against the cold window to shock himself awake. But the glass just numbed his forehead and then gradually he felt the motion of the train vibrate through it. He lifted his head away and returned it to the window with a thump. The glass wasn't damaged and his head throbbed, but he hadn't managed to wake himself up. He *had* to, though, because he knew what was going to happen. He could already hear the trickling that had come of some undreamt leak in the fabric of the tunnel wall.

He hit his forehead against the window again. No change. The image of the train that carried him didn't even falter. He could hear the water streaming down the aisle. His head thumped into the glass again. Nothing. He felt sick now, gassy in both stomach and head. He looked round and saw the water gushing towards him at seat height. His trousers were splashed and he turned frantically to the window again and beat his head against it repeatedly.

He woke up in his bedsit draped across the window ledge, one leg in the bed, the other trailing to the floor, and his head next to the window, which was marked with grease.

His head hurt like a thousand hangovers. It was a miracle the glass hadn't been shattered by his efforts.

Grimly he lowered his body back into the bed and felt the sheet to see if the same disaster had befallen him. It was damp but that could have soaked through from the mattress, or it could be sweat. He dismissed it but felt acutely embarrassed again, reminded of the earlier episode. Nobody else knew, nor would they, but still the dominant feeling was one of shame.

He slumped in the bed, depressed after the dreams. He reasoned with himself: maybe he could shake off the mood if he just determined to be cheerful. But he didn't believe it would work. He would be pretending and there was no point in that.

With alarm he identified his symptoms as similar to those of a manic depressive patient he had talked to on the wards. He forced himself to get up and fold away the sofa bed, converting the space back into a living room. He crossed to the end of the room designated the kitchen and made himself a coffee. He took his breakfast to the sofa and sat down. As he crunched corn flakes he tried to think about Clayton and what to do next in his attempt to ensnare him, but thoughts of the damp mattress and brief flashes of his dreams prevented him.

The mattress was part of the sofa bed: he couldn't detach it and stick it out of the window to dry. And as for the dreams: the women and the train came from the Delvaux book, obviously, and the water ... That had to be the bedwetting. But what caused him to do that? He hadn't wet the bed in living memory. Could it really be old Alice's death and the swill of memories it must have stirred subconsciously?

He finished his breakfast and put the dishes in the bowl to soak. His green jacket was on the back of the door. He grabbed it and left.

The streets were relatively empty. Off-season the tourists only besieged the town on weekends. A cool salty breeze blew up off the sea. He buttoned the jacket and pulled the collar up to protect his throat. He was bored with this jacket, he realized. Six months was long enough for a jacket, no matter how much he had liked it when he bought it in one of the second-hand shops off the lanes. He drummed his fingers on the air as he walked. Again, the tune playing in his head was Sonny Rollins's 'Newk's Fadeaway'. He shook his head, puzzled, but didn't stop drumming. As he approached the Treble Clef jazz club he slowed down to read the posters. He noticed a new one plastered over the lower half of the Blues Beat poster, which indicated that Blues Beat had been cancelled and replaced with Alan Barnes. Ian was pleased. Barnes was a *good* alto player. *Brilliant* for a white man.

That cheered him up. He strode off in the direction of the hospital. His luck must be changing, he decided. He could stuff Clayton before lunch, see Lucy in the afternoon when she came out of theatre, and go and listen to Alan Barnes at the end of his shift. It hadn't started off well, but it was going to be a good day after all.

At a junction of three streets he stops, rests his back against the wall and flexes his fingers, effortlessly twisting them into a breathless run up and down the keys he imagines to be there.

He emerges near the main square of the city, facing one of the many decapitated statues. Four ragged figures huddle round a flickering screen under a corrugated shelter to his left. Two of them are smoking, impossible since inhalation and exhalation are beyond their capabilities, but old habits die hard. A third man lifts a bottle to his disfigured mouth and pours alcohol down his throat; again, a useless act, given the absence of thirst and physical sensation. These men indulge their former desires out of habit rather than need.

Last Resort

When Ankers checked in to the Hotel Van Der Griend in Brussels there was a message waiting for him from Hašek: the Czech had been delayed. Ankers carried his case up to his room, then came down again and went out to get some fresh air.

Brussels was no more characterful than it had been ten years earlier when he had visited the city as a tourist and left disappointed. The hotel was situated in the Quartier Leopold. Ankers crossed the ring road into the city proper and headed for the Parc de Bruxelles, whose grim formality had not been softened by time. He wandered aimlessly in a southerly direction, past the Palais Royal and the Palais de Justice, coming into a poor area of dingy streets populated by elderly Bruxellois and immigrants old and young. Shopkeepers offered an unhappy selection of overripe fruit and vegetables and rolls of garish fabric. The few curtains that hung in this district were scraps of grimy lace. A face appeared at one window, like a smear of lard with frightened eyes scooped out.

When he'd caught up with Inger, she'd already come to a halt a few metres from the edge of the promontory. He was surprised to see that she was awake. 'I'm not asleep,' she said. 'You could have stayed in bed.' Although she wasn't sleepwalking, the incident alarmed him.

In recent weeks Inger had appeared to slip into a deep melancholy. When she did speak it was of the frozen north. Floro was too warm, she said. Ankers conceded that the temperature was perhaps a degree higher than it had been a decade earlier, but it could hardly be called oppressive.

She found old photographs of her mother and father, and stuck them on the mirror where she sat when she wasn't watching the sea.

49

Ankers offered to drive her back up to Narvik to spend some time there, but she shook her head, reminding him of what happened to his car the last time he braved the Arctic Circle. He was sure she longed to return there but without his help.

He showed his concern, asking constantly if she was happy. Did she want to go back to her parents? Was there *anything* he could do? She made noises to reassure him, which failed.

When word finally came from Hašek to expect his arrival in Brussels in a few days' time, he was excited and nervous in equal measure.

Having found De Panne on the map, he had wanted to go there immediately, but reason suggested waiting for Hašek. He didn't want to get there with only a cassette and his saxophone and find himself unable to conjure the visions. Hašek wanted to leave Czechoslovakia, and this could be the impetus he needed. More to the point, however, he wanted to play with the man. Metal tape was fine, but surely no substitute for the real thing.

Clouds built up throughout the day and finally precipitated rain when Ankers was on the western side of the city, just wandering. He ducked into a snack-bar and ordered a coffee, which came with melted chocolate and ice cream. He stirred the concoction while watching the waitress as she wiped down the stainless steel surfaces. She worked with quiet dedication. He couldn't imagine Inger doing the same job. Again the worry surfaced in his mind that Inger might take advantage of Ankers's going to Belgium to leave the wooden house and go back north to Narvik. He knew there was a real risk he might return home to find her gone. Picturing an empty house, he felt a great emptiness, which the coffee, sickly with its sugar overdose, couldn't fill.

As it was raining more heavily when he emerged from the snack-bar, he went to catch a train. The Bruxellois didn't communicate a great deal. They didn't hold doors open for each other. Nor did they apologize when they accidentally clashed in a crowded carriage. Before asking for a ticket to be produced, the controller looked to see which newspaper the passenger was reading – whether it was in French or Flemish. The city, officially bilingual, was in fact divided by the language barrier. Although most people knew enough of their foreign tongue to get by, they preferred to remain silent rather than to give offence by speaking to a Fleming in French or vice versa.

Back at the hotel, Hašek had still not arrived. In his room Ankers showered and shaved and since he was travelling light put the same clothes back on: his fisherman's sweater, woollen trousers and lightweight windcheater. He went downstairs for dinner. There were several residents dining at the same time, but even foreigners in Brussels kept their distance – though south of Oslo, it was a colder city.

After coffee Ankers repaired to the bar. He ordered a brandy and fell into conversation with the handsome Scottish barman. Wiping the counter top with a damp cloth, the barman asked him if he'd ever been to Scotland and Ankers admitted that he had not. The barman, who had visited Norway, assured him that a Norwegian would have no reason to be disappointed by the highlands and islands.

Ankers took his drink to the lounge and sat down in front of the television. He was looking around for the remote control when a tall, thin, blond man appeared quietly from nowhere. The newcomer had a frank, piercing quality in his eye; in his hand was the control box. He offered a half-smile. Ankers thanked him. The man withdrew and Ankers noticed he was wearing a cashmere scarf, which seemed incongruous indoors.

He flicked through the dozen or so channels until the game shows gave way to a news programme, but, apart from continuing ethnic strife in the Soviet Union, the world seemed quiet. Ankers killed the TV and sat staring at the blank screen for at least five minutes, wishing Hašek would arrive so they could go to De Panne. Then he returned to the bar for another large brandy. The barman said he couldn't fail to notice, when Ankers had checked in, that he carried an instrument case of some kind.

'What do you play, if you don't mind me asking?'

'Tenor saxophone,' Ankers told him.

After breakfast he checked with the desk for any messages.

'Sorry, sir.'

He asked if the hotel took any international newspapers. The answer was the same. Checking in his pocket for change, he strode towards the double doors that led to the street. As he pulled open one door, a man coming in from outside opened the other. Ankers took in the man's appearance as they passed each other in the doorway. He had shoulder-length, dark, tousled hair, and several days' beard growth. A short man, he was sure of his step.

Parked at the kerb was a strange, black car with only three wheels. The bodywork was dented and grazed in many places. Curious, he peered through the dusty back window. On the seat he could make out two or three scattered cassette tapes and a case very much like his own, only slightly smaller.

He spun round on his heel and headed back into the foyer of the hotel.

'This is slower than the trams in Prague,' Hašek grumbled. 'And the city is less beautiful.'

Their meeting earlier in the day had been effusive, embarrassing both men and the hotel clerk. They withdrew and became wary, Hašek excusing himself on the pretext of checking in to his room. Later, to escape the confines of the hotel bar, they went out and took a tram. Ankers wondered how they were going to get on. The man had occasionally shouted at him down the telephone that the Czech government was wicked and corrupt, their laws Kafkaesque and the secret police brutal beyond comparison.

'But, er . . .' Ankers took his hand from the pole and mimed playing the sax.

'Yes, I know, Ankers,' said the Czech, 'I know. Here I can play what I like.' He smiled ironically.

'You did want to leave Czechoslovakia?' Ankers asked.

Hašek paused a moment, then said in an ambivalent tone, 'Yes. Yes, I did. I said so many times, I believe.'

Ankers motioned to Hašek that they were getting off and they moved to the concertina doors. Hašek *had* said so, often. Ankers glanced at the inscrutable Czech and hoped he'd done the right thing by pushing him to leave the country. Whatever had happened afterwards was neither his fault nor Hašek's.

'You can always go back,' he said, as they stepped down on to the pavement, 'if you don't like it.'

'Yes, I can go back,' he replied sombrely. 'If I'm lucky I may only be shot.'

Ankers led the way up the street, feeling hurt and not a little foolish.

Hašek had been worrying about his friends since leaving Czechoslovakia. He had a feeling, no better defined than the memory of a dream, that the security forces had turned nasty after his departure. He'd tried to phone Vlastimil and Bedrich from West Germany but had been unable to get through. None of the newspapers and TV news bulletins he'd managed to see while crossing West Germany and Belgium had mentioned any casualties. They reported the event because the twentieth anniversary of Jan Palach's suicide was news, but by all accounts the day had passed without tragedy.

Mystified and anxious, Hašek knew he had been unfriendly to Ankers, who also had much on his mind. When they returned to the Hotel Van Der Griend, Hašek had a few drinks and relaxed, becoming almost jolly.

The proprietor, standing behind the bar with his barman, demanded to know if they *both* played the sax. He was the tall thin man with boyish features whom Ankers had encountered the previous evening. When Hašek nodded, he pleaded with them to give a recital. The barman refused to serve any more drinks until they played.

Ankers was very reluctant. 'I don't usually perform,' he protested feebly.

Hašek clapped him on the back, grinning. 'Come on, Ankers,' he boomed. 'Do not be so shy. We must oblige our hosts.'

Five minutes later Hašek slipped into the melody line of W.C. Handy's 'Ole Miss'. After seven bars Ankers took up the harmony.

They played for an hour or more, drinking steadily and delighting the proprietor, his barman and several guests who drifted into the bar. Not once, however, did they play anything remotely modern. The Czech authorities would definitely have approved.

Owing to the steady deterioration of Hašek's antique Tatra – Ankers had left the Taunus in Floro and come to Belgium by train – they did not reach De Panne until the evening of the next day.

Investigation of the immediate area produced no clues. The sea front in particular was disappointing, there being few dunes and no traces at all of either Roman-style buildings or naked, wide-eyed sleepwalkers. Inland, the town was moribund. The two jazzmen gravitated towards the railway station and loitered on the platform.

Hašek had been quiet for most of the day, not even returning Ankers's occasional glances.

Ankers leant back against a pillar and visualized Inger: her hair the colour of arctic sand, eyes turquoise as a puffin's. He pictured Narvik, where she claimed the air was purer and the light closer to what God had had in mind when He made the world.

The night was disturbed by a long, low wail, which made Ankers think of the seals he'd seen Inger observe longingly as they gathered in the rocky inlet below their house. He looked up and saw Hašek a hundred metres down the platform, his alto sax hovering under the dot of his mouth like an inverted question mark. Ankers stretched out an arm towards his case and within half a minute was breathing into an F which fitted snugly under Hašek's A flat.

The music meandered. Only when the two instruments tried to play the same note and had to dart away to opposite ends of the scale – like two trains attempting to enter a tunnel on the same track and both disrailing to mount the embankments on either side – did Ankers accept that they were playing one of Hašek's pieces, whether it be an old number or something new they were creating together. Even when it appeared to be in trouble, the harmony did not go astray. The two men continued to improvise. At times Ankers took the lead, at the invitation of the other man.

Since the vision did not come immediately, Ankers closed his eyes to speed its arrival. When nothing came and he opened his eyes again, he caught sight of an old man passing on the other side of the road from the railway station. He saw him soon enough, before the man disappeared around the corner, to recognize his preoccupied look and the circular lenses of his spectacles.

Hašek looked over to see why Ankers had stopped playing.

54

'Come on. Quickly,' shouted the Norwegian, shoving his saxophone into its case and jumping across the tracks. Hašek followed.

Rather than catch up with the old man, they elected to fall back and see where he would lead them. Soon the surroundings became familiar to Ankers, as they once again quickened their step to keep the old man in sight amongst the dunes. Hašek still claimed not to have experienced anything like the visions Ankers had described to him.

As soon as the ruins and the square came into view, Ankers could see that the sea had advanced considerably; the most vulnerable buildings were already waterlogged and high waves had begun crashing down on the steps and columns of monuments which before had been left dry.

Twenty-five metres from the edge of the square, Ankers tasted salt. He stopped when he reached a long colonnade. One of the women was walking directly towards him. She was naked, but his gaze did not move from her eyes: wide like saucers, they seemed to behold him, betraying no sign of acknowledgement or, indeed, life. Only metres away, yet separated from him by more than the width of ancient colonnade, she lifted her arms into the air, spelling signs from a meaningless language with her slender hands. In the moonlight she looked pale as a shop-window mannequin; her eyes might have been glass. But her fair hair lifted by the wind off the sea as she turned was as real as Inger's.

She was joined by a woman in a red velvet dress, and the two of them walked along the line of crumbling pillars in the direction of the surf. Bubbles of froth landed on their shoulders and caught in their hair, but they only turned away when the perimeter of the square allowed them to go no further towards the sea.

Ankers looked across the square and saw Hašek on the far side, stepping into the path of an advancing group of women. Beyond Hašek the figure of the old man could be seen walking back into the dunes.

'We must follow him,' Ankers panted, as he drew level with the Czech. Together, despite Hašek's reluctance, they hefted their cases and set off in pursuit.

'There is something in their eyes,' Hašek said, clearly awed by what he was witnessing. 'Some kind of sadness.'

Ankers commented: 'It seems to me more like absence.'

'Like me,' Hašek continued, 'they are in exile.'

'Oh, shut up, Hašek!' Ankers marched on ahead. Something apart from the plight of the sleepwalkers was troubling him and had been since before his frustrating encounter with the fair-haired woman. In the circumstances, Hašek's precocious impressions of exile were irritating.

They followed the old man until he eventually disappeared into a sprawling, single-storey building. Finding no obvious trace of the old man's entrance route, they investigated the rear of the building and came upon an unlocked door.

To allow their eyes to become accustomed to the darkness, they waited in the gloomy corridor for a few moments. There were no sounds to be heard in the darkness. The moon, just a sliver shy of full, cast a ghostly pallor on the far end of the corridor, by means, they discovered when they had felt their way down there, of a skylight. The next corridor led into a room, again lit only by moonlight, but its windows were generous, so Ankers and Hašek could not only see that the walls were hung with paintings, but were able to make out their subjects.

Every painting featured women, eyes wide and apparently walking in their sleep, most of them naked and awash with moonlight. A group of women stood around another woman lying on the ground; in the background a mysterious stand of trees. One woman wearing a long dress saw herself naked in a mirror. Another in a different painting embraced the statue of a man with no arms or legs. Women walked through a forest where giant plantains grew among the trees. Women and men, mostly unclothed, thronged about a bespectacled old man against a background of ancient buildings. A dark-haired woman lay on a chaise longue, exposing herself to the dressmaker's dummy which stood at its end.

Ankers swallowed and moved on, scarcely believing his eyes.

The next room had women in railway station waiting rooms, crossing tramlines, watching signals change. After that the women were almost always close to the sea: walking through uncompleted cities bordered by dunes, patrolling desolate colonnades, faced with staircase after staircase leading only to the sea.

Ankers exchanged a look with Hašek. The Czech seemed deeply disturbed. He mumbled something and glanced at the floor. Ankers was already heading out of the room into another corridor. The door at the end opened into an artist's studio. Canvases were everywhere, propped up against the wall and hanging on it, leaning against an unmade bed and even wrapped in a tangle of sheets. Moonlight was shed by an enormous skylight and large windows. The two men dropped their cases on the floor.

The old man looked up only briefly from his easel, which held a canvas bigger than any they had seen so far.

'I am almost at the end of possibilities,' the old man announced in French, apparently unsurprised by his visitors. 'I don't know if I can save them.'

Hašek followed Ankers when he stepped over to the painter's side of the easel. The canvas was a jumble of numbers, hundreds of thousands of numbers, painted with a very fine black brush. There was more order, however, than there at first appeared: the numbers were arranged in columns and they all had two decimal places. 21.14, 03.22, 09.37, 16.43 . . .

'It's the time,' Hašek murmured.

'*Times*. Going back years,' Ankers whispered, turning to Hašek. 'It's a tide table.'

'It will not work,' said the artist. 'But I must finish it anyway.'

'You're trying to change the tides,' Ankers exclaimed.

'After this,' the artist declared in a thin voice, 'there is only a last resort.'

Ankers leaned closer to study the progression of numbers on the canvas. The painter dabbed his brush on the black smudge of his palette and added more minuscule numbers to the list.

Shadows moved around the studio as the moon arced across the skylight and Ankers sat watching the painter. He was barely aware that Hašek had taken out his saxophone to begin playing mournful asides, and even less aware of his own actions as he reached for his instrument and joined in.

Battering against the ancient square, the waves had increased in force and depth. Though frequently splashed in the face, the women did not awaken, but walked on and around in several centimetres of water. Ankers noticed a new intensity in Hašek's playing, belying a vacant, lost look in his eyes. In the square, Ankers caught sight of the fair-haired woman whose vulnerability had moved him, and stopped playing.

In the studio alone with the painter, Ankers knew that rewriting the tide tables could not reverse such a dramatic rise in sea level. The women would drown in their sleep.

'I had to finish it just to see,' said the old man, replacing the large canvas with one of normal size. From where he stood, Ankers could not see what, if anything, was on the new canvas. 'The last resort,' the painter said, smiling, as he began filling in details.

Ankers moved to the old man's side and surveyed the canvas now on the easel.

The wind freshened, blowing his hair back from his forehead. With the back of his hand, Ankers wiped salty spray from his lips.

For the first time since he had seen them, the women, now that they were swimming in the sea, seemed to have shaken off the veil of sleep. They held hands, no longer gesticulating in a void. Occasionally, their large tail fins broke the surface and thrashed the swell playfully.

The distance between them and Ankers was growing as they swam further out, but he thought he could see a smile on Hašek's face. It seemed right that the exiled man should be allowed to go with them.

He scanned the women's faces again, those he could see through the distant choppy waves, searching to ascertain if he had only imagined one particular face in the bottom corner of the artist's canvas. A face with turquoise eyes and hair like arctic sand.

The Face Behind the Mask

Ian listened outside Clayton's door for two minutes before trying the handle. There had not been a sound: neither the whisper of papers nor the rustle of a voice on the telephone. Therefore, if Clayton wasn't there, the door would be locked. But Ian tried it anyway.

There was a sickeningly loud click, and the door opened.

For a second he didn't know what to do. Fall back and flatten himself against the wall, or run? Or walk right in, with a false pretext in case the good doctor was in. In an instant he had chosen the third option and stepped inside.

The room was empty. Or seemed to be. He called: 'Mr Clayton.' Just in case.

There was no answer – unless the tapping of leaves against the window and a dripping tap could be counted as one. Ian closed the door behind him. Had there been a key in the lock he would have locked it. As it was, he would have to be quick. Clayton would only leave the door unlocked if he was planning to be right back. Because he had something to hide. And now was Ian's chance to find out what.

There were some papers on the desk that Ian shuffled through. He found nothing unusual. He opened a drawer full of pens, rulers, empty charts. The next drawer down held a stack of letter-head and a bunch of envelopes. Nothing that shouldn't be there.

His heart was thumping, pulse racing.

Then he heard footsteps.

But when they reached the door they didn't stop, and there was no subsequent click of the door handle.

Ian looked in the third drawer, but it was empty. It occurred to him he might be looking too closely. By doing so he could miss something obvious.

On the window ledge were several cacti. Normal. Sort of.

Banal, in fact. It made sense. Clayton was banal, for all his pretensions to radicalism (claiming to support the junior doctors' protest against conditions; wearing a denim shirt under his white coat). But banality, like transplantation, was not a crime. It was all a question of how he got hold of his organs and from whom.

Clayton's room was part office, part lab. Workbenches lined two walls. A sink was an inset feature of the bench below the cacti; it was here that a tap dripped. Ian went to tighten the faucet but hesitated and drew back. Let it drip. He should leave the room as he found it – unless he found what he wanted.

Ian froze.

He had heard a click. His eyes went straight to the door handle but it didn't move.

Click.

The window. It was just a twig on the window.

As the tension broke, sweat flowed and his stomach began to haul itself up to his throat. He listened intently for a moment before concentrating once more on his search. After the sink the bench continued for several yards until it hit the wall. There was a microscope and a box of slides.

At the wall the bench turned through 90 degrees.

(*Where was Clayton?*)

On the bench, his eyes scanning from right to left, were two foolscap folders full of notes, a Filofax (*why wasn't that on his desk?*), a packet of cigarettes, a dirty mug, a pile of loose papers thin as onion skins,

(*Where's Clayton?*)

a couple of pens, a test-tube rack,

(*For a bizarre moment Ian thought he might be on* The Generation Game. *Clayton would come in and say, 'What did you see? What did you see? Did you see a test-tube rack? A cluster of Petri dishes? Two organ boxes?*)

a bottle of methylated spirit, a discarded swab . . .

Two organ boxes.

Two organ boxes. He'd found them.

(*Where's Clayton?*)

Almost hyperventilating as a result of the tension, he approached the bench, *feeling* the boxes with his eyes.

There were footsteps in the corridor outside the door.

Oh, fuck what do I do now? I could stay here and brazen it out. Say I was looking for him and the door was open. What though? What did I want him for? Or I could . . .

Before Clayton had finished opening the door, Ian had vaulted on to the edge of the sink, climbed to the window ledge, slipped the catch and jumped out.

It was only one storey. Ian heard Clayton's footsteps crossing the office floor as he fell. His landing was soft and filled his shoes with damp soil. Picking himself up agilely, he ran to the nearest shelter.

Once he had ducked around the corner of the east wing, Ian sneaked a look back. The window was still open, which probably meant he'd got away with it.

At a price.

His left hand, the thumb and the palm, bristled with spines from one of Clayton's cacti which he remembered grasping accidentally. Why didn't Clayton appear at the window? Surely a gaping window and a dislodged cactus, possibly scattered across the floor, would have raised the alarm.

He tried to pluck out the tiny spears that stung his hand, but his fingers were trembling from the nervous release and the excitement.

If only he'd had time to snatch one of the boxes as physical evidence.

He gained purchase on a long spine and tugged. *Owww!*

He shook the injured hand in pain thinking, *99 to go!* When he was able to unclench the hand he counted less than half that number, but still thought he should find something to numb the hand.

He sloped away from the east wing in case Clayton *had* seen him and was now making his way round to apprehend him. He threaded a route through the hospital car park, heading for the main buildings. He would be able to get something from Ray to ease the pain while he extracted the spines.

What he had seen, finally, in Clayton's room was the proof he needed. The organ boxes should not have been in his room in the first place. If the contents had ever been legit, the boxes would have been in the pathology department under lock and key.

But the real giveaway was the lettering on the side of one of the boxes. The alphabet was not Roman but Cyrillic.

Only recently Ian had followed a case in the news about a Bulgarian peasant allegedly tricked into selling one of his kidneys to a London doctor. Clayton could even be working through the same contacts. But whatever the identity of his associates, he was almost certainly involved in the same kind of business: paying desperate peasants under the odds for an organ they could live without as long as its counterpart didn't fail. Otherwise, why the secrecy? Why the departures from the rule book and the large numbers of transplant operations performed privately by Clayton?

Ian's head throbbed. He saw now that in addition to the forty-odd large spines there was a multitude of tiny bristles like five o'clock shadow. He entered the building at the main doors and turned right after reception.

'Ray,' Ian said upon arrival at the pharmacy store. 'I've got to have something to kill this hand while I get these out.' He showed the man the afflicted hand.

'How the fuck d'you do that?' Ray asked.

'I grabbed hold of a cactus, didn't I.'

Ray stared at Ian in puzzlement but no more explanation was forthcoming.

'Why don't you go round to casualty?'

'Ray,' Ian said impatiently. 'Please. You know how busy they are. Anyway, I'd feel a right dick. Come on, give us something.'

Ray looked doubtful but eventually ducked between his shelves of drugs. Ian looked round while he waited. At the end of the corridor were the theatres. As Ian watched he saw one set of swing doors pushed open and green-robed figures emerge from theatre number three. Even before she'd pulled off her mask, Ian saw that one of the surgeons was Lucy. Deep in conversation with another doctor, whom Ian vaguely recognized, she didn't notice him. They passed into the changing room together.

Ian frowned. A thought had crossed his mind.

When the surgeon in charge of an operation had completed the major part of the work, he sometimes left more junior colleagues to tidy up the patient in terms of suturing and cleaning. What if . . .

'Here,' Ray interrupted. 'Use this. Ethyl chloride.' He held out a small spray bottle.

'Ray,' Ian said, taking the bottle in his good hand. 'Who's just been operating in number three?'

Ray thought for a moment. 'Er, Clayton,' he said. 'I think. But I can easily check if you like.'

'No need,' Ian said.

Ian walked disconsolately to the nearest staff toilets and locked himself into a cubicle. Closing the lid, he sat down.

'Ah, fuck,' he said to the floor as he shook his head. The hand had suddenly become a minor concern, the discovery of the boxes a thin triumph.

Lucy didn't altogether share his views on private medicine, but he had thought she was sensitive to them to the extent that she did no private work herself. Now he discovered she was working privately. But that, even that, was pedantry. What stung him was that she was working with Clayton, the man she knew he despised. Ian had explained to her what he believed Clayton was up to, and still she stood alongside him at the operating table.

He felt his spirits sink lower and lower until tears began to well up from the bottom of it all. He looked at his hand. 'Aw, fuck it,' he said.

As the tears dried on his cheeks, he gripped and twisted off the cap. The ethyl chloride made his hand icy cold; he covered the affected area, then put the bottle down on the floor and started plucking out the spines. Some by now had worked themselves loose; others needed more encouragement and slipped out no more easily than fish hooks. He continued to spray the contents of the bottle over his hand, and while the effect was noticeable it failed to kill all the pain.

It took him twenty minutes to remove all the big spines, which was how long it should have taken Lucy to get cleaned up and changed. He would find her and have lunch with her and not mention that he'd seen her coming out of Clayton's theatre.

Instead, he would tell her what he'd seen in Clayton's room and see what she said. He saw it as giving her a last chance.

Ian flushed the dregs down the toilet and dumped the bottle in a bin underneath the washbasin. He gave his hands a thorough wash and felt the snag of tiny spines he had not been able to get hold of with his fingernails.

*

63

At the canteen he caught up with Lucy in the queue. 'I've got something to tell you,' he said.

'What?'

'Tell you when we're sat down.' He craned forward to see how long the queue was. 'I'll get these,' he said when they had reached the till. Lucy flicked her fringe like an irritated mare and carried off her tray.

'Come over here,' Ian said, gesturing towards a less crowded corner. Lucy's shoulders sagged and she looked heavenward. But Ian had already marched off, leaving her no choice. She followed him and sat down diagonally opposite. He ignored this small statement and moved along to face her. He half smiled and took his fork in his right hand. He stabbed a potato and raised it to his mouth. Lucy stared at him, not caring to hide her annoyance.

'Well, tell me then,' she said. 'What is it that's so exciting?'

He pointed to his mouth, which was chewing food. She became exasperated and still he chewed, widening his eyes as if to say, *You don't want me to talk with my mouth full, do you?*

Lucy made to get up. Ian stopped her. 'Sit down,' he said. 'You haven't touched your food.'

'I'm not hungry,' she answered irritably, sitting down again. 'Are you going to tell me or aren't you? I can't imagine *what* it's about.'

'Can't you?' he wondered, enjoying the dramatic irony. 'It's Clayton. Remember that stuff I told you? Well, now I've found evidence. It's not just a theory any more.' He continued eating. He carved a chunk of meat from his chop and lifted the fork to his mouth. 'I love food,' he said.

'Oh, you really are getting me annoyed, Ian. What are you going on about? You sound like a bloody policeman.'

'In Clayton's office,' he uttered, between mouthfuls, 'I saw two transplant boxes.'

Lucy burned red with anger. 'You went in Steve's office?' she demanded. He nodded, his mouth full. 'How dare you? You can't do that. That's spying.'

Ian's jaws were still working. He pointed with his finger and chomped exaggeratedly. Then, food swallowed, he sucked his teeth and exclaimed in delight. 'That was great!' he said.

'Ian!' Lucy was enraged. The long-term implications of this conversation had become evident to Ian. Lucy was not his girl, never really had been, nor would be. So it didn't matter if he wound her up. There was little to lose. He could at least extract a splinter of bitter enjoyment.

But her raised voice had turned heads right across the canteen.

'Look, Lucy,' he said earnestly. 'I now know for certain what Clayton's up to and it's not something a woman in your position wants to get involved with. So, are you in or not?'

Lucy pushed her chair back and stood up, nudging the table as she did so. The table leg barked against Ian's shin. He took in a sharp breath but held his tongue. Lucy was looking at his left hand. Against the white table top it blazed. He'd forgotten about the hand but felt the hundreds of tiny wounds again as she stared at it.

Her lips pursed in some bitter parody of victory, she looked him in the face again. He looked up at her, lifting his hand off the table at the same time and hiding it in his lap.

She whisked round and strode away from the table. He felt cheated. The moral victory had been his but he hadn't let her know it. Instead, she'd made him feel small and petty.

'Shit,' he muttered. 'Shit, shit, shit . . . *shit!*'

Something else was worrying him as well: how the hell was he going to drum when his left hand felt like a pin cushion?

He went on to the wards, reminding himself of an adage he'd once read in a banal magazine and which had stuck in his mind: you had to be alive to complain.

Some of these people couldn't even walk, yet they still managed to go on. He could walk, think straight and play the drums.

When he reached the ward where he'd held Alice's hand as she died, he realized he was humming '2nd Avenue Blue' and tapping an imaginary cymbal with his hand, his *left* hand.

Alice's bed, he saw, was empty. By evening it would almost certainly be occupied. They barely had time to change the sheets.

That recalled his own spoilt bed linen and '2nd Avenue Blue' was temporarily forgotten. He hoped the foam mattress would have dried out.

'Ian. Please.' It was the nursing sister. She called him over to the bedside of a middle-aged man with throat cancer.

'Hello, Mr Tindall,' Ian said, smiling at the patient. Mr Tindall just managed to raise a hand and the skin creased at the corners of his eyes. *Hours rather than days,* thought Ian. And then a thought struck him like a bolt. He flinched and reeled, forgetting where he was.

'What's wrong with you?' the sister asked. She was not unkindly.

Ian moaned quietly, turning away from the bed.

'What is it?' she asked.

Ian looked at her. Could he tell her? Yes . . . No . . . It was a crazy idea and he hoped it wasn't true.

'Migraine,' he said, clasping his forehead. 'I've had it on and off all day,' he lied. 'I think I'd better . . .'

'Go and lie down,' she said, firmly but with indulgence. He felt bad for deceiving her but it was necessary. He half-staggered extravagantly out of the ward. Once round the corner he picked up his heels and ran down the corridor.

It was the sight of Mr Tindall so close to death that made him think of it. And the idea of Clayton plundering old Alice's defenceless body was enough to knock him backwards.

Ian didn't know where Alice's body had been taken but guessed at the mortuary. He ran now in that direction. Pictures tumbled through his mind as he ran: Lucy emerging from the theatre and tearing off her mask, the transplant boxes on Clayton's bench, the fistful of cactus spines, the marbled toilet floor, Mr Tindall's final efforts at communication. He willed the images to continue as they masked one far more malignant which his mind could not suppress: Clayton plunging his hands into Alice's ruptured corpse, digging for gold.

Drums, thought Ian. *Drums. Sax. '2nd Avenue Blue'. Buddy Rich. Alan Barnes. Alto sax. Jazz Renegades. Philip Caramazza. Charlie Parker. Bird.*

He flung himself round a corner and dodged between two laundry trolleys that almost converged to hit him, or such was his impression.

Ian skidded to a halt, sweating as he levelled his gaze at the locked doors barring entry to the mortuary. Nurses had no business here, not even charge nurses.

Alice couldn't be anywhere else other than in the mortuary.

Unless Clayton had already operated and taken what he wanted.

But what use would Alice's organs be anyway, ravaged by cancer?

The silence in the corridor was abruptly shattered by the bleeper in his pocket. The sudden noise made him jump. Sister must be wondering where he was. He crossed the room and picked up the wall-mounted phone in the corridor.

He was connected and heard a male voice utter his name.

'Yes?' he responded.

'It's Steve Clayton here,' the voice said. 'Would you come to my office? Now.'

Ian's knees went weak and he felt instantly sick. Clayton had hung up. His manner was unequivocal: he knew what Ian was up to and now was confrontation time.

Why had Clayton used his own Christian name? Was it like the prison governor coming into your cell on death row and offering you a cigarette, saying, *Call me George*? He couldn't go. He didn't have to. He could just walk out of the hospital and never look back.

Or he could go and take the principal administrator with him, having told her the whole story.

But he had, in fact, to go alone and confront Clayton with the facts.

I know what your game is, Clayton, and I've got evidence. You're finished. You'll never operate in this country again.

Exit Clayton, head bowed under cloud of shame.

Enter Lucy, beaming with pride in discovered hero. They embrace.

The end.

It put off the fear of confrontation. Ian was only two ward lengths away and Clayton's office was drawing nearer. He kept going because he believed that he had to. He was committed now.

When he reached the door he told himself not to knock, but to march straight in as a gesture of defiance.

He knocked.

Clayton said: 'Come.'

Ian's hand twisted the door handle and for the second time that day he stepped into Clayton's room. His eyes went straight to the bench where the transplant boxes had been – and were no longer.

'Shut the door,' said an unseen voice. Ian complied. Clayton was standing behind his desk, his white coat unbuttoned. 'Come here. Sit down,' he said softly.

Ian crossed the floor and sat down where Clayton had indicated. Then he stood up again, angry with himself for becoming subservient.

'I know what's happening,' he said hesitantly, not daring to use the doctor's name. Names, he believed, were dangerous. It had taken him weeks to make first use of Lucy's name.

Thinking of her fuelled his anger.

'I know what you're doing,' he said. Nausea filled him. This was the confrontation he had feared. He wanted to leave the room and run home. But he was committed. Maybe for the first time in his life he had a real responsibility and he couldn't relieve himself of it.

Clayton had spoken. Slowly the words, still hanging in the air like after-images on the retina, echoed in his mind: 'What are you talking about?'

'What? Whaa . . .' he stuttered.

Lucy. The transplant boxes. Alice.

'What am I talking about?' He ignored the gnawing fear which threatened to debilitate him. It wasn't the possibility of violence that worried him, though as a coward he didn't relish the idea. It was just the mutual opposition of two people who were obliged to expose their quarrel. And the consequences here were considerable. Someone would win, the other would lose. 'The transplant boxes,' he said, feeling sick. 'You've moved them.' Clayton said nothing. Ian forced his eyes to look at the other man's. Clayton had managed to contrive an air of patient indulgence. This young man had fallen prey to some delusion or had been misled by a fool. 'Where are they?' Ian asked, breaking the spell.

'Mr Cunningham,' said Clayton, 'either you've made a mistake or you're inventing a story, though for what purpose I cannot imagine.'

Ian sneaked a look at the window ledge. The cactus he'd knocked over had been righted and the window closed. Clayton was just making like there had been no intruder. He had probably checked that nothing important was missing. Ian guessed the transplant boxes were stashed in the boot of Clayton's car or hidden in the bowels of the hospital.

With no conscious intention Ian moved to the back of the room and pointed to the empty space on Clayton's workbench.

'This is where they were,' he heard his voice saying, scarcely believing it. 'Two transplant boxes with Cyrillic writing on the side. Where were they from? Bulgaria? Like that doctor in London? Or Russia, or Yugoslavia?'

'That's enough,' Clayton snapped. 'You're in trouble, Mr Cunningham. I don't know what you're implying but I've had enough of your attitude. If you've got emotional problems you shouldn't bring them to work.'

'Tell me, Clayton. Where were they from? It was Bulgaria, wasn't it? You paid some poor peasant a couple of thousand quid and bought his kidney, you bastard. Then you sold it to someone who needed it and had the kind of money you were asking.'

Ian was breathless – and exhilarated. He'd never let go like this before. He took deep breaths and his head swam. He mustn't hyperventilate.

'I'm phoning security,' Clayton said, reaching for the phone.

Ian crossed the room in a flash and knocked the phone out of Clayton's hand. 'No way,' he shouted. 'That kidney,' he said. 'Was that the operation you were doing this morning?' He grabbed the lapels of Clayton's white coat. 'Was it? Tell me!' The doctor's denim shirt beneath the white coat was crumpled. He screamed: 'Tell me!'

Clayton thrust his arms forward and loosed Ian's grip. 'I've taken enough of this,' he roared and pushed Ian backwards. He tottered and collapsed into the chair. Clayton was shouting at him: Ian had no proof and was a fool to make such serious allegations without any. Ian knew his accusations were grounded in truth and he knew Clayton knew it. But the doctor had not admitted his guilt. Ian knew the man across the desk from him had won. He had caught victory's sweet scent, had grasped its slender stem. But once plucked, the flower dried up and died in an instant. Its seeds blew around the office, finding no purchase in the stony bedding of the cacti.

Ian felt light-headed. He had summoned from within himself the courage to confront the doctor, but at the critical point he had been betrayed by banal circumstance. He simply couldn't prove that Clayton had done what he knew he had done. The fighting spirit drained out of him, his hand throbbed dully and Clayton barked instructions into the phone. He heard the word 'security' but made no effort to leave his seat. Tiredness numbed his responses, the weariness of defeat.

Within moments footsteps came pounding down the corridor towards Clayton's room. There was a perfunctory knock and the door flew open. Clayton pointed at Ian in the chair and two burly men helped him from it.

Ian knew the doctor was trying to scare him into doing nothing, but without hard proof nothing was all he could do. His word, that of a black male nurse six months on the staff, against Clayton's, a consultant of five years' service. And a white man. Old resentments died hard, but he knew race wasn't a factor here. He hoped both he and the country itself had grown out of that.

The security guards frogmarched him down the long corridor. He thought of American TV movies in which he would summon strength from the well of the scriptwriter's brain and wrench himself free. He would hare back down the corridor and knock Clayton for six, produce the transplant boxes out of thin air and go straight to the hospital director. Clayton would be sacked in disgrace and prosecuted, while he, Ian, was praised and awarded promotion, swamped by admiring pressmen and Lucy's embraces.

The doors were kicked open and Ian pushed out on to a gravel path. He stumbled and collapsed. Behind him the doors were pulled shut and footsteps faded away.

He drives most of the way to the border one-handed. His left hand mimes the lower notes while the fingers of his right hand tap out the high notes on the steering wheel. The sky appears briefly between concrete walls and rusting iron roofs. Literally thousands of people are wandering about; most of them stone dead.

Although he does not possess a saxophone, he hears the melody line of 'These Foolish Things' as clearly as if he were actually playing it.

The further he goes the more concrete and rough stone dominate the ramshackle architecture at the expense of iron and steel. The dead are everywhere, walking from one construction to another, visible also through gaps in the walls, sitting watching television and playing games.

Heralds of the New Spring

No matter how many times he read the letter, it became no clearer. An invitation from Petrović to visit him in Ljubljana; but why, and for how long?

Bentinck wiped a large orange handkerchief across his forehead. He took off his glasses and wiped the bridge and then down both sides of his nose. Despite the icy air outside, he had worked up a sweat through the exertion of changing trains. According to the weather forecast he'd seen the night before at home in Zürich, temperatures throughout southern Europe were expected to rise unseasonally over the next few days. He wished fervently he were at home now. It would be cool, more than likely raining. He could walk up to the cemetery or down to the lake. Instead of which, he was stuck in an unmoving train.

His eyes caught the gaze of the young man opposite with strange little glasses no bigger than his eyes, who had smiled at him awkwardly when Bentinck had dropped his bag trying to put it on the rack. It was a big, heavy bag. Petrović had not indicated how long his stay might be and Bentinck did not know how well the Yugoslav would be able to provide for him. He figured on lasting about three weeks maximum on what he'd managed to cram into the bag.

He hated trains and distrusted other forms of public transport. Learning to drive a car had never really occurred to him. Until last year Anna had driven him everywhere. Until last year, when she started driving other guys everywhere as well. Or, until last year when Bentinck *discovered* that that was what she was doing.

At least there was something reassuring about trains. As long as the wheels stayed on the rails there could be no real problems. He just wished these particular wheels would start moving. There was already a certain frustration in having to change trains at

Veneziana Mestre and so not get to cross the lagoon to Santa Lucia and Venice proper.

In a way, though, he was glad. To see Venice the way it had become would be heartbreaking. Having spent a part of his youth in the watery city with his Italian mother had ensured him a lifelong attachment to the place.

He had written a number of unsuccessful articles about Venice; *you're a political journalist*, the editors told him, *leave environment to the experts*. So instead, over the past three years he had kept a comprehensive file of cuttings about the deterioration of the city: the gradual sinking, the desiccation of the masonry and the build-up of algae, its effects both in and out of the water. The situation had been coming to a head for some time and even now the authorities were poised to take this or that drastic course of action. Bentinck had no wish to arrive in Venice the day they decided either to drain the city or to dredge the canals, probably demolishing half of its buildings in the process.

He rooted around in his travel bag and found his copy of *Muzik*. He leafed through it until the efforts of the little man opposite to read the back of the magazine became too annoying. He stuffed it into his bag, wiped his brow and grimaced at the light reflected by the tiny round glasses.

He took out his head-set and punched the play button, happy that this was likely to irritate the other passengers. The man on his right was annoying him as well by seeming to object to Bentinck's bag taking up too much room on the seat. He felt his bag being nudged along the seat, so he pushed it back. He *would* be comfortable.

Bentinck's last published article was largely speculative and had generated a lot of controversy. The television hardware manufacturer he had accused of selling more than the allowed proportion of his stock to Yugoslavia was still demanding a full apology in the pages of the newspaper concerned. That the manufacturer had not taken steps to sue Bentinck was a sure indication of his culpability. However, since few people really appreciated why trade with Yugoslavia should be restricted, no one cared very much about the transgression of the law.

What caught the readers' imagination was Bentinck's claim that the exports were not staying in Yugoslavia, but were being sold on to neighbouring Albania. The number of units flooding into the small Balkan republic, Bentinck's article revealed, was vastly out of proportion to the population figures there. The obvious implication was that Something Was Going On.

But when no subsequent reports appeared – the hardware manufacturer sacked his entire workforce, including Bentinck's mole – the people lost interest. Unable to gain information from other sources, Bentinck also lost interest. He was a journalist, a reporter, and if something wasn't in the news it wasn't interesting; similarly, if something wasn't interesting it wouldn't get in the news.

He had a hunch there was Something Going On in Ljubljana. Otherwise why would Petrović, who knew of his avaricious appetite for scoops, invite him?

Having little appetite for travel *per se*, Bentinck turned up the volume on his head-set and sat back in his seat with his eyes closed.

As he slept, the train crept around the top of the Gulf of Venice, waited half an hour at Trieste and finally headed into the Slovenian hills. He dreamt that a major world statesman was assassinated on a state visit to Slovenia (which appeared to have seceded from Yugoslavia and become a republic in its own right) and that he, Bentinck, the only journalist present when the shot was fired, rang in with the story only to discover that his news-paper didn't exist any more.

He jolted awake with a shaking hand. The other passengers were asleep, with the exception of the little man opposite, who was looking out of the window, although there was nothing to see but darkness. Extricating his bulk, Bentinck left his seat and stood in the corridor. Hirsute men wearing vests under brown jackets stood leaning out of the windows. Bentinck took a squashed pack of cigarettes from his pocket and, straightening it, lit one. He pulled his window down. It was raining but the air was warmer than he had expected. His cigarette glowed like a poker in the rushing wind. The tension begotten of the dream went the same way as the exhaled cigarette smoke.

The train was making heavy work of wooded foothills, sounding its horn at each twist of the track. The old diesel cast a sooty wake over the carriages. Dim yellow lights burned in occasional isolated cottages. Bentinck drew on his cigarette and felt almost light-hearted.

Because the train had been delayed by ninety minutes Bentinck didn't expect to see any sign of Petrović. Nor did he when he scanned the long empty platforms and the queue at the snack-bar. He squeezed himself into a Mercedes-Benz taxi waiting in front of the station and gave the driver the address.

They drove for a quarter of an hour down wide boulevards lined with tall, denuded trees and streetlamps which splashed the road with blots of yellow. Here and there rubbish bins had been turned over and the occasional window broken. Sitting in the passenger seat, Bentinck watched the dinars mount up in green digits on the meter. Whether they represented the cost of his ride or the rate of inflation, he didn't like to speculate.

The taxi driver set him down in the middle of an area of high-density housing. As the Mercedes accelerated sluggishly away, Bentinck looked about him at the surrounding apartment blocks and realized he lacked a vital part of Petrović's address: the number of his flat. All he had was Block 25.

He soon found Block 25. And he found Petrović's nameplate by trial and error four floors up on the second staircase.

Zoran Petrović was a far warmer man than Bentinck usually allowed himself to appear to be.

'Rolf, Rolf. I'm so glad you came,' he said when he opened the door to the journalist.

'Don't get overexcited, Zoran,' Bentinck muttered, avoiding the other man's hands.

'I am sorry I was not there to meet you at the station,' Petrović said, leading the way down the hall. 'I waited an hour but there was no announcement. I didn't know how long to wait.'

'It was delayed in Trieste for some reason,' Bentinck said. 'I got a taxi from the station. No problem.' He looked around the living room. It was nicer than he had expected: potted plants, concealed lighting, recessed television and video.

'I was surprised to hear your message on the answerphone,

75

Rolf, accepting my invitation.' Petrović took the other man's coat and hung it behind the door.

'It intrigued me.' He looked at Petrović, whose face broke into a broad smile. 'What is going on, Zoran?'

'Ah, yes,' said the Yugoslav, grinning as he sat down on a floor cushion and motioned to Bentinck to do the same. 'What is going on?'

Bentinck remained standing while he waited for Petrović's answer. But the other man had switched on the television and was hopping between channels.

'We have twenty-eight different satellite channels,' he said proudly. 'The building subscribes and all the apartments are linked up.'

'Hurrah for the Socialist Federal Republic of Yugoslavia,' Bentinck observed with acerbity.

'No,' Petrović rejoindered. 'Hurrah for the Social Democratic Republic of Slovenia.' He looked at Bentinck with a frank expression that belied the irony in his voice. 'You won't find such general provision in southern Serbia and Montenegro; dishes are still rare in Macedonia.'

Bentinck knew that Petrović was not far off the mark when he used the term 'social democratic' in relation to Slovenia. The north-western republic had always been the most liberal of the six republics that made up the Yugoslav federation. Political commentators in the West had long been predicting the secession of Slovenia from Yugoslavia. That time still had not come.

The party leadership in Ljubljana, the capital of Slovenia, was a dog that often strayed from the path of ideological communism but always came running back when the federal parliament in Belgrade called loudly enough.

'If you've got twenty-eight channels,' Bentinck asked, 'why are you watching that rubbish?'

Petrović had put the remote control to one side as soon as it had located a continuous music-video channel. The current trend in popular music was 1970s revival; any tune would do, old or new, as long as those playing it wore the right clothes.

'This is the most popular,' he said.

Bentinck came away from the window and finally sat down in a soft-cushioned chair in the corner of the room.

'You're a real man of the people, aren't you?' he said.

Petrović just smiled and carried on watching the cavorting figures on the screen.

'Don't you like this music?' he asked at last.

'If we're talking about revivals,' Bentinck said, scratching his ear, 'I prefer jazz.'

'That was a popular form of music, in its day,' Petrović conceded. 'You know, you surprise me, Rolf. You say you like jazz, which is a very friendly, sociable kind of music, and yet you are not really a gregarious person, it seems to me.'

Bentinck met Petrović's gaze, astounded by his criticism. 'Well, what about you?' he retorted. 'You claim to be a man of the people and come across like everybody's best friend. Yet the music you say you like is cold and repetitive. The fact is you just pretend to like it because the people like it. You don't actually like it at all. It's an obsession with you – whatever the people like, you like.'

The two men stared at each other, both astonished at this bitter exchange. What grudges had they borne and for how long?

Petrović said: 'Do you want a drink, Rolf? I'll get you a drink.'

The tall Yugoslav left the room and Bentinck began to wonder if he hadn't been a little too aggressive. The man had a right to arrive at his likes and dislikes by whatever routes he chose, didn't he? When Petrović came back in, Bentinck was almost ready to mumble an apology. But the other man spoke first.

'When you've had this we'll go out. There's someone you should meet.' So saying, Petrović handed the journalist a tumbler containing two fingers of a thick plum-red liquid.

Outside, Bentinck observed Petrović's profile under the white streetlamps; if he allowed himself to trust anybody, would this be a face he could trust? Pointed with single-minded resolve in profile, it betrayed its ambiguity only when turned to the front. Did those wide, clear eyes and simple expression evidence a childlike naïvety, as Bentinck had always thought, or did they all but reveal his insanity?

The ability to place trust in other people was no longer a part of Bentinck's make-up. His journalistic training had undermined the foundations and his girlfriend Anna's deception struck the final blow. Not that he considered it much of a loss.

Petrović, his breath frosting on the air, crossed the yard to a white Zastava, a copy of the Fiat 500, and fumbled his key into the lock.

'Why do you bother to lock it?' Bentinck asked.

Petrović ignored him. Bentinck was dismayed; he had only meant it as a joke.

They squeezed inside and Petrović tried desperately to animate the engine without exhausting the battery. When he finally succeeded he shrugged and said, 'Cars are still very expensive here, you know, relative to everything else. The Zastava may only be a Fiat to you, but to me it's a Jaguar.'

They drove. Although unable to orient himself, Bentinck could tell at least that they were not heading for the city centre; the roads became boulevards and on either side of them stood estates like Petrović's. Here and there beyond the net of the street-lamps' limpid whiteness he glimpsed patches of wild grass and rough ground. Soon the lamps were interrupted by longer stretches of darkness and the buildings grew scarce.

Bentinck thought how the Zastava both sounded and felt like a ride-on lawnmower, but he held back his tongue.

Petrović twisted the wheel and the little car bounced down a dirt track. At the far end stood a dilapidated cottage. Petrović parked next to a Zastava identical to his own and the two men climbed out.

The air was thin yet seemed to carry scents of blooms that puzzled Bentinck: were they ghosts of the previous summer or heralds of the new spring? The front door of the cottage opened and a taller man even than Petrović beckoned the newcomers in. Bentinck was introduced, to Orel, then the two Yugoslavs bent over a table draped with a waxed cloth and exchanged remarks in their own tongue, which Bentinck was unable to follow. Their faces were serious, Orel's breaking only once into a nervous grin.

Later, the host produced a bottle of the same local brandy that Petrović had earlier given to Bentinck.

'Tonight, all over Ljubljana,' Petrović confided, 'men are gathering and talking to each other in rooms like this.' He would elucidate no further.

The three men drank while Bentinck resentfully acquiesced to an invitation to describe in a few brief words his native Switzerland.

On the journey back Petrović was silent. He hunched his shoulders over the wheel. Waiting for traffic lights to change, Bentinck pointed out the smashed windows in an institutional building across the street. Petrović just nodded and muttered, 'Tomorrow.'

Affected by tension, Bentinck could not sleep. He got up from the living room floor, where Petrović had made him a bed of cushions, and reached for the TV remote control. He flipped through the pop channels, the re-run game shows and period detective dramas, until he found an Italian station. On screen was the Grand Canal in Venice. A nasal voice explained that the government had taken the decision to dredge the city's canals without draining them. The voice pointed out that light dredging was already performed on a regular basis to remove rubbish from the canal floor, but that the job of attacking the weed growth and explosion of algae which the summer and autumn had produced would need far heavier equipment. Extensive studies had proved, to the satisfaction of the government, that no significant damage would be caused to the city's buildings, roads and bridges.

Bentinck switched off the set and sat thinking for ten minutes. Presently, he lit a cigarette and shuffled into the hallway. On bare feet he paused outside Petrović's bedroom; drawing consistently deep breaths, the Yugoslav appeared to be sleeping peacefully. Bentinck progressed to the kitchen, where he located the plum brandy in a spotlessly clean cupboard above the cooker. He unscrewed the bottle and poured himself a generous amount into a glass. He left the bottle standing and peered out of the window as he tasted the fiery liquid. It seeped into his gut like magma.

Outside, a dome of greenish light protected the city and all looked calm. Deceptively so.

Ceauşescu Blues

Gabriela Croitoru lay back and thought of Romania.

She had done little else for ten years, so it was easy. Especially now. So near to the end. One way or another.

At dawn on 10 August 1988 the inhabitants of the little village of Szarazpatak in south-east Transylvania were awoken by the rumble of bulldozers come to raze their homes to the ground. As part of Nicolae Ceauşescu's systematization programme of agricultural rationalization, the village was to be destroyed and its inhabitants rehoused in high-rise concrete blocks.

Of Romania's 13,000 villages, 8,000 would be demolished and 300 redeveloped into 'agro-industrial centres'. The declared aim was to create greater equality between urban and rural dwellers. But instead of raising the standard of living in towns and cities to meet that enjoyed in the countryside, President Ceauşescu elected to eradicate the luxuries of village life, among them self-sufficiency and property ownership.

The population of Szarazpatak was mainly ethnic Hungarian, specifically Szeklers, descended from lesser noble families going back to the ninth century. The ethnic Hungarian population of Romania had already been made the victims of Ceauşescu's cultural-assimilation policies. Hungarian-language schools had been closed down. Hungarian newspapers and books became scarce. Whenever the second-hand bookshop in Cluj got hold of Hungarian textbooks, students from the nearby university cleared the stock within minutes.

Now the final blow was about to fall on their culture and identity. As it also was in the case of the ethnic Germans of Braşov and the Romanian peasants themselves.

Gabriela Croitoru, although Romanian, would suffer the same fate as the ethnic Hungarians in the village when the bulldozers erased their past in one cowardly swathe: incarceration in concrete towers which lacked the most basic amenities.

Her husband had defected to the West ten years earlier, leaving only his smuggled jazz record collection, a few whiskers in the sink and the occasional shadow of his reflection in a gilt-edged mirror. Gabriela had made no friends in the village; it was always difficult between the two nationalities. Romanians considered Hungarians arrogant and boastful, while the Hungarians saw the Romanians as greedy and uncivilized.

She had only ever wanted two things. One was to leave Romania, and not necessarily in pursuit of her husband; simply to live in a country whose regime didn't require her to queue for bread at 5 am and regard the consumption of fresh tomatoes as a privilege to be enjoyed no more than twice a year.

Since escape to another country was out of the question – her husband's job as a Romanian Railways train driver having played no small part in his defection – she would settle for her second wish: to own a piano. She had learnt to play the instrument as a young girl living with her grandparents, and after their deaths didn't set eyes on another piano for several years. Later, as her husband's record collection grew, she paid it less and less attention, retreating, if possible, to another room when he took one out and played it. Possibly this avoidance had more to do with qualities peculiar to her husband rather than to his records, for after he left she took to playing them herself. In time she heard them all, but fell back on the pianoplayers: Art Tatum, Erroll Garner, Mose Allison. She played them at low volume so as not to alert vigilant neighbours to the presence of illegal possessions.

It seemed to her inconceivable to go along with the resettlement plan, and so on the day they demolished her cottage she gathered together all the belongings she could carry and all the money she had, and took a train to Bucharest. The collection of jazz records she left to be mashed into the soil. Maybe they would instil a little soul into the earth of the dying countryside.

She had been to the capital before but never with the intention of staying more than a few days. Her husband, to his credit, had left her a small stash of lei, which she now dipped into to pay for a hotel room.

She went to every restaurant in the city but there was no work.

81

In a rundown café in the Gara de Nord she met a robust, blonde woman who told her that if she didn't mind *how* she earned her living, she would find her some work. Gabriela explained about the hotel: she couldn't stay there longer than a week. The blonde woman seemed to decide for her and told her to sit and wait while she made a phone call. Gabriela watched the people alternately trudging and rushing around the forecourt beyond the café windows. Several trains stood waiting. Another arrived with a squeal of resignation from its airbrakes. The carriages jolted and came to rest, doors opening to release scores of headscarved peasant women and men wedged into small narrow trilbies. A woman wrapped in a brightly coloured but dirty shawl proceeded to the exit bent double under an enormous sack of potatoes.

A chair scraped on the floor behind her; she turned round. The blonde woman had returned from the phone.

'It's fixed,' she said. 'I've got you a room.'

Gabriela just stared at the woman, uncomprehending.

'You'll have to start paying for it, though. Now.'

Gabriela made no move to get up and the woman had to take her hand in encouragement.

Doina Popescu, the blonde woman, realizing that Gabriela knew little of city life, decided to educate her in two stages. First, she would teach her how to fleece foreign tourists in currency exchanges.

Gabriela was made to stand and watch while she waylaid a bewildered-looking German and took out a thin roll of Romanian banknotes. Gabriela saw the confidence on the woman's face as she peered into the German's wallet. He even pulled it apart for her and she took out a handful of notes. The German looked unsure but she nodded briskly and unrolled 300 lei. The escape, Gabriela appreciated, had to be swift but unhurried. She watched Doina walk straight across the square in the direction of the post office. As Gabriela followed she saw the German still counting his money, then he folded it into his wallet, apparently satisfied or resigned to the fact that he'd been had.

Doina explained, when they were standing in the post office doorway, that it was simply a matter of confidence. But it was important to avoid Western business travellers – who would have their own regular contacts for changing money – and pick only on tourists. They were not difficult to spot in Bucharest, a city of such drabness.

After Gabriela successfully conned a French couple moments after their train pulled in, Doina took her to the room she'd fixed up. Diagonally opposite the Gara de Nord, the room was on the second floor of a former hotel. The room was tiny, maybe four metres by two, and little brighter than the streets of Bucharest at night. A commitment to save energy meant a 9 pm restaurant curfew and street lighting along only the widest boulevards. Electricity was rationed in the home, allowing a flat to be lit for up to two hours a day in winter. Electric heaters had been banned several years previously. If Gabriela owned either a washing machine or a refrigerator she would be able to use neither. If she owned a gas cooker she would find the pressure so low that any use of it would be impossible before midnight.

Tall windows opened on to a tiny balcony, from where the depressing slabs of the railway station dominated the view.

'Thank you,' Gabriela said. She had checked out of the hotel and given her French francs to Doina to pay for the new room.

'Let's have a drink,' Doina said, producing a bottle of strong spirit. It would be easier after a few drinks to embark on the second stage of Gabriela's education.

'You've got to live,' she said, filling another glass. 'You've got rent, food and clothes to pay for.'

'You think I should work as a hooker,' Gabriela said, swallowing the spirit and burning inside. She had known what to expect. The jazz pianists had prepared her for it, instilling in her a knowledge from beyond her environment. Art Tatum's slight hesitancies and precipitous runs, Mose Allison's driving piano and vocals stretched taut across years of the jazz experience.

She knew what it would mean living in Bucharest, when the state would only provide for her hundreds of kilometres away in an agro-industrial centre. There would be sacrifices but she would survive, because she had to.

Doina kept pouring the drinks and they didn't stay long in the glass. The women shared intimacies and at the same time became paranoid, of themselves, of each other and of Bucharest. Doina wrote on a scrap of paper that there could be microphones even here. Gabriela looked at her to gauge her sincerity; it seemed complete. Doina wrote some more: 'In 1965 in Romania there were one central electronic monitoring unit and 11 regional units. By 1977 there were 10 central and 48 regional, plus 1,000 portable. Ten million microphones. Hidden in TVs, phones, ashtrays, vases.' She had learnt it off by heart.

Gabriela looked around the room, her eyes taking in two vases, an ashtray and an old television set. She looked back at Doina, who was pouring the contents of another glass down her throat. Getting to her feet, she walked across to the television. Gingerly she twisted the power knob. Nothing happened. Presently the murky screen was broken and a flickering white square expanded to fill it. Then the square darkened and the set began to whine. A shape formed and gained definition. Gabriela soon recognized the hamster cheeks and chicken neck of President Nicolae Ceauşescu. His voice rose to drown out the whine from the back of the set. She turned to Doina and they both laughed.

'It's not often he makes you laugh,' she said, pouring more drinks. Gabriela put a finger to her lips and cautioned the other woman, pointing at the room's imagined microphones. Doina laughed even more loudly and Gabriela joined in. She sat down again and took up her glass. For a while they drank quietly, smiling. Then Doina picked up the pencil again and wrote on the reverse of the paper: 'We laugh. But it's true.' Gabriela looked at her. Again, the serious look was there in her eyes.

The following morning Gabriela changed money with a West German tourist and bought a transistor radio. That evening, when she brought her first client back to the room, she turned the volume up so it masked the noise they made. Doina had told her it was unnecessary; prostitution was legal and women were 'encouraged' to pass on any information they might extract from foreign clients. You didn't have to look far to pass it on to someone; one in three people was reckoned to be an informer.

Prostitution turned out to be lucrative, but despite its legality contraceptives were unavailable and abortions against the law. Gabriela had no idea of the enormity of the risks she was really running when she became a worker in Romania's black economy. The scanty pages of the Romanian newspapers, once they had printed several pictures of the President and members of his family and listed the five or six new laws which were created daily, had little space left to devote to warnings about AIDS.

Gabriela still occasionally tricked naïve tourists out of their hard currency. Mindful of Decree 408, she went furtively about her business. There was no law against talking to foreigners. The state was subtler than that. Decree 408, unpublished but known to just about everyone, said that such conversations had to be reported to the authorities within twenty-four hours. Questioning would inevitably follow. The fine for not reporting a conversation amounted to the average worker's wages for one year.

She was able to give money to Doina for the room and still save some for herself. It took only six months of regular activity to save enough to buy an old piano.

President Ceaușescu had always maintained that because of the Romanian constitution, Romania's signature on the Vienna declaration was unnecessary. The constitution, according to Ceaușescu, guaranteed human rights in Romania. It said, for instance, that if a citizen applied for a passport and received a refusal with an official reason, the citizen could appeal to a tribunal if he or she thought the reason unjust.

Gabriela Croitoru first applied for a passport in 1975, three years before her husband left the country. She received no reply and made another application after six months. Again there was no reply. No refusal and no official reason for it. So no opportunity to appeal to the tribunal. She continued to make applications every six months until after her husband's defection, when she stepped up the rate to three times a year. By the time of her displacement to Bucharest, Gabriela had made thirty-seven applications and not received a single word, written or verbal, by way of reply. Not even the shadow of a Securitate agent beneath her window at night.

Gabriela played the piano during the day and earned her living in the small hours. Sometimes she kept the radio on while she was working, sometimes they fucked in silence. Some of the clients talked to her before and after. Some chatted away during the act, out of either embarrassment or boredom. A few grey souls remained tight-lipped throughout and folded foreign banknotes on to the corner of the piano as they left. Most of them, she learnt and guessed, were businessmen and diplomats. Few were tourists. Given that her occupation was only allowed to thrive for the intelligence information its interpersonal dealings might throw up, Gabriela wondered how the information was collected. Were there really microphones in the room? And if so, why did the owner of their listening ear continue to allow her to frustrate their efforts with a transistor radio? She saw Doina frequently and in their conversations sometimes referred to clients and the stories they told. Was Doina the one out of the three? Was she an informer? Possibly it didn't matter much either way.

Gabriela played jazz piano (reconstructing tunes from memory), worked nights, and walked around Bucharest ready to join a queue the moment one formed. Many shoppers joined without knowing what was on sale at its head. Sheep's heads, hunks of cheese and pigs' trotters – called patriots because they were unexportable and so never left Romania – were equally re-viled and desired because there was nothing else. Romania had become the second biggest sheep-rearing country in Europe after Britain, but in Bucharest there was no mutton for sale. Nor most of the time was there any beef, pork or milk, chocolate, coffee or butter. No aspirin, no soap.

The dollar shops, patronized by diplomats, businessmen or who-ever could lay a hand on a dollar, sometimes had meagre stocks of these luxuries. But Gabriela found that as time went by and she worked less intensively, she was nevertheless having to give more to Doina.

A teacher from Iaşi drove down to Bucharest in his ailing Dacia and cruised around the city's boulevards and squares. Affixed to the windows of his car were crude signs and pla-cards denigrating Ceauşescu. ('The Great Redeemer Must Fall', 'President Dracula', etc.) He was apprehended, but not before his message had reached hundreds, maybe thousands, of frustrated shoppers and loiterers, Gabriela among them. He was charged under Article 166 of the Penal Code which stated: 'Propaganda or the undertaking of any action in order to change the socialist order is punishable by five to ten years' imprisonment.'

He was generally thought to have got off lightly with the maxi-mum ten years.

Gabriela thought of him in his cell. She respected him more

than she did her husband. But she didn't have the guts to follow his example. Instead she lay alone at night and pictured him in gaol. Unable to sleep, she got up and squeezed past the piano to the windows. Tugging the net curtains aside, she saw the hideous Gara de Nord cast into cubic shadows by the Picasso-moon. A policeman smoked the only speck of colour in the whole square as he leaned against a pillar in front of the station. Would the gaoled teacher be allowed to smoke a cigarette as he followed the angle of the moon's progress across the concrete floor of his cell?

She lay down again, having left the curtains open, and the walls of the room bowed in towards her, their convexities smeared by moonlight. The piano, the largest item in the room, bent its keyboard over the narrow bed. If she sat up she would bang her head. Instead she slept and dreamed of the teacher as the sole prisoner in a gaol that resembled the Gara de Nord. There were no cells, only platforms and waiting rooms. There were dusty carriages but no locomotives. He found a can of paint and a brush and began writing slogans on the walls. He only stopped when he realized no one would ever read them.

In a waiting room he peered at a photograph of a man's head. It seemed detached from its body as if as the result of a motor accident involving an old Dacia. But the colour which confused him was not blood; it was rouge on the old man's cheeks. The legend under the picture said: 'The Great Redeemer Must Fall.' He left the waiting room, following the sound of a piano being played.

He crossed the concourse and saw a guard smoking a cigarette at the main exit. He kept his head down and entered the café where the music was louder. Behind the counter was a woman, naked, bleached bone-white by way of a skylight above her head. Her eyes were open yet she did not appear to be awake. She didn't move and there was no food in the plastic cases on the counter. Hovering in the shadows of one of the corners of the café was a dressmaker's dummy wrapped in black linen.

The piano music drew him through a doorway at the rear of the café into a large empty room, like another waiting room or a vast office cleared of desks and chairs. Light fell from a window at the far end of the room and revealed that it wasn't empty. A dark figure was seated at an upright piano. The teacher crossed the room. The figure began to turn at the sound of his approach. The pianist was another dressmaker's dummy wreathed in black cloth, with no arms to play but the music went on, a light syncopation. The suddenness of the turn wrenched the dummy's skittle-head from its neck and it fell on to the hard floor softly with no noise.

The teacher then regretted taking the action which had resulted in his incarceration.

When she was woken by the sun on her face she reconstructed the dream and doubted only the final moment of regret. The teacher's protest had been courageous and proud. His punishment, she felt sure, would be endured in the same spirit. She sat at the piano and extemporized in the hope that the dream's music would return to her. By the end of the morning she had a theme worked out, which, if it hadn't featured in the dream, should have done. She called it 'Ceauşescu Blues'.

Humming the melody, she went out in search of a queue. She walked south down the Calea Victoriei. Workmen were digging up the stumps of demolished churches and historic buildings, like dentists pulling at exposed nerves and roots stranded after hasty extractions. Halfway down the boulevard towards the Dimbovita River, police stopped the traffic. Uniformed officers moved into the centre of the road and used hand signals to divert oncoming vehicles. They then formed lines blocking side roads. Young men, their throats nicked by little-used razors, stood nervously in doorways trying to look like civilians. Their grey polyester suits hung awkwardly on narrow shoulders and sharpened their shins to thin knives. What was the point of calling them *secret* police?

Gabriela watched as a fleet of black Dacias turned into Calea Victoriei. Behind them trailed a black Mercedes. Inside it would be a member of the Ceauşescu family, but there was no telling which one. The President himself; his wife Elena, whose latest ghosted scientific treatise had just joined a dozen others in bookshop windows alongside collections of her husband's speeches; or young Nico, playboy son and party chief in the city of Sibiu.

The traffic was stopped whenever any of them moved more than a hundred metres in any direction.

The cavalcade passed by without slowing down and the police relaxed.

Gabriela crossed the bridge over the Dimbovita and felt tiny in the expansive Square of National Unity. The tune of 'Ceauşescu Blues' still tripped through her head, enlivening the uniform high-rise constructions at the edges of the square.

If there was any food in the city that day it was not for sale. During the eighties Ceauşescu had diverted virtually all home produce to the export market. Times were hard for Romanians, but they understood the strategy was to pay off foreign debt. When it was paid off they would eat well. By the end of the decade, however, the debts were cleared and conditions were deteriorating. Some said that the regime cultivated shortages in order to keep people preoccupied with survival rather than politics; others that the reasoning behind the great pay-off was so that no member of the world community would be able to tell Romania what to do.

In the poor light of late evening Bucharest, he was just another potential client leaving the Gara de Nord. Gabriela approached him at an oblique angle and when she was close enough made clear the nature of her solicitation. He followed her across the square, though not too closely, and didn't speak until he reached the door she was holding open for him. He thanked her in English, which made her long for the jazz records that had been pressed even thinner beneath the rubble of Szarazpatak.

Although she left the lights off, she made the unusual move of offering him a drink and switching on the transistor radio without immediately beginning to undress. He squeezed between the piano and the bed and sat down on its edge.

'You haven't got much room,' he said.

She struggled to understand and reply in words learnt from songs. 'All I need,' she said.

There was no light from the window to see him by. Just the faintest sparkle as he tipped his head back to receive the contents of his glass.

'Just you, the bed and the piano,' he said.

'And the TV,' Gabriela said, pointing to one behind the piano. 'But nothing to watch. Only . . .' She used her hand again to indicate the window and the city beyond it. Surrounding the city was the country, her gesture implied, and more encompassing still than that was its leader. Television programmes were broadcast between 8 and 10 pm and consisted of uplifting political material. The only face that reappeared with sufficient regularity to become a personality was that of Nicolae Ceauşescu. Opening stage-managed factories and blessing exhibitions commemorating his achievements. Giving speeches. Spreading his adoration.

The stranger had tuned the radio to a station she didn't know. 'Radio Free Europe,' he said, drawing her on to the bed. He removed her dress and caressed her back. His hands felt different. Less like other clients' and reminiscent of her husband's affectionate touch at the very beginning. He twisted his fingers under the elastic of her bra and removed it. Instead of grabbing at her breasts he massaged her shoulders and trailed his fingers down both sides of her body. She had forgotten it could be like this. There was a kindness in his hands where normally she felt only brutishness or childish bravado. His belt was thick leather and heavily buckled. She unbuttoned his trousers and slid a hand inside them. Now his hands stroked her breasts. She felt his cock swell beneath her touch and pushed down his trousers to release it. He caressed her through the silk knickers she wore and she shifted her legs to give him more room. He was still lightly squeezing her breasts with one hand, moving from one to the other and applying gentle pressures. She gripped his cock and moved her hand slowly up and down its length. Feeling it throb, she suddenly wanted to do something which she often had to do under orders. This time she did it because she wanted to, working entirely by touch. The man's features never emerged from shadow. The radio played piano music in the night and the open window admitted the smell of woodsmoke. She wondered, as she closed her mouth around his penis and flicked her tongue over its tip, if the Bucharestis had resorted to burning their furniture to keep warm.

His hands were tender on her neck and his fingers pulled through tresses of her hair. Her head rose and fell and she could almost feel him smiling. She squeezed his balls and he lifted and tensed slightly. Recognizing the warning signs, she opened her mouth and straightened up, grasping with her hand once again and increasing the speed of her movements. She heard him grunt with pleasure as his sperm struck her chest in a warm spray, cooling rapidly in the draught from the window.

He sat up almost immediately to kiss her warmly, his hand reaching inside her knickers for the first time. One finger, then two, crept inside her and stretched as far as they could, then further. She bent forward to allow deeper penetration and he used a third finger to rub her clitoris while the other two pushed further inside her.

She thought he was speaking but it was the radio. An American voice introduced another record and Billie Holiday sang a song Gabriela hadn't heard in over ten years, 'Strange Fruit'. Waves rose inside her, met others going the other way and crashed. Spume and light foamy bubbles of excitement reached the ends of her fingers and toes. Her head was all froth.

Eventually the waves withdrew, tugging gently. The tide receded but the sand remained wet and glistening.

Through a haze in the air Gabriela Croitoru heard and recognized a song on the radio. Mose Allison sang:

> I've got a right to cry
> I've got a right to cry
> All day I'm filled with gloom
> Here in my lonely room
> You treat me so unkind
> I nearly lost my mind
> I wonder if you'll care
> My life's a sad affair

She knew she couldn't rely on an isolated incident to take her life from out of the lyrics of Mose Allison's song. Whether or not the nature of the change lay in the night's activity, she realized something had changed. Things would never be the same again.

The Gara de Nord was all she could make out through the open window. Cool air drifted into the room. Gabriela gathered the sheets about her, shivering.

> My heart is aching
> Breaking

91

> I don't know what to do
> Sweetheart, all on account of you

The song was reading more into it than was there. This was just a man. A special one maybe, with whom sex was more than just a duty, but only a man at the end of it all. There was a sense of change in the air, more significant than the man himself and the feelings he'd reawoken in her.

'Things are going to change around here,' he whispered into her neck.

'Mmm-hmm?' she breathed lazily. 'What? Who?' she then said abruptly, pushing herself up and leaning on one elbow.

Apart from her, the bed was empty. He'd gone. Vanished. Had she fallen asleep and missed him leaving? There was no pile of dollar bills on top of the piano. Would he have sneaked off without paying? She doubted it.

The song was still playing. And the volume was loud enough to have masked the stranger's murmur, even to have produced it: was her mystery lover none other than Mose Allison? Later she would see that the 'you' addressed in the song was not the man she had dreamt was lying in her bed, but the one outside, all-seeing, all-knowing. The Great Redeemer.

> All day I'm filled with gloom
> Here in my lonely room

Life under Ceauşescu was unhappy and isolated, one's spouse having either defected, died of malnutrition or been 'disappeared' by the authorities.

> You treat me so unkind
> I nearly lost my mind

A third of all minds already had been.

> I wonder if you care
> My life's a sad affair

For a brief, sweet moment – to be recalled later by the dirty copper-green dawn and chill of dew – she had allowed herself to believe that a new era was at hand. The only explanation was that she had dreamed the darkly mysterious lover and the fantasy had been so potent that she had reached orgasm. She stretched and ran her hands over her breasts, wondering, if it had been a dream, where the alien, slightly salty smell had come from.

Doorway to Zero

Ankers knew Hašek was dead when he began dreaming about him.

After watching him swim out into the North Sea with the mermaids, Ankers went back to look for the painter. But the gallery and studio seemed to have vanished. He crossed a line of dunes, scanning the horizon for the low building to which he and Hašek had followed the old man. The view from the crest of the dunes held only more sand. He climbed slopes and slipped down gullies until he had lost his bearings.

As dusk fell it began to rain lightly from a yellowish-grey sky. He found himself on a ridge looking out to sea again. In the far distance the grey uniformity of the sea was interrupted by flickers of white. Hašek and his companions? Or the white horses of a local squall? On the shoreline he saw a figure briefly, stooping slightly like the old painter, which disappeared when he blinked. There were no shadows. Only his eyes to play tricks on him. The beach was empty. He turned and headed inland.

A distant line of dunes yielded the gallery building. Ankers walked.

The old man was sitting at his easel. The picture in which the somnambulist women had grown tails and taken to the advancing sea, Hašek amongst them, lay on the unmade bed. Next to it was the artist's impression of himself stooped and looking out to sea, protectively following his creations with some emotion in his eye. Ankers frowned as he noted the white horses and sickly sky.

But there was nothing to say. The old man dabbed at his palette and brushed silver hair out of his eyes before leaning forward to touch the canvas. A nod of the artist's head seemed to indicate that Ankers should sit down and wait. He sat down on the window ledge, which was wide enough to permit him to raise his legs and lean back against the wall. Lulled by the sound of brushstrokes, his body gave in to exhaustion.

Outside a window high in the far wall could be seen the red lettering of a political slogan on the roof of the adjoining building. The red letters were not lit; it was too early in the day to waste energy. RROFTE SHOKUT ENVER HOXHA PPSH.

The men around the large polished table wore suits of a drabness which suggested the business of either commerce or politics. They had sheaths of papers and piles of submissions poorly photocopied and inexpensively bound. There were some seals and bindings of tape as red as the letters outside the window.

The only woman in the room, hands poised over her keyboard, suppressed a fit of coughing. The suited men around the table had been smoking all morning, barely pausing to utter the words the woman was waiting to record.

One man, like all the others dark complexioned, held his cigarette between his teeth while he pushed a bundle of papers across the table to another man, who stretched out his arm to receive it. The first man spoke in a strange language. His words were translated into an even stranger language for the other man to understand. This man gave a brief reply, which was also translated. The woman stopped typing before the interpreter finished speaking. Possibly she was bilingual.

With knowledge of neither language being spoken, the dreamer learnt the basic nature and dynamics of the meeting by unknown means.

Representatives of the Greek government were offering part of their territory to Albania. The Balkan state, which was hosting this meeting of representatives in Tirana, was under siege by invading hordes and had already declared a state of emergency. The neighbourly offer made by the Greeks, who not very many years before had been officially at war with Albania, had come at just the right time. The island on offer was small but so was the population of Albania. The authorities expected few difficulties, however, in persuading their people to relocate to more cramped conditions, given the nature of the invaders.

Only by climbing on a chair could Ankers see out of the window down to street level. Skanderbeg Square was athrong with citizens and soldiers in green uniforms, who looked on equally confused as the invaders milled around listlessly, their numbers seeming to augment by the minute. They rarely approached people and when they did there was little or no aggression, but people felt threatened. The threat was of a far more profound nature than physical violence. It was targeted at the mind rather than at the flesh, and at the cortex, where the two became one.

Across the veneered table two men shook hands vigorously. At once smiles broke out and other handshakes were made. A tangible sense of relief dissipated the clouds of smoke and the woman breathed more easily as she strained to hear the closing exchanges of two of the representatives. Her fingers busied themselves like hungry spiders.

The offer made by the Greek government, for Albania to evacuate her people on to the island of Corfu until such time as the invaders could be repelled from Albania, had been formally accepted. The Greek army would even assist in constructing emergency housing.

Among the walking wounded filling the square was a familiar figure. His long dark hair was streaked with grey and his face was bloated and bluish. He appeared more lively than some of those around him and stopped to take in the view while they shuffled on to no particular destination. His arms lay still at his sides but his fingers flexed constantly like the woman typist's.

The letters of the political slogan on the roof of the adjoining building were spaced far enough apart to allow Ankers to stand between two of them. At five storeys the building was high enough to show the city's topographical situation: nestling in a shallow depression lined on all sides by rolling hills.

Ankers became aware of a rumbling. The sky was clear and cold. There were no major rivers. Yet the rumbling persisted. Like a million gallons of water released in sudden floods. But from where?

The old man was shaking his shoulder.

'You were dreaming,' he said.

The pounding in his head had not stopped. Out of the window he saw why. The sea was a hundred metres away, no more. The waves crashed high and the spray almost reached the gallery wing.

'It's coming closer,' the painter said. 'Everything has been speeded up. All the things we knew would happen are now happening. The timescale has gone.'

'We've got to stop it,' Ankers said, breaking into a sweat as the sea advanced.

'We can't. We've left it too late,' the old man explained.

'Then we've got to get out of here.' Ankers turned to look at the old man, who was moving his head slowly from side to side and taking a step backwards. 'We've got to,' he repeated, shouting at the retreating figure. Then he read the old man's expression, the rounded shoulders. The painter had known all along this was going to happen. Who hadn't? The warming. The ice caps. But the painter had seen it coming sooner than most. He'd painted it in oils. His women had feared it. Or he'd feared it for them. Now they'd escaped danger by swimming in it.

Hašek had been different. His sense of exile had been exaggerated. Perhaps for this reason he had drowned while they swam. The old man had painted his women into myths and ensured their survival. Presumably if the waters ever receded he could paint back their legs.

But would he still be around? Having saved his lifetime companions, he looked now as if he were ready for the deluge.

Ankers wanted to reach the man behind the paintbrush, and have a look into his mind. 'We have to,' he said for the last time, 'get out before it's too late.'

'It's high tide,' the old man said. 'It's not going to get any higher.' Ankers looked at him with misapprehension. 'The sea won't reach the building. We're safe. My paintings are safe.' Ankers didn't know whether the old man was still sane. When he'd been searching for the gallery earlier, he'd put several ridges of dunes between himself and the sea. Now the sea was practically lapping at the front door.

'I did this for you,' the old man said, as he took a small canvas from his easel and proffered it to Ankers. 'You were asleep.'

Ankers looked at the face of the woman in the painting and thought of Narvik – the frozen north to which Inger might already have fled. Where the mountains climbed higher and the fjords plunged even deeper. Where the air and the sea and all the elements were closer to purity and perfection. The painter may

97

never have met Inger but somehow he'd painted her picture.

Ankers looked at Inger's face, then back at the painter, whose own face surrendered none of its secrets. She was standing in a red dress at the bottom of a steep rift valley. Snow capped the peaks above her. The sea curled at the rocky shore, like question marks, or saxophones.

Outside, the waves appeared to be closer.

'I'm going,' he said, staring into the painter's eyes. 'Are you coming? There's a car in the town. We can drive inland.'

The old man shook his head and looked out of the window. There was a half-smile on his face that was almost beatific. 'You go,' he said.

Ankers snapped the painting into his saxophone case and strode to the door, where he hesitated.

'I want you to come with me,' he said, knowing it was useless. The painter just stood with his back to Ankers, watching the waves. Ankers opened the door and stepped outside.

The air was ice-cold and tasted of salt. Ankers tore his eyes from the towering waves and the brackish sky louring above them; he hefted his case and marched in what he hoped was the direction of the town. He climbed a stretch of dunes, behind which he had expected to see the flat plain of Flanders, but there was only sand as far as he could see. With the sea at his back he threw himself into the desert, a fresh wind picking up grit and flinging it at his face. He walked several kilometres, anticipating that each time he climbed a dune it would be the last. The wind didn't let up. His only comfort was the fact that the sea had not followed him. For some time he watched the shoreline recede in his wake as he moved further inland. Presently it was hidden by the lined-up humps of dunes he'd clambered over like so many camels. It was not long before the sea's disappearance became a source of distress, it having been his only point of reference in the repetitious landscape. He pressed on in what he hoped was a straight line.

The weight of his case and his feet in the sand soon began to tell. He slumped down on the lee side of a dune and lay on his back. It was the warmest winter of the century, according to the cries of newspaper vendors in Brussels, but this close to the sea it was hard to appreciate the statistic. Ankers was sweating from his exertion and the wind chilled his sweat. He hugged the case and adopted a foetal position on the sand. The sky was dark and the town invisible.

Across the vast square dust blew into the vacant faces of the newcomers. They didn't raise hands to protect their eyes or attempt to close mouths, which fell open naturally.

Bicycle riders found for the first time that they had to steer around people rather than relying on them to get clear. Diplomats' chauffeurs and delivery van drivers hooted their horns until the square rang with their strange harmonics.

The invaders moved en masse over the square past the Museum of National History towards the Hotel Tirana. They streamed in through the glass doors and jammed the lifts. Those who could locate them took to the stairs.

The hotel staff stood by, confusion and fear on their faces. They watched as the newcomers tried to gain entry to rooms. Where a door had been left open they would simply enter the room and one of their number would take up occupancy by sitting on the edge of the bed. The room's original occupier, if present, would protest but find his efforts to remove the interloper fruitless. Thus a stalemate was reached and only broken when the original guest left the room to go and complain to the management. He would find the door locked on his return and the staff refusing to use their keys.

Faced with locked doors themselves, the invaders squeezed into corridors until their numbers were so great the pressure forced the doors open. Sometimes the wood gave way, more often it was the lock that was weak. As soon as the management realized the scale of the invasion, a team of chambermaids and waiters was sent up to the top floor by the service lift to begin unlocking all the doors in readiness. From the upper floors the view down over the square showed hundreds more torn creatures homing in towards the hotel. Most of them were grave-weary and raggedy.

Amongst them, Hašek appeared like a fresh shrub in a forest destroyed by acid. He stopped and pivoted against the flow to study the blank faces of those passing him. He would have seen others like himself who clearly felt they were not part of the crowd. A handful of men whose eyes still took in the light of the sun. Who appeared still to have brains in their heads and hearts inside their jackets. All the same, they eventually turned and headed towards the hotel.

Hašek took a room on the seventh floor. A dark-eyed chambermaid unlocked the door for him and he walked in, cool as you like, just as if his reservation card were sitting on the manager's desk.

He went into the bathroom and turned on the taps. He didn't linger over his reflection in the mirror but returned to the bedroom and opened the wardrobe door. A wire coathanger rattled and motes of dust juddered on the shelf. He crossed to the window and unlatched it.

The influx had dried up and the square was trying to return to normal. Local people walked across the square as they always did, to and from work and home and wherever they wanted to go. Many weaved old rusted bicycles in and out of the crowd. The occasional three-wheeled van scattered pedestrians with its modest klaxon. Ten-year-old Mercs ferried men in suits from consulate to embassy, carrying news of the agreement reached that morning with the Greeks. People passing in front of the hotel stopped and looked up. Their lips moved as they spoke to each other, unsure what view to take of the invasion, the first their country had seen for fifty years. Western tourists had only puzzled the indigenous population when they began to arrive.

The new invaders had taken over the Hotel Tirana, traditional base of the tourists, and yet little resembled them. The newcomers were shellshocked and largely uninquisitive about their surroundings.

Though the Albanians stared up at the fourteen floors of the hotel, its guests did not look out to meet their gaze. All over the hotel 260 television sets had been switched on, belting out the most exciting news story in years of Albanian programming; 260 bleary, stupid faces watched the pictures. If they recognized themselves trailing into the city and pouring into Skanderbeg Square, they gave no reaction. And the commentary was in a language none of them had ever spoken. The picture switched to men in suits shaking hands.

Hašek, leaning out, glanced across at the other windows of the seventh floor. One other man was looking out. The remaining windows were closed. The man returned Hašek's stare. His eyes were like the thick glass of an aquarium obscuring some dark ambiguous shape hiding within. At the corner of his mouth a slight tic jerked the tight skin of his cheek. Hašek's eyes were drawn to this, a sign of life. The movement repeated itself but the shadows behind the man's eyes failed to come to resolution.

At a sudden rumbling, Hašek and the Twitcher both looked away. They were high enough to see the hills surrounding the city. The rumbling intensified. It sounded more natural than man-made. Hašek sensed the Twitcher's tic working two windows away. *Where was this roar coming from?*

Ankers jerked awake, head thumping. Was the rumbling inside it or outside? He massaged his brow, shivering suddenly in the freezing coastal dawn. The rumbling was his, he felt, rather than the dream's, and it presaged disaster.

He looked about. The sun had risen and already vanished behind grey stratus. Where the clouds were of a lighter shade, though, he saw the town he had lost the night before clinging to the earth as if afraid for its solidity.

In the opposite direction a broken white line represented the modest breakers of the North Sea glimpsed between rows of dunes.

Beset by a sudden doubt, Ankers unfastened his saxophone case. The painting was still there. He took it out. Inger looked back at him as his yearning invested her with life. He looked at the snowy peaks behind her head and worried that wearing only a red dress she would suffer exposure or even catch pneumonia. But he recalled the rocky cove in which he had seen her for the first time, wearing only light clothes in winter and her arms dripping with freezing water.

Why the red dress? he thought. As far as he knew she didn't possess one. He put it down to the painter's reinvention of her as one of his own women.

A flash of light appeared in the distance away from both the sea and the town. A muffled crack followed. It was all the warning he needed that there was no time to spare. The painting went into the case and he hauled himself to his feet, and set off in the direction of the town.

He had the keys to the car because he and Hašek had shared the driving from Brussels. He was glad, doubtful that he would have been able to work out how to hot-wire the Tatra.

He hugged the coast and reached Ostend before the shops opened. He passed into Holland after a one-minute stop at the border. The sooner he reached Bremerhaven and boarded a ferry for Oslo the sooner he could begin to relax. Worry for Inger was turning his stomach upside-down at every bump in the road. He pictured her walking naked off a cliff top before he could stop himself conjuring the vision.

At Utrecht he decided to divert to Amsterdam and book his Bremerhaven ferry from Centraal Station. It was a mistake. The office had ceased taking bookings because of storm warnings. The clerk couldn't even tell him whether boats were still sailing; the computers were down.

Dejected, he left the station and entered a bar. Despite the mild winter the streets were almost empty of the lonely musicians, nude acrobats and genuine eccentrics who performed round the clock in warmer months. They had taken up residence instead in the city's bars, clubs and foyers.

A young man in a felt hat played a mournful saxophone in the corner while Ankers sat with a glass of beer. His music was not particularly pleasing and yet the bar seemed to need it. Without it there would be no reason to sit in this bar rather than that one. Ankers recalled what his mother (long since dead) had once read him from the Norwegian edition of *Reader's Digest*: that to lift your mood you must first listen to music which reflects it, before switching to something livelier and more cheerful.

He watched the young man and found himself wishing his own life were as simple as he imagined his to be. He played slowly and harmlessly – not unlike Ankers, who would be the first to admit he'd never been an adventurous player and in whose musical development the most exciting phase had begun when he first duetted with one of Hašek's recordings – but clearly the young man remained untroubled by fantastic visions portending doom.

Ankers now regretted the visions that before had been welcome evidence of a world which existed outside of his experience. Now, with Inger reduced to a face on a canvas and his friend Hašek drowned, he wished he'd never seen them and been drawn to De Panne. He felt a sudden burst of anger directed against the old painter. But it was useless, short-sighted fury. The painter's function was far from clear. Was he creating the world to be or was he part of a larger pattern in which his duty consisted in reporting on the future? What about Hašek's death? Was it accident, suicide or murder? Only the first of these required no motive. Where did it leave Ankers with regard to Hašek's music and its secrets?

It left him sitting in a bar in Amsterdam listening to a younger, more innocent version of himself indulge the bell end of his saxophone.

It brought him full circle and left him going round in one.

Women sat in windows, leaning back in chairs and opening their legs. Sometimes they leaned forward and smirked at passers-by. They walked from café to 'hotel', from bar to whore-house, and felt the cold on their thighs. They let their robes fall open to offer a glimpse of the merchandise.

Ankers wandered in the vague direction of the car, unsure if he had entered the red light district by accident or choice. He felt himself stiffening as tall women in windows seemed to bend and offer their breasts to him. Should he feel turned on by them? Was he betraying Inger by looking? Did he miss sex or Inger? Or sex with Inger?

When she sleepwalked at the edge of the sea she was sexless. Naked, but cold and unfeeling as a statue of herself. In bed with him she was pliant, the sculpture become the clay that made it.

They had never really made love. They'd kissed and touched and had sex occasionally. But never really made love together. She would lie there, his to do with as he wished. She seemed to have no great feeling for her own body. It mattered as little to her as those of the sleepwalkers did to the women painted by the old man. The capacity for this disregard passed naturally on to Ankers. He had channelled his energies into solving the riddle of the somnambulists.

One minute he was a window shopper, the next a customer. In an upstairs room he found a woman who undressed for him. She presented her breasts to him in a manner that was half proud and half lascivious. Holding out an arm and smiling, she invited him to come to the bed, but he remained sat in the chair, only able to watch.

Some time later, she sat on the edge of the bed turned away from him, her head down. He put the painting of Inger back into his case and asked the woman her name. She said it was Leanna.

He stood at the end of the bed looking first at the back of her head, then at the floor as he left.

Standing on the cobblestones he stared into the murk of the canal and became aware of an emptiness entering him. It felt like water, seeping into his gut, carrying silt and bacteria to corrupt the flesh and clog his arteries. As it rose it rumbled, stirring fears and vague recollections. He clasped his head in his hands and pressed on his temples, as if to squeeze out the illusion. His eyes swam and as they focused again he saw the water was not in him but without.

The level of the canal had risen by at least a metre. And was still rising.

He remained rooted to the spot as the scum and algae climbed, aspiring to street level.

He shook his head, pressed his temples. The water crept over the edge of the bankstone and trickled towards his shoe.

The emptiness inside him which had turned to water now ran thick as adrenalin.

The canal ran over the toes of his shoes. He looked down the straight bank and saw that its former sharp definition had disappeared. The level continued to rise and the canalside shops and bars were flooded within seconds. His shoes were waterlogged. When he finally quit his trance he found it almost impossible to move.

The sky was blue and clear, not a raincloud in sight. The air was fresh and still. It was the water that chilled him, cut to the bone and filled his shoes with cement. He pulled with all his strength and shifted one leg. Now he had leverage and was able to twist the other leg and lift his foot a fraction.

Facing the other way, his back to the canal, he looked up at the brothel from which he'd emerged not fifteen minutes before. His eyes found the third floor and Leanna standing at the window looking out, a blue silk robe gathered around her shoulders barely concealing her breasts. Her eyes were as empty as he had felt when he'd taken from her and given nothing, only money. Even now, he felt something drain out of him as the sides of her robe fell away and he looked at her, imagining Inger in her place.

Could he have loved this unknown woman as he loved Inger? Was it as arbitrary as all that?

He felt something like the blood in his veins ebbing and when he looked down the cobblestones were dry. He turned and looked at the canal, which was back in its proper place.

He rang Bremerhaven himself from Centraal Station: all sailings to Scandinavia had been suspended. The remaining option was to drive to France and take a ferry to England. Then he could drive north and cross from Newcastle. As it got late and he still had not reached France, he thought about taking a room at the Van Der Griend, but decided against it on the grounds that time was short and he could well be delayed there by the charismatic proprietor and his smouldering barman. Instead he pulled off the road and nosed into a hedgerow.

The Tatra's back seat was not a comfortable bed. He dreamt only briefly of Hašek in Albania. So many more casualties had arrived that thousands of locals had seen the sense in relocating to Corfu. Tirana was emptying from the centre outwards, a small proportion of individuals hanging on, not to oppose the invaders but rather to make a go of it with them and see what might come of the change.

As the housing stock soon proved inadequate, the new arrivals found the energy to throw together ad hoc constructions of breeze-block and corrugated iron. As long as there was somewhere to plug in a TV, which was acquired as a priority, and other useless items such as freezers, cookers, microwaves.

The strange rumbling, which again had no perceptible source, woke Ankers in a sweat.

It was bitterly cold in the car and he started to shiver, his teeth to chatter. After hugging his knees and thumping himself, he clambered into the front seat and started the engine. He let it run for a while, then switched on the heater. It belted out warm air, which he hogged with his marble hands, but soon blew cold.

He reached into the back for his case and took out the picture. It didn't work, however. No warm glow. Just more anxiety.

When the sun came up he stepped outside to take a piss and a short run up and down the side of the road. Although he had stocks of neither, he thought to check the water and oil. The latter was low but not yet dangerously. The radiator, on the other hand, gave him cause for concern and he wondered if he should have emptied his bladder into it instead of on to Belgian soil.

Feeling marginally better – and despite the water shortage – he took to the road again, heading for France. Defeating his curiosity, he avoided De Panne by staying inland as far as Lille, then he cut across to Dunkirk, planning to go down the coast towards Calais for the shortest crossing.

He stopped in Dunkirk and had some breakfast in an airy café on the rue de Douvres. A man with a heavy beard and a thick pipe stood at the counter, pushing a cup of coffee up and down on the zinc top. The cup made little scratching sounds on the counter as if it had trapped a few grains of sand from the beach Ankers could see out of the window. There was another sound, softer and moist. Ankers studied the man and saw his pink lips, which emerged from his beard like a shellfish, twitch regularly as he sucked on his pipe and exhaled blue smoke.

As he continued to move the coffee cup on the counter the man stared out through the windows at the sea. Despite his glasses and the shadow cast by the beard, Ankers could see a gleam in the man's eye.

Ankers followed the man's gaze to the sea and thence to the horizon. The sea and the sky were both blue; too clear and bright for the season. He heard the rumbling again. It was like thunder but clearly wasn't. It seemed to come both from the horizon and from within him. He turned to look at the bearded man, who remained inscrutable, still staring out to sea and scraping sand on the zinc top. The rumbling abruptly became louder. Ankers snatched the small bottle of mineral water he'd purchased with his dwindling francs and strode out of the café.

He ran across the road and on to the beach. He came to a halt about fifty metres from the waterline, blood pumping furiously in his temples, heart thumping fit to burst. The noise had stopped, he realized as he took several deep breaths. There was now just the terrible stillness there had been before. In panic he whirled round and looked in the direction of the café a hundred metres away. The lenses of the bearded man's glasses glinted back at him.

And he could hear the grains of sand being ground into the counter top as clearly as if he were standing right next to him. He told himself that it was impossible but his ears took no notice and carried on listening to the scratching.

He saw the Tatra parked up at the top of the beach. Could he make it back to the car before the rumbling began again? A seagull wheeled over his head and screamed. Behind him the thunder returned. He ran up the beach. The sand sapped his energy and crept into his shoes. The door of the café opened and the bearded man stepped outside. He could still hear the scratching, which proved it was all in his mind. But the volume of the rumbling increased.

He reached the car and flung open the bonnet. Fumbling the top on the plastic bottle, he poured the contents into the radiator. The bonnet snapped back into place. The bearded man was coming his way. In a ludicrously futile gesture he threw the empty bottle down the street towards him and jumped into the driving seat, jabbing the keys into the ignition.

Only once he was moving did he allow himself to look in the mirror. The man had picked up the bottle and was brandishing it as if to admonish a litter lout. Ankers stepped on the accelerator and followed the sign for Calais and the Tunnel.

Four kilometres out of Dunkirk he pulled over and cut the engine. It died slowly, shaking the car with its final twist. Ankers became aware of the silence. He wound down the window. The air outside was balmy and still. There were not even any gulls. On one side of the road was the sea, on the other, several hundred metres distant, were the uniform warehouses and workshops of local industries. Everything seemed so ordinary and undisturbed. The incident in Dunkirk was receding like a dream.

Ankers was seized suddenly by the desire to play music. His hand went to his case, but he held back. He couldn't afford the delay. The clock was still ticking.

He started the car, checked the mirror and regained the road.

The closer he got to Calais, the more signs there were of building work on commercial and residential property. And the sicker he felt in his stomach. His plan wasn't going to work and something was going to go horribly wrong.

He drove past a demolition site where mechanical diggers roared as they bit into the ground. Whole walls collapsed as the machines undermined them. The tumbling bricks rumbled and the diggers didn't let up – they attacked a chimney-stack which toppled and fell to earth with a clap of thunder.

But when the bricks were on the ground the rumbling went on. Ankers bit his lip until it bled. He was frightened. He looked at the sea. It rumbled innocently. From beneath the sea, from inside his head, the rumbling intensified. He pressed his foot down, hoping to drive through it.

The railway came in on his left and soon he was skirting the uncompleted Tunnel terminus. He kept on going, down the slip road that followed the railway as far as it went towards the mouth of the Tunnel. The rumbling grew like a great corrupted flower blossoming. When the road went no further he stopped and gazed into the black maw of the Tunnel. The ground beneath his wheels trembled as the rumbling came nearer and louder. Blood trickled from Ankers's nose. His ears popped. In his gut everything seemed to churn and he felt himself sinking into primeval nightmare as the menace and the pressure increased and he diminished in relation to them.

He struggled to raise his eyes above the Tunnel entrance to the sea. It was calm as it had been, and blue. But on the horizon a black line had appeared. Impossible to tell if it was the sea or the sky. Maybe neither. It looked like nothing he'd ever seen. Neither an angry gathering of clouds, nor the sudden spread of an oil spillage. It was more like a void. A doorway to zero. The edge – or the end – of the world.

Then the rumbling passed the pain threshold and Ankers ground his teeth, failing to stop a scream which forced its way out. It struck the windscreen and pierced his skull on the rebound like a thin blade.

Outside the car the world was changing, the planet avenging herself. Out of the Tunnel roared the dream. Within seconds it would engulf the Tatra and Ankers would never play the tenor again.

He had a flash of enlightenment in which he saw that it was

the saxophone that had caused this. The catastrophe had been inevitable but not in so short a time. The visions and dreams, the cross-fertilization and the irrationality, had triggered the deluge. Ankers pushed his hand against the tide, reaching for the ignition, hoping, at what seemed like the end, that he might hold on to life.

The man takes out a small map of the vicinity and begins drawing on it. 'Look. This is where you should meet them.'

It is like a gulch between two massive skeletal blocks of rough concrete apartments. The lights are purplish and glimmering. An ex-army Jeep lurches up the rough road, throwing its two occupants about inside.

'Why do you want to join us?' asks the driver, who has been so badly burned he appears to have no skin stretched over his scorched flesh. He wears a loose-fitting, torn and patched military uniform.

'I went over on my own without much success,' Hašek replies without turning his gaze from the mountains. Even here the city climbs the slopes in prefabricated units and haphazard constructions, on which endless lights shine thickly. The sky is spider-webbed with reception aerials.

All Over by Lunchtime

Bentinck awoke to the tinny sound of pop music. He scratched his scalp and glared in confusion at the television, but it was blank. He took a moment to refamiliarize himself with the strange surroundings before he realized the noise was coming from the kitchen. Groggily, Bentinck pulled on his trousers, cursing his bulk. In the top of his bag there was a fresh orange shirt. He tossed the cushions on to the sofa and stumbled towards the door.

'Good morning, Rolf.' Petrović was cheerful again after his serious, intense mood of the night before.

Bentinck grunted.

'Did I wake you up? It's time to get up, anyway.'

Bentinck pointed at the portable TV and twisted up his face in irritation.

Petrović grinned and opened the fridge door. 'Do you want some breakfast?' he said, producing half a melon.

Frowning, Bentinck turned round and shuffled back towards the living room. He drew a squashed pack of Kents from the pocket of his jacket and lit one.

'If you want to take a shower,' Petrović called from the kitchen, 'you've left it too late. We've got to go soon.' He switched off the TV. 'In a minute or two, in fact.'

Bentinck inhaled deeply and felt a sharp kick as another branch snapped off his lung tree. *That's what I smoke for,* he reminded himself as his head swam.

'I'm glad,' he said. 'If only because it means you have to switch off that row. I can hear myself think at last. Perhaps now you will tell me where we are going and why you invited me to Ljubljana.'

'You will need your notebook and pen . . .' Petrović broke off and cocked his ear. 'What's the time? I haven't got my watch on.'

Bentinck fished in his jacket pocket. 'Eight o'clock,' he said.

There was a muffled bang outside and then another, louder and more distinct. Bentinck had jumped but Petrović's eyes were gleaming.

'Let's go,' said the Yugoslav, in a voice with new edge to it.

'What the fuck's going on?' he yelled as Petrović disappeared into the hall. Bentinck delved into his bag and pulled out a pocket camera and a small attaché case. Petrović emerged from his bedroom in a leather jacket, still pushing an automatic pistol into the pocket. Bentinck's heart began to race and he clutched the attaché case tighter. Obviously, he was going to need it before the morning was over.

Once Petrović had got it to start and both men were crouched in the Zastava heading citywards, the tall, thin, suddenly electrified man explained a little of what was Going On.

'The bombs you heard were a diversion,' he said, as he waited for lights to change.

'You've got a gun in your pocket, there are bombs going off, and you're waiting at a red light like it was a Sunday morning.' Bentinck shook his head in disbelief. The lights changed and Petrović accelerated calmly.

'Perhaps,' he said, 'you have a romantic idea of revolutionaries and how they should behave. Have a look under the back seat.'

Bentinck squirmed round, releasing himself from the seatbelt, and lifted the rear cushion.

'Jesus Christ!' he muttered.

'Put the seat back,' Petrović said. 'It's getting busier.'

The streets here were alive with people going to work. Petrović pulled up behind a Škoda in a traffic queue. A group of factory workers crossed between the cars and looked in through the windscreen at Bentinck. He thought he might as well be wearing ammunition belts and bristling with grenades plucked from the arsenal under the seat behind him. The men just passed by and the traffic began to move.

'Do they know?' Bentinck asked.

'Not these ones maybe. Some of them. There are many of us.'

Bentinck sat for a while and thought. Most of the other cars on the road were identical to Petrović's; were they all carrying the means to overthrow the state? When they stopped at a junction, Bentinck stared at a woman alongside. White Zastava 500. Same car. But she looked as if she were driving to school where she taught bright kids about EC agricultural models, and surpluses and requirements.

She caught Bentinck's gaze and looked away again. He took out a pack of cigarettes and lit one.

'So are we going to the police station or the parliament buildings?' he asked. 'Or the law courts?' he added, thinking of the youth magazine editor held in the cells there pending the outcome of his treason trial.

'Others are going to those places,' Petrović said. 'We're going to the railway station. The city has got to be closed off.'

'Who else knows about this?' Bentinck asked excitedly. 'What about the press here? What about *Mladina*?'

'We couldn't trust them. Belgrade's people are everywhere. Even *Mladina* we couldn't be sure about.'

Petrović turned into the bus terminus in front of the railway station and for the first time looked nervous.

'So I've got a real scoop?' the journalist asked.

'I should say so,' agreed the revolutionary as he passed the station buildings and bounced over the cobbles into a yard where there were two postal vans and another white Zastava.

Petrović and Orel, the man Bentinck had met the night before, entered the station master's office confidently and levelled machine-guns at its occupants. An official spluttered and remonstrated, but raised his hands and stepped out from behind his desk when ordered to do so.

Orel explained to the official what was taking place and the man relinquished authority for his station, but not without some reluctance. Orel had him explain the Tannoy system, which he then proceeded to use.

'We've got people on the platforms,' Petrović explained over his shoulder to Bentinck. 'Orel's telling them we've taken control. They'll make sure the public react safely.'

'But there'll be police and soldiers here within seconds,' said Bentinck.

'Hopefully not,' Petrović said. 'The bombs outside the city will have diverted them. They're very jumpy at the moment because of the *Mladina* trial and they're too stupid to suspect a diversion. Naturally,' he added, 'we've got our own people in the security forces, too. Right the way up to the top. We can't fail.'

Bentinck sat at the station master's desk – 'You don't mind?' 'Not at all, go ahead'; once he knew there was no personal danger, the station master was pleased to co-operate – and opened the attaché case. Inside was the state of the art in reporter's notebook and pen – a top-of-the-range IBM.

'Slovenia seceded from Yugoslavia today as an armed coup was staged in the republic's capital, Ljubljana,' Bentinck wrote. 'At 7 am two diversionary bombs were detonated 4 km east of the city, drawing large numbers of soldiers and police out of nearby barracks and stations. At 7.10 groups of men armed with automatic rifles, machine-guns and grenades stormed the parliament buildings, main police stations, army barracks, courthouse and railway station. Aided by hundreds of sympathizers among the Communist Party and the security forces, the rebels took control of the republic within minutes.

'Soldiers and police continuing to support Belgrade were disarmed and where necessary overpowered. Although shots were fired it is thought there were no serious casualties.

'The Slovenian Party leader, Konstantin Krunić, went live on Ljubljana Radio and Television at 8 am publicly to declare Slovenia's secession from Yugoslavia. "The Democratic Socialist Republic of Slovenia announces its independence from Belgrade and the Yugoslav federation," Krunić said, in a voice that barely concealed his emotion.

'Sources suggest that Krunić was secretly behind the coup from the beginning.

'The most liberal and Westernized of the six Yugoslav republics, Slovenia has been straining at Belgrade's leash for years ... SUB-EDITOR TO GET RESEARCH AND CONTINUE.'

'What about the border with Serbia?' Bentinck asked Petrović later, as they drank victory brandies at a bar on Cankarjeva Street. 'Serbia has dominated Yugoslavia for too long to give up a republic just like that. Belgrade will send troops, surely. Milošević is too proud to let this happen without flexing his muscles. Isn't he?'

Slobodan Milošević, charismatic leader of the Serbian Communist Party, had made himself a folk hero by leading the crusade against the ethnic Albanians in the Serbian province of Kosovo. They complained of persecution and brutality. So did he. And he had the newspapers on his side. He stripped Kosovo of its autonomy and silenced the ethnic Albanians for a while.

'We've got troops defending the border,' Petrović assured him. 'But I don't think he'll do anything. It would be civil war and Yugoslavia can't afford it. Especially now they've lost Slovenia. We contributed 60 per cent of the federal economy. In military terms they could defeat us but it would break them. They'll just have to accept that things have changed. This is history.'

Both men drained their glasses.

'What about your story?' Petrović asked.

'I plugged into the phone lines at the railway station. They should have been able to reset the front page and get another edition out this morning. It should be on the news-stands now.'

Bentinck lit a cigarette and inhaled deeply. There goes another one, he thought. He smiled to himself as he imagined the reactions of his critics and rivals to seeing his byline under the biggest scoop of the year. The only pity was that he couldn't be at home to bask in the attention.

'This place will be crawling with hacks within hours,' Bentinck said. 'And photographers and TV crews. You won't be able to move. Time I was somewhere else, I think,' he added. 'Do you suppose much will happen now?'

'No, I don't think so,' Petrović said, leaning back with his brandy. 'Belgrade's supporters will cool off in the cells. We made room for them by releasing all political prisoners, including Mikulić, of course.'

'And will Mikulić continue to edit *Mladina*?'

'I expect so,' Petrović nodded. 'As for Milošević, he'll blow his top to the media about the whole thing, the coup and the secession, but there'll be no war.'

'So,' Bentinck mused, straightening a crumpled cigarette and lighting it, 'I don't really need to stick around Ljubljana any longer?'

'Nothing much is going to happen.'

Bentinck drew on his cigarette and kept on inhaling until his head felt about to burst. Then he took a swig of brandy and swilled it around his mouth as he exhaled through his nose. He was slowly realizing that events in Yugoslavia were not going to be issues on the sidelines and he was going to get to them all before anybody else. This wrenching of one small wheel from Yugoslavia's rusted mechanical nightmare was but a divertissement; of this Bentinck was convinced. The best was yet to come. He made a mental note to call his assistant, Böll, and have him send all his material about the West German TV manufacturer whose exports to Yugoslavia attracted the attention of the state trade inspectorate. He could see he was going to need it. To think that if Petrović hadn't written to him he might have missed out on so much that he now saw before him. He looked at Petrović, who was mellow with brandy, leaning back in his chair, grinning broadly. If he wasn't so strict with his own emotions, he would reach over and give that thin, lunatic face a kiss.

Petrović caught Bentinck looking at him. 'Where will you go?' he asked.

'South,' Bentinck said, making the word a circle in his mouth. 'Something certainly Happened here today. And in the south there's Something Going On. I'm sure of it.'

'Kosovo?' Petrović asked.

'Kosovo.'

'Makes sense,' he nodded and swallowed more brandy.

'I'll go to Belgrade first. I suppose in this godforsaken country I've *got* to go through Belgrade to reach the south.'

'Unless you've got your own transport,' Petrović said.

'Sadly I am reliant upon Yugoslav Railways,' he sighed. 'Let's go.' Bentinck rose too quickly to his feet so that he felt dizzy. 'We'll get a cab,' he said, pulling 5,000-dinar notes from a roll and dropping them on the table.

'That won't be enough,' Petrović said. 'The price will have gone up while we were drinking.'

'While the barman unscrewed the cap, I should imagine,' he agreed, adding more money to the pile. 'What will you and your comrades do about that?' he asked, as he propelled Petrović towards the door.

'About what?'

'The economy. Inflation.'

'Rolf. Don't you see?' he said, like a drunken schoolteacher. 'Slovenia is rich. Always has been. But we had to subsidize the poor regions. Macedonia. Montenegro. Kosovo. You see? Now they can go fuck themselves. It's simple.'

Bentinck hailed a Mercedes taxi and dived in, almost leaving Petrović stumbling victoriously on the pavement.

'So that's your democratic socialism, is it? Long live the revolution.'

Petrović grinned elastically, then frowned and muttered. He looked green enough to start throwing up.

Bentinck called out to the driver the name of Petrović's district and the car swung back into the roadway.

He helped Petrović to the bathroom, then grabbed his bag and the plum brandy from the kitchen and left the flat, pulling the door to quietly behind him. Petrović's groans drifted down the stairway after him. Bentinck had told the taxi driver to wait.

'The railway station,' he said, settling down in the back seat.

Tunnel Visions

Ian's hand was trapped between his leg and the gravel. Slowly he lifted his weight and sat on the step. His hand was red. He massaged it gently and tried to imagine it holding a drumstick. '2nd Avenue Blue'. He tapped a cymbal. It felt good but defeat tasted sour. Lucy's face came into his mind, tearing off her surgical mask. He shook it away and stood up. The sun was shining but there was still a chill in the air. He shivered briefly through the thin white coat, which he wasn't used to wearing out of doors, and wondered if he should go back for his jacket. *Fuck it!* He'd never liked the jacket. What was in the pockets? Tissues, a bit of change, an old bus ticket, a crappy novel: he could live without all that.

So he left it behind like an old skin and strode away from the hospital in his white coat. A fair swap, he thought. His wallet and keys were in the pockets of his trousers. He could leave it all behind – Lucy's betrayal, Clayton's petty wickedness, Mr Tindall's final hours anaesthetized by painkillers – and start afresh.

As he got closer to home, crossing streets that became more and more his territory, he became morose. The sloughing off of the old life was a feeble gesture. Clayton had beaten him and was still stealing lives to line his pocket. He had changed nothing.

Despondently he twisted his key in the lock and opened the door. The flat smelt of the previous night's mishap and made Ian grimace. He went round opening all the windows, then grabbed a pair of sticks and left the flat, still wearing the white coat. He marched down through the tail end of the town towards the sea. He could taste the salt and hear the seagulls as they wheeled and cried above the sea front. He saw a fish and chip shop and crossed the road to pass through its aura. The smell was so good he doubled back and stepped inside for a bag of chips. He felt the sticks in his back pocket as he reached for a pound. He liked having them there; just two sticks of wood but they represented the only thing he could do half well. As he shook more salt on to his chips and sprinkled on some vinegar, two youths who were giving their order stared at him. He wondered if it was his black skin or his white coat that drew their thin veneer of contempt.

The chips were good. At the sight of white horses skimming the sea, his spirits lifted. He hummed the flute melody from the beginning of '2nd Avenue Blue'. He scrunched up the chip wrapper and tossed it into a bin on the sea front. The wind caressed his skull and billowed the tails of his white coat. Seagulls hovered and dropped through the air like fighter planes. He went down the steps and jumped on to the pebbly beach. There were few people about. He turned round and watched people on the promenade leaning into the wind as they walked across his field of vision like targets on a funfair shooting range. A man was pulled along in the other direction by his outstretched scarf.

Ian turned back to the sea and stuck his tongue out to taste the salt.

In his mind he played the guitar solo from '2nd Avenue Blue'. Buddy Rich resisted the temptation in the song, on the whole *Tuff Dude* album, in fact, to do a solo. A good drummer would always do a few solos, a great one didn't have to: Rich led the band from the back, marking time, driving the beat. He did solos as well, the best in the world.

The sax came in, its tenor voice full and with just the right harshness of edge. Ian went down towards the waterline and small waves splashed on to the stones like cymbal rolls. He walked towards the pier and the piano came in just as he passed beneath it. He sat down on a rock by a rusted girder. Taking the sticks from his jeans, he accompanied the piano and allowed the bass to come in and take over. Then the piano returned and Ian drove the rhythm on to the end.

It wasn't a fast finish but he was sweating. It was the excitement. His life had changed and he was beginning to live for the moment, to savour every sensation. His defeat at the blood-soaked hands of Clayton would yet turn to victory. He wasn't meant for Lucy; maybe he wasn't even meant to carry the responsibility of exposing Clayton's racket. Nor was he meant to hold the hands of dying patients in their last moments – it hurt him too much because each time it was too late.

There was only one thing he had ever been really good at: hitting skins with sticks.

He was free now, could go anywhere and do anything. Play drums for whoever would have him. He began playing 'Newk's Fadeaway' on the girder, Sonny Rollins's tenor sax melody almost as clear as the applauding seagulls. Kenny Drew ran up and down the keyboard and left Ian a few bars' drumwork before Rollins came in again. Ian imitated the Art Blakey rhythm perfectly, delighting in the syncopated thrash just before the fade-out.

He looked at the horizon and thought that he could go abroad if he wished. He might be able to get work on the Continent. Maybe speaking English was an asset in the European jazz environment. Being black might help. It was, after all, black music, or had been in the beginning. As it fell out of vogue it became the province of middle-class whites. That was fine, but now that jazz was fashionable again maybe people would accept the return of the black man.

Ian sat beneath the pier as the sun went down. He ran through 'Newk's Fadeaway' again on the girder, then played another favourite Sonny Rollins tune, 'St Thomas'. The sun sank lower and Ian drove his imaginary band through '2nd Avenue Blue' again, without once feeling the chill left behind by the sun; not even when the drums fell quiet for the bass solo did he shiver. The song over and the cries of the gulls dying in his ears as they fled the darkening beach, Ian pocketed his sticks and stretched his arms and legs. All at once he felt the cold bite through his thin clothes, so pulled the white coat tightly around his neck. He dug his hands in the pockets and discovered he still had his bleeper. Swinging his arm back and then flinging it forward, he propelled the little box into the black sea. Unable to see the splash he fancied he had thrown it the length of the pier.

Then he turned and walked up the beach towards the town, slipping once or twice on the larger stones. Waves chased him up the beach: the tide would not delay long before coming in. At the top of the beach he stopped and looked back before climbing up to the promenade. It was quite dark now, the sky gaberdine blue, the sea black as leather. Ian felt a tug from the beach and the sea.

All he had to do was go back and sit under the pier and beat the bass drum of a funeral marching band while the tide swiftly smothered him. It was so dark, so inviting. The *swish-thump-swish* of the waves became the drumming pattern of '2nd Avenue Blue'. Cymbals and bass drum driving the blood round the body of the song. *Swish-thump-swish.* The heart of the night was beating. *Swish-thump-swish.* He thought of his mother. And of himself as a child clinging to her for long hours before she went away. He remembered the wet street, the upstairs curtain pushed aside by tiny fingers so he could watch. Not the flashing blue light itself but its reflection in the slick tarmac. The two men entering the house and leaving it as one long shadow cast by the hall light. Carrying something between them.

When he was fourteen, Ian asked his father why he had not driven his mother to hospital, or at least gone with her in the ambulance. The old man had looked down and spoken so quietly Ian had to strain to make out the words. 'I couldn't move from this chair,' he had said, tapping the arm of the chair. Tears had filled his eyes as he recalled the day the boy's mother was taken away to die. 'I just couldn't get out of the chair.' Tears had fallen on his cheek and he began to sob.

Ian's fourteen-year-old heart grew thick with contempt: he thought his father a coward.

Years later he grew to regret this ready condemnation. His father was no coward; just a broken man whose reason for living had been taken away. He had cared for Ian's mother for months as she lay more and more hours of the day in bed. She had not wanted to burden the hospital services with a cancer she knew would eventually kill her. Twice before, she had had tumours removed and twice recovered. But this time, she knew, would be the last, so what was the point of having it taken out?

Ian learnt all of this five years after the first conversation with his father. With this knowledge he looked back on the past and saw his mother slowly becoming bedridden and his father exhausted with looking after Mother, him and the house, but never letting Mother know. The ending was the same: Mother was taken away and she never came back.

When he was nineteen, Ian thought again about that first conversation with his father and realized the accusation of cowardice was completely unfounded. His father had been in the grip of the most terrible sadness. If his life's purpose had been to care for Ian's mother, that purpose had been removed. The gap it left could not be filled.

So, the second conversation took place, and the ground was cleared for a *rapprochement* between the boy and his father. But it was too late. Ian's father failed to wake up one morning. Cause of death was listed as unknown. But Ian knew what had killed his father and he blamed himself.

Now, six years later, standing on Brighton sea front, staring at the oily black sea and blurred skeletal pier – tears streaming down his face – he felt the self-recriminations could cease. He could make peace with himself and his past. He wanted to say out loud, 'I love you, Father', to the sea, with some romantic idea that the waters would carry his words to a place where his father might hear them. He wanted to, but when he opened his mouth to utter the words he felt too self-conscious. He kept the thought inside his head, where his father was just as likely to hear it.

Ian buttoned up the white coat and headed back into the town centre.

Outside the Treble Clef several groups of people milled around as if unsure whether or not to go in. Ian's white coat drew one or two remarks as he passed between them to get to the door. Snorts of laughter followed him into the foyer. As he dug in his new pocket for the entrance money he could hear music inside. An alto sax was playing the chorus line of 'Billie's Bounce'. It sounded so much like Charlie Parker himself it could only be Philip Caramazza. Ian smiled in anticipation as the young man in the booth pushed his change and a ticket under the glass.

He pushed the swing doors open and stepped into the warm smoky fug of the club. On the small stage at the far end of the room was indeed Philip Caramazza. A white boy barely eighteen from the look of him, yet he could play Charlie Parker as well as Parker. He flung his instrument into the music in the same way. The result was almost vocal, as if he had been singing and the saxophone got in the way. Occasionally he overreached himself; either his young lungs couldn't hold the breath he needed, or his fingers tied themselves in knots as they raced to press the key-pads in the order dictated by instinct and genius.

Ian got a pint of Guinness from the bar and moved slowly to the front, stopping occasionally to gulp his drink and savour the boy's playing. 'Billie's Bounce' was wound to a close and the audience elbowed their pints in order to clap. Ian recognized the drummer when the latter stood up and reached for a mike. 'Thank you, folks,' said the drummer. 'Philip Caramazza there on alto sax. He thanks you. And the rhythm section: Roger Barnes, Terry Davies and John Richardson. They thank you so much.' Ian clapped. He remembered the trio now though he couldn't recall where or when he'd last seen them. 'Phil's going to stay up for another number,' John Richardson continued. 'And he'll be joined by Al McGuire on baritone sax.' There was a ripple of applause from those punters who had seen McGuire before, Ian among them. He was another young player but he played the baritone with assurance. It seemed to Ian that one had to coax melody lines out of the baritone sax, unlike its smaller cousins, but Al McGuire made it seem effortless. He and Phil Caramazza played together on Gerry Mulligan's 'Reunion', Phil Caramazza substituting his alto for Chet Baker's mellifluous trumpet. Ian took a mouthful of Guinness and glanced around. Most of the faces he could see were wreathed in smiles, including his own, he realized. That, he thought to himself, was the single most important reason for liking jazz: it made you smile, it made you happy. In spite of everything: Lucy's betrayal as she ripped her mask off, Alice's death, Mr Tindall's inevitable death, Ian's dismal failure to expose the doctor's crimes, and Ian's ejection from the hospital. In spite of the cancer that killed Ian's mother and the ignorance and blindness on Ian's part that isolated his father and eventually helped break and kill him. In spite of all that shit he couldn't help grinning as Phil Caramazza and Al McGuire swopped solos on 'Reunion'.

Ian's father had been a jazz fan. He owned a great many records. But he stopped listening to most of them after he had a conversation with his fourteen-year-old son in which his son called him a coward and turned his back on him. He sold them all when the son went away to art college, a year before the second conversation.

Ian shouted with everyone else for more when Philip Caramazza and Al McGuire stepped off the stage. But John

Richardson asked the audience to throw their hands together for Alan Barnes. The alto player in the familiar powder-blue jacket came on to a warm welcome and tuned up with pianoplayer Roger Barnes. Ian wondered if they might be father and son: they were not unalike. He went to the bar for another pint and the quartet began to play Sonny Rollins's 'St Thomas'. The barman gave Ian's white coat a look but said nothing. Ian finished the pint before the quartet finished the song. He ordered another. He drank an inch so he could carry it without spilling any, and made his way back towards the front. Alan Barnes finished a solo and was applauded. Roger Barnes took a few bars. Ian watched John Richardson as he drank, studying his drumming pattern and comparing it to his own, or to his ideas for the song. Richardson was a good drummer. Ian couldn't fault his technique and he admired his style. Next they played an Alan Barnes composition, 'Man Goes'; more than just a clever title, the song featured a strong hook and some fine syncopated percussion.

Ian took a deep draught of his Guinness and moved with the music. The band found a groove and dug it. They all took solos, even the skins got a good pounding. Ian got more and more into the music and with the aid of the drink became ever mellower. Soon he'd polished off two more pints and was determined to go off and play drums professionally. He'd done it before but at the time lacked the stamina required to keep looking for work. He never made it into a regular band and soon gave up playing for nursing.

They played 'Freedom Samba', another Alan Barnes tune. The pace was frenetic and Ian could only just keep up on his mental drum kit. His fifth pint glass was empty, on the floor.

He had to start playing again, but perhaps not in Britain. Maybe jazz was getting too fashionable too quickly and he would find it hard to compete. He recalled the pull the velvet sea had exerted on him. Should he go to Europe? It wasn't far, after all, and there was a lot going on. He could travel, work if necessary, and create opportunities to make his mark. He'd managed to save a bit of money living cheaply and working overtime.

Alan Barnes swapped his alto for a tenor and led the band into another Sonny Rollins number, 'Tenor Madness'. Ian took his sticks from his jeans and drummed against his legs. They played for another forty-five minutes, joined on stage by Philip Caramazza and Al McGuire for two encores. Ian drummed until his thighs were bruised. His head was whirling with the alcohol and the excitement. When they finally stopped playing his ears were ringing. The people who passed him on their way out were wearing big stupid grins: the gig had been a great success. Eventually Ian pocketed his sticks and followed the stragglers out. The night was cold but Ian was still high. He wrapped his white coat tightly around him and set off in the direction of home at a brisk walk. Though drunk he was dimly aware of the salty smell of the sea impregnating the town. The route home from the club was like a corridor, or tunnel, down which he strode. He desperately needed to empty his bladder but wouldn't stop. He had never pissed in the street and was determined not to break his duck now. The bedsit was only ten minutes away, in any case.

Once inside he felt how cold it was. All the windows were open. He ran round and closed them before going to the toilet. He stood urinating for at least two minutes, intent on the stream falling into the pool and the steam rising out of it. His mind was fogged and could only cope with one thing at a time. He was finished for now but knew there would be more later. Flushing the toilet automatically, he moved to the washbasin and splashed his face with cold water. He looked at the mirror and tried to single out his own reflection. For a moment it appeared to take form from out of the blur but then melted away again. He stared hard but could not decide which of the two Ians was him. In fact, including himself there were three. 'Oh, fucking hell,' he slurred and left the bathroom. He leant back in to switch off the tap.

His bedsitting room was freezing. He needed 50p for the meter. He went through his pockets, found coppers, a twenty and a pound, but no fifties. There were none scattered on his bookshelf, where he usually looked. None in the kitchen drawer. Suddenly he remembered where there would be one: in the pocket of his green jacket which he'd left in the hospital.

He gave up, too drunk to continue the search. All he could perceive was a tunnel, at the end of which was his bed. The mattress was already unfolded. Without bothering to undress he yanked the duvet free of a heavy book. It was the Delvaux book;

his tug opened it at the colour plate of three women in a railway station waiting room. He scowled and kicked the book. It slid a few feet across the synthetic carpet but remained open at the same page.

Ian threw himself on to the mattress and pulled the duvet over his head. Even through his clothes he felt the damp chill retained by the foam. But the discomfort was momentary. All he was aware of was the tunnel. At one end were six pints of Guinness. At the other, oblivion. The tunnel was straight and despite a terrible throbbing din there were no obstructions. His head fell into the pillow and went straight through it, falling down and down into the deepest darkness.

The train made its own racket but that could barely be heard above the noise of the tunnel itself. A heavy beat which made the tunnel quiver and resound like the inside of a bass drum.

There was a framed picture on the wall of the carriage. It showed three women in a waiting room; one, wearing a low-cut dress, stood behind a counter, the other two, standing opposite the counter and reclining on a couch, were naked. All three appeared to have been caught in mid-gesture by the artist. But the gestures would have done nothing to bring the three women into contact with each other: they were all looking in different directions.

Through an arched doorway in the far wall Ian could see a train standing at the platform, steam rising from the engine. He left his position of artist's eye view and crossed the floor of the waiting room. As he reached the doorway he fancied he heard a sliding, a rustling behind him. Unaccountably frightened, he turned round slowly. The women did not seem to have moved. Maybe he had heard merely the eructations of the steam engine acoustically enhanced by the high ceiling of the waiting room.

He swept his white coat in an arc and left the waiting room with a flourish. The train was ready to leave. He climbed on board and it rattled out of the station.

He knew he'd seen the scenery before. The pines, the sand, the dunes. But he couldn't stop it unfolding before the train. The same classical ruins appeared, incongruous in the middle of the dunes. More women sleepwalking naked in the moon-washed square. Then the same lurch to the left and the jolt as the train headed down into the earth.

The tunnel levelled out and the lights came on. The first thing Ian saw was the framed print on the wall. Then he noticed that the interior of the carriage was streamlined and modern. The train he had boarded at the station had been distinctly old-fashioned.

There was a terrific din coming from outside the train. Ian's head, tender already, was pounded relentlessly, so that soon the beat seemed to be literally inside his skull.

Well, wasn't it all a dream?

He knew that already but there was no waking from it. The train bucked and rolled, buffeting his head against the seat. The roll was so accentuated it made Ian think of a boat tossed on a heavy sea. Just then his worst but unspoken fear was stoked.

He noticed water lapping at the soles of his shoes.

He had known it was inevitable but the shock hit him hard like a blow in the chest. He pressed his fists into the chair, raising his body an inch or two, and twisted round to look up the aisle.

The water was coming.

He panicked, jumped to his feet and sprinted up the aisle away from the water. His precipitous action seemed only to encourage the stream to grow. He heard it gush as it flowed inexorably towards him and flooded each of the spaces between the seats. He thrust out an arm to open the door at the end of the carriage. The door was heavy and jarred his shoulder. He elbowed it shut and before passing into the next carriage looked back through the little window.

A torrent of water slammed into the glass only inches from his face. His heart flipped over. The force of the water had cracked the glass like creased parchment. Adrenalin rushed into his mouth and he reacted swiftly to the danger. He twisted round and opened the connecting door, dived through and ran for his life.

It's only a dream, a part of his mind kept telling him. But somehow he knew the significance was much greater. If he drowned in the train he might never wake up.

Two carriages up he stopped for breath, panting. He slumped on to the arm of a seat, wondering if it wouldn't just be easier to give up and wait for the water to claim him.

He sniffed the air: there was an unmistakable tang of salt. Brighton's sea air must be falling in on him through the window. But he knew there had to be more to it than that and when he heard the water splashing against the door at the end of the carriage he knew what it was.

As he got up he noticed another framed print hanging in the same place as before in the carriage where he'd been sitting. Like the other it was a Delvaux. More of his familiar marble women were sleepwalking through a jungle of ferns and plantains. They were accompanied by men who were equally pale and wide-eyed.

The water distracted him. There was a hiss where the pressure had built up and forced a leak around the door.

He threw a final glance at the picture. He could even remember where in his book it was. So why the hell couldn't he wake up?

The hiss was getting louder.

He ran.

As he ran and tried to imagine where this flight might be leading, a phrase from '2nd Avenue Blue' suddenly came into his head. It was the transition where the piano hands over to the bass and Anthony Jackson feels his way into the solo. It repeated itself a few times, then it was gone. He didn't stop running. He left that carriage and secured the door just as the door at the far end gave way and the water plunged in, covering the distance to the door he was closing in no more than four seconds.

As he picked up his feet to run he felt weary. The water level rose behind the door. The picture on the carriage wall showed the women sitting in chairs in two rows facing each other on either side of a narrow road that led downhill to the sea. The women were naked to the waist, then covered by discreet robes from the waist down. Ian wondered what the blankets hid from view. As the water rose behind him and the hiss of the first leak was heard, he tried to snatch the print from within its frame, but the frame was screwed to the wall and glass protected the picture. He couldn't understand why when the flood was only a few feet behind him, but he jabbed his elbow hard into the glass. It cracked right across and left a small gap. He pulled a drumstick from his back pocket and prised the pieces of glass further apart, then levered one out of the frame. It fell and smashed on the floor like a tumbler of water. He teased at the picture until he gained a purchase and was able to remove it. It slid out and he folded it into the same pocket as his sticks.

The water was squeezing through. A thin stream hit his leg. He heard the door crack and ran. It gave way before he reached the next one. While he was still pushing it open the floodwater reached him, splashing up the back of his legs. He'd opened the door and allowed the water through. He tried to push it shut behind him, but couldn't. He couldn't stay in the middle between carriages. Water was pushing up between the steel plates under-foot. Obviously the only clear space left in the tunnel lay ahead in the front carriages. He could hardly lift his feet. The water covered his shoes and dragged at his trousers. He released the catch on the door to the next carriage and the water flooded in, himself with it. A surge came from behind and he was bowled off his feet. The water boiled beneath him. He rolled and gulped a lungful of salty water, rolled back and coughed up as much as he could, swallowing the rest, then retching. His foot hit a seat and he realized how high the water had risen. The carriage ceiling was only two or three feet away. The waters swelled and lifted him clear of the seat.

It's only a dream! It's only a dream! It's only a dream!

A cold wave enveloped him. He twisted underwater, trying to surface. He opened his eyes and saw the seat fabric glowing viv-idly through the bubbling green. It seemed to him suddenly that it could be so beautiful if he stayed underwater. An enormous white-bellied skate appeared beneath him, making him jump and shriek a great white gasp of surprise into the rushing water. But the skate was only the tails of his white coat billowing in the flood. This brought a swift stream of images flashing through his mind: old Alice's shrunken cheeks, Clayton's tight red face con-torted with anger, Philip Caramazza's alto sax twisting like a snake caught between his mouth and his hands.

Then the waves rolled him again and he broke the surface, spluttering for air. There was precious little left between water and ceiling. The survival instinct urged him to swim. He splashed wildly, the realization of his peril begetting panic, and thrust his body forwards to the front of the carriage. He had to dive to locate the door handle. As he struggled to reach the handle, having almost to upend his body in the water, he pictured the nature of his predicament in his mind's eye. Outside the tunnel the huge expanse of the sea exerting enormous pressure. Inside too was water, a tunnelful. In the tunnel the train was filling up rapidly from the back. Only the front carriages still contained oxygen. If he kept heading for the front he might still be breathing air by the time the tunnel reached land and surfaced. Even in dreams a tunnel had to end up somewhere. He just had to press on. He stretched another inch, holding his breath till his head felt like an overripe fruit, and he managed to catch hold of the door handle.

It wouldn't turn.

He exhaled in shock and the bubbles tickled his forehead as they rose to the surface. The door wouldn't open. Which could only mean one thing.

He was already in the front carriage.

There was no further escape.

Disbelieving, yet desperate for air, he lunged for the surface. The cold was beginning to hinder his movement. He shuddered uncontrollably. As soon as his head left the water he gulped at the remaining air. There was barely a foot between the water level and the carriage ceiling. He had never craved air so desperately. Suddenly it was the most precious thing in the world and there couldn't be too much of it. *I'll never take it for granted again*, he prayed. *If only you let me out of here before I drown!*

A wave splashed up into his face and he shook his head. His teeth were chattering so violently he feared they might shatter. Paddling with one numb hand and treading water, he wiped his eyes and nose. His eyes were stinging. His clothes weighed him down but there was no point in shedding them now. He shivered convulsively and thought quite calmly, *I'm going to die*. A sort of resigned calm fell upon him and he felt his body relax. The shivering and chattering stopped. He continued to tread water languidly. Looking back the way he'd come, he estimated the carriage was about a hundred feet long and twelve feet wide. The average height between the water level and the ceiling looked about a foot. That made 1,200 square feet of air left. So if he only used a square foot every minute, that meant he had 1,200 minutes, divided by sixty made twenty hours. Except that the water was still rising and he could only breathe the air at his end of the carriage.

I must wake up! I must wake up! I must wake up!

The water lapped at his chin. He had already bobbed to the centre of the carriage where the ceiling was highest and his head was now scraping against it. Splashes of froth momentarily blinded him and he could no longer raise his arm to wipe them. He watched the level rise still higher through eyes that felt like they'd been sanded and rubbed with vinegar. Mouth closed, he sucked in breath through his nose. The smell of salt and soaking woodwork was overpowering. He tilted his head backwards and his whole body swung to the surface so that he was floating on his back.

With the ceiling only six inches from the tip of his nose, he fluttered his hands desultorily to remain afloat and waited for the end to come. The tails of his now discoloured white coat flapped upwards and wrapped themselves around his hands and body like a shroud. He could still feel the two drumsticks in his jeans pocket nestling against his left buttock. Aware of these hard testaments to reality he tried again to overthrow the tyranny of the dream.

I must wake up! I must wake up! Wake up! Wake up! Wake up!

A small swell pushed water up his nose and panicked him. He snorted and splashed his arms and as a result began to sink. He went completely under and tipped over sideways. The seat colours were dimmed by the extra depth of water but still inviting – *why don't I just sit down on one of them? They look so comfortable*. But he pushed down and managed to roll on to his back again. His head hit the ceiling. Even leaning back as far as possible he was only an inch clear.

He expected now to see a stream of images pass before his eyes unbidden. Scenes from his life or just pictures from his last, disastrous day at the hospital. But instead all he saw were the murky images of the drowned seats beneath him in the carriage. He hoped when his lungs filled with water that he would be lucky enough to fall on to a double seat and be comfortable in death.

He wondered if in his bed in Brighton he had already choked on his own vomit.

The green squares and orange triangles of the seat covers shone dully through the water.

Wake up! Wake up! Wake up!

He saw the ripple of another wave and reckoned it would be the last. Even at the end he was still pretending there might be a chance of survival as he took a deep breath before the wave washed over his face.

There was no more air left between the water and the ceiling.

Lungs full, he kicked his legs behind him and swam down through the water. The seats looked so inviting.

Smoke issues from a side street and a vehicle exits under its cover so suddenly that the squad's Jeep has to veer sharply to the right to avoid a collision.

The first they know is a scream from the East German on Hašek's left. Two spikes of a grappling hook pin him to the Jeep's bodywork, one through the shoulder, the other through his forehead and skull. A chain taut from the stem of the hook disappears into the smoke, stretching to the other vehicle.

A second hook thuds into the bonnet and drags the Jeep off course. The Russian driver attempts to regain control but the aggressor appears to their left and smashes heavily into the side of the Jeep. Hašek and the East German, freed from his hook, open fire on the Yugoslav army unit. A grenade bounces off the Jeep's bonnet and explodes away to the right. The Russian passes something back to the East German, saying, 'Use it. I can't aim while driving.' The East German has a look; it is a thermate grenade. But before he has a chance to lose it, his whole body jerks backwards, pivoting at the neck. Hašek twists his head round. A soldier has jumped from the other car and is riding on the back bumper, holding on to a garrotte around the East German's neck. The garrotte works too quickly, slicing through neck and spine, and the Yugoslav falls away clutching the head. Hašek catches the grenade and lobs it high so it drops into the Yugoslav vehicle and explodes on impact. The thermate flashes brilliantly, silhouetting the three remaining soldiers as they are carbonated.

Moment of Flight

Only once had Gabriela seen Ceauşescu.

It was the day after she dreamt the dark stranger into her bed and she was out walking. The roads had been cleared, which meant one of the Family was about to be driven by. Thin young men stood awkwardly in their polyester suits, eyes swivelling like oiled parts of a machine. A few passers-by watched the empty road; others, more cautious, studied the pavement. Scarcely any would try to look into the tinted windows of the limos as they arrived, for fear of actually seeing Ceauşescu. It would be like beholding the Godhead. Or Satan. Either way the effect would surely be terrible.

Because of the stilled road the noise of the cavalcade's engines could be heard several blocks away. It droned through squares and boulevards, growing louder. Among the plainclothes men lining the route uniformed men had appeared, submachine-guns slung across their chests. Gabriela stepped back beneath the awning of a store that appeared to be selling yellowed posters of Bohemian castles, or trips to them.

The cavalcade appeared in the distance like a blot of ink on a pen drawing of the perspectives. The cars were drawn a little closer as if on a string. She felt her insides being tied into knots.

Over the road a uniformed gunman shifted position and the plainclothes men nearest to him made plaits of their sightlines.

She was suddenly convinced again that the stranger existed and was in Bucharest to assassinate Ceauşescu. Even now he was focusing his sights on the tyrant's limousine.

The cortège nosed into a shaft of cold sunlight. Stripes of chrome dazzled and sliced up the pen and ink drawing. A young security policeman, an angry rash on his neck from shaved acne, winced and shielded his small eyes.

Gabriela began to shiver with suppressed excitement and fear. But the line of cars was still a hundred metres away.

Ceaușescu's security advisers used the old trick with the glass hidden beneath one of three cups and you have to guess which cup. Following the first police Dacia were three identical limos, all with tinted windows and no identification marks. Clearly, the Chicken was in one of them, but which one?

You immediately ruled out the first one as being the most vulnerable. The second, sandwiched by the two others, was too obvious. The third was discounted as everyone knew Ceaușescu was too vain to follow behind.

It became popular belief that the Chicken rode in the middle car for maximum protection.

Gabriela saw the three limousines approaching, midnight-blue Dacias in front and behind. Her heart began to thump. When would the shot ring out? Would he use a silencer? She pictured a neat hole punched into the tinted glass and a strangulated cry squeezing its way out, as if through a child's mouth rounded in shock.

How would the assassin know which car to hit? How would he even know he would get Ceaușescu and not his feared wife or hated son?

The excitement was like a child whirling a favourite toy round and round her stomach. She felt giddy and couldn't believe it didn't show. The eyes of the onlookers either side of her had glazed over, cheeks sagging and chins drooping. The Bohemian castles curled even yellower behind the microscope-slide-glass of the shop window.

Gabriela had become a corporeal Venice, her body an intricate system of canals down which fluids coursed. As the frenzy in her grew, long-neglected, desiccated waterways were invaded by ethers briefly warmed the previous evening for the first time in years.

Her legs felt weak, her brain curdled.

The limos went by and she saw him in the middle car peering out of the window. No shot rang out, no cry of protest was raised.

She had dreamed the whole episode with the stranger. But this was no dream. Ceaușescu was alive and well and living in a limousine. Nothing had changed nor ever would. Her despair was total. She didn't bother to hide her tears and hysterics. Great waves ebbed out of her. Her knees gave way and she slumped against the shop window.

The train drilled deeper into the night. Gabriela had spoken to none of her companions in the malodorous compartment, nor had they to anyone else. Most train journeys were undertaken in silence, since paranoia hung in the air like a moist sticky fog wherever people gathered in groups of more than three.

Gabriela glanced slyly at the five other passengers in the compartment. Statistically, at least one of them should be stooge.

There was a girl her age or younger, wearing a leather jacket. Her eyes were bleak and shifty, which could mean anything. Next to her was a middle-aged couple. They looked ordinary and downtrodden, the husband in particular. But they could be friends of the local party secretary in their home town. Or related to him several times removed: it would get back, it always did. They sat opposite Gabriela. Next to her, also facing the couple, was an old man. He hadn't removed his small black trilby since boarding the train. She wondered what resentments and intentions that hat contained. Beyond the old man a younger man occupied the corridor seat. With his side parting and glasses he looked like a student. But was he a radical or a conservative?

She looked at them all once more under the jaundiced lighting. It could be the middle-aged couple. Their down-trodden look could be a pretence to lull dissenters into a false sense of security.

But it could just as easily be the young woman or the student, eager to grab a few favours in the struggle to keep heads above water.

Her only safe ally, she decided, was the old man, who would have known Romanian life before hardline communism.

The compartment smelt but it was hard to say of what. She might have said cleaning fluid but that there was no evidence of any having been used.

The old man had nodded off beneath his hat. The student too appeared to have closed his eyes behind his glasses. The young woman stared into the dim corridor, her jacket creaking whenever she moved. Opposite Gabriela the middle-aged woman dozed off intermittently. Each time she woke up she scowled at her husband, presumably cross that he had allowed her to drift off. Barely heeding her reprimands, he stared mournfully out of the grime-streaked window at the darkened farmlands. The moon, in its first quarter, emerged infrequently from behind strips of purple cloud.

The train was heading west to its eventual destination of Timişoara. But Gabriela would leave it before then.

She'd seen Ceauşescu in the flesh and again on the television later that same day when a choir dressed in white had sung his praises.

She wondered if he fantasized about going to heaven. She hoped so because she knew they would never let him in and the rejection would hurt him.

The next day she had withdrawn what money she'd managed to save for herself from inside the piano. She closed the lid so that dust would not settle between the keys and walked across the dismal square to the Gara de Nord. As she settled into her seat, waiting indifferently for the train to leave, she heard the station Tannoys wheeze. The jingle they sounded was absurdly jaunty and cheerful in such drear surroundings, like some privileged infant of the First Family blowing his little heart out on a toy trumpet. Her indifference had stiffened for a moment into malice.

Gabriela had taken a blow. She had dared to dream of change. But it was the last blow she would take. She was determined to try to escape from Romania even if it meant she died in the attempt. One way or the other she would get out. Her indifference applied here also.

She slipped out of the compartment when the train plunged into a tunnel. She brushed against someone's leg – the old man's, she thought – and hoped she could trust him not to raise the alarm. As the train rattled through the claustrophobic darkness, she felt her way down the corridor towards the rear.

The train was due to stop at a number of small stations close to the border with Yugoslavia, but she thought if she disembarked her every move would be watched. She crouched in the shadows, which hung thick as curtains in the last carriage.

Still she didn't say anything. Halfway between Reşita and

Bocsa she slipped the catch on the door and hung for a moment over the rushing ground. She didn't care if she died in the fall. Leaning out slightly, she felt the wind catch her hair and shout its secrets in her ear. The ground was a treacherous river of lumpy grass, rocks, stones and railway sleepers.

It was probably her lack of concern that saved her because it meant her body was relaxed. As she tumbled, her mind emptied and she felt free. It would have been worth it just for this moment of flight. But the earth took her, couching her fall in spongy grass and tossing her some little way away from the train. Within seconds it was a rat-tat-tat in the distance and was drowned out by insects and the pounding of her blood. The ground was warm and she was tempted to sleep. An image of the train compartment entered her head. The young woman, the student, the middle-aged couple and the old man. In her seat was a shadow, an after-image on the retina.

For the first time in her life she was hidden. Not a soul knew where she was. For a moment the thought unsettled her, but soon she cherished it, clasping the idea to her glad heart. The insects chafed and chirped close to her ear. Flowers stood colourless in the moonlight but they smelt no less sweet. She brushed pollen from her face and slowly rose to her feet. No bones broken, she walked towards the thick blanket of firs which swallowed her tiny form.

Shafts of moonlight intruded between tree-trunks like the marble columns of her dreamed station-gaol. As she passed black trunks and white pillars, she imagined light piano music coming from somewhere behind the forest. The ground rose and fell like the melody of the blues she had written. She wasn't carrying a map but she had memorized one before setting out. Her intended route would take her between two minor roads towards the border. When she came within sprinting distance there would be one road to cross, joining the villages of Co-morişte and Cacova.

She ran for short stretches where the forest was least dense. Elsewhere the trunks seemed to gather in groups and intimidate her as she passed them. If she ran here they might try to stop her. In the moonlight anything could happen. She was scared by the possibilities. As she ran through clearings, she exhilarated in the flight and imagined herself breaking free, leaping clean over the fences to another life. She walked like a princess through strange gaudy cities, her body exclusively her own, no longer for sale.

Then she became entangled in knots of branches and roots and felt certain she would fall only to wake up back in Bucharest on sheets reeking of a man's sweat.

The trek to the border took more than four hours and for most of that time she wavered between wild hopes and indifference.

She crossed the little road without realizing it and almost ran headlong into the border fence hidden in a dark thicket. She stopped and panted for breath. Blood pounded in her head and she imagined it covered the hasty footsteps of border guards rushing to disable her.

But none materialized.

She tested the wire fence gingerly and, when she was satisfied it was not electrified, began to climb. Near the top her slick fingers lost their grip and she almost fell back down to the forest floor. She clung on. The desire to escape unharmed burned fiercely inside her now. It threatened to impede her progress as the fear of capture made her fumble and begin to tremble. At the top of the wire she pivoted for a moment and could have gone either way, but she leaned more heavily in the direction of freedom, and was soon scrambling down the Yugoslav side of the frontier. She didn't stop but sprinted into the thickest bunches of trees where the moon cast no light, but, as the fire within her burned so brightly, she found the way ahead lit clearly.

Downhill most of the way, it only took Gabriela an hour to reach the village of Vršac. There she lay down on a patch of grass and fell asleep for a short time, until the sun woke her very early in the morning. Teeth chattering, she started walking down the main road to Belgrade, which was still seventy kilometres away, and stuck out her hand whenever she heard a car approaching. After half an hour a truck driver stopped and took her to Pančevo. From there it was a short hop over the Danube to Belgrade. An office worker gave her a lift and she reached the city in time for a late lunch.

PART II

Tenor Madness

That same day, full of indelible impressions and emotions, we were received by the disciple and loyal continuer of the work of Lenin, Joseph Vissarionovich Stalin, who talked with us at length.

From the beginning he created such a comradely atmosphere that we were very quickly relieved of that natural emotion which we felt when we entered his office, a large room, with a large table for meetings, close to his writing desk. Only a few minutes after exchanging the initial courtesies, we felt as though we were not talking to the great Stalin, but sitting with a comrade, whom we had met before and with whom we had talked many times. I was still young then, and the representative of a small party and country, therefore, in order to create the warmest and most comradely atmosphere for me, Stalin cracked some jokes and then began to speak with affection and great respect about our people, about their militant traditions of the past and their heroism in the National Liberation War. He spoke quietly, calmly and with a characteristic warmth which put me at ease.

– Enver Hoxha, *With Stalin* (The '8 Nëntori'
Publishing House, 1979)

Garden of Unearthly Lights

The Tatra's engine caught, though Ankers could neither hear nor feel it above the tunnel's ear-splitting roar. Everything shook: the rear-view mirror, the steering wheel, Ankers's arms as he tried to control the car, and the body of the vehicle itself. Veins stood out on his forearms and temples like thick cords. He clamped his teeth together to protect them. Blood poured from his nose on to his fisherman's sweater.

He managed to get the car into reverse and backed away from the tunnel. He meant to watch the rear-view mirror to make sure he wasn't going to drive into a fence post, but the sight of the yawning tunnel kept drawing his gaze through the windscreen.

The dream emerged from the mouth of the tunnel in a sudden rush. The dream was made of water.

An enormous black column of water shot out of the tunnel and struck the railway line, the sidings and the road all at the same time. It hit the ground with an incredible crash and splashed thick fans of spray right over the top of Ankers's car. He pressed his foot down to the floor and the back end of the car veered wildly from side to side above its single wheel.

If the flood streaming impossibly out of the uncompleted Channel Tunnel and surging towards his car frightened Ankers, what he saw next struck terror into his soul. At the centre of the deluge, just now leaping from the dark tunnel, like the stamen of a terrifying watery bloom, was a train.

It landed badly and skittered forwards, half on and half off the rails, swept along by the unabating tidal wave. Water spewed from the cracks around windows and doors. Ankers could see the level dropping inside the front carriage as more water escaped. He wondered if there might be anyone on board, before reminding himself that the train couldn't even exist. How could a train emerge from a tunnel that hadn't been dug?

But he suddenly remembered something else. A hundred metres further up the road there was a level crossing. If the train reached the crossing before he did it would cut him off and the flood would engulf his car. Reversing was too slow. He twisted the wheel and jammed the brakes on. He was going too fast to avoid hitting the wire fence behind the car. Something was stuck in the mesh. He pressed his foot down and the tyres screamed like banshees. Out of the side window he saw the wall of water moving up the road towards him. It was spreading out to cover the surrounding land also but the road offered an immediate channel. He flung his weight forward trying to pull the car free. Something gave. The car shot forward. He swung the wheel round and hurtled in the direction of the crossing. The train was now in front but he was gaining on it.

But the floodwater had more power than the old car and when the crossing came into sight Ankers could see that the train was only seconds away. If he didn't start to apply his brakes they might collide. He would have escaped the sea only to die on the road. Still he accelerated, however, shouting and screaming at the car to go faster. Even when he saw that there was no way he could beat the train across, when it was too late to avert disaster, he raced towards the junction of road and rail, and life and death.

The train faltered on the threshold of the crossing. The locomotive appeared to trip as if the points were set against it, then it ploughed into the barrier post and its back end jerked into the air. The Tatra bounced over the rails just before the engine completed its somersault and crash-landed on the track.

Ankers pulled his left hand down and slammed on the brakes. The first carriage had been squeezed off the railway and had fallen on to its side on the slope. Sea water had begun to gush from its many shattered windows, and Ankers had caught a glimpse of what looked like someone inside.

It didn't matter that it was impossible. If someone was trapped in the train, Ankers couldn't just drive away. He hoped the flood would subside. The long line of crashed carriages should act as a temporary sea wall.

Ankers left the car and waded through the shallows draining from the first carriage. He reached an open window frame and gripped the metal bodywork. It was solid, like all the worst nightmares, no suggestion at all that the thing had no earthly substance, except for the unreal circumstances that had brought it here.

As Ankers pulled himself up to peer inside, something lunged out. Ankers cried out and fell back. Crouching in the empty frame was a young black man in a white coat, alternately heaving out lungfuls of dirty water and gasping for air. His eyes had rolled up into his skull, exposing the whites. He began to overbalance.

Ankers caught him as he fell. The man's efforts to breathe had ceased. Ankers ran with him to a patch of dry rubble beyond the car and lay him on the ground. He pressed down on his chest and pushed. Water splashed from his open mouth like a dying fountain. Ankers pushed again and again, until there was nothing. Then he pinched the man's nostrils shut and gave him the kiss of life. The man responded on the second attempt, coughing and spluttering and trying to sit up.

It was beginning to look like Norway was beyond reach, at least for the present time. Ankers wanted desperately to get back to Inger, but his dreams in which Hašek rummaged and poked his way around the Albanian capital of Tirana had become so vivid that he knew the pictures were not only in his head. His empathy with Hašek was as strong as the concern he had felt for the painter's somnambulist women in danger from the sea. Hašek was in Tirana – drowned, resurrected, undead: he didn't know, he didn't care – and he needed his help. The responsibility was unquestionably his. He had encouraged the Czech to defect. If he was the only person dreaming of Hašek, he was the only hope the man had.

The Englishman was a new player in the game. Fully revived, Ian Cunningham wanted to know where he was.

'You're in Calais, France,' Ankers told him, matter-of-fact.

'How?' was the young man's response.

Ankers couldn't explain any better than he could himself. Ian insisted on being driven to the nearest built-up area to see for himself. *Boulangerie. Charcuterie. Café-tabac.* He agreed that they appeared to be in France.

'The weird thing is that I had decided I wanted to go to the Continent,' he said. 'Only yesterday. Then I went to the jazz club. I got pissed. Went home and dreamed I was on a train.'

'Your dream came true,' Ankers said.

They went in a café and ordered a couple of beers. Maybe, Ian thought, with a few beers inside him he would begin to accept what had happened without wanting to understand it. The two men drank and talked. Ian told Ankers about his failed efforts to expose the crooked Clayton and about his final day working at the hospital. The Norwegian spoke about Hašek, relating the story of how he had first heard the man's saxophone playing and been enchanted. When he described the dreams that blossomed out of playing harmonies with Hašek's tapes, Ian couldn't believe his ears.

'That's Delvaux,' he said, aghast. 'You're dreaming images from Paul Delvaux's paintings.' As he said this he remembered that he himself had dreamt of the waiting room and the naked women wandering in the classical ruins surrounded by dunes. He felt in his back pocket and withdrew the picture he had snatched from the carriage wall. The sea had destroyed it. Ankers looked on amazed as it fell apart along the creases where Ian had folded it.

'It's only a print,' Ian said, placing the discoloured remains in the ashtray.

The two men swapped notes on their dreams, slowly realizing that something was happening that was bigger and more mysterious than either of their individual experiences. They discussed the dreams in detail and the possible reasons why they might be dreaming the same dream. Whichever route they chose, they wound up in a dead end. Since they couldn't go back and explain what was happening, they decided to go forward together: Ian would join Ankers on his journey to Albania.

An immediate plan formulated, they ordered more beers and got on to music. Ian listened with rapt attention as Ankers talked about the European circuit and his experience of it. 'That's what I wanted to come here for,' Ian said, grinning. The tension was flowing out of him now. He was excited by events and revelations and expectations.

'Drink up,' Ankers said. 'Then we can have some more.'

'You know what happened last time I got drunk,' Ian pointed out with a broad grin.

'What would you want to go back for? You're here now. That's what you wanted. Maybe that's what the dreams are about. Yes!' he shouted, as if he'd hit on the real reason for them. 'They're about wish fulfilment.'

They knew there was more to it than that, but the simple answer would do for now. As he ordered two more *demis* from the waiter, Ankers asked about a cheap hotel. The waiter said there were a few close by, but *les messieurs* would have to *faire gaffe*.

'What's he saying?' Ian asked.

'He said we must be careful.'

'Careful what we dream, you mean.'

Ankers smiled.

They walked out into the mild night. The air smelt of the sea. Ankers wondered if the floods had retreated and the tunnel filled itself in. Three youths slouched in a doorway like abandoned puppets, lowering their voices when Ankers and Ian walked past. The hotel was cheap and looked it. They booked into the same room and Ian let Ankers have the bed.

'I slept well on the train,' Ian joked with a drunken snigger.

Breakfast wasn't included in the price, which would have doubled if it had been. Both men were nursing headaches and Ian still felt a little drunk. They had coffee, and ham and cheese croissants at the café before setting off. Few words were exchanged. Ian wondered if Ankers regretted allowing Ian to accompany him. When the bill came, Ankers took care of it and waved down Ian's offer to pay his half.

They were somewhere between Troyes and Dijon when the Tatra died in the outside lane. It took all Ankers's skill at the wheel to coast between lines of traffic to the inside lane without any casualties.

'That's the end of that,' Ankers said.

Ian wasn't sure if he meant the Tatra or the journey to Tirana.

'Do you know much about cars?' Ian asked.

'Nothing,' said Ankers. 'How about you?'

'Less than that.'

Ankers walked to the emergency telephone. After that they settled down to wait.

'How long will they be?' Ian asked.

'Up to an hour, maybe longer. They couldn't guarantee how long.' Ankers looked out at the cars flashing past. 'We could listen to some music. Oh, unless . . .' He checked to see if the electrics were working; they were. 'That's good,' he said. 'We can listen to Hašek.' He took a cassette from his top pocket and slotted it in.

Hašek's distinctive mournful tones filled the car, sliding over each other, almost finding a low, ponderous melody, then hitting a brief flurry at the top end of the register like a flash of reflected sunlight. Ian listened intently to this strange, formless jazz and felt he could give it some shape without detracting from its sense of freedom. He pulled his sticks from his back pocket and just felt the weight of them in his hands for a moment, unselfconsciously. He began tapping with his right hand against the glass covering one of the Tatra's dials. It was an adequate high-hat.

Ankers listened too. He was surprised. The music on this tape had seemed the most amorphous and unmelodic of Hašek's themes. But Ian was tracing lines around it with his off-set beat, not trapping the music but rather freeing it. He drew out the patterns that Ankers hadn't deciphered. There was a melody, a deceptively simple refrain which was repeated over and over. It started again before it was properly finished. Ian tapped on, shaping and reshaping the sound.

Ankers reached into the back for his instrument case. He moistened the reed and attached the mouthpiece, moving his chair back to give room to the saxophone. He waited for the cycle to be complete and start again, and was too late because it had already started. He saw why the melody had eluded him: it almost wasn't there. It was a tune which had started to consume itself. Anticipating the next *rebondissement*, he slipped into the pattern, immediately broadening its scope. He varied his speeds, playing fast where Hašek went slowly and losing pace when the Czech speeded up. Ian tapped on, and on, adding more layers to his percussion.

The music swirled around the car, increasing its hold over its

148

makers. All thought left their minds. Soon they were as good as unconscious. Their bodies had become part of the music, fed by the concoction of rhythm and melody as much as they bled into it. Ankers saw vast stretches of sand dunes, the wind blowing tunes between them. Ian was in a tunnel upon whose tight skin the sea beat its tattoo. In a moment of heightened awareness he distinguished an exterior noise: a hand tapping on the window beside his head – no doubt the serviceman. But his attention withdrew just as quickly. He emerged from the tunnel into a dunescape. The music went round and round. Sand drained through his fingers. A desert passed between them.

Then Ankers was with him on the sand. They were conscious. The music had stopped. There was still a beat, of waves upon the shore. The sand was a beach. Ian looked at Ankers for two or three moments, then pocketed his drumsticks and walked slowly towards the shoreline.

Ankers pulled his saxophone case towards him and opened it. Inside was the picture given to him by Delvaux of Inger in a red dress, her hair tossed by bitter-cold winds and her soft features vaguely threatened by the sharp geometry of the mountains behind her. He put the saxophone away and snapped the case shut. Seconds later he had joined Ian at the water's edge.

'Where do you think we are?' Ian asked. He had initially been frightened by the sudden new surroundings, but now accepted he was dreaming. It was the same dream as the one in which he had crossed the Channel in a tunnel that didn't exist, the same dream in which he met a man who shared his dreams of Delvaux's naked sleepwalkers.

It wasn't a dream at all, but the laws it followed were those of the imagination, in which the world reinvented itself constantly. It was a dream and yet it wasn't a dream.

Ankers just shook his head slowly. The smell of the sea when the music stopped had said Norway to him. But it was too warm and flat for the far-flung north. He bent down and put his hand in the water; it was not cold. They turned and surveyed the land beyond the beach. There was a line of trees and large hotels. Beyond and to the left was a town, and behind that were hills terraced for crop-growing. Greater hills shimmered purple in the hazy distance. Ankers thought he recognized the landscape, but until they knew for sure where they were he kept his thoughts to himself.

They walked across the beach in the direction of the town. Even when they crossed the first road, there was no one about. No traffic, no locals out on foot. The main street was deserted. A few shops were boarded up as if their owners had been forced to evacuate the town at short notice and hoped to come back when it was all over. When *what* was all over? Some doorways were open and tins of fish could be seen scattered on the floor inside.

'It's like a ghost town,' Ian remarked, as they continued warily down the length of the dusty main street, like two gunslingers suspecting the hidden presence of bounty hunters.

Ankers saw the name of the town in a shop window: Durrës. As he had guessed: they had landed in the Albanian resort thirty kilometres to the west of Tirana.

Ian asked, 'Are we in Albania?'

'Yes, we are,' Ankers answered. 'We have to get to Tirana and find Hašek.'

At that moment the peace was shattered by the appearance of a Russian-built Jeep containing four men.

Ankers and Ian stood their ground in the middle of the road, expecting the Jeep to stop. It didn't even slow down but came right at them, accelerating. The four men, the driver included, looked dopey. Ian was rooted to the spot, staring through the windshield at the driver's face. There was something about it that filled him with horror, transfixing him. Ankers shoved him power-fully in the left shoulder, pushing him out of the way. Ankers himself dived the other way and sprawled on the unmade road, losing his saxophone case. One of the back-seat passengers leant out with a scythe as the Jeep passed between them and swung at Ankers's foot. The tip of the blade scratched his ankle bone, causing him to yell out in pain. The Jeep snarled to a halt at the end of the street and began turning round. Ankers grabbed his case and got to his feet. Ian was dazed and had to be helped up. The Jeep had completed its turn and was coming at them again.

'Quickly,' Ankers urged him. He half dragged the younger man to the side of the road and the partial shelter of a tree-trunk. The Jeep came as close as it could and the man with the scythe lashed out although somewhat languidly, almost as if it were sport and he knew he'd bag his catch eventually. This time he sliced into the tree-trunk and the blade nearly stuck fast, threatening to pull him out of the Jeep, but it came free and the Jeep sped off.

'They'll turn round again,' Ankers said.

'Who are they?' Ian asked.

'Come on. We've got to lose them,' Ankers said. 'We can be quicker on foot.'

They ran up the street in the same direction as the Jeep. But the Jeep would be turning round and going back the other way. Trees stood five metres apart in a line between the road and the pavement. Their foliage was sparse but the trunks themselves meant the Jeep couldn't mow them down on the pavement.

Ian was thinking about the driver's face, its torn features blurred through the dirty glass, the two gaping nostrils. He couldn't imagine how the man could bear such wounds.

The Jeep made another pass at them but they didn't stop running. Fifty metres ahead there was a turning. They reached it before the Jeep had even turned round. Ankers and Ian ran down the side street. The saxophone case was slowing Ankers down but he knew he couldn't get rid of it. They were still able to turn left down the next street on the left before the Jeep had reached the side street. Ankers pulled Ian down an alleyway and into a small courtyard. They rested against a wall, panting. The Jeep buzzed like an angry bee two streets away.

'We can't stay here,' Ian said.

Ankers pointed to two rusty bicycles propped against a crumbling wall.

'Bikes are very common here,' he said. 'There's no private transport, but that doesn't include bikes.'

'How far's where we're going?' Ian asked.

'Thirty kilometres or so. Not far.'

For the moment Ian was content to get his breath and inhale the strange warm smells of Albania. There were scents of blossom he had never known. The months were going by faster than ever before. He was so confused he didn't know what month it was. Out of the corner of his eye he saw Ankers looking at him, and smiled.

'I don't even know your first name,' Ian said.

'It's Edvard,' he said. 'But hardly anyone uses it. We ought to get moving. Grab a bike.'

The sound of the Jeep was no longer to be heard.

'Edvard,' Ian began doubtfully. 'Do you think we can cycle thirty kilometres without these psychopaths in the Jeep catching up with us?'

'We've got to try,' Ankers said. He was concerned about Hašek. And worried for themselves until they could reach Hašek and he could protect them. They were not, after all, enemies of the men in the Jeep. But the men saw them as targets. Ankers thought he knew from his dreams what the men in the Jeep were after, but to tell Ian would only make him more nervous.

They moved out of the courtyard, wheeling the two rusty bicycles. At the end of the alleyway Ankers held his hand up, telling Ian to stop while he peered up and down the street. Finding it empty, he beckoned to Ian. They mounted their bikes and pedalled cautiously up the street away from the sea. They turned several corners before appearing to have reached the edge of the town. The street they were on petered out into a patch of waste ground. Beyond that lay countryside – farmlands, a railway line and in the middle distance a road leading diagonally inland. The two men pushed their bikes again. Suddenly Ian said, 'Stop! Can you hear that?'

They listened. Ankers shook his head.

'Listen,' Ian commanded.

Ankers strained his ears and eventually distinguished one irritant from the tapestry of birdsong and insectile hum. It sounded like someone using an electric razor behind a closed door.

The Jeep burst into the serene picture 300 metres away as it left the town on the road which cut across the fields.

'Get back,' Ankers hissed.

They pulled the bikes into the shadow of a wall as quickly and quietly as possible, then crouched to watch the Jeep. The four men bounced like dummies as the Jeep hit a rut. One man in the back slumped forward, hitting his head on the seat in front.

'I don't think they've seen us,' Ian whispered.

'I think you're right. If we just let them go they'll probably return to Tirana, and a lot faster than we can. It'll be safe to follow them in five or ten minutes.'

Ian sat down next to his bike and picked up a little stone, which he tossed into the middle of the road. He looked across the fields at the disappearing Jeep and wondered what he was getting involved in. He pictured the driver's face again and shivered involuntarily.

'Are you thinking about England?' Ankers asked him.

Ian looked at Ankers for a moment. 'No,' he said. 'I don't miss England.' *Clayton's sordid exploits, Lucy's unmasked betrayal, the terminal patients.* 'I was wondering if you've told me *everything* about this trip. Well, I'm fairly sure you haven't. But I don't know what's missing.'

Ankers sat down with a sigh. He scratched absently at the rust on the handlebar of his bike. 'I was going to tell you in the car when we got near to Albania. But I was overtaken by events. Suddenly we were here. You know? It'll make more sense when we get to Tirana.'

'Yeah, but having just met some of the locals I'm not sure if I'm still that crazy about going to Tirana.'

'We'll be OK once we've found Hašek. In fact, I don't think there'll be any danger to us at all. There are thousands of people in the city, not like here. We'll blend in.'

'Not if they've all got their faces torn apart,' Ian remarked. 'I saw the driver of that Jeep. He looked like a fucking zombie.'

Ankers hesitated just a moment too long.

'Aw, come on!' Ian protested.

Ankers couldn't think of what to say.

Ian picked up a bigger stone and hurled it across the street.

'It'll be OK when we get there,' Ankers said with little reassurance in his voice. He wished he'd told Ian everything while they were still in France. 'We stick out here because Durrës has obviously been evacuated and not yet colonized. The men in the Jeep weren't expecting anyone to be around.'

'Is this whole thing a dream?' Ian asked.

'We're here, aren't we? This is happening. The dreaming just brought us here.' He paused a moment. Ian looked unhappy. 'I think we should go now.' He stood up and offered Ian his hand. Ian took it and Ankers pulled him to his feet. Ian looked across the fields at the hills. The air shimmered. There were patches of purple near the hilltops. Beyond that line of hills the city awaited.

If he was dreaming it was very vivid, very real. He noticed the red comma on Ankers's ankle where the scythe had scratched him. Ankers saw him looking and said, 'It doesn't hurt. It's only superficial.' Very real and tangible. Cause and effect held sway in this blighted paradise.

'At least the weather's nice,' Ian said. 'It was winter in Brighton. Suddenly it's summer. Everything's in bloom. The bees are busy.'

'We are further south,' Ankers pointed out.

'But still. I think the clock has speeded up.'

Ankers shrugged and straddled his bike. Ian followed him down a cinder path that led towards the road.

Only a few minutes out of town they came to a junction. The road to the left was signposted Shijak, Vorë and Tiranë; straight on for Tiranë only. They exchanged a glance and went straight on. Neither man was anxious to pass through more towns than was necessary. The reception committee at Durrës might not have been a one-off. They cycled abreast of each other. A single-track railway line ran alongside on the left. Soon there was a second choice of routes. Straight on to Kavajë or left for Tiranë. They worried as they took the left turn in case they were going to be diverted via Shijak and Vorë, like it or not. After a few hundred metres the road bent sharply to the right and continued straight. A smaller road joined theirs on the left. They kept a permanent look-out for interlopers. There was now a river on their left. Small birds swooped and dived. The fields on either side of the road were dotted with pillboxes each the size of a man. The landscape was extremely attractive and unspoilt. Ian's tension trailed behind the bicycle and left him altogether. His sticks were in his back pocket; he felt them with every revolution. The hills loomed closer. The road was heading straight for them. He hoped there would be a pass between them.

For Ankers the ride was less pleasant, as he had to accomplish it one-handed. He decided he would have to rig up a strap in Tirana in case of further occasions like this one. But he was glad that Ian seemed happier than when they had left Durrës. He wanted the man's spirits to be high; they might need to be to give him strength. Ankers feared for their lives in Tirana.

The road began to climb into the hills. On either side the ground rose more steeply, indicating that the road would indeed

154

cut between two hills. There were fewer birds now. Larks skipped and jumped through the perfumed air but their twitterings were drowned out by the creakings of the old machines, no doubt unused to this kind of treatment. Ankers struggled with one hand wrapped around his instrument case. Ian was panting for breath as the gradient increased. The road grew darker as the hills reached higher into the sky. The sun was sinking behind them. Soon the ground fell away on the left-hand side of the road and their climb became steeper. A river meandered in the valley to their left; cloaked in shadows it was inscrutable. Ian stopped for a rest and Ankers pulled up next to him. They drew deep breaths as they looked down into the valley. When their breathing returned to normal they listened for any sounds. The hillside was quiet. There were neither birds nor insects. When he concentrated Ian could make out the rustling of the river in the bottom of the valley.

'Shall we push on?' Ankers suggested.

The road seemed to reach its highest point about 200 metres ahead. The two men leaned into the incline, cycle chains creaking under the strain, saddles squeaking. When they reached the brow of the hill they stopped again and dismounted.

The hills sloped gently into a verdant depression like a soup bowl, in the centre of which nestled the city. A pall of brown smog hung over it. Here and there gaps between the hills allowed shafts of late sunlight to penetrate the smog and create glowing pockets. At this distance the city was silent and the air on the hills was still. They saw the railway line snaking out north-east of the city towards the only real gap in the hills that surrounded it.

Ankers turned to look back the way they had come. The hills rolled down to the plain which stretched to the sea. A deep, gilt-edged blue, the Adriatic was like a velvet coverlet draped across the earth as far as the sandy pillows of the beach. The sun was sinking below the horizon like a segment of an enormous blood orange. Ankers tapped Ian's shoulder. Ian jumped and laughed when he saw it was only Ankers. 'Look at this,' Ankers said.

The two men crouched on the road to watch the sunset, squeezing the orange dry as if they feared it might be their last. With a mere sliver still visible above the darkening horizon, the sun threw its last javelins of light high into the clouds, turning them crimson as fresh wounds. Then it was gone, eclipsed by the suddenly black sea.

Ian felt a stab of regret. Was it that the sunset might be his last? Or was it the wine-dark sea, that intoxicating reminder of his life's losses? His mother taken from him so early and his bond with his father broken so soon after. Those years when he and his father lived separately in the same house. His enlightenment which arrived too late to mend his father's broken heart.

His more recent efforts to give meaning to his life seemed futile distractions: Steve Clayton, Lucy Bayley. Too many doctors. He was well out of the medical profession.

He remembered the joy he'd rediscovered at the jazz club, the conviction he'd formed. Then the drunken descent into nightmare which took him under the sea to Europe and unimagined adventure.

Was he still dreaming in his bed in Brighton? It wouldn't be the first time he'd dreamt a vast epic in a single night.

Awake or asleep, he'd never felt more alive.

He heard noise and looked up. Ankers was tinkering with the chain on his bike.

'We ought to go,' Ankers said.

Facing the city again with the sun gone from the sky, they saw it differently. Thousands of lights burned through the smog from buildings, streetlamps and headlamps of vehicles that moved through the city like extraterrestrial grubs. The overall effect was like one of Bosch's visions of hell.

'Looks good, doesn't it?'

Ian heard the falsely light-hearted note in Ankers's voice.

'A dream of a place,' Ian replied.

They cycled to the beginning of the slope and let gravity take them downhill.

In Kosovo Polje they break up an anti-Albanian demonstration and chase a small group of terrified Serbs into a dead end. One of the Serbs produces a weapon and fires at the Russian. The bullets pass through him uselessly and Hašek swings his club into the man's knees, disabling him.

Hašek threatens the Serbs with an automatic rifle while the Russian steps forward and slits the throat of the man on the ground. The other men become hysterical and start to flee. Hašek shoots at their kneecaps and the Russian makes busy with his knife. 'The boxes,' the Russian says. Hašek goes back to the Jeep for the transplant boxes and when he returns finds the Russian already at work. A set of surgical instruments lies unwrapped on the ground. The Russian replaces one instrument and takes a small hacksaw. He works at the Serb's skull, being careful not to saw too quickly and damage the brain. He has to keep wiping his burnt hands on his coat to prevent the scalpel slipping in his grasp.

Hašek experiences a small jolt of discomfort. He tells the Russian he lacks the experience and sits out on the operations. The Jeep is parked between two imposing but essentially characterless buildings, in juxtaposition to which Hašek seems almost to come alive.

His hands mould around his remembered saxophone and his fingers warm up on a few scales before slipping into Sonny Rollins's 'St Thomas'. As he improvises, the killing fields of Kosovo seem very far away.

City of the Dead Things

The further downhill they went on their rusty old bikes, the darker their surroundings became. Patches of grass and waste ground bordered the road. In the distance the glowing city of Tirana loomed closer. Ankers and Ian had not spoken during the spin down from the hills. Each man was trying to cope with his growing nervousness.

The road took them past the football ground, the TV station and Radio Tirana, and into the university district. The tall streetlights had a slight yellowish cast to them. The faculty buildings, built in polished off-white stone, shone the colour of old bandages. No lights burned in the windows. By now the sky was indigo over the hills they had crossed, graduating to a curious brownish purple over the city and jet black over the louring hills to the east and south.

Something lurched into the road and Ian braked suddenly, losing balance. Ankers braked and jumped off his bike, eyeing the shape moving across the road. Ian was on the ground holding an injured knee and watching the figure in terror. Ankers tugged at Ian's arm and helped him up. The shape disappeared behind a line of trees.

'Did you see his face?' Ian gasped.

'No. What did you see?'

'– I don't know, damn it! Something. It was sickly and yellow.'

'That's just the light, Ian. Look at me.' Ian looked at him. 'Pretty frightening, huh?'

Ian just shook his head, staring into the darkness after the figure.

'We have a tendency to hallucinate when we're in a state of heightened expectation. Believe me, it's just the odd light. Plus, he gave you a shock, coming straight out into the road like that.'

Ian got to his feet. 'When a whole crowd of these creatures is tearing us limb from limb,' he said, 'you'll be telling me not to worry.'

'I think we ought to get moving or we'll attract attention. Let's go.'

Cycling slowly and keeping their heads down, they rolled into a small square. There were university buildings on three sides and a tree-lined boulevard leading off from the east side. In the centre was a series of fountains, lit with coloured bulbs, playing into a large oblong pool. Around the edge of the pool on a stone border dozens of dark figures sat facing out at the square.

'I think we should lose the bikes,' Ankers whispered.

Together they backed out of the square and wheeled the machines around the back of one of the grand faculty buildings.

Ankers looked doubtfully at Ian. 'I'm not sure about your white coat,' he said. 'The in colour seemed to be black. Perhaps you should leave it with the bikes.'

'I don't really want to leave it,' Ian said. 'I don't think the bikes are going to stay here. Someone's going to take them. Don't you think? I'm quite attached to my coat.'

Ankers shrugged. He took his own jacket off and reversed it to expose the darker lining.

'Where are we going to look for your friend?' Ian asked, smearing his coat with leaf mould and soil from around the base of a tree.

'A hotel. There can only be two or three big hotels. He's in one of them. I think.' He paused, in thought. 'OK. Let's go. Are you OK?'

Ian nodded.

'Just walk slowly with your head down. Show no interest in your surroundings. Try not to catch anyone's eye.'

They walked into the square and past the fountain. No one looked up at them, as far as they could tell. On the boulevard they stayed in the shadow of the trees. Figures passed them; some appeared normal and healthy, others shambled along like drunks.

The air beneath the canopy of trees was warm and green. Ankers and Ian walked at medium pace. Their hearts raced whenever they sensed someone coming towards them, but no one accosted them. In front of the university library a large crowd had gathered around a bonfire. Ian looked at Ankers.

'Let's take a look,' said the Norwegian.

They approached warily. No one took any notice of them, however. All attention was focused on the bonfire. As they joined the edge of the crowd, Ian looked around. The flames danced in the eyes of those who still possessed them. Some craned faces with empty sockets closer to the fire to feel its heat or hear its crackle. Others had eyes but their ears had been torn off or their nose had rotted and fallen away. One creature's face trailed off beneath its nose. The upper jaw was intact, the bone ingrained with dirt, but the lower jaw was lying in some grave.

Many wore rags which were falling apart and stank of corruption. Some had acquired new clothes which they draped about themselves with little regard for appearance. A man only an arm's length away from Ankers was wearing a check shirt still stiff from its packaging, but he hadn't bothered to fasten the buttons, so that Ian could see the way his ribs had been crushed and splintered. Tatters of flesh remained attached to some of his bones. His one eye was milky with cataracts but it watched the conflagration. Wisps of hair on his pitted, patchy scalp were whipped this way and that by the currents of heat.

This is not happening. I am asleep in bed in Brighton. I am dreaming. Please, God, let me wake up!

Ankers had dreamed these sights already and so had known what to expect. But the dreams had concealed from him the smells of putrefaction and earth, the rasp of coarse clothing against flaps of skin, the useless wheezing of punctured lungs protruding like bellows from a man's cloven chest. He hadn't known how repulsed he would be by the accidental touch of a rotting limb swollen to near bursting point.

A sightless woman threw a book on to the fire. Ankers watched the flames clutch at it and begin to transform its pages into black butterflies which tried to flutter free but were caught and sucked back. The woman tossed another book on to the fire and Ankers noticed that the entire bonfire was constructed out of books. Now he realized it he saw a figure emerging from the library carrying a pile of books. Inside, through the plate-glass window, he saw people sorting through books. Some were put on one side but most were thrown in a pile by the entrance. Ankers stared into the fire and was able to read the writing on the spines of those books not yet consumed. The books which were not by Enver Hoxha featured either his name or Stalin's in the title. So the pyromaniacs had a grudge against old communists.

Another pile of the former Albanian leader's works was thrown on top of the burning books. Flames and sparks shot out and Ankers shielded his face, seeing Ian do the same. The front rank of dead things did nothing to protect themselves. Consequently, the flames caught their parchment skins and tinder-dry flesh and ignited them. Several dead things combusted and collapsed into the fire, fuelling it like bunches of bony twigs. A pair of lungs popped like a puffball, showering sparks, which a handful of the dead things stepped back to avoid. Something else burst and spurted fluid into the heart of the fire, hissing and spitting like a wild cat.

When more books were loaded on to the pyre, Ankers withdrew and beckoned to Ian to follow. The younger man looked sick. Ankers led him away with his arm protectively around his shoulder.

'Try to think of it as a dream,' he said. 'In a sense, that's all it is.'

They walked up the boulevard, less concerned now with concealing their faces from the locals. They passed the Palace of Congresses on the left, the People's Assembly on the right. Both men, with no prior knowledge of Albanian, were able to understand the words on the plaques. The next two buildings bore no official identification, but were of a similar imposing aspect. Across the doors of one a protester had painted the slogan NO TO SECRET POLICE.

They crossed a side road and were startled by a car horn. It was not them but a group of dead things walking down the middle of the boulevard that were being addressed in this way. The car was a black limo with CD plates. Sitting in the back in a row were three bloodless faces. When the limo passed, Ian watched it go and saw dark, sooty bullet wounds in the backs of the necks of the three men. The dead things in the road stepped out of the way to let the limo go past. Ian wondered who the men in the back could be to get driven about like ambassadors. He couldn't see the point of a revolution if the new leaders took on the same airs and graces as their predecessors.

They glanced at the Enver Hoxha Museum set back on the

right-hand side of the boulevard. Most of its plate-glass had been smashed and the enormous statue of Hoxha daubed with paint. Outside the Hotel Dajti Ankers stopped and studied the exterior.

'Is this it?' Ian asked. He hoped so.

'I don't think so. The place I dreamed of was higher, more modern. And it had more space around it.'

The statues of Lenin and Stalin which had faced each other across the boulevard and now lay in disgrace beneath their pedestals offered no clues.

They pressed on, oblivious to stares from passers-by, past two Ministry of Defence buildings and into Skanderbeg Square. A statue of the medieval hero astride his horse stood proud, unblemished by vandals. The square was huge and completely free of vehicular traffic. There was a smell of woodsmoke from nearby chimneys. The youth centre away to the right had been reconverted into a mosque.

Ian remembered when his mother was alive and they lived in a flat in south London. One time he was told to dress up smart because they were going into town to meet distant relatives. For some reason they went to an art gallery and his mother and father and their distant relatives walked round large airy rooms full of paintings where you had to whisper if you wanted to talk. Not much was said. Ian trailed behind, confused by adults who stood and stared at a painting as if it were a television. He could have told them the picture wasn't going to move. But then he glimpsed a picture that made him stop and go back for another look. It had appeared to move. Little stick figures walked this way and that across the picture, leaning into their stride or into the wind.

His father, who had come back to find him, placed his hand on Ian's head and said, 'That's a Lowry.'

He felt now as if he were looking at a Lowry. Skanderbeg Square resembled the street outside one of Lowry's mills: people coming and people going, and people passing by. Even this late in the evening the square was full of pedestrians. Most of them stank of the grave – some smelt fresher than others – but among them walked keen-eyed, relaxed Albanians, those who had stayed on.

Ankers appeared to have spotted something. 'That's the Palace of Culture,' he said, pointing to the long, cool-looking building on their right with the colonnaded frontage. *I know,* thought Ian. He was dreaming this every bit as much as Ankers now. What would happen to all these people when he or Ankers woke up? Would they cease to exist, in the way that philosophers had said the world ceased to exist when one is not awake to perceive it?

At the far end of the Palace of Culture stood the Hotel Tirana, a tall, drab, featureless building lacking the classic elegance of the Hotel Dajti. But as he stared up at its many storeys, Ankers knew this was where he would find Hašek.

They walked into the marble foyer and looked about them. A few dead things stood about staring at the floor. On the left was a bar, on the right the reception desk. A television had been brought down and a group of tattered creatures watched a Greek news programme. They showed no reaction to any part of the broadcast, but stared with glassy eyes and lolling heads at the screen. Ankers and Ian understood Greek no better than Albanian, yet they both knew what the newscaster was saying. There were pictures of a border post on the Greek–Albanian border taken from the Greek side. The voice was saying that there had been an extraordinary increase in trade in Albania, or in imports, to be precise. Huge orders had been placed with wholesalers of consumer goods in West Germany, Austria and Greece.

There were some still pictures taken from Corfu with a very long lens. The skyline of the Albanian town of Saranda had been transformed. The roofs of apartment blocks and hotels bristled with TV aerials and radio masts and satellite dishes. What was going on? the Greeks wanted to know.

The audience sat in silence. The news programme ended and a string of commercials came on followed by an imported sitcom dubbed into Greek. Ankers and Ian drifted away from the reception area.

'We could look upstairs,' Ian suggested. They were walking in that direction.

'There are fourteen floors,' Ankers pointed out. 'We wouldn't know where to look. I've seen him in his room. I think I even saw the number on the door but I can't remember it. I know it was high up, but that's all.'

They were at the base of the main staircase now. A man with a bloated green face was coming down, leaning heavily on the mock-marble banister. A stringy web of saliva drooled from his mouth and adhered to his chin, giving him a sort of lace handkerchief beard. He paused on the last step, looking at Ian, then fell forwards. Without thinking, Ian put out his arms to catch the man. His fingers sank into swollen, dead flesh and sickeningly he felt his nails puncture the skin. The man was heavy, making Ian stagger. He remembered helping an obese heart patient who fell over in the hospital toilets. The patient had been at least twenty stone, beyond Ian's capacity to lift, but he knew he had to lift him or he might die.

The consequences were different but the challenge was the same. In fact, the dead man was lighter. And he was dreaming, wasn't he? He could do anything in a dream, couldn't he?

Bending his knees, he jerked the man upwards and on to his feet, then disengaged as quickly as possible. The dead man ambled off towards the bar, leaking some unpleasant fluid on the marble floor. Ian looked at his discoloured hands, from which globs of grey flesh hung on threads of perished skin, and immediately felt his gorge rise. He wanted to vomit. Ankers had grabbed his shoulder and was pulling him towards a sign beside the staircase that indicated the presence of toilets. They went down a flight of steps and through a door into a washroom that smelt of the sewers.

Three times Ian retched, bringing up a thin dirty-brown swill and very little solid food, which reminded him as he clutched the filthy toilet bowl that he couldn't remember the last time he had had something to eat.

Ankers helped him clean up at a washbasin. 'At least we know these creatures don't mean us any harm,' Ankers said. 'He could have bitten you if he'd wanted to.'

'I don't know,' Ian said between gargles. 'What about those things in the Jeep?'

Ankers shrugged his shoulders. 'Maybe they were fresher. Maybe like us they're not all the same. Some are violent, others wouldn't hurt a fly.'

'They probably eat flies,' Ian grimaced. 'I'll never get these hands clean.' He scrubbed them under the tap with a cake of industrial soap.

'What made you go for him like that, anyway?'

'I don't know. I couldn't watch him fall on the floor. Helplessness is such a terrible thing. No one should ever be abandoned.' He rubbed at his wrists. 'I suppose it's just working in a hospital. You see so many helpless cases and you know you've got to do something.' He knew it went deeper, however. It had to do with his abandonment of his father. He had decided to put that behind him but he knew he would never earn his own forgiveness.

'But this man – this *thing* – was already dead. What does it matter if it falls on the floor and cracks its head open?'

'We all die. Lots of us, in a way, are already dead. Either because we're going to die soon or because we aren't really living life. Death is only a state of mind.' Ian shook his hands in the sink and looked about for a towel. There was none, so he rubbed them dry on his trousers. 'What about Hašek? We've come here to help him, yet he's already dead. If you believed he was beyond help you wouldn't have wanted to come to this hellhole to find him.'

Ian was surprised at his speech and he could see Ankers was slightly taken aback. Ian began to feel foolish. Ankers was staring at him as if he'd grown two heads.

'Look, forget it,' Ian said, wanting to defuse the atmosphere. 'I'm just blathering. Ignore me. OK?'

But Ankers was still staring. He whispered something.

'What?' said Ian.

'Listen.'

Ian listened. He soon heard it too.

Jazz.

Someone was playing jazz. Jazz saxophone.

Ankers was the first to the door. Ian followed him. Outside, it was clear the music was coming from further downstairs, from the hotel basement. Ankers took the steps three at a time but slowed down as he got nearer the bottom. Ian was next to him as they reached the bottom and turned left into a dimly lit cellar bar. Both men had recognized the tune as Charlie Parker's 'Bluebird'.

Ankers held his breath. Slowly his eyes got used to the light. Dead things and, he thought, a scattering of Albanians sat at round tables and at the back of the room in little alcoves, all looking one way. 'Bluebird' finished and those who could delivered a round of applause. It was thin but sounded genuine. After a couple of moments the opening phrase of 'Koko' galvanized Ankers; he wanted to clap to show he recognized it.

On a small stage at the far end of the bar a fat-faced, untidy, sick-looking parody of Hašek was holding an alto saxophone and moving his fingers on the keys as he would to play 'Koko'. He held the instrument in the way Bird always had and *appeared* to be playing the song. He even had a mike for verisimilitude. But he was miming. The music was on disc.

Behind the bar was an enormous stack of the most expensive up-to-the-minute stereo equipment. Even from where he stood Ankers could see the green laser reflecting off the spinning disc in the CD player. No one in the bar was being fooled: there was full group backing on all tracks but Hašek was alone on stage.

Ankers moved to a table that had empty seats. He and Ian sat down. Hašek 'played' 'Perhaps'. The CD sounded like a selection of Bird's best-known recordings. After 'Perhaps' there was 'Red Cross'. Ankers and Ian clapped with everyone else and Hašek acknowledged the applause before stepping down unsteadily from the stage. The barman was slow and the opening riff of 'Klaunstance' escaped to the loudspeakers before he pressed EJECT. Hašek stumbled to the bar and the barman produced a glass, which he filled with thick orange liquor. Hašek took the glass, held it up to the light – Ankers and Ian watching every move – and poured it down his throat. The barman refilled the glass. People around the room focused their attention on their own little groups. Ankers made a sign to Ian to follow him.

Ankers approached Hašek from the side. He put a hand on the Czech's shoulder but met with no response. Heart beating wildly, he pulled at his shoulder and Hašek moved. He turned slowly. Coloured lights behind the bar slithered across his moonface scarcely disguising its blue tinge.

Ankers absorbed the shock and spoke his friend's name. Recognition flickered on Hašek's face. 'Hašek, it's me, Ankers. This is Ian.' Ankers beckoned to Ian, who stepped forward and stupidly realized he had put his hand out. But Hašek took it and gave it a small squeeze.

'Ian,' he said. Then, turning to Ankers, his face broke into a smile and he embraced him as warmly as if he were alive. 'You came to see me play,' he murmured with obvious irony.

Ankers felt close to tears but Hašek's dark joke made him grin. Hašek pulled away and was grinning too, which made Ankers laugh. Ian began to laugh as well. Soon there were tears in Ankers's eyes.

'Nderim,' Hašek addressed the barman. 'These are my friends. Give them a glass of ponç. Ponç,' he turned to Ankers and Ian, 'is an Albanian liqueur. I'm told it tastes wonderful, like oranges.'

Ankers looked quizzically at him as Nderim poured the thick orange drink into three glasses.

'I can't taste it,' Hašek declared. 'How can I? But old habits die hard. I've always enjoyed a drink. And I thought it would be nice to sample what these kind people have to offer. I'm sure it's superb. Your health!' He raised his glass. Ankers took his and passed one to Ian. They toasted Hašek and tipped the contents of their glasses straight down as they had seen Hašek do.

Ian had an instant coughing fit and doubled up. Ankers spluttered and went red in the face. Hašek enjoyed the joke. True, he couldn't taste the ponç, or feel its effect, but he knew it was strong stuff.

Crossed Lines

The first thing Bentinck did upon arriving in Belgrade was find a newspaper stand. There was no sign of his paper. The vendor spoke no German, nor any English. But when Bentinck enunciated clearly the name of his paper the man shook his head and turned to someone else.

'Asshole,' Bentinck muttered. He marched off, as quickly as his big bag would allow, in search of another news-stand. He couldn't find his paper at the next three stands. Angry and frustrated, he decided to ring either Böll or his editor and find out what was happening. It was possible that resetting the front page would have delayed the paper's appearance. Maybe he would have to wait until tomorrow for copies to reach Belgrade.

He found a phone a couple of hundred metres down the road on the other side. While he was crossing the road a man approached the call box from the other direction. Bentinck trotted the remaining distance and reached the door before the other man, who glared at Bentinck. Holding the door open, Bentinck swung his bag into the kiosk and dug in his pocket for change. He pulled out a handful of Swiss francs. He reached into his trouser pockets but found only low-denomination Yugoslav coins, no good for the phone. The man outside rapped on the glass and Bentinck flapped his hand in the air. He was beginning to sweat and to swear; the two often accompanied each other when Bentinck got hot and bothered. Turning round with difficulty in the tiny box, he jerked open the door and asked the man in a mixture of German and mime if he had any coins. He offered some of his Swiss francs but the man had begun shouting and waving his arms about, attracting the attention of passers-by.

'You're an asshole,' he told the man in Swiss German, so that he couldn't understand but so that Bentinck was in some small way satisfied. He dragged his bag out and brushed past the man

168

on purpose as he left the kiosk. The man roared his anger and strode after Bentinck. He grabbed Bentinck's arm and the larger man – Bentinck – whirled round. He was going to shout back when he saw over the man's shoulder that someone else had stepped into the phone kiosk. Bentinck laughed out loud and, while the man was turning round to see what the big joke was, Bentinck hailed a passing cab. As the taxi drove away he lit a cigarette and watched the man banging on the kiosk, terrifying the woman who had thought it was free.

Bentinck told the driver to take him to the best hotel in Belgrade. Now that he was riding the crest of a top news story, he felt justified in the extravagance. The paper would pay. He wiped his brow with a damp blue handkerchief and gave a big sigh. He would take a hot bath and have dinner in the hotel restaurant. He felt he'd earned it after the seven-hour haul from Ljubljana. He had cursed the train for being so slow and so uncomfortable. At the point where the line crossed from Croatia into Serbia there was a delay and a great many uniformed guards milled around outside the train, poking batons into its undercarriage and squinting through the windows. Some of the guards were armed and a check was made on all passengers. Some, Bentinck saw as the train finally pulled away, had been detained on the station platform.

He watched Belgrade go by from the window of the cab. The atmosphere seemed relatively calm, considering what he knew of Serbian nationalist feeling. Certainly this didn't seem like the capital of a republic at war.

The cab driver left him outside the Intercontinental Hotel. The thickset Serb behind the reception desk accepted his credit card and took down his details with a shade of disdain in his eyes. Bentinck noted the prices with a smile. As long as someone else was paying it was something to smile about. He was about to ask a porter to carry his bags up, when he remembered where he was and bit his tongue.

His room on the fourth floor was comfortable. He rang down to check on the times for dinner. There was enough time for a quick bath before going down. While the water was running he unpacked his bag. His orange shirt and his blue shirt he refolded and placed in the wardrobe. He put the copy of *Muzik* by the

169

bed. He had read most of it on the train but there were one or two potentially interesting articles left. If he didn't have too much to drink with his dinner or afterwards in the bar, he might read them before going to sleep. He took Petrović's plum brandy out of the bottom of the bag and put that next to the magazine. He undressed in the main room and draped his trousers over the back of a chair. He hung his shirt in the wardrobe, stuffed his socks into his shoes and left his boxer shorts on the bed. Taking his toilet bag from out of his big bag, he walked into the bathroom. Steam billowed up from the bath. He turned off the tap, felt the water and ran some cold.

Enjoying the luxury, he stood astride the toilet and pissed straight into the middle, something he rarely allowed himself to do, in case anyone might be within earshot. The room cost such an extortionate amount he would be stupid not to do just as he wished. Especially since he wasn't paying.

The bathroom was thick with steam. He rubbed his hands over his body, taking pleasure from the slick feel of the hair on his chest. His hands slid down over his stomach and thighs. With his right hand he cleared a section of mirror and looked at himself. He liked to think he was well built rather than fat. There were no scales in the bathroom, so he couldn't get a second opinion.

He realized he hadn't got long and stepped into the bath. He immersed himself and sat up smoothing his hair back. One of the several white towels served as an excellent flannel, with which he scrubbed his entire body before letting the water out and standing up.

It took him only a few minutes to get dried – patting himself gently with the thickest towel – and dressed in his orange shirt. He was down in the restaurant five minutes before they stopped taking orders. He had the most expensive steak on the menu and a bottle of Cabernet Sauvignon. In his head he composed his letter of acceptance for the Reporter of the Year award.

Bentinck was drunk by the time he rolled into the bar and ordered a double brandy. He lit the first of the evening's cigarettes. Piano music was coming from somewhere – jazz piano. He took his brandy and sank into an armchair. The civil war felt a long way away. A good brandy and good piano. But where *was* the piano?

He looked all around and finally spotted it unlit in the corner of the bar and so moved to another chair to be nearer to the music. He was surprised to see that the pianist was a woman. Soon he was on his third double brandy and had formulated a plan. He asked the barman to give the pianist whatever she would most like to drink. During a break between numbers the barman took her what looked like a champagne glass and they exchanged a few remarks too softly for Bentinck to hear. When the barman presented Bentinck's drinks bill it was confirmed that the lady pianist had indeed ordered champagne, and not just any old champagne but the best.

After her next number she came over and said hello. His mouth watering and his mind spinning fantasies, Bentinck offered her a cigarette, which she declined, and he invited her to sit down.

They got it wrong from the start. Gabriela, through force of habit, thought he was just another client. Consequently she came on strong and straightforward. Bentinck decided he was dreaming or had died and gone to heaven, until she mentioned money, which brought him back down to earth.

In a moment's clarity they both saw their mistake. Fortunately, they were both sufficiently drunk to get over their embarrassment quickly and laugh about it. Bentinck was drunk on brandy, Gabriela on an evening's playing and a glass of champagne. When the barman suggested they leave as it was time to lock up the bar, Bentinck mentioned that he had a bottle of the finest Slovenian plum brandy in his room. Gabriela looked at him to gauge his intent.

'Brandy and a chat,' he said, lighting up again.

When they swapped stories they both found themselves confused about significant recent events in their lives. With his newspaper's no-show, Bentinck had begun to doubt he had actually witnessed the secession of Slovenia from Yugoslavia. And Gabriela couldn't actually swear she hadn't slept with a stranger who had left her bed to go and shoot Ceauşescu.

Bentinck was able to confirm there had been no talk of the

Romanian president's assassination in the press, and he felt sure it would be worth a mention.

Gabriela smiled at his irony, but reminded him that the media had also failed to pick up on the Yugoslav crisis.

Touché.

When the plum brandy was finished and the sun was pushing the night from the sky, they agreed that *something* had happened in Slovenia, even if it wasn't quite secession. And that Ceauşescu was still very much alive. Either the stranger who had shared Gabriela's bed had been romanticizing, or Gabriela had completely imagined him.

If confirmation were needed, it was provided when Bentinck switched on the television. A breakfast news programme broadcast from Vienna showed a recent picture of Ceauşescu and talked about how his systematization programme was going ahead despite protests from foreign pressure groups and a letter from a leading dissident published in a British newspaper.

'See,' Bentinck said. 'And that's only the second or third item on the news. He's alive and well.'

'More's the pity.'

'Indeed.'

On a West German channel there was a report about the Armenian–Azerbaijani clashes. They watched through a fug induced by alcohol.

'Don't you want to go there and get a story?' she asked him.

'No. There are stories here.' He burped and lit a cigarette. 'The world's changing. I can feel it. Maybe what I saw in Ljubljana was a prophecy.'

'Do you believe in that stuff?'

'Only when I'm drunk.' He burped again and scratched behind his ear. 'And when there's no reasonable explanation.'

The next item made Bentinck sit up and see straight. There had been rioting in Kosovo with dozens of fatalities. The information source was Tanjug, the Yugoslav news agency, so it was inevitable that the ethnic Albanians were blamed. The only casualties declared were Serbian. Many of them were indeed terrible: the reporter spoke of disembowelments, even of heads being cut open and brains removed. The ethnic Albanians had always been violent and had started riots many times before, but never had

172

they mutilated their victims and displayed such savagery. It confirmed even the most pessimistic forecasts made by Serbian commentators in the past. Slobodan Milošević had been proved right in the eyes of the world. So said Tanjug. But then they would.

Bentinck was suspicious.

'Why would they mutilate people?' Gabriela asked.

'I don't think they would, that's the thing,' Bentinck said. 'The Serbian media have been waging a hate campaign against the ethnic Albanians for years. Maybe they just decided to up it several degrees in order to justify the awful repression that is bound to follow.

'I've got to get down there today,' he added with determination.

The Kosovo report was followed by a piece on the North Sea. The rising sea levels combined with the tail end of a tropical hurricane had hit the Channel Tunnel and placed 'certain operations' at risk. There had been substantial erosion of the White Cliffs of Dover and severe flooding in the Netherlands. Parts of Amsterdam had been evacuated.

'You see,' Bentinck cried. 'The world's changing. It's in a state of flux.'

Gabriela could see that he thought it was all tremendously exciting. His face was lit up like that of a child at Christmas lucky enough to have a few presents to open.

She went with him to Prishtinë because she had nothing better to do and she quite liked him, for all his sarcasm and irascibility. She'd escaped from Romania with no real goal after Belgrade. Wherever she went she could never be as unhappy as she had been in Szarazpatak, before and after her husband left, and later in Bucharest. She had no desire to play hunt-the-husband. She just wanted to live for herself and see some of the world. If she occasionally got to play the piano, then that would be fine.

They took a train from the main railway station. She had assumed Bentinck would have a car, a Mercedes or a BMW. He scowled and declared that he preferred the train. It was slow but Gabriela didn't care: she had all the time in the world.

'You know,' he said to her as they trundled south, 'it took a lot of double brandies before I had the courage to buy you that drink. That sort of . . . I don't do that sort of thing. It's not part of my make-up.'

She watched the scenery, aware of him wiping his forehead with a big orange handkerchief. 'So what was different about me?' she asked.

'I don't know. A combination, I suppose, of being in a new place, believing I'd got a hot story, the drink I'd already had – and the music.'

'You were drunk,' she said, reducing his eloquent confession to one of its parts.

'Oh!' he muttered and cursed under his breath. He'd known it was a mistake to be so forthcoming. He pulled out of his bag the most recent available edition of the newspaper he believed himself still to be working for. He fussed noisily with the crease, getting it just right, and buried himself in foreign news.

'I'm sorry, Rolf,' she said after a while. He grunted. 'I didn't know how to take someone being nice to me after so long. I just assumed you were a john. It's a question of what you are used to, I guess. And I'm not used to advances that are purely friendly in nature.'

'I didn't take you for a prostitute.' Bentinck sounded hurt.

'That's what I'm saying. You thought I was an easy lay so you bought me a drink.'

'Aw, hey, come on,' he protested.

'I'm joking,' she said. 'Take a joke. It's you that makes me like this, you know. Normally I don't answer back. In my life it's rarely been necessary.'

They let the rattle of the train fill the silence between them. The country and towns of Serbia passed them by.

'Look out there,' Bentinck said.

Gabriela was already looking.

'Tell me what's wrong with it,' he said.

She looked and wondered what he meant.

'It looks OK to me,' she said.

'Well, to me it looks like late summer. Look at those trees over there. What are they? Beech? Lime? I don't know. But whatever they are, they look like they're about to shed their leaves. Wouldn't you say?'

'I don't know. I guess so. Maybe. They don't look very fresh.'

'What month is it, Gabriela? May? June? July? I don't even know. I'm a reporter. I should know. I should know the date and the exact time. But I don't. When I left Switzerland it was still cold. Now it's summer, yet only a few weeks have passed.'

'So you lost track of time.'

'Time's all fucked up.'

She looked at him, trying to relate his observations to her own life. She had lost track of time, but that was nothing fantastic. That was living in Ceauşescu's Romania, where time was completely abstract. You lived day by day and the days mounted up. After 365 of them you had a year. But what did another year mean? There was never anything to eat, nothing to do except work. Nothing ever changed. All you had were your dreams.

She couldn't really say she'd dreamed of escaping. Rather, she'd been driven to it by the endless years of stagnation followed by the illusion of change and the shattering of the illusion.

She remembered a dream about the Gara de Nord turned into a massive prison in which a dissident painted slogans on the walls. There had been a guard who smoked a cigarette and a naked woman who was asleep standing up. A cloth-bound dummy played light patterns on a piano in the station café.

Even as the sun burnished the golden beech trees across the fields, Gabriela felt a chill and shivered involuntarily as she recalled the skittle-head that tumbled softly from the neck of the dummy pianist.

'And that stuff on the TV news this morning,' Bentinck said, interrupting her thoughts. There's some Weird Shit happening in the world right now. Environmental changes are taking place that should have taken years to come about.'

'So what is it? What's causing it?'

The minibar was wheeled past their compartment, bottles of minerals clashing in the metal baskets and water sloshing against the necks.

'It's irrational,' Bentinck said excitedly. 'Some irrational force, if any exists. Chaos perhaps. There's a whole science devoted to the study of chaos.' He thought for a moment before adding, 'But that's bollocks. This stuff is just happening.'

The sun's angle took on more of an acute slant. Parts of the countryside fell into shadow.

'Maybe the Balkans is at the heart of it,' Gabriela said.

'You may be right, Gabriela. Time will tell. Maybe, if there is a pattern to what's happening, sooner than we think.'

Larry is an American dealer but he will buy organs of any nationality.

The electronically controlled gate swings open and the Russian steps through, closely followed by Hašek. Larry is waiting for them at the door, with his woollen plaid shirt and large, overhanging belly. They file in and down a number of corridors. In the nerve centre of Larry's operations a television set is tuned to American football. On the floor by the battered armchair facing the TV are three cans of American beer and a dirty polystyrene food container. On the other side of the room is a bank of monitors and computer terminals. One screen displays details of relative currency changes around the world. Another gives the correct time in major capital cities. Several transplant boxes stand waiting on a wooden bench.

'Well, come on, fellers,' Larry says, picking his teeth. 'Let's see what you got.'

Larry examines the contents of the cylinders and announces he will take three kidneys, two livers, two sets of lungs, one set of testicles and a brain. He explains he can't take the risk on the remaining viscera, since he can't predict how soon he will find buyers. He pays them, in dollars, and returns to his chair to watch the football and crack open a beer before they have even left the room.

Back in the Jeep the Russian splits the money. Hašek works out how much he will need for an alto saxophone and the visa documents. He can hear 'Now's the Time' playing in his head.

Consumer Society

In the cellar bar of the Hotel Tirana they got through two bottles of ponç and three steaks between the three of them in an hour and a half while Hašek explained things a little. Because he couldn't hold air in his lungs, his voice never rose above a rasping whisper. Occasionally Ankers and Ian had to strain to hear what he was saying.

Albania had become a lodestar for the victims of Stalinism throughout Europe. They unearthed their corpses from mass graves in Russia and Poland. They rose and walked from cemeteries in Lithuania and Romania. They got down from their mortuary slabs in East Berlin and Prague. Wherever a Stalinist regime had made its country's people suffer, the dead, whether murdered by the state's evil servants or killed slowly by deprivation, left their leaden beds and suddenly found themselves somewhere else.

The migration focused on Tirana and gradually spread to other towns and cities, squeezing the indigenous population out of the country. The Greeks offered the Albanians the island of Corfu as a temporary home. Most left but some of the natives stayed and found they could live side by side with the dead things.

They were hungry, these dead things. Hungry for what they had been denied. Freedom they now had. But they wanted money, and things to spend it on. When word got about that you could make a great deal of money selling live human organs it became the national pastime. A sense of decency and fair play spared their hosts, the Albanians, who proved willing helpers in this drive to capitalism. They showed the dead things the Republic of Serbia and its autonomous province Kosovo, in neighbouring Yugoslavia. Serbs hated Albanians, who formed a substantial ethnic minority in Serbia (in Kosovo they actually outnumbered Serbs by eight to one), and had begun to persecute them. Nationalist sentiments were being whipped up by the Serbian leader

Slobodan Milošević, a dangerous man who incited hatred of the Albanian minority.

Serbs would make excellent organ donors and the dead things could make a quick return on their investments by selling to the West. In Kosovo the dead things were directed to the Serbian strongholds and taught how to recognize ethnic Albanians and so leave them intact.

Organs were sold to dealers in Yugoslavia who would sell them on to the West. The dead things got rich and began buying consumer goods. Seriously. They dealt with West Germany, Austria and Greece, acquiring televisions, radio receivers, stereo equipment, video recorders, satellite dishes, washing machines, dishwashers, computers, fax machines, sophisticated telecommunications. It didn't matter that many of these goods were perfectly useless to them. Possession became an end in itself.

Not all the dead things wanted the same consumer goods. Some had individual wishes. Many thousands wanted to watch soap operas and old videos; just as many wanted to watch their rags going round and round in a washing machine. Some wanted to read books banned in their own country. Others wished to hear music by artists considered decadent by their former leaders. Hašek wanted to play the saxophone again.

First of all he had to get the money to buy one, since his own was at the bottom of the North Sea. Then all he needed was air in his lungs to play it. Here capitalism revealed itself a disappointment. You couldn't buy back life. But he could buy a forged visa for Hella to leave East Berlin and visit him in Albania.

Which was where Ankers and Ian came in. The postal service was in disarray and could not be trusted with irreplaceable documents which had cost a small fortune to acquire.

'I want you to take the documents to East Berlin and give them to Hella,' Hašek explained to Ankers.

'Why can't you take them yourself?' Ankers asked, puzzled. 'You seem quite fit – considering.'

'We can't travel. One night plundering in Serbia and we're completely wiped out for the next day. Anyway, look at me. I'm blue. I should be laid out in the morgue. Imagine you're an East German border guard and I want to enter your country. Do you wave me through? Or do you reach for a gun? I know which I'd do.'

'What about dreaming?' Ankers asked.

Ian took a mouthful of ponç. He swirled it around his mouth and swallowed it slowly.

'We don't dream. I haven't dreamt since I got here.'

'I mean "dreaming" you to East Berlin with the music. That's how we got here, you know. We played together with your tape in the car. Ian's a drummer – a good one too. We lost the car but ended up on Durrës beach.'

'Fine,' said Hašek, not outwardly impressed by their impossible journey. 'But you forget – I can't play.'

This obvious fact dampened Ankers's spirits. Ian wanted something else to eat – the food was excellent – but didn't like to break up the group. He had another drink instead.

'So where are the documents?' Ankers asked. 'I mean, I, we, would be perfectly happy to go to East Berlin. I just wanted to help you get out of here yourself.'

'Sure, I know. I could walk out tonight but I wouldn't get very far. The important thing is this' – he patted the saxophone – 'I want to play again.'

'How can Hella help?' Ian asked.

'Hella is my ex-wife. The only person I've ever been close to. But she thought this came first.' Again he reached for the saxophone and this time cradled it in his lap. 'Maybe she was right, though I didn't think so at the time. Only she can help me now.'

'How?' Ian persisted.

'With a kiss she can put air back into my lungs and I'll be able to play again.'

'But why does it have to be her? Why couldn't it be . . . well, Ankers?'

Ankers poured himself another glass of ponç.

'You're obviously not a romantic, are you?' Hašek said to Ian. 'Ankers and I have never been close. At least, not that close.'

Ankers had too much ponç inside him not to grin. Ian thought about Hašek's remark. He supposed the dead man was right. Lucy had shattered any romantic delusions.

'Don't you think I tried that?' Hašek was saying. 'As soon as I got here and had realized my situation – and once I'd squeezed three litres of the North Sea out of my lungs – I went to see a whore. Several girls stayed when we all arrived. Maybe they thought business would pick up. After all, Tirana is hardly Amsterdam. Or maybe they were just curious.

'I was advised to frequent the basement bar in the Hotel Dajti. The Dajti is quite different to this place. Visiting diplomats used to stay there, or drink in the bars. Some still do, in fact.

'I felt foolish at first, with my blue face, buying drinks I couldn't swallow properly or taste at all. But like I said before, some habits you just don't lose when you cross over.

'I drank there for three evenings, listening to Beatles songs played endlessly in the background somewhere before I caught her eye. She'd been there on and off the previous two evenings but I didn't feel it would be right to make an assumption. It's funny, I've no qualms about killing Serbs for their internal organs, but I couldn't bring myself to approach the woman for sex. But when I caught her eye she came over to me. She accepted a drink and made no comments about my appearance. When she'd finished her drink she asked me if I had a room in the hotel. I told her I was staying at the Hotel Tirana. *It's nicer here,* she said. So I booked a room – they managed to run the place pretty much as normal, unlike this hotel, which was overrun – and I followed her upstairs.

'We got into the room and she began to undress immediately. She'd taken off her red dress and dropped it on a chair before I was able to stop her.'

Hašek paused. Ankers and Ian were staring at his face, watching his lips intently. Otherwise the bar had emptied. Even Nderim had gone. His coloured lights, of which he was so proud, had been switched off.

'Go on,' said Ian, clearly interested in the outcome of the story.

'Maybe I should let you go up to bed,' Hašek murmured. 'You need sleep, you living things.'

'No,' Ankers roared as he swallowed a mouthful of ponç. 'Go on with the story.'

'Where was I?' Death had not robbed Hašek of his sense of humour.

'She took her dress off,' Ian prompted him.

'Yes. She had an exquisite body.' On Hašek's parched, burred tongue the *exquisite* cracked like a dry branch underfoot. 'There was moonlight in the window. It fell across her like a négligé. *What do you want me to do?* she asked me. I don't know what I said to her. *Nothing*, I think.'

Ankers gulped another mouthful of ponç. Ian crossed his legs.

'I placed my hands on her breasts – I hadn't intended to touch her, but the temptation was too great – and moulded my palms and fingers to their comforting shape.

'A great sadness filled me then, because I couldn't feel a thing.' Hašek stopped again.

'What did you do?' Ian asked.

'I asked her to put the dress back on. Then I went over to the window. I tried to pluck up courage to ask her what I'd wanted in the first place. She straightened her dress, not knowing what to do. I think she was about to leave when I asked her to kiss me, to pass a little air into my lungs. She came to the window and put her lips to mine. She blew lightly into my mouth and kissed me. I could tell from the way she moved that it was a passionate kiss, but again I couldn't feel it. I remembered the moist slide of Hella's lips, the warm intrusion of her tongue. But with this girl I felt nothing.

'When I'd paid her and she'd gone I went into the bathroom and switched on the light. I leaned over the washbasin and tried to breathe on to the mirror. The glass didn't mist over. It was then that I knew that if I was ever to blow air into a saxophone again I would have to see Hella.'

Hašek had finished. The three men sat in silence for some time before Hašek suggested they go up to his room. In the lift Ankers became aware for the first time of the smell that emanated from his friend. They had to resurrect him. And quickly.

'Where's the visa for Hella?' he asked.

'I don't have it yet. I know where I can get it, but I haven't got the cash. One more night in Serbia and I should have enough. Do you mind waiting?'

'We can look around,' Ankers said. 'There must be a lot to see.'

'There are things to see,' Hašek agreed.

Badly hungover, they saw very little the following day. Mid-morning they looked out of Hašek's bedroom window at Skanderbeg Square filled with pedestrians, cyclists and three-wheeled delivery vans. The square resounded with the hooting of horns. The air was warm and smelt of woodsmoke and strong Albanian cigarettes. Private enterprise had become popular very quickly. Albanian men opened suitcases filled with blank video tapes at random points across the square. Dead things stopped and bought some.

The dead man felt well enough to go out and do things, while Ankers and Ian regained their beds, sincerely regretting their discovery of ponç.

When the atmosphere of sweat and sweet corruption became insufferable and the act of facing the day was preferable, they went down and sat in Skanderbeg Square on the steps of the Palace of Culture. They drew stares from passing groups of Albanians and walking corpses as they peeled oranges from the hotel kitchen. After ten minutes or so of being stared at, Ankers decided to try an experiment. He smiled at a group of Albanian men who were standing near by. Typically they were wearing brown flared trousers and jackets with lapels that would have been fashionable in the West fifteen years earlier. Momentarily surprised, they stared at Ankers. Then, suddenly, they smiled back. Ankers nudged Ian. He looked up and saw the men smiling but his own worried expression remained unchanged. The men moved on; occasionally one of them would look back still smiling.

'What's wrong, Ian? They were smiling back at us. Being friendly. We've no reason to fear them, or the dead things.'

'No, I know,' Ian said, frowning.

'Then what's wrong?' Ankers pressed him, slipping a segment of orange into his mouth and biting on it with his back teeth. The juice squirted on to his tongue.

'A clash of loyalties,' Ian said. Ankers waited for him to go on. 'Remember I told you about that doctor at the hospital in Brighton? He was importing live organs to do transplants on wealthy patients. There's nothing wrong with that in itself, though I don't think the issue of a transplant organ should depend on how much you can pay for it.

'The point was that he was doing so many transplants I became convinced he was obtaining the organs illegally. I broke into his office one day and saw two transplant boxes on his workbench. They had Cyrillic writing on them, which I connected with either Russia, Bulgaria or Yugoslavia. Now I know they were from Yugoslavia. Torn from the bodies of innocent Serbs, probably while still alive.

'These people – Hašek and all his dead friends – have been massacring innocent people, all in the name of profit and greed. And we're condoning it by being here.'

'It's not that simple,' said Ankers. 'The dead things don't have any concept of morality. To them the Serbs are just envelopes of guts waiting to be slit open. After all, these people,' he spread his arms to encompass the square, 'know that being dead is not such a big deal.

'Look, maybe it is simple after all. The Albanians have been victimized by the Serbs for years and years. And they've had to put up with the Belgrade-controlled media saying it's the Albanians who persecute the Serbs. They're fed up. This is their chance for revenge, you see. I know it's not very nice but when you've had your head pushed under for a long time you develop an instinct for revenge and come up fighting.

'It's like the struggle that women lead against male domination. They don't just want to be granted access to the clubs and institutions that have excluded them. They set up their own exclusive retreats. Women-only bookshops, performances of plays, screenings of films, publishing houses. You can understand it.

'It won't last for ever. Sooner or later the Serbs will get sick of their people being wiped out and they'll rise up.'

'The way I see it,' Ian countered, 'is if the killings continue and they are confined to Serbian areas of Kosovo, Belgrade is going to lay the blame on the ethnic Albanians there and accuse them of genocide. There could be a war. Or just a massacre.'

Ian threw his orange peel in the gutter and spat out a pip. Ankers sucked shreds of fruit flesh from between his teeth.

'I think,' Ankers said, 'this is a situation which is bound to change soon. So don't worry about it. It's in no way your responsibility. It's all *his* fault.' Ankers was pointing right across the square to the felled bust of Stalin. Ian scowled. 'It is,' Ankers emphasized. 'This is all about him and what he did to the world.'

They sat for a while longer watching the microcosm go by, then returned to the hotel to await Hašek.

*

He had been to put his name down for one of the death squads crossing into Serbia that night. He suggested to Ankers and Ian that they walk up to Enver Hoxha's grave on one of the hills overlooking the city. Long before the Change, Hoxha's grave had assumed the nature of a shrine. It was guarded twenty-four hours a day by armed soldiers but you were allowed to approach it and sit in the great man's presence. In the world's first atheist state, he had effectively taken the place of a god – at least in his own imagination.

Ian drummed against his legs as they walked up the hill. His white coat-tails flapped behind him as he danced to the rhythm of 'Buddy's Cherokee'.

'He looks like Cab Calloway,' Hašek said quietly to Ankers, who smiled.

Hoxha's burial place was no longer under guard, but nor had it been desecrated as one might have expected. Hoxha and Stalin had been mates, and Hoxha's Sigurimi secret police had a human rights record any ruthless dictator would have been proud of. Maybe the Albanian people still had a grudging respect for the man who had in fact achieved a great deal of good in terms of education and social welfare. His people had never been treated as shabbily as Ceauşescu had treated the Romanians.

Hašek sat down on top of the grave itself. Ankers hesitated. A mixture of superstition and good manners told him it was wrong to sit on top of a grave. Hašek beckoned him, a small smile curling his stretched lips as he appreciated the irony. If Ankers was going to sit next to one dead person, he might as well sit on top of another.

'I should get the rest of the money tonight,' Hašek said. Ankers glanced at Ian, who looked away. 'I'll sort the visas out in the morning and you'll be able to go.'

Ankers thought of Inger. He should be with her, not engaged on an absurd rescue mission, that for all any of them knew could leave them stranded in the middle of nowhere, dreamed figures in the mind of a dead man.

He thought about the picture Delvaux had painted for him. There was something unnerving about it. At first he had thought of the picture as something talismanic, almost totemic. Now it felt more like a warning. But of what? He wanted to take the picture out and examine it, search for clues in Inger's expression. But he'd left his instrument in Hašek's room at the hotel, thinking it would be safe there.

'Yes,' he said slowly. 'The sooner we go the sooner we bring her back.' He thought for a moment. 'What if she doesn't want to come, though?'

'She'll come. I believe she'll come. If you tell her what I need. It's so simple, such a small thing for her, but it's the gift of life to me. She once said to me, "I'm always here if you need me." I need her now. She'll see that.'

'I hope so,' Ian said, breaking his silence. He still hadn't recovered his spirits since Ankers and he talked outside the Palace of Culture.

Ankers looked away from Ian to the city. He saw it as they had first glimpsed it when they arrived. He realized it was less than twenty-four hours ago, yet it felt as if they'd been there a week. The domed brown cloud of smoke and dust sat on the city's shoulders like a familiar.

'Hella left me several times. When we were together.' Hašek was talking again. Ankers had to lean closer to hear him. 'Sometimes I knew she would come back the same day or the next day. Other times, I knew I'd have to wait a week or so. A couple of times I just wasn't sure. She betrayed nothing in her eyes. The last time was like that. She had become asthmatic from the anxiety. I was an asshole. I just kept on cleaning my saxophone. After she'd gone I thought to myself I should have tried to persuade her to stay.'

Ankers felt sorry for Hašek. It must have hurt like hell. Especially in retrospect. He would have replayed all their conversations over the last two months, since she had become pregnant, listening for signs of betrayal or disingenuous signs of commitment. The worse thing would be if he hadn't actually found any.

'It was hard because she left that day and didn't come back. I had to send her things to East Berlin. She spoke to me on the phone but wouldn't tell me anything about what she was doing. She said I could ring her, and if there was another man he never answered the phone. It was some time before I learnt about Trefzger.'

Hašek had finished. He seemed to have run out of strength.

186

'Save your breath for tonight,' Ankers said. Then he realized what he'd said and looked at Hašek. There was an approximation of a grin on the dead man's face. And something else too. Ankers thought for a moment he saw the glint of a tear in the corner of an eye. He looked away, sure that Hašek would not want to be seen crying. But he *couldn't* cry. And when he looked back there was no sign of any emotion at all.

The three men sat watching the view as the sky above the hills to the west changed colour and the brown cloud over the city took on a purplish hue. Presently a wind got up. They were exposed on top of the hill. Ian's white coat was thin. But apart from that something else was bothering him.

'Why isn't he up and about?' Ian asked, pointing with one drumstick at the grave.

'He wasn't a victim,' Hašek whispered hoarsely. 'He was a perpetrator.'

Ian thought for a moment, then said, 'You weren't a victim either, I thought. You had already escaped when you drowned.'

Hašek looked at Ian, and Ankers turned to watch Hašek.

'I've been thinking about that too,' Hašek said. 'But maybe the whole thing goes back to the conditions in Czechoslovakia. Otherwise why would I have escaped and why would I have gone to Belgium, of all places?'

'Because of the dreams,' Ankers said.

'Yes, but I was having dreams before you wrote and told me about yours. In prison.'

'You were dreaming about Delvaux and the women?' Ankers asked excitedly.

Hašek shook his shaggy, bloated head slowly. 'No,' he said. 'I was dreaming about a place where the dead went to watch television and buy things they don't need. They seemed to be driven by an obsession to possess things. Things that were no good to them. But still they had to have them. I was dreaming about this place.'

Ankers was stunned. Ian had no answer.

'Shall we return to civilization?' Hašek asked. 'You must be getting cold up here.'

Strange Fruit

They entered a building tucked away behind the Hotel Dajti and the art gallery. In the lobby, rats scampered from beneath their feet. On the way back from Hoxha's grave to the hotel Hašek had said that he wanted them to meet some people he knew. Both Ankers and Ian now regretted agreeing to the slight detour. The building stank more atrociously than any other quarter of the city they had yet investigated. Flies buzzed in the sluggish air just above their heads. It was warm and close.

Ian felt uncomfortably hot and uneasy about Hašek's leadership of their little group. He didn't know if he could trust him. Possibly because he'd only known him dead. He might be a completely different man alive.

He knew Ankers liked the man considerably and so for the time being was prepared to go on that trust.

They passed doors that stood ajar. The darkness inside the rooms seemed liquid and glutinous. Ian gripped his drumsticks like a baton. They would be useless as a defence weapon, he knew, but he needed something to cling on to.

At the end of the corridor they stopped beneath a bare yellow bulb festooned with cobwebs. There was a closed door in front of them. Hašek turned round to look at Ankers and Ian before opening the door. He briefly studied their faces. Ian fancied he saw the ghost of a smile pass across his fattened-up face, but it was impossible to be sure.

Hašek opened the door.

The stench rolled out in waves, turning their stomachs. Darkness flooded the corridor and drowned the feeble yellow glimmer. Hašek stepped into the room and uttered a greeting. They wanted to run out into the cool of the tree-lined boulevard, the brightness of the square, but something drew Ankers and Ian forward into the room. There was a wide-screen TV stranded in the middle of the floor. Its flickering images cast enough sporadic light to see by once their eyes had become accustomed.

Ian saw the shapes first and instantly bent double as he threw up a bitter gutful of orange and coffee on to the thin carpet. Ankers felt as if he'd been punched in the throat. He sucked in air sharply and felt his head swim.

The shapes on the low settee pushed up against the back wall of the room could have been dummies taken from the shop of a Tirana gentlemen's tailor, if it weren't for the stick-like arms and legs. And an almost imperceptible stirring.

Ian was heaving on to the floor and cursing Hašek. Ankers was taking abnormally shallow breaths and would soon hyperventilate. Hašek was aware of the discomfort caused to Ankers and Ian and vaguely regretted it. He looked at the dead men. Their bodies were dressed, though their clothes fell in tatters about them. The neck stumps, originally knife-sharp and flat as mirrors, had been adversely affected by partial cremation and subsequent decomposition.

'Maybe I shouldn't have . . .' Hašek's voice trailed off. It was the first time since their arrival in Tirana that Hašek had seemed unsure of himself. Ankers understood that the man felt guilty. He thought he knew now how badly Hašek wanted air in his lungs, how acute was his need to play jazz.

Crouched down near the floor, Ian wiped his mouth. His position allowed him to see one of the severed heads. It sat upright on the floor and was in better condition than the bodies. The eyes were open; one gazed in the wrong direction; the mouth was twisted down to one side.

'Good evening, gentlemen,' Hašek whispered. 'Living friends of mine. Jazzmen. They're going to help me.' He sat down on the settee next to one of the bodies and placed his hand on the thing's shoulder. 'They can't hear me,' he said, addressing his remark to Ankers and Ian. 'At least, I don't think they can. They are not equipped for hearing. Yet I speak to them in case they can understand me. They are dead, but no more dead than I am. Just a little more tired. You see: they move.'

Ian was studying the thinning carpet. Ankers, still breathing too quickly, was already watching. He couldn't take his eyes off the barrel-chests on the settee. They *were* moving, as one might

189

in a conversation, edging forward, sitting back, inclining slightly to one side or the other.

'They have a television,' Hašek pointed out. 'They sit in front of it all day. I don't know if they take anything in or if they keep it as a status symbol. They would never have owned a TV before, you see. These men were guillotined in the 1950s by Walter Ulbricht's regime in East Germany. It's maintained that sixty-two people were beheaded between July 1952 and January 1960 in the Nazi-era People's Court in Dresden.'

Squatting on the floor, Ian listened. He had caught sight of the other two heads. One sat on a chair, the other lay on its ear on the floor at one end of the settee. They looked like motorcycle helmets casually left lying around until they were next needed.

'In the early hours of the morning,' Hašek continued, 'victims were led from their cells to the execution chamber. They were strapped to a plank, without a blindfold, and guillotined. The bodies were taken to be burned at a crematorium, but the job was never finished. As you can see.'

As Hašek finished speaking one of the torsos seemed to relax and lean back, as if it had been listening.

'These men . . .' Hašek began again, but stopped suddenly and looked at the television. 'Look,' he said, as he leaned across the lap of the cadaver nearest to him and seized the remote control. He punched the volume button. Ankers had turned to watch the screen on Hašek's instruction. Ian moved around to where he could see the picture but stayed as far from the three corpses as he could.

On the screen a column of tanks was rolling into a city square. A voice spoke in a language Ankers failed to recognize, and yet he understood every word. Even this far into the adventure he was forced to admit it was a dream. His own or Hašek's. Or Ian's.

The voice identified Tiananmen Square in Beijing. The tanks belonged to the Chinese People's Army. They were coming into the city to break up a peaceful pro-democracy demonstration that had been going on in Tiananmen Square for days. The demonstration was led by students and comprised ordinary workers, intellectuals, dissidents and merchants.

Albania had once enjoyed particularly close links with China.

For a time the Chinese had practically moved in, but relations were severed when Hoxha formed the view that China was straying from the communist straight and narrow. They left behind the terraced hillside farming method and thousands of three-wheeled delivery vans, little more than glorified scooters.

Suddenly on the television screen a man ran out from nowhere and stood in the middle of the road in front of the first tank. The tank braked suddenly, swerving slightly.

One sensed it was a crucial moment.

Tanks further back in the column shuddered to a halt, trying to avoid mounting those in front.

The young man who had stopped them – a student, the reporter said – stood pertly to attention, leaning forward slightly, as if a degree of intimidation would convince the soldiers of his sincerity. They were *not* to enter Tiananmen Square and disrupt the demonstration. It meant too much. It had acquired greater depth of meaning with each new sunrise over their improvised statue of liberty. It said, 'That's enough' to the rulers of the country.

One man against a column of tanks.

But the world was watching. They wouldn't have the balls to run down a defenceless student in cold blood. Moreover, the young man driving the first tank wouldn't *want* to. He couldn't be that much older than the student. His aspirations couldn't be *that* different.

In the low-ceilinged dark room the heat was becoming overpowering. Ian, who had already emptied his stomach, felt nauseous. It smelt something like a house that had been undisturbed for four months. Piles of trash in the kitchen had decayed and turned to foul sludge. In an upstairs room the body of Ian's father lay in a pool of rot, leaking through the mattress to the floor, soaking the carpet. The first thing he'd smelt upon entering the house had been damp carpets.

Damp carpets.

The boy stood in front of the tanks. The first tank edged forward to within two metres of him. He still clutched a white plastic bag. Ian wondered what the bag might contain. His books? His drawing or writing materials? A musical instrument?

The tank lurched closer, trying to frighten him into retreat.

Ian pictured his father four months dead. It was the most horrifying thing he had ever seen and probably ever would see. He had put it to the back of his mind, but these obscenities on the settee, and maybe the boy holding back the tanks, had recalled it vividly. Ian fought to maintain equilibrium in his mind. He didn't *need* the guilt that sat familiarly on his shoulders like the smog on Tirana's rooftops.

The tank was less than a metre from the boy. He was still leaning forward. The world was holding its breath. Even the reporter had fallen silent.

The thousands of lives in Tiananmen Square depended on just one boy. Just as one lonely, broken man's life had depended on his son.

Ian's head reeled. He felt himself falling. Someone caught him. He hoped it was Ankers. Or Hašek.

Ankers saw Ian begin to collapse as the boy on the screen was pulled out of the way of the tank. Whether by friend or foe wasn't clear. Ankers twisted his body to catch Ian before he hit the floor.

'He's fainted,' he announced to Hašek. 'We must get him outside.'

Hašek spoke to the corpses as he got up and opened the door to the corridor.

As Ankers hauled Ian to his feet, one drumstick fell from his pocket and rolled under the foot of one of the corpses. Ankers lowered Ian to a sitting position and, without shyness, lifted the thing's leg. It felt soft beneath the cloth of its filth-caked trousers. Strangely he didn't mind. Looking up as he retrieved the drumstick, he was certain he saw the torso lean forward, as if to see what was going on.

Ankers hefted Ian again and half carried, half dragged him to the door. Between the settee and the side wall Ankers noticed a smart, matt-black stereo system. He kept his thoughts to himself as he carried Ian down the narrow corridor towards the light.

Ankers blinked in the relative brightness of the evening. He sat Ian down on a bench by the entrance to the art gallery and mopped his forehead with a clean section of his coat. Hašek was hovering.

'It was too hot in there for him,' Ankers said, to appease

Hašek's apparent feelings of guilt. 'I don't think the television pictures helped. I think Ian is very sensitive to tension like that.'

Ankers alternately wafted air in Ian's face and stroked the back of his head.

'It wasn't your fault, Hašek,' he said.

'Well, I thought . . .' the dead man murmured.

'Forget it.' Ian's eyelids fluttered open and he looked frightened, disoriented. 'It's OK,' Ankers soothed him. 'We're here in Tirana. Me, you and Hašek. And we're safe. Nothing to worry about.'

Ian steadied himself on the bench and looked back at the house. The doorway beckoned like a coal cellar, or a gateway to hell.

'It was the heat,' Ankers said to him.

'Yes, partly. The heat was only part of it.' He hadn't forgotten the pictures and the smells. How long had they lain in waiting in the darkest pit of his mind? Would he never be free of the consequences of his immature grievance against his father? 'That boy,' he said. 'He was so brave.'

Ankers nodded.

'What happened to him?' Ian blurted out. 'I didn't see what happened.'

'He was led away. The tanks didn't touch him,' Ankers said.

'What about the tanks? The demonstrators in the square?'

'They're almost certainly dead now,' Hašek remarked.

'What? You mean . . .'

'Those tanks wouldn't have stopped again,' Hašek said.

There was silence for a few moments.

'Will they come here?' Ankers asked.

'No,' Hašek replied. 'Chinese rulers may have affected the lives of many more people than have suffered under Stalin's influence – a fifth of the world's population is Chinese, after all – but Stalin was different. He changed the world. He really did change the world. Look at him now.'

They followed Hašek's gaze to the bust felled from its plinth. The stone man's victims had set about his head with a sledgehammer. He was scarred almost beyond recognition.

'People are angry,' Hašek said. 'You have to have experienced one of his experiments to understand their anger.'

'He sounds like the worst monster that ever walked the earth, the way you talk about him,' Ian said. 'What about Hitler?'

'Stalin was a monster and so was Hitler. Really they're incomparable. If Hitler was evil – and that is beyond doubt – Stalin was callous; but callous on an inhuman scale.'

Ian prodded the dusty ground with his sticks. Ankers looked at Hašek, who was watching the sky get darker.

When Hašek had left in a Russian Jeep for the plains of Kosovo, Ankers and Ian descended below ground to the hotel bar. They had Nderim pass them a bottle of ponç and Ankers asked him to put something on the stereo. The barman picked out a Milt Jackson CD apparently at random and slipped it into the machine. Ankers noticed that there was no cassette deck, only a CD player and amp.

The first track was 'Bags Groove'. The two men settled at a table. Ankers knew there was something on Ian's mind, because the rhythm of the music was very infectious, yet Ian's fingers barely twitched. Ankers gave the younger man a chance to speak first while he poured out two glasses. Though clearly on edge, Ian said nothing.

'What's eating you?' Ankers asked him.

'That boy,' the words came out in a rush. 'That Chinese boy who stopped those tanks. He was such a slight figure and the tanks were so huge and threatening. Yet he held them up. How did he do it? He must have had something infinitely powerful inside him.' Ian stopped peremptorily as if he expected Ankers to say something, perhaps to provide the answer. Ankers didn't know what to say. 'I mean, he must have known they wouldn't touch him. Something must have given him that confidence.'

'Maybe it's faith. Maybe he knew what he was doing was right, and the soldiers didn't have that same conviction in their own actions, or their own orders.'

Ian didn't relax. When they had had half the bottle between them Ankers suggested they call it a day. Climbing the stairs, he watched Ian from behind. The young man's shoulders seemed less broad than when he had first been surprised by his body lurching out of a train window in Calais; his head hung lower.

When they reached Hašek's room Ankers pretended to go to sleep. Ian's breathing gradually slowed down, and when it eventually levelled off, Ankers rose quietly from the floor, reached for his saxophone case, and crept out of the room.

Although they didn't have to sleep in the normal way, the dead things tended to rest at night-time, largely out of habit. Consequently, Skanderbeg Square at two o'clock in the morning was almost deserted. Two or three figures walked aimlessly around the central fountains while a determined silhouette strode across the boulevard that led north-east to the railway station. The air was pleasantly warm and redolent of strong Albanian tobacco. Reception aerials glinted in the yellowish glow cast by the street-lamps. They formed a spiky spider's web over the city, creating an illusion of security.

On Stalin's nose an old Albanian man sat enjoying a cigarette. Ankers wondered what an old man made of recent events in his country. A welcome overthrow of the old regime? Or a descent into an even greater madness? The old man looked happy enough smoking and scuffing his worn shoes on the tyrant's face. The bust of Lenin had been felled less cleanly. Half of his face remained, like something by Francis Bacon. The busts had been tall, more than twice life size, and the plinths were monolithic, like truncated columns in a ruined classical frontage. Ankers was made to think of Delvaux's women. Their marble features inevitably conjured a vision of Inger: her cold, pale face, sculpted and polished, eyes shining like turquoises.

Ankers hurried past the ambiguous remains of Lenin and slipped down by the side of the art gallery. His heart was beating faster and sweat broke out along his hairline. He pushed open the door and paused a moment to listen and accustom his eyes to the darkness. There were faint noises but they could be from outside. Feeling his way along the wall with his left hand and clutching his instrument case with his right, Ankers approached the door at the end. His mind had emptied of all thought and had become a screen upon which flickered images of the three headless men beyond the door.

'I'm doing this for Inger,' he thought as he eased the door open, held his breath and peered through the gloom. The television was switched off.

Two of the dead things sat on the settee as before, but now they were perfectly still.

Ankers felt sick.

The third corpse was nowhere to be seen.

Since the room contained an abundance of shadows and not a few places to hide, the thing could be waiting for him. Maybe it had heard Ankers coming down the corridor and had secreted its overripe bulk in a dark recess from out of which it would lumber into an attack. Ankers remembered how soft one of the legs had been to the touch. He wanted at all costs to avoid being forced into an embrace with a torso and feeling its innards begin to seep through old scars before the whole sickening thing burst.

He couldn't see the third dead man from the door, so he stepped into the room. Earlier with Ian and Hašek, he had not been seized by the terror which affected Ian, but neither had he particularly enjoyed the company. Spotting the cassette deck on the way out, he had formulated a plan for action after nightfall, without quite appreciating how nerve-racking its realization would eventually be.

The heat was barely less intense than in daylight and the smell for some reason was even more vile. Ankers walked forward gingerly, eyes peeled, senses alert.

He tried to convince himself that the corpse had gone out for a stroll round Tirana. He stretched out an arm and hit the power button on the amp. He hesitated a second, then switched on the cassette deck. From his pocket he slid the cassette into the machine and pressed PLAY.

The two torsos sat motionless in their miasma of reeking putrescence. The third was still absent. The music flowed from the speakers like a tincture to act against the nightmare – the nightmare of the whole situation and the two nightmares on the settee.

And the nightmare in waiting.

Ankers unfastened the catches and took his tenor from the case. The instrument felt unwieldy in his slick hands; his fingers fumbled fleshily on the keypads. Sweat dripped from the tip of his nose on to the floor. Hašek's music continued and Ankers blew mute notes in accompaniment, lacking the courage to sound them.

Inger's face appeared in the shadows clinging to the settee. It hovered disembodied, then floated down on to the shoulders of one of the cadavers. Ian shivered. Someone was pressing ice shards from a Narvik glacier against the base of his spine. The torso twitched. The material of its shirt had rotted and become enmeshed in its flesh. Stretched tight in the ghostly light shed by Inger's face, it looked like old bandages stretched over terrible wounds.

Feeling panic growing inside him, gripping his bowels and squeezing his heart, Ankers blew life into the saxophone. He worked instinctively into Hašek's difficult melody and was relieved to see the spectre of Inger fade and snuff out like a candle flame. He had felt sure it was just a hallucination rather than a transportation either of Inger or of the room in which he was playing. Its disappearance confirmed that.

He played and played but was unable to relax into the music. His eyes darted constantly to the darkest corners in search of the third dead man.

He wasn't deserting Hašek and Ian, he reassured himself. He just wanted to see Inger, know that she was OK, and come back. He could be back before morning.

Soon, there being no sign of the third man, the music was just pouring straight out of him into the saxophone. Ankers knew this was a good one. He pictured Inger and willed himself to Norway. But the room around him stayed solid. He brought forth images of mountains, fjords, snow and ice, but the temperature in the charnel house remained constant. He summoned recollections of Inger: stooping over the salt-pools at a rocky shore, arms bare and dripping with water; her obvious discomfort in an expensive Oslo restaurant; the emptiness of her eyes as she neared the edge of the cliff in her sleep. Again he willed himself to her.

The music flowed like a river. He was merely a channel. There were eddies where the tune turned on its own tail and chased itself back into the mainstream, and gushings of white water when the notes tumbled over each other at high speed.

It was going to work. Any minute now he'd find himself on the promontory looking up at his house. Inger's face would shine like the moon in her favourite window. He might even land *in* the house. Wake up in his own bed and wonder what he'd been dreaming about. He felt arms slide around his body and embrace him.

'Inger,' he said breathlessly as the music stopped. He felt warm and safe, as if he'd returned to his hearth after a long and tiring journey. The dream was over. The dead were once more at rest. And he lay in the arms of his lover.

He opened his eyes to smile at her. Instead he smelt her.

She smelt something like the deck of a Bergen whaler awash with blood.

His stomach turned over. The thing tightened its embrace and Ankers screamed. His head had been resting on its rumpled neck stump. As the hideous thing squeezed him he felt its mass yield, again, as if it might burst. As Ankers struggled to get free he raked the fingers of one hand across the dead thing's chest. They sank in up to the knuckle. He wrenched his hand free, quaking with terror and disgust. Over the thing's shoulder he saw the other two bodies shifting on the settee. Were they preparing to join their efforts to those of their friend?

Ankers finally pushed the thing away. Its legs buckled, causing the torso to fall against the stereo unit. It made no immediate attempt to get up. The other two were still seated.

Maybe it hadn't attacked him. It had come in from its walk and bumped into him.

Still shaking, Ankers ejected the cassette and pocketed it. He dismantled his instrument and stowed it in the case, minutely aware of every stage of his own actions. He realized he was bitterly upset at his failure to reach Norway. Why was his home country inaccessible? He only wanted an hour with Inger to be reassured of her feelings and commitment. He wasn't just scared that she would run off to Narvik and her parents. Something else worried him deeply. But all he could isolate was his vague unease about her affinity with the sea. Would he lose her to the *sea*? With no one to restrain her, might she not sleepwalk over the cliff?

Delvaux's painting too made him anxious. The mountains behind her seemed to hold as much menace as the sea.

The dead thing on the floor gripped his ankle with a weak fist. His reaction was to kick it away, but he thought it probably just wanted help getting to its feet.

Slowly it hauled its bulk from the floor, using Ankers's leg as a rope. Ankers was petrified. He didn't know if the thing was going to attack him or walk away when it had managed to stand up.

It walked away. To the settee.

Its walk was uneven, like a crane fly that had had a leg ripped off by a child. When it reached the settee it sat down heavily at the far end. Ankers backed towards the door, keeping his eye on the settee. The torsos moved no more than might fruit dangling in the breeze.

Outside, he gulped at the warm, pleasantly scented air of the city at night. His effort to reach Inger had failed but in the end he was glad to have escaped unharmed from the headless men. Whether they wished him any harm at all he couldn't be sure. But they frightened him because they were a perversion of the nature he had grown up believing in. Hašek was too, but he *looked* OK. Relatively. These *things* should be lying in wooden boxes under six feet of earth.

Entering the hotel he heard commotion from the television lounge. A TV set still sat on the reception desk and it was switched on, but no one was watching it. Ankers approached until the pictures became clear. Thousands of people were demonstrating in city streets. But it wasn't China. He moved closer and read the slogans on their banners. The words were German. Excitedly he twisted the volume knob.

'. . . at least 300,000 here on the streets of Leipzig,' a reporter was saying, 'and the story is much the same in East Berlin. Thousands more escaped to the West earlier today on special trains from Prague, where they had camped out for days in the grounds of the West German embassy.'

Something had to give, Ankers thought. People were on the move and things were changing.

He walked up to the mezzanine, where a large crowd gathered around two TV sets. There was stamping of feet and death-rattle cries of support and sloshing of foaming steins as dead East Germans cheered on their living compatriots.

Ankers wondered how long it would be before Honecker sent in the tanks and ended the demonstrations in a bloodbath.

Walking upstairs, he heard the urgent voices of news reporters and commentators coming from televisions in rooms. Ian, however, was asleep. Ankers put down his saxophone case as quietly as possible and crept beneath his blanket.

Hašek returned with the cash, a cassette recorder and blood-stains on his coat, which Ankers hoped Ian wouldn't notice. Hašek asked if they'd seen the reports on TV from East Germany.

'They're going mad outside in Alexanderplatz,' he said.

'What do you mean?' Ankers asked.

'Different nationalities have tended to stick together in Tirana. They have created their own ghettos. The East Germans colo-nized a small square in between the diplomatic neighbourhood and the railway station. People tend to refer to it as Alexanderplatz.'

'Is there a Czech area?'

'Yes, in the south-east corner of the city, but it's not very big. I prefer to live here in the hotel, where the mix is more cosmopoli-tan.' Again, that ironic grin stretched the corners of his mouth. But it soon disappeared. 'You've got to get her out of there before it all goes up,' he said. 'She's my only hope. And you're her only hope.'

They had breakfast in the hotel dining room, where meals were still served upon request. Hašek played with a crust of bread. 'Apparently,' he said, 'a group of people stormed the border last night between Albania and Kosovo. But from Kosovo into Albania. Probably the first time it's ever been done. No one knows who they are. Could be ethnic Albanians – they aren't allowed to visit Albania and most of them would dearly love to.

'Or they could be Yugoslav troops. I think trouble is brewing. Conflict in the Balkans has been on the cards for a long time. This could be it on the way. And there's nothing to stop it becom-ing an all-out war.'

Ian drained his glass of orange juice and looked around for a waitress. Ankers shrugged.

'Excuse me,' Ian said, getting up. 'I guess it's self-service. Can I get you anything?'

Hašek shook his head. Ankers said he wouldn't mind another bowl of tinned fruit.

'Is he OK?' Hašek asked when Ian was out of earshot.

Ankers considered Ian's back. 'Yes,' he said. 'He's just distracted. Like the rest of us, I think he just wants to play jazz. Perhaps he doesn't understand what's going on.' Ankers looked at Hašek and laughed grimly. 'As if I do,' he added.

Shqiperia! Shqiperia!

Bentinck and Gabriela arrived in Kosovo Polje in the late afternoon.

Bentinck was ready to whip the IBM out of his bag and file a story from the front line – Kosovo Polje, a railway station and surrounding district, was one of the Serbian enclaves in ethnic-Albanian Kosovo. But all was quiet.

Still confident that the newspaper would pay, despite the disappointment and bafflement over the Slovenia story, Bentinck insisted they took a cab into Prishtinë. It was only three kilometres along a straight road, alongside which greengrocers tempted passers-by with huge watermelons, splashes of green and red in an otherwise grey-brown colour scheme.

Bentinck booked two rooms at the Grand Hotel Priština and they dined in the restaurant. Gabriela regretted the absence of a piano.

'A colleague of mine told me how to find the best nightspots in Prishtinë. We can go after dinner,' Bentinck suggested. 'Maybe we'll find a piano in one of them.'

They found no pianos – just taped music wherever they went – but they did find pleasant company. Bentinck located Besnik's Pizzeria in a covered precinct ten or fifteen minutes' walk from the hotel.

'We've eaten,' Gabriela said, seeing the sign.

'They don't actually serve pizza, or so my colleague told me. In fact, it's not a restaurant at all, but a bar.'

Besnik himself solved the conundrum. He was a tall, dark man with arched eyebrows who stood proudly behind the bar and occasionally turned over a cassette, while his barman Kujim saw to the customers' needs.

'I went to London,' Besnik explained, 'and worked as a waiter in the Deep Pan Pizza Company in Ilford outside London. Do you know London?'

Bentinck shimmied his hand in the air. He'd been there but had little knowledge of the place. Gabriela shook her head.

'When I came back here and opened the bar I called it my pizzeria. Just a small joke.'

Bentinck began asking Besnik about the riots and Besnik said he should speak to Leka. 'He works for Prishtinë Television,' said Besnik, pointing to a brown-haired man with expressive features who resembled a young Jean-Paul Belmondo. Leka seized Bentinck's hand, delighted to meet a fellow journalist.

'This is Gabriela,' said Bentinck, 'from Romania.'

'Congratulations to you on being here rather than there,' Leka proclaimed as he shook Gabriela's hand as well.

'So what about the riots?' Bentinck asked, handing round a pack of cigarettes from which only Leka helped himself.

'What about a drink first? What would you like? *Kujim!*' he called the barman.

Kujim provided drinks. Bentinck had more brandy while Gabriela asked for a vodka. Kujim gave her a double with bitter lemon, and Leka began talking about the riots.

'There *are* riots,' he said. 'But they're not so violent. The killings you've heard about are nothing to do with the riots.'

'Then what?' Bentinck asked impatiently.

'Bands of mercenaries are crossing over from Albania during the night.'

At the mention of Albania, Kujim shouted out the Albanian word for his homeland: 'Shqiperia!' Several people cheered, including a striking auburn-haired girl whom Bentinck noticed for the first time.

'He's very patriotic,' Leka said. 'They're coming over from Albania and attacking groups of Serbs on the streets of Kosovo Polje and other Serbian areas.' Leka took a mouthful of his drink. 'They're killing them and removing their organs.' He tipped the remaining contents of his glass down his throat.

'Why are Albanians doing that?' Bentinck asked, raising his voice above the crashing drums of the folk music.

'They're not Albanians. I've got footage. I've seen them. They don't look like Albanians.' He hailed Kujim, who refilled his glass with whisky. 'They're like nothing I've ever seen before. They're a *mess.*'

'What do you mean?'

'Like they've just climbed out of their graves.'

Bentinck looked at him in bafflement. Leka drained his glass. Bentinck did the same.

'Have you shown the footage?' he asked.

'No.'

'Why not?'

'If I show it the Yugoslav army will invade Albania. They'll do it in a flash. Whether the assailants are Albanian or not, they're crossing into Kosovo from Albania.'

'And if you don't show it?'

'If I don't show it, the killings continue. We have suffered too long under the Serbs. Milošević is a madman. A fascist.'

'But everyone thinks it's the rioters. The army will retaliate against your people here.'

'They are doing already. They don't need a miserable excuse like a few disembowelments. They've been wanting to fight us for years. Anyway, the footage isn't that good. They'd say it was fake. A bit of make-up from the TV drama department.'

'This is incredible,' Bentinck said. Gabriela polished off her vodka and bitter lemon. Besnik turned the volume up on the folk music. Kujim began beating his fist on the bar in time with the bass drum as he refilled Gabriela's glass.

'Have another drink, Bentinck,' Leka shouted above the music. Bentinck nodded. 'Incredible,' continued the young Belmondo, 'but undoubtedly true.' Leka swept up his glass as soon as Kujim had filled it. *Wham-bam-bam* went the drums. It was stirring, passionate music, impossible to dislike. Unless you were hung-over or infirm. But for drinking to it was perfect. It stirred Bentinck's blood and *his* wasn't Albanian.

'I thought Kosovo was supposed to be the poorest region of Yugoslavia,' he said to Leka.

'It is rich. We are rich in minerals. But the federal system takes all our money for worse-off areas of the country, so we end up with almost nothing.'

'Yet . . . all this.' Bentinck swept his arm to encompass the bar, its smart décor, the fashionably dressed, well-fed clientele, outside, the precinct with its smart boutiques and carefree air.

'Simple,' said Leka with a broad grin. 'We Albanians know how to enjoy ourselves. We love life.'

The last part of Leka's explanation was almost drowned out by Kujim, who delivered a thunderous 'Shqiperia'.

The auburn-haired girl jumped up and down on her seat, laughing and sweating. Gabriela had moved to sit next to her and it was Gabriela who had entertained her.

'She says she has written a song, "Ceauşescu Blues",' the girl said to Leka.

'You never told me that,' Bentinck shouted across Leka and the girl.

'You never asked,' laughed Gabriela.

'"Ceauşescu Blues"?'

'"Ceauşescu Blues".'

He paused a moment. Leka and the auburn-haired girl were watching him. Gabriela too waited to see what he would say next.

'What's it about?'

Everybody laughed, but only because the drink was taking effect.

'Who is this charming lady, anyway?' Bentinck asked.

'Violeta Pexhepsagig,' announced Leka proudly, appearing to stake a personal claim. 'The best singer in the whole of Kosovo.'

'You're a singer?' he said.

'Yes. I am. I sing and I play bass guitar here in Prishtinë. I make records and play on the television.' She spoke with an easy charm and was totally unaffected. Bentinck felt his stomach muscles clench for the first time since Anna. He didn't know Violeta Pexhepsagig, but he liked her.

'Gabriela plays the piano,' he started, but the looks they gave him made him realize his mistake. 'But you know that already.' They all laughed. 'Have a drink, Violeta. If that's all right,' he added with a look at Leka.

'Oh, that's all right,' she said, putting her arm round Leka and planting a kiss on his cheek. 'Leka and I are very good friends. He would do anything for me.'

Bentinck looked at Leka: he threw his head back and swallowed another tumbler of whisky. 'Kujim,' he called.

Kujim came over with the whisky bottle. But he didn't want a drink.

'Shqiperia,' he shouted.

'Shqiperia,' Kujim joined him.

'More drinks here,' he said, indicating Bentinck and Violeta.

Bentinck ordered a brandy for himself, a vodka and bitter lemon for Gabriela, and looked at Violeta. She named a drink. Bentinck touched Leka's shoulder but the journalist declined. 'Not if I'm driving,' he said. 'I've already had six. That's enough if I'm driving.' He turned to Kujim and together they shouted, 'Shqiperia.'

Those with drinks drank. Bentinck asked Violeta what kind of music she played.

'Popular music.' Did that mean she liked the same music as Petrović? he wondered. 'Pop music and folk music.'

'What about jazz?' he asked. 'Gabriela plays jazz.'

'Music is music,' she said with a wide smile. 'Music frees people whether it's jazz, folk or pop. Or classical. Or opera. It frees the mind and the heart. Makes you fly. Makes you dream.'

'You're right,' he said, swallowing a mouthful of brandy. 'You're so right.'

Drink continued to flow as freely as the chat. Attempts to discuss theories of music were soon abandoned in favour of chants of 'Shqiperia' and boisterous singing along to nationalist folk songs. Those who didn't know the language soon picked up the key words. *Shqiperia. Parti. Enver.*

In the middle of the night Besnik opened a door behind the bar. Streetlighting glowed on a dilapidated courtyard where a car stood waiting. Bentinck saw Leka reach into his pocket for keys.

'Shqiperia,' roared Kujim, reaching up for two bottles of liquor. Gabriela made a comment which Bentinck didn't hear but Violeta Pexhepsagig laughed from deep in her throat. Through an alcoholic haze, Bentinck thought he knew what was was happening. And he was more than happy to let it happen. He lit another cigarette and thought nostalgically about his big bag in the Grand Hotel. He would miss his orange shirt, his IBM and the copy of *Muzik*, which still contained one or two unread articles. He looked at Gabriela: she returned his look knowingly. Maybe Violeta had said something to her. Bentinck wondered how premeditated this trip was.

'Shall we go for a drive?' Leka shouted, jangling his keys.

Still singing, they passed out of the bar. Kujim handed the bottles and two cassettes to Leka. Gabriela and Violeta climbed into the back while Bentinck sat next to the driver. Leka started the car and they rolled on to the road. Leka drove with one hand on the wheel slung down at the bottom, almost resting in his lap. Frequently he turned round to make comments to Violeta. Bentinck stopped worrying after a while and placed his life in the hands of chance. A bottle was opened and passed round. Leka refused, watching the road.

Soon they climbed into the hills. Leka said he had one of Violeta's songs on a cassette. She begged him not to play it and led them into a traditional patriotic song instead. Leka beat the drum pattern on the steering wheel.

Traces of gunfire or small explosives silenced them as they coruscated momentarily in the distance. Leka shouted 'Shqiperia' and they took up the song again. The sky was velvet black like the coat of a panther. The beast roared and spat on distant groups of Serbs as more and more bands of mercenaries made fire on the skyline. The car bounced over ruts and tumbled in and out of potholes. The four small people in it sang and stamped their feet, as it carried them out of the world they knew and into the dark land of their dreams.

The singing crescendoed and reached a peak as the car smashed through the barriers at the frontier post. Thereafter it died away to a whisper of reverence. The mountains dwarfing the little car were the same as those in Kosovo, but they *seemed* different.

Gabriela saw her first dead thing five kilometres inside Albania, though she didn't know it. She glanced behind as the car passed a derelict building on the outskirts of a tiny village, and saw a tattered head poke out of a broken window to watch the car. She shivered, thinking the poor creature to be a local vagrant or victim of the hostilities. She didn't know he was a long-dead victim of Stalin's purge of Lithuania and that the mess in the middle of his face was the exit wound of the bullet that had killed him. But the mere sight of him made her shiver.

By the time they rolled into Tirana they had all seen dead

things. Leka said that whatever accounted for the appearance of these people, they were as ragged and dirty as the figures on his film.

When they found a hotel they realized they were too exhausted to be curious any longer. It required a generous bribe to secure two rooms for the four of them. They only found out later that dead things had been kicked out of the rooms and it was they who had left the sheets cold.

Although sexual relations seemed not to exist between either couple, Bentinck shared a room with Gabriela, while Leka and Violeta went together.

They slept through the day. Once every hour or so Leka woke up to the sound of shuffling footsteps and car horns hooting. The air in the room he shared with Violeta was warm and stuffy, but he was too tired to get up and open a window. There was a sweet smell like burnt sugar which he couldn't ascribe to either of them. Violeta lay alongside, sweating in a bunched-up T-shirt, occasionally twitching the corners of her mouth. Some dream agitated her eyes beneath their lids.

They had been friends for years, ever since one damp morning when he'd needed a warm shoulder to cry on more than he'd needed air to breathe or eyes to see. A woman to whom he had given his fragile love had turned round one night and rejected him. *Fuck you, Leka. I can manage on my own.* He had left the woman's apartment as tears hot as sparks burst from his eyes, with no bed of his own and no life worth living.

He had camped out on the steps of Prishtinë Television and Violeta found him the following morning on her way in to do some work on a show. They were already friends but then she devoted herself to him, caring and nursing him back to a kind of happiness.

He had never repaid her, though she said his friendship was the greatest reward, where none had even been required. But he had continued to feel in her debt and here in this country of their dreams, Albania, he would protect her from the unknown elements he intuited around them.

He drifted back to sleep.

In the early evening they gathered in Bentinck and Gabriela's room. Bentinck smiled shyly at Violeta as he offered her a cigarette. She declined with a smile of her own.

They decided to have a look outside before getting something to eat.

Their walk lasted only a few minutes.

In the square outside the hotel they saw abominations: walking skeletons ragged with shreds of flesh; children with decomposed arms; a woman with a blurred, mushy face; a young man with a gash in his neck and dried blood streaking his filthy peasant's clothes.

They ran in terror back to the hotel.

Hašek turned round from the television – which was reporting on abnormally high temperatures throughout northern Europe and warning of possible mosquito infestation – and saw the four frightened figures run in past the reception desk. He recognized them as living mortals and stepped forward, blue, swollen face notwithstanding, to calm them.

He persuaded them into the bar, where he began slowly to explain.

The Beast Pauses for Breath

Hašek had gone off to get the visas from one of the old embassies. Since the only qualification now was cash, the embassies in Tirana sold visas for their own countries and for others, plus an agent's fee, of course.

Ankers spent the morning duping Hašek's cassettes on the tape-to-tape, so that in case of emergency he wouldn't run out of music.

When Hašek came back triumphantly clutching the visas, the three men went up to his room on the seventh floor. Ian was nervous.

'I like this place,' he said quietly, standing by the window looking out over Lowry's Skanderbeg Square. A Chinese tricycle-van hooted and a crowd of bystanders moved slowly around each other to one side, like cells in an organism. The fountains played continuously in the centre of the square. On the steps of the Palace of Culture an Albanian folk group had struck up a rousing tune, drums crashing, clarinets wailing.

'We'll be back soon,' Ankers reassured him. 'Nothing can go wrong.'

Hašek set the tape going. Ankers had the visas and Hella's address in his back pocket. He began to play. Ian tapped the window experimentally and kicked the wall for his bass. Had he turned round he would have seen that Hašek was joining in, miming to his own music as if it were a TV show.

It crossed Ankers's mind briefly that he might be able to divert them to Norway. Just a quick visit, then they'd be on their way to Berlin. But he knew he couldn't deceive Hašek. The Czech had said: it was vital to get Hella out of East Berlin fast. In any case, if his nocturnal effort was anything to go by, Norway was out of bounds.

His playing became automatic. He could hear Ian getting into it on the window sill, only using the glass pane as a light splash, presumably for fear he might shatter it.

They were at the bottom of a cutting by a railway line. Ian was still drumming, on the steel rail instead of the hotel woodwork. Immediately Ankers noticed the difference in the air. There was a smoky smell, but it came not from strong cigarettes. It was pungent, acrid, much less pleasant. They climbed up the rough slope where straggly weeds poked up between the stones. At the top they viewed their surroundings in silence. Ankers unfolded the piece of paper bearing Hella's address.

'Ever been here before?' he asked Ian. The drummer shook his head. 'Let's see what we can find, then.'

They climbed over a low wire fence. Ian handed Ankers his saxophone case. Ankers offered Ian a hand to get over. Ian could manage but he accepted Ankers's hand nevertheless. They were here now and he might as well make the best of it.

The streets were lined with small, cheap-looking cars: Trabants and Wartburgs, mainly. There were more cars than people. Maybe it was too early in the morning, though it had been midday in Tirana. Ian had lost his watch on the channel crossing, but hadn't missed it. What was the point of a watch when something was seriously screwing up the passage of time? Midsummer had arrived before spring was due to end. And it wasn't just coming south to Albania, Ian was convinced. The elements seemed to be in a state of flux. He thought it must all be part of the dreaming.

He didn't consider the idea that the dreaming might be a symptom of the flux.

As they walked, the streets became busier and with directions they soon found themselves at the address Hašek had written down. It was close to the centre of the city.

Hella accepted the pared-down version of their story and invited them in. She heard all they had to say and to her credit, as far as they were concerned, seemed to believe it.

'You'll come?' Ankers asked her.

She would not say one way or the other. It was all a shock. She needed time to think about it. Ankers told her how concerned

Hašek was that the Honecker regime might do a Deng Xiaoping and send the tanks in. 'I need to think,' Hella repeated.

She said the city was theirs and suggested they return at 6 pm, by which time she would have reached a decision. Ian looked at Ankers, who shrugged his shoulders. 'The city is ours,' he said.

They walked to the real Alexanderplatz, after which the East German ghetto in Tirana had been named. They had even told Hella about that and she had grinned uneasily.

'Maybe she thinks the whole thing is completely made up and didn't believe a word of it,' Ian said abjectly.

'Quite possible,' Ankers agreed, 'but we've got to take her at face value.'

Buffeted by strong winds that lashed the wide, empty square, the two men sat down on a bench. Neither of them had much of an appetite for sightseeing. Ian took his sticks and began tapping out a rhythm on the arm of the bench. The piano did twelve bars in his head and the flute came in. He hummed the flute melody and continued to snap his stick down on the rim of the side drum and mark every alternate bar on the high-hat. A sax had joined the flute.

Ian looked round at Ankers. He was humming the same tune.

'"2nd Avenue Blue",' Ankers said. 'I love that song.'

'Yeah? Really?'

'Yeah. Love it. It's one of the best.'

'That's weird,' Ian said. He had stopped drumming. Ankers quizzed him with an eyebrow. 'Well, it's one of my favourites as well. A lot of people have a go at Buddy Rich, simply because he's the best. He's the king, and people always like to knock a king off his throne, you know?' Ankers nodded. 'He is the best, though. And the prince is Art Blakey.'

'I'd go along with that,' Ankers nodded. 'I could get my sax out and we could play,' he suggested.

Ian thought a moment. 'Better not,' he said.

Ankers was relieved Ian said that. It wouldn't be fair to take him to Norway. He'd freeze in that thin white coat. But they probably wouldn't even get there, anyway.

'I mean, we *could* go back to Tirana and then come back in

time for 6 pm,' Ian said. 'But it's probably not a good idea. We should stick around.'

Ankers was glad to see Ian embracing the team spirit. He leant down to the catch on his case and snapped it open. Withdrawing the painting, he said, 'Look, I've got something to show you.'

Ian looked at the painting and his eyes opened wide as saucers.

'Fucking hell!' he gasped. 'That's a Delvaux. Look! There's his fucking signature.'

Ankers nodded vigorously. He knew.

'Shit. I just got that print from the train. This is an original.' Ian shook his head. 'You didn't tell me he'd given you a painting. I assume he gave it to you.'

'Yes. He gave it to me.'

'And I don't know it. Is it a new one?'

'It's new. His most recent picture. He did it while I was in his studio. You obviously like his work a great deal. What do you think of it?'

Ian looked closely at the painting. He took it from Ankers and turned it to get the best light. 'It's great,' he said. 'It's vintage Delvaux.' He turned the picture again and studied it. 'It's like *Chrysis* with the woman taking up the foreground and looking straight at the artist. But different. For a start she's wearing a dress.'

'Yes,' Ankers said.

'Or *is* she? There's something not quite right about it.'

'You know who that is?' Ankers asked.

'What do you mean?'

'The woman in the picture is Inger. My girlfriend.' Ian looked at Ankers and the Norwegian nodded. 'Inger,' he repeated.

'When did Paul Delvaux meet your girlfriend?'

'He didn't.'

'You gave him a photograph.'

'I gave him nothing. He's never met Inger. But that's her. Absolutely no mistake.'

The wind whipped across the square. Ankers saw Ian's grip tighten on the picture and smiled.

'How can he paint your girlfriend if he's never met her?' Ian asked.

Ankers lifted his hands palms upwards to the sky. 'The same way he made me dream about his women, I suppose. Maybe it's all Hašek's doing. Though I guess it's not that simple. Who knows how it all started to happen? Except that it did happen. There's no doubt about that.'

'I thought *you* thought this could all be somebody's dream. Yours or mine. Or Hašek's. Or Paul Delvaux's, for fuck's sake.'

'Yes, but even if it is . . . It's still happening, isn't it? We're here. You're holding that picture.'

'You'd better put it away before I drop it,' Ian said, handing the painting to Ankers.

'I know you wouldn't drop it.'

'It's beautiful,' Ian said.

'He got it slightly wrong,' said Ankers. 'Inger doesn't have a red dress.'

'Artistic licence.'

'Yes. And these mountains behind her. I don't know where they're supposed to be. Delvaux's idea of Norway, I guess. But there's something about them, about the way he's painted them, something I'm not sure about.' Ankers put the picture away in his case.

They walked around to pass the time. Ian beat his stick against his legs. Near the Brandenburg Gate they encountered the beginnings of a demonstration. People were massing in the space between the street and the Wall. Ian saw a few banners still unfurled and clasped by the sides of their carriers. A green van arrived and disgorged a number of policemen, who formed a line of defence between the demonstrators and the Wall. Ankers asked a boy the time and beckoned to Ian. It was time to make their way back to Hella's. They walked side by side against an influx of people going to join the demonstration.

'I hope they don't send the tanks in,' Ankers said.

Most of the people who passed them were young and had the greater part of their lives before them, whichever side of the Wall they lived them on. They were living now, Ankers thought. *I hope they go on living. They're too young to die.*

'I've decided,' Hella announced, taking a sharp breath as she showed them into the apartment. 'I'll come with you.'

On the walls were framed art prints and shelves stacked with so many books they sagged under the weight. Ian looked at the names on the spines. There were hundreds of political works, in German, the whole suggesting a left-wing bias.

'You're interested in politics,' Ian remarked.

'That's my boyfriend,' she said. 'They're mostly his books.'

'Where is he?' Ian asked.

'He's not around,' she snapped, and drew a short breath.

'Sorry.'

'He's in prison. Here in East Berlin. They got him at the Wall. He was trying to escape. It was a crazy idea. It was never going to work.' The speech had left her breathless.

Ankers waved the visas limply. 'You don't have to try to get over the Wall,' he said. 'I've got your escape route here. All legal and aboveboard.' She looked away. 'Nearly,' he added.

'I've packed a bag,' she said. They saw it, a small, tight hold-all standing by the desk at the far end of the room. Hella was taking short, shallow breaths, and appeared anxious.

'Are you OK?' Ankers asked her.

'I'm OK. Let's go, shall we.' She was nervous.

'You have asthma, don't you?' Ankers said.

'Yes, I do. So what?'

'Well, I reckon if you were to relax a little, you'd find it easier.' Ankers remembered from his mother's *Reader's Digest*s kept by the spare bed that anxiety is a frequent cause of attack for asthma sufferers.

'Thank you,' Hella replied icily. 'But I know how to change my own condition.'

They fell into an awkward silence, broken only by Ian playing an imaginary cymbal – *Ts ts ts ts ts.*

'So, you got a car?'

'Sadly, no,' Ankers said. 'We go from Zoologischer Garten.'

'That's in the West.'

'Yes, I know.' Ankers waved the visas again. 'That's why Hašek had to raise such a lot of money. These things aren't easy to obtain.'

'For a Czech living in East Berlin, they're the stuff of dreams,' she observed. 'It's ironic to think,' she added, 'that in order to escape East Germany, people have been fleeing to Prague. Hašek knows that Czechoslovakia is not such an easy country to leave.'

'Unless you're East German and you take refuge in the West German embassy. I don't think the West Germans would welcome the Czechs or the Romanians with such open arms.'

Ts ts ts ts ts.

'No,' she agreed. 'The fatherland looks after its own.'

Ts ts ts ts ts.

'How do we get there?' she asked.

'It's your city,' Ankers said, spreading his hands. She gave him a look. 'We cross over to the West at Friedrichstrasse,' he said.

Ts ts ts ts ts.

When they crossed the frontier at Friedrichstrasse U-bahn station, Hella was obviously excited, although she pretended not to be. In spite of her resigned shoulders and introverted mood, her eyes sparkled with the joy of discovery. She was like a little girl taken somewhere by her parents and determined not to show her enjoyment.

Ian attracted stares from fellow passengers by drumming on the edge of the seat. *Tick tick ti ti tick ti tick tick ti tick.* He showed less interest in their surroundings than Hella.

'What do you think is going to happen here, Hella?' he asked unexpectedly.

She looked at him in surprise. 'I don't know,' she said. 'Either the Stasi and the army will crush the demonstrations like in China. Or the government will give in to the protesters and introduce reforms. They may open the Wall.'

Ian and Ankers laughed. Of the possible consequences, opening the Wall was the one that seemed most unlikely. It was the kind of thing that wouldn't be conceivable for ten years, or five at the soonest.

The train slowed down as it passed through the ghost stations between Friedrichstrasse and the Wall. While most passengers stared at the floor, Hella, Ankers and Ian looked out at the desolate platforms and each entertained private thoughts.

Hella lost some of her inhibitions when they emerged in West Berlin. She turned and craned her neck at advertisement hoardings and gross displays of wealth. Zoologischer Garten station was crawling with vagrants.

'I wish we had time to look around,' Hella said.

'The train leaves in ten minutes,' said Ankers. 'We could grab something to eat but that's about all.'

They got a bagful of junkfood and boarded the Vienna train.

'Vienna,' said Hella, enjoying the word. 'Wien. We might see Harry Lime.'

She was excited now and appeared quite relaxed. Her breathing was normal and quiet.

The journey to Yugoslavia – via Vienna – proceeded largely without incident. They talked but in no great depth. They watched the countryside go by the window with no special enthusiasm. For Ankers and Ian the novelty of travelling by train in the real world soon wore off. Ian played with his sticks and Ankers was tempted to get his sax out, but the thought of leaving Hella stranded on the train stopped him.

In Ljubljana they switched trains to go to Belgrade. There were no interruptions where the line passed from Slovenia into Croatia, then into Serbia. They slept most of the time. Ankers dreamt of the Albanian coastal plains, the land dotted with pillboxes and out of each one stepped a marble replica of Inger. Her eyes shone at him like those of an elk he had once caught in the headlamps of the old Taunus.

Ian slept badly. He was troubled by vague coagulations of darkness, which almost formed into recognizable shapes, then fell apart again into chaos.

He was woken up several times by the smell of damp carpets.

Each time he stared in terror into the darkest corners of the compartment, but could make nothing out of the huddled forms slumped there.

Hella dreamt of a golden-haired little boy, her son Karl, who stood before her and laughed away the sooty bullet hole in his forehead. His laughter bubbled like a spring and filled her with so much joy she thought she might burst. As he laughed, the wound smudged and became lighter in colour, as if an animator were erasing an imperfection from his hand-drawn character. When it had completely disappeared he stopped laughing and ran off, skipping and jumping towards a high whitewashed wall. 'No!' she screamed after him. 'Stay away from the Wall. Stay away!' A crack resounded dully in the warm air and the black-ringed hole reappeared on the boy's forehead. He cocked his head and started to laugh. Running back to his mother he laughed and chuckled, pointing at the bullet hole. She gnawed at her fingers, biting the knuckles raw till they bled. But the boy laughed and when the wound started to fade again she felt the pain leave her and happiness begin to flood into her heart.

So it went on.

In Belgrade they stepped down from the train like empty husks. They drank small cups of bitter black coffee in a vain attempt to revive their bodies and spirits. The train to Niš in southern Serbia was slow and extremely uncomfortable. The other three seats in their compartment were occupied by thickset men of varying ages, but all old in their attitude. A bookbuyer from Macedonia asked Hella where they were going. Ankers answered for her: 'Prishtinë.'

'Priština! Priština!' The bookbuyer scowled. 'You're going to see the Albanians.' Ankers just returned his gaze. 'They are animals,' the man said with distaste. 'They have ten, fifteen children and they run around without shoes.'

It didn't sound like bestial behaviour to Ankers but he kept his own counsel. In his experience, prejudice could rarely be challenged head-on with any success. After a while the bookbuyer gave up and sat back in his seat, muttering some remark to the old man in the next seat, who merely grunted and cleared his throat of phlegm.

In Niš all the signs and names of shops were written in the Cyrillic alphabet. With an hour to kill before their connecting train to Prishtinë, Ankers, Ian and Hella walked into the town. They passed a siding where two huge steam locomotives rusted quietly. The streets were dusty and hot. Ian was particularly downcast.

'It's the Cyrillic,' he explained when Ankers asked him. 'Seeing it reminds me of the transplant boxes.'

'It's not your fault, what's happening,' Ankers pointed out. 'It's just happening. You can't expect the dead to have any morals. And we're doing our bit to bring it all to an end by helping Hašek. He dreamed of Albania first, remember. Who knows, when Hella's kissed him and he can breathe and play again, maybe we'll all wake up. The dead will rest again.'

'Yeah. Maybe,' Ian grimaced.

They sat outside at a restaurant and ordered three salads. The waiters wore traditional dress which seemed at odds with the glum, modern décor. The salads came in small bowls accompanied by a pitcher of water with half a lemon floating in it.

It wasn't that much further to Prishtinë, but the train was a local diesel and very slow. It was packed with Serb families returning to Serbian towns and villages between Niš and Prishtinë. Ankers and Ian and Hella attracted a great deal of curiosity from the other passengers. Sitting opposite Hella, Ian drummed his hands sullenly on the seat. Slowly the train emptied and night fell. They stopped at tiny stations decorated with row upon row of beautifully scented blooms. An attendant would appear from a dark doorway smoking a cigarette and the train would pull its doors shut and set off again.

With the windows open the night was an animal, roaring and exulting in the chase. When they stopped at a station the beast paused for breath, exhaling great wafts of warm air into the train and recovering its strength for the next bout. Its sleek velvet coat was the jet-black sky, its eyes stars or the moon twinned with a lantern burning in a cottage window.

Prishtinë was hot and throbbing. The train disgorged them into the animal's belly. Its liver and lights shone with a purplish hue.

The plan was to find the Grand Hotel Priština, where a reservation would have been made in Ankers's name. Someone would arrive to pick them up within a few hours.

The hotel appeared to be the tallest and newest building in the city. Although it was the middle of the night, there were people milling around in the foyer area. Journalists or businessmen, Ankers guessed, most likely journalists. Prishtinë, as the capital of Kosovo, had become the main focus of media attention in the province.

The rooms had been booked. One for Hella, one for the two men. Ankers put his ID away and the desk clerk handed over both keys. 'Breakfast is at 8 am,' he said with a smile that was slightly askew.

'*Faleminderit.*' Ankers thanked him in Albanian.

Hella said she was going to bed. Ankers said to knock on the wall if she needed anything; he and Ian were next door. While Ankers stretched out on one of the twin beds and kicked his shoes off, Ian went to the window and looked out.

'It's like Tirana,' he said. 'A bit.' When Ankers said nothing Ian turned to look at him. The tenorman had fallen asleep. Ian washed in the bathroom, examining his face in the mirror. He looked tired. Overall, he was happy to be here. His life had changed completely. He relied more on himself now than he had done before. He didn't need another person's approval in the way that he'd needed Lucy's. He was becoming a stronger individual while at the same time contributing more to others.

He worried a little that the team placed so much faith in Hella. She was a likeable woman, feisty and independent, yet quite unfathomable. She was holding something back, some hurt or betrayal. Maybe it was just the change in her circumstances, however, and the strangeness of the task she had been asked to perform.

Ian used the toilet, then did a dozen sit-ups before getting into his bed. It was good to feel sheets and blankets next to the skin again. They smelt of fresh laundry. Ian smiled and lay awake waiting for a tap on the door before he too drifted off to sleep.

Like a Million Wasps

Hella woke Ankers and Ian at 8.10 by knocking on the wall. Ankers groaned and turned over. Ian said, 'Nnnnn,' and stretched. He felt as if he'd only been asleep five minutes. Hella knocked again. 'What do you think she wants?' Ian asked.

Ankers sat up and rubbed his eyes. 'I feel like shit,' he said. 'I wish I'd taken all this off.' His clothes were crumpled and sweaty. 'I'll go and see.' He levered himself out of bed and cracked a joint standing up.

Ian got up and pulled his clothes on while Ankers went next door. He was washing his face when the Norwegian returned and muttered, 'She only wanted to wake us up for breakfast. I just want to go back to bed.'

'I think some breakfast will do you good, though,' Ian said, drying himself. Ankers hesitated. 'Is Hella ready?'

'Yeah.'

'OK. Well, we'll go down and get a table. You have a shower and join us in a few minutes.'

Ankers considered this and smiled weakly. 'OK,' he said. 'Sounds good.'

'How long do you think we'll have to wait?' Hella asked Ian, as he poured her a second cup of coffee.

'For Ankers? He'll be down soon.'

'For the people who are picking us up.'

'I don't know.' Ian took a roll and broke it in half with his fingers. 'Ankers said it wouldn't be a long wait.' He buttered the roll and took a bite. 'I love food,' he said. Hella was distracted. At that moment Ankers appeared, in a state of excitement and carrying his case and Ian's white coat.

'What kept you?' Ian asked.

'They're here,' he announced. 'They're waiting close by, about ten minutes' walk away. They rang up; I spoke to someone.'

'We can finish our breakfast, can't we?' Hella asked. 'We've been waiting for them. They can wait for us a little.' She had gone white in the face. Presumably she was nervous, Ian thought.

'No, we've got to go,' Ankers insisted.

'Ankers, why don't you just have a cup of coffee? You'll need it. Later you'll wish you'd had it.'

Ankers looked at Ian. 'What about Hašek?' he said, with a simple plea in his face that made it look as if they were boys deserting a friend in some schooltime adventure.

'I'm sure he'd want you to have some breakfast. Sit down for a few minutes.'

Ian was persuasive but gently so, Ankers thought as he crunched a crusty roll. He was all right; he liked him.

'Where's my coffee, then?'

'In the pot,' said Hella.

Ian poured him a cup. Hella seemed combative this morning. Why couldn't she just relax? Ankers unsnapped his case and took out Ian's sticks.

'You left these upstairs,' he said.

'Thanks.' Ian grinned. 'I knew they were there.' He prepared to play a roll on the coffee pot. Ankers smiled but Hella seemed detached from them. He slid the sticks into his back pocket.

'Shall we go?'

They walked past the reception desk. Ankers had already handed in the keys. Bright sunshine assaulted them in the street. Old men in tall dome-shaped white caps stepped lightly through the dust of the main shopping street. There was no tension, apart from at their sides: Hella was fairly humming like an over-stretched guitar string.

'It's not far,' Ankers said. 'Are you OK, Hella?'

She just stared straight ahead. Ian touched Ankers on the arm and said quietly, 'She's OK. Just leave her.'

Ankers pointed in the direction they were to go in and Hella strode off first.

'What's wrong with her?' he said to Ian.

'Nerves. She's just nervous. Think about it. We've convinced her she's going into the lion's den and she's frightened about it now the time is imminent.'

'I don't know,' Ankers mused. 'She's hiding something. I can't help feeling she's keeping something back. Like she's playing cards and she's got a couple up her sleeve.'

'Nah, she's OK,' Ian said. 'I wasn't sure at first, but I think she's just shit scared.' He rolled up the sleeves of his coat. 'Come on, or she'll be going without us.' They trotted after her. Two soldiers with red stars on their caps watched them lazily.

They turned left off the main road into a shopping precinct. There were small boutiques run by young people wearing fashionable clothes and hats. Teenagers stood around in groups chatting and smoking. Boys perched on window ledges to talk to girls serving up crêpes. Ankers ducked into the entrance to Besnik's Pizzeria and spoke to the tall man behind the bar.

'This is Besnik,' he said to Ian and Hella. 'He's helping.'

Besnik opened a door at the back of the restaurant and they filed out. In a small yard a battered Citroën stood waiting. The driver flashed his uneven teeth at them and said, 'I'm Fatos. Get in. Let's go.'

The Citroën must once have had good suspension, but years of punishment around the poor-quality Kosovo roads between Prishtinë and the Albanian border had taken their toll. They hurtled south on the main road to Skopje and soon swung off to the right through the villages of Lipljan, Stimlje, Crnoljevo and Blace. Hella's breathing became laboured. As they sped through the town of Prizren – where Albanian flags fluttered outside some houses – Ankers wondered out loud how the road came to be so clear of military patrols.

'This trail has already been blazed,' Fatos called back from the front seat. 'People started entering Albania two nights ago. For so long we have been kept out. The Serbs always talk about us wanting to annex Kosovo to Albania. It was not true. We wanted Kosovo to become a republic, within Yugoslavia, like the other republics.' He took a corner between two high walls at 65 kph and Ankers began to sweat, Hella to pant. 'But now the government in Albania has fallen we can go there and not have to give up our cars, our clothes, our money.'

'What about the dead people?' Ian said. 'Don't they put you off going?'

'Why should they?' Fatos asked gleefully, as he accelerated out of the town and into a long straight. 'Enver Hoxha has been dead for four years, but his spirit is rampant. We Albanians know what ghosts are. Sooner or later they all lie down and die.'

As they approached the border and were waved through by Albanian guards, Ian felt he was returning home. Then he noticed the tears pouring down Fatos's cheeks. In the back seat Hella was wheezing each time she drew breath.

For Hella it was a journey into hell. Yes, she was terrified of confronting the dead, but she was more profoundly distressed by the plan she had formulated: to contrive a split from the Norwegian and the Englishman and go in search of her son Karl. When she had found him – hopefully in the East German ghetto 'Alexanderplatz' – she would use whatever breath remained to her to resurrect him. Then she would proceed to the Hotel Tirana to pass on the gift of life to Hašek. But only if the act of resurrecting her son had not exacerbated her asthmatic condition so far that she was unable to do so. Rationally, she still didn't believe this nonsense, though if it might restore her son to life, she would do it.

It was becoming increasingly painful and difficult to breathe. Her lungs seemed to have shrunk to the size of an apple and her windpipe had become as narrow as its stalk. The closer they got, the more anxious she felt and consequently the asthma attack became more severe. The air in and outside the car changed, grew thicker, and soon it was grainy like a photograph taken on fast film with a long lens. It buzzed at her like a million wasps until her head began to hurt. She wondered if she was trapped in somebody's nightmare.

It was evening but still light when they finally descended from the hills into Tirana. A tyre had been shredded on fallen rocks between Murë and Lis, requiring a change of wheel. Subsequently the gear box almost disintegrated on a particularly steep uphill section. But Fatos proved himself more than competent and the minimum of time was lost. Ian and Ankers both noticed how Hella's condition deteriorated as they neared the city. They were solicitous but powerless to help. She had medication but its effectiveness had been tested and broken.

224

Hella had decided that since neither of the two men knew she had a son – not even Hašek had been told – she could simply ask to be put down at Alexanderplatz while they went to tell Hašek she had arrived.

'I think . . . it might . . . give him too great . . . a shock . . . just to see me . . . without any warning.' Ian looked round at Ankers. 'I think . . . you should warn him . . . first . . . Also . . . I'd rather get used to . . . looking at . . . these creatures . . . before I . . . see Hašek.'

She knew what she said made perfect sense. They were bound to agree to it.

At first it looked like any other poor city with its stores and tenement blocks. She was struck by the earth-coloured dust, which emphasized throughout the city that the countryside was never far away. Where she came from in Czechoslovakia there were just patches of green recalling the rural landscape to the memory of the city dwellers. In Berlin, of course, the very centre of the old city was now a grassy, rubbly waste land bisected by two parallel walls.

Then she noticed the virtual absence of private cars and the knots of unkempt men tied to street corners. She didn't know if they were natives to the city or abominations out of dreams.

They passed through an enormous square and Ankers tapped her on the shoulder to point out Hašek's hotel. He said she was to come back there within fifteen minutes. Did she have a watch?

'I can estimate a quarter of an hour,' she said.

'You can't get lost,' the Englishman told her. 'The city is too small and all roads lead back to Skanderbeg Square.'

'I won't . . . get lost,' she gasped.

They dropped her in Alexanderplatz, which was basically two or three blocks of flats and an old official-looking building. When the Citroën had disappeared she went into the old building, pulling a photograph of her little boy from her back pocket as she climbed the short flight of steps. If she found it difficult to walk, climbing was excruciating.

Shutters and blinds had been closed and the only light came from power switches and dials on electrical units, and from TV screens. At first she couldn't see anybody. It was like being in a

225

haunted electrical-goods showroom in the middle of the night. Haunted because she could sense the presence of others.

Moving out of the lobby and into one of the rooms she caught sight of a number of people, but they were no more than disembodied faces suspended near the base of a wall, or propped up in an armchair. The faces flickered in the light of a dozen TV sets crammed together at one end of the room. The televisions all showed different pictures. Frequently a channel would be switched and Hella noticed the shadowy, drab bodies to which the faces belonged, as they pointed a remote control at the wall of televisions.

In the cacophony it was impossible to distinguish the sound coming from any one television. The hum and throb of dishwashers and washing machines from the lobby and other rooms added to the confusion.

Aware that she only had so much time before they came looking for her and determined to locate her son, Hella ignored caution and threw the switch for the lights in the centre of the room. Three bulbs came on out of a possible six and the dead things stirred.

Hella took as deep a breath as she could and spoke out loud.

'I'm looking . . . for a little boy,' she said. 'He's eight years old . . . small and thin . . . blond-haired . . . Has anyone seen him?' She looked at the faces, which returned only blank expressions. 'I've got a photo,' she said, holding it out for those nearest to see. She wondered if she could be heard above the racket and was relieved when one or two men muttered in reply, even though the responses were negative. She switched the lights off and left the room.

Other rooms on the same floor offered the same prospect. She thrust the photograph before vacant stares but nobody betrayed any sign of recognition. She had wasted at least ten minutes. At the foot of the stairs she looked up and wondered if she could make it. Then, very clearly, she pictured Karl standing next to an upstairs window, evening light falling across his forehead, spinning a web of shadows around the bullet wound. She found the strength to climb the stairs.

Inside a room piled high with big cardboard boxes bearing the names of Japanese hi-fi manufacturers three men sat around a table drinking and shuffling papers. Much more alert than the creatures watching television, they turned to look straight at Hella as she entered their room. One man started to draw all the papers into one pile as if they were confidential. He only had one eye. The left socket was a black hole leaking matter and pus. In this perverted evolution she supposed he was a recent victim, shot at the Wall or clubbed at a Leipzig demonstration, while the things downstairs had been dead for years.

'This boy,' she said. 'My son . . . Have you seen him?'

The three men studied the picture. The one-eyed man took it carefully between thumb and forefinger. A lengthening silence exasperated Hella. She drew a breath, sharp as razor wire.

'It looks like little Karl,' the man said, showing it to his nearest companion. 'Don't you think?'

'That's his name!' she shouted. 'Where is he?'

'He's your son?'

'*Where?*'

The man stood up and beckoned to Hella as he moved towards the window. From downstairs the noise of the televisions suddenly unified as if all the viewers had suddenly decided to select the same channel.

'Across the street,' the man said and pointed to the third storey of a dismal block of flats. 'Second window from the end, I think. He's really your son?'

But she was already out of the room and half running, half stumbling downstairs. Ragged cheers went up from the TV lounges on either side of the lobby and Hella caught snatches of commentary: 'Wall . . . Communists . . . opened the Wall . . . incredible scenes here . . .' She realized dimly what must be happening but could only think of Karl. At least twenty minutes had elapsed since Hašek's friends had left her. It wasn't that she wouldn't happily resurrect her ex-husband if indeed such a thing were possible, but she had to reach her son first and give him what she could. If there was anything left over, Hašek could have it, but Karl came first. Karl was her flesh and blood; Hašek was a memory.

She ran across the street, her lungs now the size of a plum and diminishing. In the doorway to the building she bumped into a shaggy form and left it sprawling in the dust as she raced for the stairs. She counted the floors, convinced she was going to pass out before reaching the third. Down in the street a car honked its horn and squealed to a halt. She went the wrong way down the corridor and whirled round. Two doors from the end she burst into a darkened, sweltering hallway. There was a sweet smell which she attributed to her own exertion. Footsteps rattled up the staircase behind her. She slammed the door shut, praying silently, wild eyes scanning the options. Only one door was ajar. She ran to it and shouldered her way into an empty, stinking room. Back into the hallway. She twisted the next doorknob. Locked. She doubled back and tried the one on the other side. The door opened and she saw inside. Her knees went completely weak and she used the doorknob to pull herself up.

He stood exactly as she had pictured him. By the window. The bullet hole ringed with burnt flesh and soot.

Fists pounded on the door to the flat.

Breathing like a small, inefficient machine, she approached her son. 'Karl.' She spoke his name in her head. His eyes were glazed over but she knew he could see her.

The flat door was kicked in and men rushed into the hallway, giving chase in that heavy-footed, indignant way that only men can.

Little Karl. If she kissed him he would live again.

And grow into a man.

Like any other man.

Like the men behind the door. Like Trefzger, her ex-lover, father of Karl, who had stubbornly taken their son with him when he attempted to flee across the Wall. She had begged him not to. Had forbidden him to take Karl. He took no notice.

'*He's not going to rot here like you. He's coming with me to the West.*'

'*It's not where he is. It's who he's with, you selfish bastard.*'

'*He's coming.*'

'*He's staying.*'

'*I'm taking him and you'll have to kill me to stop me.*'

In the event Trefzger was wounded in the foot and banged up in gaol. Karl was shot in the forehead. They told her he died instantly.

The door splintered.

She drew a breath that almost burst the plum and clutched

Karl's body, steeling herself against the feel of his cold flesh.

The door gave way. But too late. She had already pinched her son's nose and breathed as hard as she could into his mouth.

PART III

Now's the Time

'When I paint, I am in fact in the painting.'

– Paul Delvaux

Lovers' Embrace

Ankers had broken the door down but Hašek was the first to step through into the room. Just behind, Ankers and Ian flanked him like lieutenants. In the corridor Bentinck and Gabriela, Violeta, Leka and Fatos jostled for space.

Hella's eyes met Hašek's. Her face had turned a shade of peacock-blue from the effort of resuscitating Karl. The look between them was charged with knowledge and desperation. And anger: betrayal tasted just as sour to a dead man.

He took a second step into the room. Hella, still clutching Karl to her, twitched backwards. She took a final shuddering breath and blew into her son's mouth.

Even from outside the room they could see the boy's chest swell as the air entered his lungs.

As soon as he had set eyes on the boy, Hašek had worked it out. This explained why Hella had always refused to talk about her boyfriend. He'd given her a child and the child had died. At first, when the boy was alive, she would have wished to avoid hurting Hašek by telling him. Later, after the boy's death, remaining silent would have protected her from an added dimension of grief.

Hella's grip on the boy loosened and her legs crumpled, causing her to fall backwards and collapse on the floorboards.

The boy swayed a moment, then his mouth twitched and he coughed. Hašek watched in dumb amazement as the cough grew worse but at the same time brought colour back to the boy's face: two bright scuffs of scarlet on his cheeks. The boy eventually controlled the cough and began to laugh. The light in the room faded another shade and he laughed louder. It was undoubtedly a trick of the twilight, but Hašek could have sworn he saw the bullet wound on the boy's forehead smudge and disappear.

Hašek looked forlornly at the deflated figure of Hella lying on the floor like an old coat at the back of a cupboard. His chance to live and play again had been and gone. He felt bitter regret twist in him like a gutting knife.

The boy ran between Ankers's and Ian's legs to the door and escaped into the corridor still laughing. Hella didn't stir. Everyone stood rock still as Hašek took two more steps into the room. It was almost possible to hear dust settling and the scrape of long shadows as they slid over the floor.

Suddenly Ankers moved. He marched across the room, into a cloud of dust motes suspended in the window's light. The air swirled about him. He grasped Hašek's shoulder and turned the man round to face him. He looked into his eyes for an instant and was appalled by the resignation he saw in them. Hašek had been broken.

Ankers hoped it wasn't too late as he clasped his hands behind the other man's head and placed his lips on Hašek's. He tightened the embrace and kissed him as closely as if they were lovers. He felt his own lungs deflate like bellows as his gift of life entered Hašek's body. The man's chest expanded and Ankers hugged him tighter to squeeze the air out. Second-hand air fed back into his own lungs and he breathed through his nose. He blew again, relaxing his hold slightly while Hašek's lungs filled up, then tightened his grip.

They clenched and unclenched in the middle of the room like lovers.

The others held their breath in anticipation. The crumpled form of Hella shifted slightly and squirmed like a cat under a blanket.

The tension broke when Hašek first resisted Ankers's tight embrace. He tried to push the Norwegian away, but Ankers held on, not knowing if he had been successful or not and anxious that he shouldn't have wasted his breath.

But Hašek pushed him roughly away and staggered towards the door. Those in the doorway parted to let him through. He stumbled down the corridor. Ankers listened carefully to his fading footsteps and was filled with great joy to hear a very faint cough echo in the crumbling stairwell.

Excited and relieved, and nervous – they didn't know why

Hašek had fought to get free – they let him run off into the night.

Hella had got to her feet and made uncertainly for the door. They let her go too.

She had found her long-lost son tonight: she didn't want to lose him again.

Drifting back to the hotel, they broke out into groups and tried to deny the general feeling that the resurrection had been an anti-climax.

Ian, who had been watching Gabriela since her arrival in Tirana, was enormously flattered when she fell into step with him and began to talk. She asked him where he was from and what he was doing in Albania. He answered her questions hesitantly and didn't know how to phrase his own. As they entered Skanderbeg Square waves of warm, cigarette-scented air rolled over them. The grand buildings and the less grand tenements made soft echoes of the hundreds of footsteps crossing the square this way and that.

Bentinck walked into the square with Leka and Violeta. His enthusiasm for the Kosovar musician grew exponentially as he spent more time in her company. Leka talked to him about stories they had both covered from their different points of reference. While he was interested in what Leka was saying he couldn't concentrate as long as Violeta was walking beside him. He heard the gentle plod of her canvas shoes and the brush of her denimed legs against each other. He didn't know if what he felt was love or lust. But whichever, it made his heart beat faster and his breathing erratic.

At one point when Bentinck turned to Violeta to ask her something, Leka looked around and couldn't see Fatos.

Ankers found himself on his own and couldn't help feeling that the others were avoiding him. Perhaps they weren't sure what to think about his action on Hašek until they knew if it had worked or not. Maybe they had been shocked or repulsed by the precise nature of what he had done, or was it just the idea of resurrection that disturbed them?

He peered into the dusty, yellowed streets that radiated from the square and wondered down which one, if he went looking, he might find Hašek. Surely the man was alive – his cough was evidence – but how had he taken to it? What if he couldn't handle coming back to life? Had Ankers been too rash?

These thoughts worried at him and with sudden clarity he realized he hated this sultry southern city with its fine, insidious earth and stifling air, and its life-and-death paradoxes. Norway was cleaner and simpler. You knew where you were in Floro. Living people walked around and said good morning. The dead lay still under the earth.

And Inger vacillated somewhere in the middle.

He ached for her as he crossed that alien square. He longed to see her turquoise eyes with the yellow ring around the pupil. He still didn't know if that ring disappeared as the pupil dilated, or if it was merely stretched too thin for his eye to see. He wondered if Delvaux knew.

He had to return to Norway and find her. He felt it was inevitable now that she would have left their house in Floro and gone back to the north. He had originally feared she would seek refuge in the arms of her family. Now that was his hope, for nightmares were forming vaguely in his mind in which she was a passive, almost willing victim. In his separation from her he had become firmly convinced that she was in some undefined way linked to the sea. When she sleepwalked it was always in that direction. When she sat and stared out of the window at the sea it was with the most heart-rending yearning in her eyes.

He was scared because he didn't understand. She had some deep knowledge or instinct that he had only glimpsed. Delvaux's picture in which she and Hašek swam with the mermaids had unsettled him, but the one he carried in his case had become a source of terror. He felt certain it contained a terrible prophecy.

When they got back to the hotel Ankers watched Bentinck, Leka and Violeta head towards the downstairs bar, and he himself approached the stairs. He ran up to the fourth floor and was panting by the time he reached his room. He pulled the saxophone case out from under the bed and unsnapped the catches. But he stopped before opening the case and pulling out the picture.

He had been in such a hurry to get at the saxophone case he hadn't noticed it at first, but there was a strong smell in the room. A smell of salt. And something else too. The second ingredient was elusive. Ankers sniffed the air like a dog but couldn't identify it, though he felt sure it was a familiar smell and that he would kick himself when he realized what it was.

He took the picture out and looked at it. The canvas felt almost alive in his hands. It was tense like a skin over a drum. The colours seemed more vibrant than ever before. The red of her dress was more vivid; the stark chiaroscuro of the peaks and troughs behind her even more pronounced. He held the painting close to his face and examined her eyes. The artistry vanished: it was exactly like looking into her actual eyes. The pupils were dilated and at first Ankers thought the yellow rings had disappeared. Then he wasn't sure. There was a hint of yellow. But that could be just because he imagined it there. Or it could be that Delvaux had somehow managed to paint yellow rings thinner than the finest down.

Her irises shone with the blue of the sea and the grey of the sky.

Ankers couldn't be certain that her pupils hadn't dilated further while he'd been looking at the painting. They now looked big enough to fall into. He wished he could do so and thereby look out and see what was frightening her. The backdrop looked unthreatening to one familiar with the wild northern coastline of Norway: sharp peaks and deep gullies in which ice slides glistered and glaciers creaked.

She looked so frightened. He felt so protective towards her.

Dropping the picture, he grabbed his saxophone out of the case. He just blew – played anything – hoping against hope that it would work. There was no reason why it should, since it hadn't worked playing with Hašek's cassette in the hot, stinking room where the three headless corpses sat out the decade. There was no reason why it should, but Ankers thought it just might. After all, no one had believed the Berlin Wall would fall, but it had, that very day. Maybe the time now was right and it would work.

He played. Improvised according to his instinct.

It must work!

But it didn't. The walls of the room stood firm. He saw nothing.

The smells seemed less strong now. But that could have been because he had got used to them. Whatever it was mixed in with

237

the smell of salt was still a mystery. Ankers put the saxophone back in the case and lay on the bed holding the picture to his chest. Sleep came.

He was awoken later by a great commotion in the square. Climbing groggily on to one elbow, he looked out of the window. The square was a seething mass of bodies seemingly dancing and swaying in celebration and waving flags. The sky above the western side of the square was florid like Turner's greatest excesses. The colours of the flags as they caught the first rays of ruddy sunlight were the red, white and blue of Czechoslovakia. *Now the world really is going mad,* he thought.

From rooms around his, excited commentators' voices blared out of TV sets. There were thousands demonstrating on the streets of Prague and risking their lives. What was there to prevent Wenceslas Square becoming another Tiananmen Square?

Suddenly there was a banging on Ankers's door. He jumped out of bed and stood behind it timidly. A voice boomed his name. It was Hašek. Ankers opened the door. The Czech stood there, red-cheeked and breathing great draughts of air. 'Ankers,' he cried and clasped the taller man to him in a bear hug. Ankers's heart filled with emotion. 'Thank you, Ankers. Thank you. This is a night to be alive. Have you seen them?' He swivelled Ankers round to face the window.

Ankers nodded. 'I've seen them,' he gasped.

'Get your sax,' Hašek ordered. 'We're going to Prague. This is history. I want to be there.'

Ankers thought furiously while he quickly pulled on his clothes. He took the case from under the bed and glanced round the room to see if there was anything he'd missed. The temperature in the city seemed to have risen still further, but he grabbed his fisherman's sweater and tied it around his waist.

Downstairs the foyer was overflowing with dead Czechs celebrating: they thought their hour was at hand. Hašek led Ankers down to the bar, where he was welcomed by Bentinck and Violeta – she was sitting on Bentinck's lap and pouring drinks down her throat – and Leka, who looked on in amusement. Bentinck looked delirious. Ian and Gabriela were sitting in a corner huddled over a table. At some remark he sat up and looked at her face. She stretched a hand to his cheek and gently stroked it.

'Let's play,' Hašek said to Ankers, leading the way to the far end of the room where Ankers and Ian had seen him on their first day in Tirana miming to the barman's CD collection.

Hašek blew his first note and immediately Ankers recognized the unique style that had attracted him to the Czech's playing in the first place. He was reminded of the adventure they had embarked upon together in the dunes of Belgium, where a painter played god with the lives of those he touched.

Ankers sat down on a chair to play and kept his case on his lap, since he wanted to make sure he took it with him. It still smelt of salt and . . . what?

He began to play.

Ankers didn't know if it would be possible for them to play together yet go to different places. He felt confident. If this strange phenomenon was headbound, as he believed it to be, there shouldn't be any problem. He would go where he wanted to go. And Hašek would go to Prague. He didn't think the Czech would miss him once in Prague: he would know people there, maybe meet up with the rest of the Jazz Group.

So he played his tenor in pursuit of Hašek's alto, occasionally leaping out in front to lead the way for a spell. Cigarette smoke and the sticky aroma of ponç drifted over them from the audience, but soon all Ankers could smell, as he screwed his eyes tightly shut, was salt – the sea splashing on the rocks, fish gathering in shoals, seals bobbing in the shallows, seaweed straggling over the sand – and something sharp and tangy like the smell of ozone in an electrical storm.

Something *like* that.

Waves of Pleasure

Bentinck couldn't believe his luck when Violeta, who in the bar had sat in his lap and easily outdrunk him, suggested going up to his room for half an hour or so.

Half an hour or so! Why so long? Bentinck thought to himself gleefully. He looked forward to *several hours* of sustained lovemaking of a kind he had not known for some time, that is, with someone other than himself.

He didn't pretend to her or to himself that he knew her at all well. There was obviously no need. They were getting to know each other better. Lust was not wrong, as Anna had told him. How right she had turned out to be. He only wished he could tell her.

Throughout the day Bentinck had been out examining Tirana with his meticulous reporter's eye. At first he had observed the dead things warily, but as soon as he sensed their torpor and lack of aggressiveness he found himself going right up and scrutinizing them. He tried to talk to members of the native Albanian community, but found them unwilling to discuss much beyond football. Even then they restricted their contributions to reeling off lists of favourite players' names.

'Matthäus. Völler. Lineker. Baggio.' They pointed at Bentinck's chest as they repeated the name of the West German centre forward, Matthäus. Bentinck resented the implication that they thought he was German himself.

'I'm Swiss,' he told them. 'Swiss.' The small, clean and proud, independent country's name seemed to mean nothing to them, which he considered curious given the circumstances of their own sovereign state.

He walked all over the city, longing for his IBM and his camera. He had witnessed a miracle but had been unable to report it. He felt like a storyteller whose tongue had been torn out. Frustration had built up over the day until it melted away in the bar thanks to Violeta's attentions and a great many glasses of ponç and raki.

Leka did his best to persuade Bentinck that reporting the events mattered less than simply experiencing them at first hand, which is what they had had the opportunity to do. So they were fortunate. It was an argument that appeared more and more attractive as the evening wore on.

When Violeta whispered into Bentinck's ear that half an hour or so in his room might not be a bad idea, he glanced at Leka, hoping the man would be looking elsewhere and oblivious to what was happening. But Leka winked salaciously at Bentinck. Unable to stop himself, Bentinck grinned back and Violeta urged him to his feet.

Hašek and Ankers seemed to have disappeared but music was still playing through the barman's loudspeakers. Bentinck noticed a few tables away Gabriela smiling at Ian. He looked happy but nervous. Bentinck followed Violeta to the door.

She started kissing him in the lift up to the sixth floor. So clearly delighted with events, Bentinck worried for a moment if he wasn't presenting a slightly pathetic spectacle. He determined not to become overwhelmed by Violeta's greed. He didn't want to lose face.

Once inside his room Bentinck tried to slow things down a little just to give him longer to fantasize about their imminent clinch.

'Leka,' he said. 'He doesn't mind?'

'Leka and I are very good friends,' Violeta replied ambiguously. She undid the top button of his blue shirt. He lacked the willpower to resist any longer. She undressed him swiftly and needed no more than ten seconds to take off her own clothes. He revelled like a boy in the sight of her body, but she had already crossed to the bed.

They made love quickly. After only ten minutes Bentinck was flat on his back with Violeta sitting astride him wondering where it had all gone. All that boyish enthusiasm and childlike excitement gone in ten minutes. And she had been quite fond of him: it wasn't *just* an exercise in sexual gratification.

*

He was drifting off on waves of pleasure. It had been without question the finest fuck of his career. He wanted to file a story on it but remembered his IBM was in a different hotel in another country. His mind freewheeled in pleasurable delirium, a state of mind he experienced all too infrequently to ignore.

But there was something he'd left undone, something unfinished. *What was it?* Violeta was still sitting on him. She'd squeezed him out and drained him dry: she was an accomplished lover. But there was still some vague part of the whole operation left undone. *What though?*

Violeta shifted slightly and looked away from Bentinck. When he lay on his back his face became even more jowly and his abdomen puffed up with fat. She didn't mind his size – on the contrary, fat men were an occasional pleasure she liked to indulge – it was the way he had flaked out after coming. It was rather like delivering a speech on stage as if it were a soliloquy, while the other person on stage, who had been acting her little heart out, was left suddenly speechless.

She had to regard it as fairly typical of his sex, however, so shouldn't be too surprised. It was only one of the ways in which men demonstrated their remarkable selfishness. They were still children; they took all the honey and sweets they could get their hands on. They didn't know how to stop. Nor how to share or give back. It simply wasn't part of their make-up.

Not all men were like that, Leka had told her on so many occasions. But in her experience they were. And Leka, though she loved him dearly, was no exception.

In the dim quarter of his mind that had not yet succumbed to sleep, Bentinck realized what it was he had forgotten – to smoke a post-coital cigarette.

Languidly he considered it now, but thought he would have some trouble holding it between his lips.

Violeta climbed off the bed, regarding him with detachment. She looked at his trousers, which lay extended but crumpled on the floor like the trousers of one who had spontaneously combusted.

A large orange handkerchief protruded from the right-hand pocket.

She left Bentinck's room and found Leka still in the bar. He was stretched out on a bench seat, the table nearest to him piled high with bottles and glasses. She looked at the empty platform at the end of the bar, where Hašek and Ankers had played together briefly. The echoes of their music could still be heard above the sound of Leka's deep breathing. She wanted to play again herself but her bass was in Prishtinë. Tired after her quarter of an hour in Bentinck's room, she too lay down on a seat and went to sleep.

When she woke up the bar was resounding with harsh noise. She looked about anxiously but it was only the hotel staff cleaning up. They simply swept dirty glasses off table tops into big brown-paper rubbish sacks. Leka was drinking coffee.

'How long have you been awake?' she asked him.

'Half an hour. You looked exhausted, so I let you sleep. You want a coffee?'

'You know I never drink anything, or eat anything, until after 11 o'clock. Why should this morning be any different? Do you think our journalist friend might have dehydrated me?'

'What was he like?' Leka asked.

'Like?'

'Was he as good as me?'

She considered this for a moment, then said, 'He could have been.' He raised his eyebrows but she shook her head. 'One question only,' she said. 'You know the rules.'

He laughed. 'Here,' he said, pushing his coffee cup across the table in her direction. 'Have some.'

'I told you. Not before eleven.'

'But it's not before eleven,' he said, enjoying having the upper hand back. He showed her his watch. 'It's almost midday.'

'Shit!' She jumped up. 'It's late.'

'What for? Nothing's happening. Hašek and Ankers have vanished. I want to look round Tirana, but ... when you're ready ...'

'Let's go,' she said, grabbing his cup and swallowing the remaining coffee.

*

243

They went first to the city art gallery. The doors were unlocked and no one was about. Leka worried about the safety of the collection but when they got inside they could see nothing had been stolen. The dead things obviously had a healthy respect for art.

The Museum of National History also was untended but the exhibits looked undisturbed. Several dead things were wandering around casting a glum eye over models in peasant dress and displays of early agricultural tools.

They walked freely into the government buildings and Leka sat in the chair that Hoxha himself would have occupied before his death in 1985.

'We still don't know what's happened to Fatos,' Leka said to Violeta, his voice echoing in the great chamber.

'Maybe he's found himself a nice little place to move into,' she suggested with a grin. Fatos's only known ambition had been some day to live in Albania.

They spent the rest of the day snooping around, seeing how people had lived in this city they had dreamed of so many times and never been able to visit. It was, in many places, a beautiful city; in other areas it looked like a half-finished housing estate.

The Albanians smoked strong-smelling cigarettes on street corners. There wasn't much to buy in those shops that were still open for business. There was a constant buzz of sound from thousands of televisions tuned to the various countries from which the dead things had been exhumed. Their voracious consumption of television after death suggested a bizarre form of womb nostalgia. Hašek had explained it as part habit, and part catching up on lost time: if they hadn't been allowed to watch certain things in their lifetimes, there was nothing to stop them now. The more curious pointed their aerials and dishes in all directions to pick up whatever signals they could.

It occurred to Leka that with all this hardware available to those with cash, he could probably secure himself a basic video camera and record everything on tape for Prishtinë Television. But, as he told Violeta, being in Albania had changed him.

'I no longer have to report on "being",' he explained in a low voice. 'I can simply "be". This place is about life itself. It's an essential place. You have to live in the present. When you're reporting, you're constantly thinking about the future, how it will look on the screen. It feels good to have thrown that off.'

She nodded her understanding and sneaked a sidelong glance at his profile. Maybe this would be their chance to make a go of it together. No more one-night stands and casual affairs. She had always wanted him to commit himself to her and he had shied away. If she asked for the same kind of commitment now – a pact for the future – his reaction would be the same. But if she changed her demands and looked for a commitment in the *present* tense, maybe Leka would seize the opportunity. She knew the future had always frightened him, and framing it inside a TV screen had always been his way of dealing with that. He should find the present easier to accept.

And the present gives rise to the future as surely as it flows into the past.

'By the way,' she murmured. 'Bentinck *wasn't* as good as you.'

He looked at her suspiciously. 'You said he could have been.'

'I was lying. They've never been as good as you. And you know it.'

They walked back slowly in the direction of Skanderbeg Square and at one point, just before they disappeared behind a plane tree thick with summer foliage, he took her hand.

'He Has Come!'

Prague was a city intoxicated. And on edge. Like an occupied city that knows a liberating army is marching on it and is due to arrive any day.

When Hašek came to, he was sprawled across a gravel path in the big old Jewish cemetery to the east of the city. He gathered himself up and slung his alto round his back on its cord, and looked around for Ankers. There being no sign of him, Hašek imagined he might have taken the opportunity to go home to Norway. He knew Ankers was anxious to locate Inger. He just hoped he would be able to get back to Tirana without the tenor player's help.

The air tasted different but it was as warm and heavy as in Tirana. Hašek walked towards the exit, passing Franz Kafka's grave and giving it only a glance.

On the boulevard he was swept along in a great stream of excited Czechs carrying flags and banners and heading west. There were chants of 'Freedom! Freedom!' and 'Free elections!' One large banner not unfurled until they were closing in on the city carried Mikhail Gorbachev's appeal for perestroika in the Soviet Union: 'When, if not now?' And as the march progressed the message became stronger: 'We don't want the Communist Party!', 'Forty years are enough!' and 'Jakeš, this is your end!'

The size of the march was growing all the time. Hašek was just one among many thousands. People who had been watching the demonstration on their televisions switched off and joined in.

The column streamed along the bank of the River Vltava and was met by troops and police with dogs. Národní Street, a main thoroughfare leading from the river to Wenceslas Square, was blocked at both ends by police. Thousands were trapped and they continued to wave flags and banners.

Hašek experienced a tightening of the chest. He knew the

situation was dangerous but he wouldn't have missed it for the world. If by playing his saxophone he could return to Tirana and save his skin, he would just as soon toss his reed into the deep waters of the Vltava.

He was, after all, a Czech, not an Albanian.

The police began charging indiscriminately into the crowd and using batons to beat bystanders.

Sections of the crowd charged the police in attempts to escape attack. Some inroads were made and demonstrators, Hašek among them, slipped into side streets.

The city centre rang with derisory shouts and whistles and calls of 'Murderers' and 'Gestapo' directed at Party leader Miloš Jakeš and Prague Party chief Miroslav Štěpán.

From balconies high above Wenceslas Square people waved their support. A hotel chef threw his white hat into the air. Customers and staff in coffee houses, hotels and bars shouted encouragement from doors and windows. A sausage vendor abandoned his stall and followed the crowd.

'It's the end, Miloš!' and 'Jakeš out!' the cries went up. One middle-aged man in a peaked cap raised a banner proclaiming simply that 'truth will prevail', and the thousands packed into Wenceslas Square raised their voices to sing the national anthem.

Hašek thought about providing instrumental support but decided instead that the circumstances called simply for him to add his voice to those of his countrymen.

People rattled keyrings every few minutes to signify the death knell of the communist leadership. The more agile demonstrators scaled telephone boxes and newspaper kiosks to wave their banners. Scaffolding on the side of a building had become an enormous climbing frame.

From inside trams that had been caught in the great sea of humanity, old men and women leaned out of the windows holding candles and waving, tears streaming down their faces. The tram drivers rang their bells in sympathy.

Rumours flew around that the city had been surrounded by tanks, but the collective euphoria was so great that fear could find no fertile ground. Everybody could recall the Tiananmen Square massacre but that had been before the Berlin Wall came down. There was a sense in this city that the Wall's demise had changed Europe irrevocably and that the fall of the Czech government was just a matter of time.

Hašek knew that somewhere in that surging press would be his old friends from the Jazz Group. He had wanted to find them and share the excitement with people he knew, but the feeling of community in the crowd was so strong that he already felt he was with friends. It was possible too that Hella had found her little boy after he had run off and had brought him back to Prague rather than Berlin. Wherever she was, Hašek wished her well. She had been faced with an unenviable choice and he didn't blame her for making it in the boy's favour. It was the natural thing to do.

A huge roar went up from the crowd, followed by a quickly building chant of 'He has come! He has come!' Heads turned to one side of the long thin square and Hašek saw an unmistakable figure standing on a balcony, lit from one side and stretching his arms wide as if to embrace the city and its people.

The former Czechoslovak leader Alexander Dubček had waited twenty-one years for this moment. Ousted for his part in the Prague Spring of 1968, when he attempted to introduce 'socialism with a human face', Dubček had been 'exiled' to Bratislava, where in his every move he was treated with extreme suspicion by the security services. Now the time had come for his return. For him to appear could only mean one thing. 'Long live Dubček! Long live Dubček!' the crowd bellowed.

When the crowd allowed him to be heard he spoke succinctly, but his message was historic.

'Everyone is responsible for the future of this country and the future of our children. We must find a way to democracy and we will fight for it, because it will not be easy. This country has experienced many military interventions and we will not be frightened this time.'

The people cheered him. Hašek's voice rose with those of his countrymen.

'It is only a dream perhaps that everybody – the people, the workers and the army – should stand together but I am sure we are still able to make our dreams come true ... our beloved Czechoslovakia will be free again.'

At this the masses erupted with a chorus of 'Goodbye Miloš'.

They sensed the imminent departure of the Party leader and mocked him publicly in front of the world. It was a measure of how confident they had become. Hašek knew that even now – especially now – it could turn sour. It had before. If the tanks came . . .

But they stayed away.

The celebrations began in earnest while the sackings of Miloš Jakeš and his entire politburo were still rumours kicking around the streets. Someone had painted huge English letters on the back of a newspaper kiosk in the heart of the square: 'It's over! The Czechs are free!'

Before daylight the government had been swept away.

Hašek stayed in the square with thousands of other revellers. His mind kept returning to the twentieth anniversary of Jan Palach's supreme self-sacrifice, when he and the Jazz Group had played and then he had slid through the police lines to escape the city in a second-hand Tatra. Maybe the subsequent massacre had been more than a dream. It had perhaps been a vision of what could have been or could be in the future. Or had it been a prophecy of Tiananmen Square?

He didn't know: he'd only dreamt it.

Almost a year had passed since that flight from his own country. Ten months squeezed into as many weeks. The calendar had been reduced to a flux. The seasons were tied in a muddle and now in Prague in November it was warmer than the hottest July afternoon at neighbouring Hungary's Lake Balaton.

Dead men had walked in Albania. Not only that but they had created distinct social groups and an economy, one based on a plentiful but ultimately limited material. They ate and drank instinctively and habitually. But they couldn't play the saxophone. He would always be in Ankers's debt. Life was infinitely sweeter than death and Ankers had made him a gift of it.

At some point in the morning Hašek walked out of the city centre to the south. He found his flat with no difficulty and let himself in. Even in a state of exhaustion he was affected by the strangeness of the flat. It felt as if he'd borrowed a key to somebody else's apartment. He walked around touching things: a dirty mug, a clock that was still keeping the time, a pile of sheet music, his favourite cushion on the sofa. The familiarity of these objects felt like a conspiracy.

Eventually he dropped the saxophone on the sofa and kicked his shoes off. He peeled off his clothes and collapsed into bed. The sheets were so soft he thought he'd been wrapped in cotton wool. As his eyes closed he caught a glimpse of Ankers striding up the side of a mountain, his face white as snow and eyes haunted by fear.

Once asleep, however, Hašek dreamt of Albania. He saw himself tramping through Skanderbeg Square, pausing for a while at the foot of Hoxha's statue. He wanted to touch the great foot like a child would. He reached out. The foot was hot. He snatched his hand back with a low grunt. Then he looked up at the giant and gasped. It was ablaze. It shimmered scarlet and purple and threw off little darting tongues of orange. Hoxha stood proud inside his aura of fire, radiating power over the vast square. It was still his domain.

Old dictators never die. They just get cast in bronze.

Licks of green played about Hoxha's fleshy lips. His eyes were lit up for a second and were cast instantly into shadow. The sun had slipped behind a tall block of flats on the western side of the city. The statue was suddenly dark and foreboding. But still alive to the touch. Hašek tried to grasp the loose material of his trousers and found it warm but unyielding. With no conscious intention he climbed up on to the pedestal and clung to the leader's legs.

The sun chose that moment to emerge from behind the block of flats. So close to the horizon and refracting through veils of pollution, it shone a deep, lusty red. Hašek looked up at Hoxha. The man was aglow, like a hot poker. Hašek felt the heat pass into him and hugged his legs a little tighter. He pressed his cheek against the bronze and watched the sun slide slowly beneath the horizon. Soon there was just a bloody thumbnail remaining and then that was gone too.

Hašek held on to the dictator's legs for some time more, as he gradually cooled and returned to his statuesque nature. He reasoned that some of the heat must have transferred into him because by the time the great man was cold as a corpse, sweat was rolling off Hašek on to the dusty ground beneath their pedestal.

When he woke, Hašek was bathed in sweat but it was Ankers's face he saw in his mind's eye. The desperate man was still climbing his mountain. Hašek lay on his back worrying about Ankers. He hoped he was safe and that he'd found Inger, and that Ankers's fears for her safety had been unfounded.

Light leaned inwards from the windows. His flat never seemed to get any direct sunlight. The corners and angles of the furniture he could see from where he lay looked soft and blurred. The walls were the colour of hessian. One or two prints hung where he couldn't quite make them out. It still felt like someone else's flat. And he wasn't impressed with the owner's taste. He noticed a pair of shoes on the floor by the narrow, understocked bookcase: they looked so cheap and forlorn he just wanted to be out of there and finding his own life again.

There was an alien smell in the flat. Something he didn't remember from before. Rolling over and stepping out of bed, he padded round the bed-sitting room in search of the smell's source. He sniffed the walls, his few books, the dusty shoes, before he spotted his discarded clothes slung over the back of an ancient armchair. He approached them and recognized the smell of Tirana. As he realized it he felt a pang of regret. It was, after all, the city of his rebirth. He felt a strong pull to go back there and play in the hotel's basement bar and see again the people he'd only briefly got to know.

Pulling on fresh clothes, which were musty but clean, he took up his saxophone from the sofa. He knew he needed Ankers to duet with him, but began to worry that even with Ankers maybe the trick would no longer work. If they had been able to dream themselves around Europe while playing music together, it was probably because the continent was in a state of flux. But now the changes had occurred: the fall of the Wall and the sweeping away of the communists in Czechoslovakia. Europe could produce no more earth-shattering events than those. Hungary, Poland and the Soviet Union were changing gradually in their own sweet ways. Bulgaria was rock solid and change in Romania was unimaginable. Stalinist Albania, the strangest country, had hosted their shared dreams, but would surely by now have reverted to its true state. Chaos had run amuck, felling the Wall and the Czech communists, but now reason would have returned to claim back its land, chasing away the dreams and re-establishing its tyrannical laws of nature.

He blew anyway and thought only about Tirana.

The fact that within a very short space of time he found himself back in the Hotel Tirana sitting on the edge of his foul-smelling bed meant that the reign of chaos was far from over. The march of unreason had advanced so far that he now no longer needed an accompanist to make his fantastic voyages.

He lay the saxophone down on the bed and stood up to look out of the window. The same mixture of ragged dead things and host Albanians swarmed over the square like ants under a rock. Stalin still lay sprawled across the road. Heat rose from the baking surfaces in shimmering waves. He looked for the statue of Hoxha. That was still standing, overlooking the square from a commanding position. Skanderbeg too remained aloft astride his mount.

Hašek left his room and went downstairs in search of life, in the midst of death.

Touch of Velvet

Gabriela had been drawn to Ian by his skin colour and his youth.

During her working days in Bucharest one of the very few enjoyable jobs had been when the Zimbabwean ambassador to Yugoslavia, on a visit to Bucharest, had sought her out on a recommendation. He was the first black man she had slept with, practically the first she had seen at all, and the experience struck her as subtly different; almost pleasurable, in fact. He had been so indulgent and deferential towards her, and later so sensitive.

She didn't know if it was his being black or of ambassadorial class, but it meant she was curious about Ian. More than curious: it seemed inevitable they should sleep together, as if she'd dreamt it.

Also, Ian looked so vulnerable, like a boy out of his depth. Even in soaring temperatures he hugged his now filthy white coat to him. It seemed to offer him some protection against the unpredictability of Tirana. If he had enjoyed the city's diversions at one point, he seemed tired and withdrawn now. She couldn't deny she felt a strong maternal instinct towards the boy – he must be at least fifteen years her junior.

She felt, in fact, an intoxicating mixture of the maternal and the erotic. It excited her to invite him up to her room after an evening spent in the bar. She sat cross-legged on the bed while he sat on the stiff-backed chair by the table.

'You can't be comfortable there,' she said. He said he could. What she failed to appreciate was that he liked her a lot and found these come-ons enormously exciting, but was too nervous to show it. 'Why don't you take your coat off and come and sit on the bed?' she said.

He couldn't answer.

'Come on,' she coaxed him.

He stared at the floor.

She stretched out an arm towards him. He knew he had to respond or offend her. So he joined his hand with hers but looked away. She pulled gently and laughed quietly when he offered slight resistance. Eventually he allowed her to pull him on to the bed where he sat awkwardly.

'You don't need to wear your coat indoors,' she said, pushing it slowly off from his shoulders. He didn't co-operate. The coat came off anyway. 'Ian,' she whispered. 'Do you like me?'

He was burning inside, passionately wanting to respond to her advance, and couldn't quite work out why he was so nervous. He'd made love before and he'd been rejected before. Neither possibility should frighten him unduly. He wondered if it was Lucy's betrayal but couldn't believe it played a part. It dawned on him that he hadn't felt fear like this since being trapped in the train. How could the train have anything to do with it?

Gabriela was making small, quiet movements behind him. Reaching to unzip her dress at the back, he finally understood that he was scared. Why scared? Did he think she would laugh at him? He felt certain she would not. Why should she? Unless it were all a trap. But he'd have to be paranoid to believe that. Which he wasn't.

A considerably attractive woman was getting undressed behind his back, and she was doing it undoubtedly for him, and for herself. He was aroused. That wasn't the problem. He'd been aroused sitting next to her in the bar, admiring her white arms and velvet dress. He'd brushed his hand against her dress on two occasions, saying he liked the touch of velvet.

He was made to feel dizzy, as if by the motion of the train. Then he felt her hand on his shoulder. She leaned forward and said, 'Help me.' He forced himself to turn slightly. She had turned as well to offer him her back. She wanted him to unfasten the clasp of her bra. He waited. She waited too, bending forward. With trembling fingers he undid the catch surprisingly easily. In a flash she pulled the bra forward and turned round before he turned away. She grabbed his head and pressed it into her breasts. He resisted only for a moment. She smelled enticingly of sweat. He could feel her heart beating fairly fast and thought she might be nervous too.

They'd broken the ice but Ian still had a vague feeling of

foreboding. She found his sticks in his back pocket and hit them playfully on his leg. He grinned. 'We ought to play together,' he said.

'Oh, we will,' she smiled. 'We will. Stand up for a second.'

He did as told and she unbuckled his trousers. They and his shorts were round his ankles before he could even think about being embarrassed. Her speed and efficiency made him think of what he knew she had done for a living in Bucharest. But he wasn't put off. He felt strangely proud instead. All the men she must have screwed out of obligation and still she wanted him.

Ian's heart was beating so fast and furiously he thought it might burst.

'I love your dress,' he said, caressing it where it lay on the bed next to her left leg. She looked appraisingly at his body. He looked shyly at hers. She was bigger than him and very beautiful. He knew that in a moment he would touch her skin, feel it brush over his: it was a delicious moment of anticipation. With great slowness he saw his own hand stretching to touch her wrist. It ran slowly up her arm, with a lightness of touch that Gabriela found extremely arousing. She wanted to feel his body pressed against hers. She stepped closer. Their legs touched near the top, then their stomachs and chests. Her arms slid around his back and pulled him towards her. He gripped her just as tightly and squeezed.

Lying alongside each other on the bed they swapped long and sensuous kisses. His fear had gone and Gabriela was still calming his nervousness. Her hand ran up and down his back, over his buttocks and across the backs of his legs. She moved down the bed a little and kissed his chest. He looked at the top of her head and saw the thousands of tiny hair follicles in her scalp. At any other time they would be ordinary, but to him now they represented the mysterious perfection of the human being.

He was aware that she had taken hold of his aching cock and was caressing it softly with the palm of her hand. He kissed her head, luxuriating in the feel of her hair. It smelt of cigarette smoke from the bar, but underneath was the warm smell of her body. He grasped handfuls of her hair and covered his face with it. He ran a hand down the side of her body towards her waist and stroked her stomach. She moved her head and looked up at him.

'In my bag,' she said, motioning to the side of the bed. Puzzled, he reached behind him for a small sponge bag on the floor by the bed. She pulled out a condom packet and looked at him again. *Yes, yes,* he tried to say with his eyes. She tore the wrapper and withdrew the condom. Using only one hand she rolled it on to his cock and he was glad to have been spared the task, which always required his two hands and made him regain all the self-consciousness he might have managed to lose.

She kissed him again, sensing his hesitancy and wanting to put him at ease. His erection had lost some of its rigor. He returned her kiss with enthusiasm, but Gabriela broke away and rolled on to her back. Ian sat up. She was still stroking his leg.

'Come in me,' she said quietly, opening her legs a fraction.

He looked for the first time at the dark triangle of hair at the top of her thighs and felt his resolve returning. Gabriela's legs opened a little wider and Ian felt something else growing within him. He could hear something, a rustling. The dark tunnel between Gabriela's legs beckoned and the fear washed over him again. He could hear water rushing now. Gabriela was looking at him in concern. Couldn't she hear it too? He looked down at her.

'Don't be frightened,' she said, sitting up to hold him around the waist.

His eyes were wide in terror. 'Can't you hear it?' he hissed.

'Yes,' she said. 'I can hear it. But it's all right. It'll go away. It's up to you.'

Ian was confused. If Gabriela was the tunnel, then she was trying to trap him. If he went inside she would drown him. One of her hands reached into his lap and gripped his cock.

It was still firm. It had to stay that way. She clasped his face in her hands and kissed him on his forehead, his nose, cheeks, lips and his throat. She stroked his head reassuringly and climbed to her knees to hug him as tightly as she could. He cried out. She tried to soothe him with kind words. He looked momentarily perplexed. She seized her moment, pushing him down on to his back and was on top of him in a second, easing herself down on to his erection. He struggled to get free but she had him in a clinch. She thrust hard into his body and thrust again and again, using her muscles to squeeze his flesh.

The train was in the tunnel and Ian flailed about in the darkness. The rushing of the water was getting louder. The door at the end of the aisle was caving in under the pressure. With an almighty crash the water was through into his carriage. He ran between the seats but the wave caught him and brought him down. It roared past his ears and he knew it was all over. He allowed the force of the water to push him on to a bench seat; he lay back on it, drawing last desperate breaths before the level rose above his seat. He didn't have the willpower to fight this time.

Level with his chin, the water surged forward in another wave. Ian took a deep breath and ducked under, clinging to the seat rather than floating to the surface. He opened his eyes under water and peered through the murk at the green-and-orange patterned seats and the small scraps of marine detritus floating about his head like dust motes in the air.

When he woke up, Gabriela was stroking his forehead. She smiled at him. 'You slept for hours,' she said. 'And I'm not surprised. That was an incredible night.'

The way Ian had made love once he had conquered his fear had recalled the stranger in Bucharest. Indeed, he was even more sensitive and attentive. She trusted him and gave herself to him in the same way. Could the stranger have been an emissary from the future?

Ian felt as if he'd just woken up from a nightmare and was still shellshocked. Gabriela kissed him and placed her hand on his chest. He took it in one of his own and kissed it. She drew him towards her and held him tight.

'That was amazing,' she said. 'When can we do it again? You were like a rocket.'

Not quite, he thought. *Not quite a rocket. But almost.*

He grinned as she pressed his head against her breast. He felt like he'd exorcized an old demon – or had had it exorcized for him. Perhaps he was falling in love. And maybe, just maybe, it would work out this time. He kissed Gabriela's breast, aware of the infectious rhythm of her heartbeat, and hugged her as hard as he could. Tracing his fingers down over the lovely swell of her stomach, he hesitated only a moment before sliding two fingers into her.

Gabriela sucked in a breath and arched her back slightly.

Ian smiled.

The touch of velvet.

A Place in Heaven

The line-up was complete except for one man. Ankers was still nowhere to be found. Hašek knew he had to be in Norway but could only hope he was safe, and that he had found Inger unharmed. Everyone else was present and spirits were high. They had acquired some instruments and even two or three accompanists from one of the local folk groups. He looked down the line and saw Gabriela sitting at a borrowed Korg and next to her Violeta, tuning an ancient-looking double bass. Ismail, a dark, quiet man with lugubrious eyes and a downturned mouth, perched on a stool, a flute in his hands. Behind Hašek, Ian was still exploring the different sounds available to him on a drumkit assembled with help from the Palace of Culture, the Tirana Radio Orchestra and a local acoustic group. A smiling Mehdi Bajri waited with his shiny guitar, on which he normally played Beatles covers in the basement of the Hotel Dajti. Two more Albanians stood by with drums strapped round their necks that looked straight out of New Orleans.

They had already decided on '2nd Avenue Blue', which had been Ian's suggestion. Gabriela and Violeta started together and Ian soon came in and gave the nod to Ismail, whose flute playing was exquisitely languorous. The air in the bar was already thick with smoke and alcohol fumes. There was a low murmur of chatter. Hašek could see Bentinck and Leka sitting at different tables, both watching Violeta intently as she laid the foundations beneath Ismail's flute and then Mehdi Bajri's guitar as he advanced hesitantly into his guitar solo.

For Ian the song evoked Brighton beach. Because he was playing rather than humming or merely hearing the music in his head, the memory had the texture of actual experience. He imagined he could feel the breeze on his cheek and smell the salt, and the seaweed and sewage. When Hašek came in to appropriate the tenor solo on his alto, he played deliberately low in the register and produced a sound that was as smooth and luxurious as the sky had been that night in Brighton.

The pain of earlier years was now a memory. He had successfully come to terms with his guilt and had managed to step out of the past and into a confused but exciting present. Gabriela, for the time being, was his support in this new world. Her piano solo was next, Ian remembered. As Hašek's counterfeit tenor faded away Ian listened for Gabriela's Korg.

She was leaving it late. Maybe she was letting Violeta take the bass solo first. But then he realized he couldn't even hear the piano in the rhythm at all.

He opened his eyes. The band had stopped playing. Gabriela's piano stool was still there behind the Korg, but she wasn't on it. Ian's head sank on to his side drum; he couldn't believe this was happening to him. Just when he had thought he had found something extraordinary it was taken away from him.

Shouts erupted from outside the bar. Sounds of excitement.

Gabriela's disappearance.

It was impossible.

Not Romania.

After East Germany, it was possible Czechoslovakia might go. But not Romania. Nothing could possibly change in Romania.

Plunged into the thick of a huge crowd massed in front of the Presidential Palace in Republic Square, Gabriela instantly had full knowledge of what her friends back in Tirana would be watching on television. She knew, as a dreamer knows, that an anti-government demonstration in Timişoara had prompted a vicious crackdown by the security forces that was unprecedented in Romania's communist history. There had been a massacre. Estimates placed the number of dead between 200 and 5,000.

The gathering in Bucharest came later but time was no longer the linear constant she had known before her escape from the country. Everything seemed squashed into a continuous present.

The people in Republic Square had been brought in to show popular support for Ceauşescu. He needed to restore his credibility in the eyes of the world. His complacency, coupled with past experience, led him to believe it would be easy. The Chinese authorities had massacred thousands in Tiananmen Square, but it wouldn't be long before the world conveniently forgot. Already senior American officials had popped up in Beijing to extend the hand of forgiveness, smiling for Chinese TV and toasting Li Peng, mastermind of the massacre. The world's memory was short. Timişoara would be forgotten like a bad dream. All it needed was an adoring crowd and a brief public appearance.

People in the crowd held banners aloft declaring their unswerving support for the regime. A man in a cossack hat and thick overcoat appeared on the balcony of the Presidential Palace and the crowd murmured its reluctant approval, because each person knew that a potential informer would be standing within arm's reach. Fear was a great motivator.

Gabriela felt something sharp twist inside her when she saw it was Ceauşescu who had stepped on to the balcony. She almost didn't dare look at him. Fluids began to circulate in her body but her mouth was dry. Her feelings were mixed up. The only one she could name was fear.

But there was another emotion burning in the breasts of those present: hatred. Of course, they'd hated him for years, students and young workers for their entire lives. But events in Timişoara had poured fuel on their fires. Some sensed that a new stage had been reached. Timişoara had changed something in the guts of the country.

Gabriela watched in amazement as a few brave individuals threw down their banners and touched-up enlargements of the dictator and his wife, and began shouting things out. Ceauşescu had never once been heckled. She feared the students would be swiftly dealt with before their protests could be heard above the noise of the crowd and the public address system through which Ceauşescu droned.

But the students continued to barrack the dictator and workers joined in, dropping their loyal banners and their pretence. They shouted 'Libertate! Libertate!' and 'Yesterday Timişoara, today Bucharest'. Scores of people tore up the national flag. Gabriela felt a great tide welling up inside her. Part excitement, part fear, she determined not to give in completely to emotion lest she miss something crucial.

On the balcony Ceauşescu had stopped speaking and was waving his arm at chest level as if to swat an irritating swarm of gnats. He was suddenly transformed from the devil incarnate into a frail old man confronted with an unimagined challenge. He clearly didn't understand. His top security chiefs told him day after day that the people loved him and he apparently believed them.

Gabriela felt convinced that her whole life had been leading up to this. Seeing the feared dictator so obviously hurt, she almost began to feel pity for him. But she saw the danger in that and squashed it. This was a man she had hated. He alone was responsible for the misery of millions of Romanians. Because of him she had lost her home and sold her body to survive. The knowledge that she had the capacity to feel sorry for him was enough to earn her a place in heaven. So she turned her pity into righteous anger and screamed her protests alongside tens of thousands of others. They shouted, 'Tell us what happened! Tell us what happened!'

Then the police responded with tear gas. They were trying to disperse the crowd. Ceauşescu had disappeared from the balcony. The demonstrators retorted, 'We are here to stay.' But the security forces sensed the explosive potential of the demonstration: it could easily turn into revolution, which had to be avoided at all costs. They sent in tanks, armoured vehicles and helicopters. The Securitate unleashed a brutal assault on the crowd, knowing that if Ceauşescu fell they would face death themselves. For the first time in their history the tables had been turned and they felt fear. Students fell as automatic fire rained down on sections of the crowd. Those who went to rescue injured friends were mown down by armoured personnel carriers. Tanks rolled into the crowd crushing people like wicker baskets.

Gabriela managed to evade assault. She ran out of the path of one armoured vehicle and ducked behind a building when she caught the eye of a sniper aiming his rifle.

The city descended into chaos. The flux of which Hašek had spoken seemed to be twisting time itself. Gabriela had a distinct but inexplicable impression that time was passing at great speed whereas it appeared not to be progressing at all. The sky had not changed colour since she had arrived in Bucharest: the grey, wintry clouds had a strange green cast to them, which she had seen only once before, after her visit from the stranger.

Soon there were tracer bullets describing orange parabolas in the air over the square and surrounding streets as the Securitate troops fought to put down the threatened revolution. She was aware that people were dying around her, yet she felt strangely detached. Her head was swirling. The battle was soon over but it seemed to have gone on for hours. Buildings were on fire, cars overturned and alight, corpses littered the streets and there was a pungent smell of smoke. The army had switched allegiance from the state to the people and now tanks advanced on Republic Square, carrying students and workers who believed their hour had come. The crowd regrouped in front of the Central Committee building. Gabriela jumped on to the back of a tank and rode into the mêlée. She thought of her beautiful black boy in Tirana and hoped she would see him again before she died. She had imagined him before finding him and he was even more exciting than her fantasy. This bound them to each other: she knew they should be together.

The crowd swelled and pressed against the main entrance of the Central Committee building until the doors gave way and the most adventurous spirits rushed in. Armed guards made no attempt to stop them, saying, 'We cannot shoot the people.' The revolutionaries accepted their offer of weapons and began to take over the building.

Gabriela watched from her position in the middle of the crowd outside, exhilarated by the moment of revolution. More and more people streamed into the building, but suddenly all heads in the square tilted upwards to the roof, where figures were rushing towards a waiting helicopter. She gasped as she recognized the silhouette of Ceauşescu and glimpsed the shape of his evil wife Elena. Bodyguards scrambled with them into the helicopter and demonstrators swarmed on to the roof as the craft was taking off. They jeered but were too late to prevent the escape.

She had worked herself up into a frenzy at the thought that they would get him and tear him limb from limb right there on the roof. She felt like she had while coaxing Ian into making love to her: awash with fluids real and imaginary. The despair that filled her when the huge winged bug took off with its cargo of vermin safely aboard was total. She seemed to be drowning under an unstoppable tide of filth and was only barely aware that she was about to faint. The last thing she heard was the crowd singing an adapted football supporters' chant: 'Where's Ceauşescu? There's no more Ceauşescu.'

Everything was dark. Out of the darkness came a buzzing. It grew louder as it came closer like a blowfly or a wasp. But it was still dark: she tried but couldn't see the silvery sheen of an insect's lacy wings.

She felt no physical sensation and didn't know if she were vertical or horizontal. There was no discomfort. She wondered if she might be floating, or flying.

The buzzing increased in volume. She was aware of an emptiness inside her, something lacking, a need to be fulfilled. But she couldn't identify it.

The buzzing suddenly got much louder. She thought she could feel a vibration against her cheek. Then it cut out and became a slow whirr, then died altogether.

She was sitting in the back of an old car being driven along an empty road in the middle of nowhere. The driver's white hair was combed back from his crown and ended in a ragged line above his frayed collar, exposing a band of well-scrubbed neck.

She knew he was a doctor and that he lived locally.

His head turned suddenly to the right. She followed his gaze and saw a helicopter standing in a field. The rotor blades were turning but slowly. The pilot sat motionless at the controls.

The doctor stopped the car abruptly. From the roadside a dark huddle of figures approached the car. The man who had signalled for the car to stop lowered his arm and opened the back door. Elena Ceauşescu got in first and moved along to sit next to Gabriela. Neither woman acknowledged the other's presence, prompting Gabriela to wonder whether she was actually there or dreaming. Ceauşescu climbed in next, knocking his cossack hat askew on the car roof. He looked old and harassed. The bodyguard sat in the front.

Gabriela held her breath. She was terrified but fascinated by the very proximity of these evil icons that had dominated her life.

The guard waggled his pistol in the doctor's face and told him to drive. When the car had been moving for a few minutes Ceauşescu leaned forward and said to the doctor, 'We're going to organize a resistance. Are you coming with us?' The wretched doctor was shocked but he tried to string a few words together: 'I am old. I am ill. I have children.' Then he made a big mistake and said, 'I am not a Party member.'

Ceauşescu clenched his fists until they were white, and his face became red with anger.

Later, the car broke down and the bodyguard slipped away. Ceauşescu flagged down another car and this time sat in the front seat. Gabriela sat behind the driver, and Elena next to her, behind Ceauşescu.

She wanted to kill them but elected to bide her time. Their demise seemed inevitable now. Airborne, they might have fled the country and sought refuge in Iran or China. But reduced to commandeering passing cars they no longer looked a safe bet.

Ceauşescu turned the radio on quite loud and everyone recognized the distinctive voice of the poet Mircea Dinescu. Hearing what he said, Ceauşescu slumped forward on to the dashboard and stayed there for a few seconds. Suddenly he said, 'Turn it off!'

As they came into Tîrgovişte, Ceauşescu observed their surroundings and in a melancholic voice said, 'I built them all these factories and they still don't want me.' Elena was tougher: she put a gun to the driver's head. Ceauşescu kept looking at his watch, then at the sky and back at his watch. They stopped at an agricultural institute, where the deputy director locked them in.

In captivity Ceauşescu continued to look from his watch to the sky and back again, as if he expected salvation to emerge from the greenish clouds.

Gabriela was held in a state of nervous suspension. She did not feel the passage of time, yet heard Ceauşescu pacing and his wife clucking under her breath. She saw that white stubble had appeared on his stringy throat.

She was convinced that everything she had seen had actually happened, but couldn't deny the impression that her attendance was less than real. Her physical self had not become insubstantial, yet they couldn't see her, or if they could they paid her no attention. She could feel the dull light from the window smear lightly across the left side of her face, and taste the musty air that hung around the long-undisturbed maroon curtains. Dust motes floated down through shafts of sickly light like dead cells in the eye.

Without her having been aware of any displacement, the curtains had been replaced by wooden shutters. They were pulled back to reveal the sky as green as before. The room had become narrower and longer, and the ceiling lower. The tyrant and his wife were seated on a bench and a considerable number of people had appeared, some in army uniforms; others could have been revolutionaries. Their ages were mixed, though Mr and Mrs Ceauşescu appeared to be senior to all present. One man smoked a cigarette, the end of which glowed when he drew upon it in the penumbra away from the windows. At the far end of the room were vague man-shaped shadows like headless bodies or dressmakers' dummies. Into Gabriela's head unbidden came the melody of her own 'Ceauşescu Blues'.

Questions were fired at the couple in the form of accusations. Gabriela gathered that a tribunal was in session. The charges included causing the genocide of more than 60,000 people during their twenty-four years in power; hiding more than a billion dollars in foreign banks; and ruining the national economy and heritage.

Ceauşescu argued angrily with his interrogator. 'I do not recognize this court,' he declared. 'Read the constitution.'

'We've read the constitution,' replied the interrogator. 'We know it better than you.'

Ceauşescu retorted: 'I will not answer a single question. I will answer nothing. I will sign nothing. I will not recognize this court.'

'Who authorized the shooting of the people?'

'I will not answer a single question,' Ceauşescu insisted. 'Do not interpret my silence as answers.' He stared occasionally at the ceiling and touched his wife's hands. Her face betrayed no emotion. Gabriela scarcely dared breathe in case she missed something. 'I will only answer to the working class,' he continued. 'I will tell the people. I will answer to the working class.

'The people should fight to destroy this band,' he screamed,

266

'which together with foreign powers wants to destroy the country and has carried out a coup.' He pointed a finger at the interrogator as he ranted.

'What possessed you to reduce the people to the state they are in?' asked the interrogator. 'Not even the peasants had enough wheat and had to come to Bucharest to buy bread. Why did the people have to starve?'

The man in the shadows pulled on his cigarette.

'This is a lie,' Ceauşescu said. 'Think carefully. It is a lie and proves the lack of patriotism currently in the country.'

'You destroyed the Romanian people and their economy. Such things are unheard of in the civilized world.'

'We do not intend to argue with you,' Ceauşescu said, looking at the ceiling. 'The population had everything it needed. I will answer only to the people's parliament in connection with treason and the coup and how things happened in Romanian history, and you will all answer to the people.'

Elena, who was slumped on the bench, said, 'How can you let them speak to you like that?' Referring to herself she asked him, 'Will you allow them to speak to an academician in such a way?'

'Let Elena Ceauşescu tell us,' the interrogator picked up the thread, 'about the costs of publishing her books abroad.'

Gabriela turned to watch the reaction of the woman she had begun to suspect might have been the driving force behind the tyranny.

'I gave my entire life for my people. Our people,' she stated angrily, making chopping motions with her hand like those Ceauşescu had made on the balcony when the students had started to barrack him. Then she fell into a morose attitude, staring dully in front of her. Her husband touched her leg in a poignant demonstration of support, but she didn't react.

'On the basis of the actions of the members of the Ceauşescu family,' the interrogator said, 'we condemn the two of you to death. We confiscate all your property.'

Gabriela searched for a reaction in their faces. Elena's forlorn stare didn't falter. Ceauşescu appeared calm.

'We tried to get you a lawyer. Your crimes were such that you merit the biggest penalty.'

The Redeemer of the Romanian Peoples tried to comfort his wife by patting her hand.

'You have not only deprived the people of bread, but imprisoned the Romanian spirit. You call on the people. How can you face this very people?'

Elena laughed – a sudden dry laugh like tinder catching fire.

'This laugh says all that needs to be said about you. It is unanimously decided that Ceauşescu Nicolae and Ceauşescu Elena be given the maximum sentence for genocide against the Romanian people and the destruction of the Romanian land.'

Ceauşescu spoke again, his voice almost perfectly level. 'I refuse to recognize this court.'

Elena said, 'We want to die together. We do not want mercy.'

Gabriela sat in a daze. The smoker had lit another cigarette, a dancing firefly indifferent to the solemnity of the occasion. The notes of her own composition still filtered into her head from somewhere. Chairs were pushed back, scraping on the floor. People rose. Soldiers began to lead the condemned couple outside. Elena said to one of them, 'I was like a mother to you.'

He replied, 'What sort of a mother were you, who killed our mothers?'

Gabriela joined the line of people shuffling towards the door. Her insides were churning. No one spoke any more. There was a short passage to the exit. Outside, a line of soldiers stood waiting as if the outcome of the trial had been entirely prejudged. They held rifles in their hands. The small party shuffled out of the passage and a young man led the prisoners to the barracks wall, where he instructed them to stand.

Gabriela watched them with rapt attention and tried to imagine what might be going through their minds. Would they pray for forgiveness? They were unrepentant before the people. Would they show the same contempt for wherever they went next? Or did they believe death was the end of it? Could a life spent exercising such power and amassing fortunes really end in a hail of bullets? Did the lights just go out and never come on again?

She recognized the beginnings of pity. Soon she would be pleading with the tribunal for clemency on their behalf.

In her jacket pocket was Elena's gun. Confiscated from her

during the trial, it had been carelessly left lying on a table. Gabriela had picked it up on her way out of the room, when all eyes had been on Ceauşescu and his wife.

She crossed to join the firing squad and no one attempted to stop her. She lifted her gun as the soldiers raised their rifles to their shoulders. An older man in a military uniform barked the command and the guns rattled off their fire.

Ceauşescu and Elena slumped against the wall and fell to the ground. There hadn't been time to look into their eyes and taste their fear. As she watched one of the executioners go forward to check for signs of life, she wondered whether her lust for revenge was healthy or perverse. The official reason for conducting a summary trial and concluding it with the execution of the accused would be that it was necessary to convince the Ceauşescu-loyalists to abandon their counter-revolution. Surely the real reason was the same as hers: revenge, pure and simple.

Nicolae and Elena Ceauşescu had bled the country dry, and now the country demanded their blood.

Gabriela went up to the bodies. Ceauşescu's tie was tight. How could he have faced a firing squad with such constriction around his neck? His eyes were open and the right side of his head was stained with blood that was also spattered over the stone wall.

Again she could hear 'Ceauşescu Blues', softly but as clearly as if she were playing it. Bass and drums provided the rhythm. One of the marksmen had lit a cigarette. The smoke drifted over, masking the tang of spilt blood and the acrid stench of the guns. She dropped the gun she had used by Elena Ceauşescu's body. The executioners' chatter died away to a murmur so that she could no longer distinguish words. As well as cigarettes she could smell alcohol. The music became louder and the buzz of conversation sank lower as if they were listening to her playing. She rested and there was a bass solo, after which she swapped eight-bar breaks with the drummer. Smoke from the bar curled into her nostrils while she watched the drummer. Lithe and slick, he had an urgent touch on the side drum. The veins stood out on his forearms and temples. Sweat beaded on his forehead. The almost maternal tenderness she had felt for him at first had grown into good honest desire, and what made it special was that she desired his body, and not just the rest of him.

Unexpectedly, Hašek came in for a sax solo. She and Violeta and Ian continued to play the rhythm. Out in the audience Bentinck pulled on his cigarette. It glowed like a tropical bug in the darkness. She tried to make out other faces but they were all in shadow like a collection of dummies in a back room in some forgotten city.

The Red Dress

It *looked* like Norway. But the weather was too mild.

The rock beneath Ankers's feet was strong, hard, Norwegian granite, but it was warm to the touch. The month was November – or was it December by now? But it felt like midsummer, at the equator.

The sky was overcast and threatening. The sea, on his left, was a terrifying mixture of colours: earthy greens and browns blending with gunmetal grey. There was no wind as yet though a storm looked likely – the sea, swollen as it was, appeared turbulent and dangerous. The sea and the sky seemed to be pressing against the land as if they wanted to swallow it and meet up to form a new world with one less element.

As soon as he found himself in Norway, Ankers had gone straight home to Floro. As he approached the house from a distance, he felt certain it was empty. But there was just the smallest possibility that Inger might still be there, sitting in her favourite chair watching the sea. His mood fluctuated between dread and optimism.

He wrestled with the lock on the front door and raced through the ground-floor rooms, bounding up the stairs. He saved the most likely place till last so he could still cherish a glimmer of hope as he searched. But the house was completely empty. He sat outside on the cliff edge sweating. It was little cooler in Norway than it had been two and a half thousand kilometres further south in Albania. The tide was very high, he noticed, looking down and failing to spot any of the high-tide markers he knew so well.

The Taunus wouldn't start. He got out, looked at the engine and cursed it, got back in and tried again. Nothing. He beat his fists on the steering wheel and swore at the old car. Anyone watching from the house would have seen a useless tin box rocking from side to side while the man inside threw his weight around, tiring himself out like a boy at a scrap-heap.

Some time later, because cars are like that, the Taunus started and Ankers revved the engine up as high as it would go. On the back seat was the case containing his saxophone and the painting Delvaux had given him. Every time he looked at that picture he became more convinced it held the key to a part of the mystery, past, present or future.

After two hours' heavy going in a northerly direction he pulled over and took the picture out of the case. He laid it against the steering wheel and studied it for the hundredth time. There was something not quite right about the mountains behind Inger. He thought so each time he looked at the picture. But he couldn't say what it was.

And then there was the red dress.

He thought he'd give anything to have the painter suddenly appear so he could get him to explain it. But the hills on either side were as desolate as the road ahead. He started up the car and continued his journey. It was a thousand kilometres from Floro to Narvik. Soon he was sweating. He opened all the windows and hoped the engine wouldn't overheat. He wondered if it were possible that he – or someone else – were dreaming even this episode. There were no signs of life: no people at the windows of distant cottages, no animals on the slopes, no birds hovering above the peaks. Just the louring clouds, the oppressive heat and, when it next emerged on his left, the sea which looked strangely discoloured. The road steepened; he changed down to second and accelerated.

When he switched on the radio and tried to tune it to a station, all that came out was static.

It was almost midnight when he reached Inger's parents' house. The sky was only a shade darker than before. The endless northern night was not a feature of this perverted winter. But neither was there an arrow of midnight sun. There was still more colour in the sea than in the clouds.

The house was silent.

On the road by the house – and indeed all around him – were scattered bits of rock and earth. He noticed a trail of displaced

272

material which followed the road for a short way, then veered off across a patch of grass when the road rose higher to climb a small hill. The trail seemed simply to go downhill. Bewildered, Ankers walked up to the little house and knocked on the door. As he had expected there was no reply. He tried the door and found it open. Stepping inside, he called out, 'Hello. Hello. Is anybody there?'

The house was empty, the stove cold. Beside the double bed a book lay open at page 68. He flipped the cover to see if it was something Inger might have been reading. Knut Hamsun's *Victoria*. Possible; he knew she liked Hamsun. He had once refused to read *Hunger* because he understood Hamsun had been a fascist. But that was his problem. To Inger politics had been completely irrelevant, a distraction from the important things in life, like the sea.

He bent over the sofa where they had spent their first night together. He touched it delicately, almost expecting it still to be warm. He felt nothing but he did detect the distinct smell of grilled bacon.

In the bedrooms again he checked the cupboards. Wooden coathangers hung empty apart from a few old jackets and shirts that had seen better days. The top two drawers of a handsome chest under the window were empty. The bottom two had been left untouched.

It looked like a house that had been left in a hurry.

Ankers went outside and walked to the toolshop. That too was unlocked. A hammer and chisel lay on the bench. A thin beam was jammed in the vice. A pile of shavings lay on the floor. Parts of an old Saab took up the rest of the floorspace. Ankers noticed a mug left at the far end of the bench. He walked over to it and peered inside. There was only a thin skein of mould growing over the remains of the last cup of coffee Inger's father had enjoyed in his old toolshop. They couldn't have been gone long.

Ankers decided to get some rest. If there was anyone left in Narvik they might well be in their beds at this time. He would get a clearer picture in the morning. Taking a quilt from the bed, Ankers slept on the sofa, his mind full of images of Inger sleep-walking towards the sea, not heeding his desperate cries, which soon became the screams of seagulls.

He was stunned by the silence when he woke in a slightly brighter room. The gulls had returned only to his dreams. He got to his feet and looked out of the back window at the sea. It resembled a bruise on the tender flesh of the beach. Then he noticed how little beach remained exposed. The thin strip of sand was like a snake of Inger's hair.

He looked at his watch and saw it was past 9 am. He washed and dressed and thought about taking the Hamsun book, but left it in case it encouraged the reader to come back. The car started on the second attempt. While it warmed up he had another look at the picture. A clue was definitely hidden in the mountains but he couldn't make it out. It seemed to him that the colours had changed since Delvaux had given it to him. But having come up with the idea he knew it could just as easily be his imagination. It seemed as if there were streaks of white paint where there hadn't been before, further down the gullies between the mountains. Even if it were true he didn't have the remotest idea what it could mean.

Narvik was a ghost town. No one answered his calls. When he knocked on doors he heard only hollow echoes inside. The only cars left on the streets looked like non-starters. And everywhere was littered with the debris he had first noticed outside Inger's parents' house: chunks of rock and clay, shards of slate, and even scatterings of sand. It looked like the aftermath of some moderate natural disaster.

He drove north into the mountains. He was following his instinct now. It seemed most likely the inhabitants of Narvik would have gone south, but Inger had northern blood in her. He drove until the car ran out of petrol. With calm determination he dragged the case out of the back and set off on foot. He would find Inger or die somewhere in the mountains between the sea and the sky. They seemed to want to become one as they pressed inward and threatened to swallow up the land. The sea appeared to swell each time he looked to his left. It had risen considerably; of that he was certain. The air was unnaturally still. Behind a uniform layer of cloud were rumblings and great dark shadows like continents drifting into each other. From somewhere in the mountains came a terrible creaking, groaning noise. Norway was thousands of kilometres from the nearest active fault lines. But

274

the world was changing drastically. Why shouldn't the whole of northern Europe suddenly find itself ripped away from the surface of the earth? There were no more rules to play by.

Ankers wiped sweat from his face and looked back to see how far he had climbed. His car had disappeared. The town of Narvik was a far-flung speck. He put the case down and took out the picture. In the stillness he could smell it again: salt from the sea, and the tangy, sharp smell he hadn't been able to identify before and still couldn't. It reminded him of ozone and electrical storms. Maybe that was it. The storm which appeared to be raging above the cloud layer would rend through the veil and do battle on the land. He might be struck by lightning. Anything seemed possible in the context of the painter's imagination. Or in the context of this fluctuating world which the painter had accurately foreseen.

He actually felt more powerful not knowing which it was: prophecy or creation. The ambiguity allowed him to believe he could still exert his own influence. He had to believe that, or he wouldn't be climbing the mountain. If it was a dream then it was either his own, or one in which he was granted some power over his own destiny. He hoped the dreamer – whoever it was – was a benign or indifferent god, and not a malign force.

The further north he climbed the more fervently he hoped this, because he had begun to feel like a fly working its difficult way towards the centre of a web.

From the distant gullies came terrible groans and creaks, like a giant pulling huge nails out of enormous blocks of wood. Ankers pressed on, the saxophone case by now a definite burden, but he knew he couldn't leave it behind. Each time he thought he'd reached the top of the mountain, it was only the crest of another bluff and the slope extended beyond it. The air was thick and the sea bloated. Clouds barged into each other and the mountains continued to creak and squeal periodically. Ankers was sweating and his head had begun to hurt.

When he saw a red spot in the distance to his left it didn't mean anything at first. He just kept climbing. Then his head shot round and his mouth went dry. His legs weakened so that he almost fell to his knees.

He snatched the painting from his case. The mountains rearing up behind her were the same as the ones in the picture. The sea, out of picture, was rising steadily to cut her off.

A narrow chasm separated her from Ankers. He would have to run back, covering quite some distance in as short a time as possible, then make his way towards the slopes that would, sea-level permitting, lead to Inger.

He turned back and ran downhill. The air was so heavy it resisted his headlong rush and soon he was exhausted. Still he battled on because he could see the red spot growing larger. What was she doing out there in the middle of nowhere? He started breathing in small gulps and he felt sick from apprehension.

Inger was standing on a small rise at the foot of three sharp peaks separated from each other by deep gullies. The sea was climbing towards her. If Ankers was not quick she would be cut off from him and her only escape route would be upwards. The peaks were unscalable and the glaciers that filled the gullies far too dangerous. He had to reach her and bring her back down before the sea cut them both off.

From behind Inger came a sharp crack followed by a deafening groan as if from the earth itself.

Ankers looked at the glaciers and realization dawned on him, flooding his mouth with the very real taste of fear. The painting *had* held the clue all the time: the changing colours in the gullies, the shifting streaks of white. The glaciers were on the move.

He wanted to take the picture out and examine it again but saw that he didn't need to because he was looking at it directly ahead. This was the picture exactly as Delvaux had painted it – or the world as the painter had created it.

Ankers scrambled past the point where the sea had threatened to cut Inger off from him, knowing that they might both be trapped. He glanced at the roiling sea and climbed faster, getting as close to a sprint as the steep slope would allow. Even now he didn't jettison the saxophone case, aware that it was the only possible insurance he had. He lifted his head and looked at Inger. Her eyes were wide open, staring beyond Ankers at the sea. They shone with an unnatural brightness and from twenty metres away the yellow rings around the pupils glittered like icy fire. She was fast asleep.

The glaciers moved behind her, scoring and rending the earth. They groaned like huge prehistoric creatures. The sea swirled vengefully at Ankers's back. He understood what changes the warming had wrought and had done so far sooner than all the predictions: the glaciers here were melting and scattering their debris further south; in the furthest north the ice caps were fast becoming part of the world's oceans. Amsterdam and most of central London and the Channel Tunnel would have been flooded. All this because of a few dreams, some music and a couple of paintings. But when dead men rise to their feet and walk there's no reason why the world shouldn't just stop spinning and go the other way.

The sharp, tangy smell was not ozone but human blood. The dress Inger was wearing had been white and now it was red. He was level with her and could reach out to touch her but was terrified of waking her. What terrible wounds had been sustained beneath the dress? Though asleep she was trembling. He looked into her eyes. They might have been glass for all the life he could see in them. The sea was reflected and rising all the time. He took hold of her arms which hung limply by her sides. Their softness surprised him: she had looked so much like a statue. But no life stirred within her body. Her legs below the dress were freshly cut and still bleeding. He assumed she had fallen on the rocks while sleepwalking. What he had always feared was now so close. The sea, he knew without looking down, had cut off their retreat downhill. To attempt to swim back the way he had come up would be suicide. The only hope of escape lay in reaching higher ground. But he would have to wake Inger. The clouds crashed into each other in fury at the very idea.

He looked into her eyes again. Unfathomable terrors seemed to lurk in them. Or was it just the reflection of the sea? He turned to follow her gaze. She appeared to be looking at the rocks currently a few metres short of the waterline, which had now risen alarmingly close to them. He watched the water boiling over formerly proud granite and wondered if he should just give in and wait for the sea to claim them both. His would be oblivion and maybe Inger would find the happiness that had eluded her on dry land.

But as the water lapped closer he saw an object glinting on the rocks and wondered dreamily if Inger had dropped something.

Aware of the urgent need for action to get them out of there, yet attracted like a jackdaw to this shiny prize, Ankers jumped down to a lower ledge and lay down on the rock to reach for the lost item. When his fingers entered the water he hissed in pain and withdrew his hand. The water was not hot enough to scald, but it had shocked him.

He could see the object now more clearly. It was a fishing knife with a long blade, serrated on one edge, razor-sharp the other. The sea had washed it almost clean, but a tenuous red string remained, pulled this way and that in the changing currents. As he watched, this last shred of evidence was tugged free and swallowed by the sea. The knife itself was dislodged and swung through ninety degrees. Ankers thrust his hand into the water again and his fingers danced a frantic can-can as he stretched for it. A wave was coming that would not only wash the knife out of his grasp, but might also splash over his body. He shot a glance upwards and behind at Inger – her eyes seemed to meet his squarely but with no flicker of recognition.

The wave hit him. But when he pulled his hand out of the water it was holding the knife by the handle. Whipping his head from side to side to shake some of the water away, he climbed back up to Inger's level, slipping on the suddenly wet rock and narrowly avoiding disaster. She was frozen in the same position despite the recovery of the knife. Someone had attacked her and she'd gone into shock, Ankers presumed. He slipped the knife into his back pocket and gently shook Inger's shoulders. She didn't respond. It occurred to him that her injuries might be so bad that she wouldn't be able to move even if he succeeded in waking her. He felt through the sticky dress but couldn't tell. He would have to lift the dress. Something held him back: partly it was fear at seeing terrible wounds, and partly a reluctance to expose Inger's body when she was so utterly defenceless. With trepidation he lifted the hem of the dress; it was still dripping blood.

The sea curled around their feet.

Her thighs were criss-crossed with gashes. The flesh was split open and some wounds were still bleeding; others had clotted. Ankers bent double and had to turn away. He threw up a thin stream of bile into the sea. He didn't know how she was able to keep standing. Preparing himself for the worst he lifted the dress up higher.

Behind Inger the glaciers roared.

She had sustained similar stab wounds all the way up to her waist. Some were angry red scratches, others were deep slashes. No part had been left untouched. Ankers silently promised to avenge her. He dropped the dress and reached down to open his saxophone case. He took out the instrument and slung it across his back. The painting he looked at once more and cursed before skimming it into the sea. He left the case gaping on the ground and lifted Inger off her feet. He carried her in front of him across his arms, wading carefully out of the shallows. The mingling smells of blood and salt were almost overpowering. The ground began to rise but Ankers strode forward with determination. She might be seriously wounded and unconscious, but she was alive: he had heard her heart beating.

The sea was still rising but Ankers advanced more quickly. The exquisite dangers ahead approached. Ankers was no climber and he knew that with Inger in his arms he couldn't even try. So the traditional route to the peaks was not an option; the rock face rose sheer in all three cases. The only possibility of getting to the top – where they could wait until the waters subsided or levelled off – was to mount the charging beast itself and attempt to climb the glacier.

He talked to Inger as he walked, murmuring to save his breath, telling her he would never leave her again, what had happened was his fault, he had been weak enough to be seduced by dreams. But as he said these things he kept thinking of the artist and his painting. He saw again in his mind the first image of Inger in one of Delvaux's paintings – when she had appeared to swim as a mermaid with Hašek and others into the North Sea.

'I love you, Inger. You're everything to me,' he muttered. 'You're my life. Trust me and wake up. I'll never let you down. I'll dedicate my life to you. I'll give myself to you.' He was raving and initially unaware that Inger had spoken. 'The sea won't get us, Inger. I won't let it. We'll get to the top and it will never reach us. I promise you, I won't let it.'

They were on the glacier now. Its surface was deadly slick but pitted and spotted with rocks and glacial drift, so that progress was difficult but not impossible.

'We'll get there, Inger. Keep hanging on.'

'The knife,' she whispered. This time he heard her.

'Inger! Inger! You spoke!' He was frightened he might have imagined it. He kissed her on the lips. Unlike everything else, they were cold. 'Inger. Please, speak to me.'

'The knife,' she repeated. 'Where's the knife?' She blinked several times and suddenly she was looking at him and seeing him. Life returned to her haunted eyes. 'Edvard,' she said.

His heart lifted like a balloon. 'Oh, Inger!' He hugged her and kissed her. 'Inger, what happened to you? I'm so sorry. I'll never leave you again.' He was so full of emotion he felt as if his whole body had been filled with gas and if he let go of her he would float away. His head was spinning and his breathing was fast and shallow.

'The knife, Edvard. Where is it? I didn't finish.'

He went cold as the ice beneath them. 'Inger, what are you saying? I've got the knife.'

'Give it to me, Edvard. I didn't finish.' Her eyes entreated him.

'Didn't finish what?' He didn't want to know the answer.

'Give me the knife.' She was still weak and perhaps delirious. The attack had traumatized her.

'Inger, you're going to be all right. When we can get down from here I'll find a doctor. You need cleaning up. But you'll be all right. I promise you.'

Her head fell back and her eyes rolled. His stomach leapt; he thought she was dead. But from her mouth came a low, growling wail of despair. He was made to think of the seals whose company she had always craved. Meeting his eyes once more, she asked him for the knife again.

'Somebody attacked you, Inger.' He didn't want to believe what was becoming increasingly clear.

She shook her head slowly. Just then the ice shifted beneath them. There was an enormous *craaaaack*. The shock rippled through them, jarring their bones. Everything slid a few metres and created a terrible grinding sensation. Humans were never meant to ride melting glaciers. Ankers felt panic try to snatch hold of him. Had he made another error, a fatal one this time? He had promised Inger they would be all right.

'Before it's too late,' Inger hissed. 'Give me the knife.'

'What did you do?' he asked her.

'Give me the knife! I want to go back.'

'Go back where? We will go back as soon as we can.'

'Back to the sea. I belong in the sea. Now give it to me.'

'What did you do to your legs, Inger? Tell me.' Out of the corner of his eye Ankers could see the sea rising steadily. They had to get moving again.

'They're not real, Edvard.' She was almost shouting. The clouds pressed down on the ice, smothering the two lost people. 'I want to go back where I belong.'

His mind had worked out what she was saying but didn't want to accept it. It was fantastic. He had thought he was awake but he must be dreaming again. Delvaux had given her a mermaid's tail, then taken it away again. Now she wanted it back. She did belong in the sea. Her legs were awkward, cumbersome, unwanted. Ankers felt sick to the bottom of his heart. She had tried to cut the flesh of her legs away to find the scaled, tapering tail underneath, believing that her real body was hidden beneath this human veil. Isolation had driven her insane. He felt as guilty as if he had wielded the blade himself.

'Inger,' he said. 'I love you. I'll do anything for you except help you to destroy yourself.' So saying he took the knife from his back pocket and hurled it into the frothing sea. She let out a heart-rending moan which echoed against the towering peaks above the glacier. Then she fell silent.

'Inger, we've got to move,' he urged her. She lay still on the ice. Her eyes were grey because of the colour of the sky, but the yellow rings were undimmed. They were her vitality. 'I'm going to pick you up. Please try and help me.' She didn't respond so he took her arms and placed them around his neck. She helped by holding on. His knee joints cracked like the glacier as he hoisted her.

They worked their way slowly up the potentially lethal ice slide, falling once when Ankers lost his balance. The glacier made no sudden movements of its own. The sea followed them but more slowly. They reached the top of the glacier and Ankers laid Inger down on a cluster of small rocks with great care. He looked over the lip and saw how far the monster had moved. In its wake was a trough fifty metres deep and hundreds of metres long. The sides were deeply scratched and loose boulders and dirt were scattered on the bottom. The glaciers that had melted away through Narvik must have been considerably smaller.

He sat down next to Inger and stroked her head. Her eyes were open but gave nothing away. The sea crept up the slope. He knew it wasn't going to level off and he was no Canute, despite the promises he had made to Inger. He swung the saxophone round to his chest and took off the mouthpiece shield. He was going to test the power of belief. Their lives were at stake. He knew it shouldn't work because he didn't have Hašek with him, or one of his cassettes, but just maybe, if he believed it strongly enough – if he wanted it strongly enough.

He lifted Inger so that she was lying across his lap and began to play. He imagined Hašek's music and, hearing it in his head, played with it.

Inger moaned quietly. The sky rumbled and the sea climbed towards it. Beneath them the glacier suddenly seemed to lurch.

Night in Albania

As if the world had been waiting for the song to end, when Gabriela played the last vibrato chord of 'Ceauşescu Blues' the bar erupted into noisy celebrations. There were bursts of applause, which she sensed were for more than just their performance. It was Christmas Day and the tyrant Ceauşescu was dead, and a song, after all, was just a song.

She had heard two saxophones swapping solos just before the finish and wondered if the missing tenor player had returned.

Ankers lowered his instrument, a thread of saliva stretching between lips and reed like a lifeline. The saxophone had saved their lives. He looked at Inger where she sat next to Leka. The Kosovar was offering her a drink. While her dress was still as red as it had been against the ice, the cuts on her legs were healing. He thought of Hella's little boy and the way the sooty bullet wound in his forehead had smudged and gradually disappeared. Ankers's heart swelled again at the core as he saw Inger accept a drink from Leka with a smile. Soon the core would melt the ice that locked it in. She looked tired but she was alive. He had feared that bringing her out of the nightmare of melting glaciers might have isolated her and thrown her even deeper into the gaol her mind had made of itself. She tipped her head back and swallowed the thick orange liquid.

'Merry Christmas,' Leka laughed, clapping her on the shoulder.

She grinned, first at Leka, then, turning to the stage, at Ankers. The eyes, once so cold, shone with warmth and passion and Ankers felt a small thaw begin within himself. Tears melted from the ice in his chest and sprang from his eyes. They were streaming down his face when Hašek came over to embrace him and wish him a happy Christmas. There was no need for words between them. Each knew where the other had been and what had befallen him.

Ian got up from behind his drums, sweat glistening on the planes of his face, and walked over to where Gabriela sat hunched over her Korg. When he touched her arm she looked up and smiled at him through floods of tears.

'I can't believe he's dead,' she declared with a small choke.

'It's true,' Ian said. 'And what a day for it.'

Everyone had put down their instruments. There would be no more playing for a while. Ian and Gabriela stepped down from the little stage and began threading their way between tables to the door. Ian stopped and turned round: he had forgotten his white coat, which he had shrugged off during a solo. Gabriela squeezed his bare arm. *I don't need it*, he thought and pushed open the swing door.

The hotel lobby was thronged with people celebrating, passing bottles round and singing. Outside, the square was muggy. The sky was tangerine-coloured, but it could have been dawn or dusk. The red letters PPSH glowed above the university building at the end of the boulevard. Small knots of people passed Ian and Gabriela as they walked hand in hand, and Ian realized that they all looked like Albanians. The dead things were nowhere to be seen. Clouds of Albanian cigarette smoke perfumed the air.

'I was scared I might never see you again,' Gabriela murmured as they watched the illuminated fountains in the little university square. Ian faced her and looked into her eyes. The look of invitation was unmistakable. He lived in the present now instead of clinging to the past or worrying about the future.

'I love you,' he said, aware that she might leave him within three months and he would be devastated. But also aware that she might not. It wasn't exciting not knowing – it in no way added to her appeal – but it wasn't an obstacle to committing himself, at least in the present.

She smiled at him and he saw that the tension in her eyes had disappeared. They walked past the university and the road began to climb the hill to Hoxha's tomb. Still there was no sign of the dead hordes who had colonized the city.

'Maybe it's all finished,' Ian said. The guilty had been punished in East Germany and Czechoslovakia and Romania. The world had been turned upside down for a short while, tipping the dead out of their lead-lined cots and mass graves, and then it had been righted again. 'They have returned to their graves to rest in peace.' Gabriela simply nodded and held him tighter round the waist.

At the top of the hill they turned to look at Tirana. Gabriela gasped at the sight. Ian had seen it from here before but this time it looked different. The pall of smoke and soot was still in place, but in the gathering orange twilight it shimmered with purplish and lilac hues. Red stars and other communist insignia were visible through the haze and between the trees. It was a beautiful city and Ian hoped when it fell, as it inevitably would, that it would remain unspoilt. The communists might be morally bankrupt and corrupt, but the Western developers and grasping industrialists were no better. It all came down to selfishness, greed and indifference – symptoms all of megalomania.

Behind them something stirred. They both turned and scanned the raised terrace where Hoxha lay buried. Their eyes pierced the gloom and Gabriela whispered, 'Look!' There was something moving on the actual grave, a squirming tangle of shadows.

Fear gripped their bowels and they sank to their knees. Ian had been wrong. Only the innocent could rest. Now was the time of the guilty. The old rulers who had brought such misery to countless millions – it was their turn now. Gabriela envisioned an old couple climbing from their unmarked grave, blood and soil smeared over their grey, knotted faces. Mr and Mrs Ceaușescu – how they would relish turning the terror back on the revolution, aided in their wicked work by the indestructible Securitate.

Stalin himself would appear, the deceptively friendly uncle, and avenge the destruction of his legacy in the emerging democracies.

But Hoxha would be first.

Ian edged closer, terrified but fascinated. He wanted to see. The shadows swirled around the shape lying on the grave. It was clearly a man.

'Ian. Come back,' Gabriela hissed.

He held up his hand.

Then he began to chuckle. Their imaginations had got the better of them. The exhumed corpse of Enver Hoxha was no more than Fatos, the patriotic ethnic Albanian from Prishtinë and sometime Citroën driver, tossing and turning in alcohol-soaked dreams. By the tomb were several empty raki bottles. There had been no desecration to the grave. The man had simply wanted to get to the very heart of Albania. Thwarted by an immovable tombstone, Fatos had drunk himself into a maudlin stupor. Ian and Gabriela left him and walked slowly back to the hotel.

The musicians were back on stage and playing short snatches of songs while waiting for them. The guitarist Mehdi Bajri had run to his tiny two-room flat which he shared with his mother, his wife and their two children, and returned with a traditional Albanian skirt and white cotton blouse for Inger. No one was happier than Ankers when he saw how pleased she was with the gift. She changed in the toilets and came back to the bar with a broad smile on her face. She sat with Leka, and Bentinck, who had decided to stop sulking and was pleased to find Leka as welcoming and friendly as before. Bentinck passed round a pack of Camels. Leka accepted one but Inger shook her head. On stage embracing her double bass, Violeta was amused. Gabriela settled on her bar stool and Ian ran his sticks over the different drums and cymbals. Hašek announced into the microphone that the quintet and their guests were going to do 'Night in Albania'. There was low sprinkling of laughter. It seemed appropriate as long as Europe's freak winter continued to resemble a Tunisian summer.

On the Korg piano Gabriela started quietly and built up slowly as Violeta joined her on the bass. Soon Ian was tapping out the beat on one of his splash cymbals, muting it with his free hand. Hašek listened to them and watched the audience intently.

He felt overwhelmingly benevolent. Dying and being resurrected was a tonic. In his old life he had grown used to everything. Nothing had surprised him any longer. Now everything seemed new. Even were he to watch some machine perform a repetitive action, he would become aware of the change in the light as time passed, or he would notice dust motes dancing and the effects of friction between parts of the machinery.

But the bar was full of individuals. He watched a dark woman in a halter top lift a tall glass to her lips without once taking her eyes off Ian. The glass caught a reflection and the colourless liquid shone like mercury.

At a table down in the front sat Leka, Bentinck, Inger and Mehdi Bajri. Bentinck and Mehdi Bajri were watching Violeta, but while Mehdi Bajri was obviously concentrating quite hard, Bentinck seemed detached. His eyes, usually inexpressive, were swimming with some undefined emotion. Leka's eyes were closed, but he occasionally smiled at Ian's syncopation as he pulled on the cigarettes Bentinck was feeding him. Bentinck had lit a cigarette but left it smouldering in the ashtray.

Inger's eyes were wide open and sparkling with vitality. When Ankers took a solo, two high spots of colour burned on her cheekbones. An empty glass stood before her. Hašek wished he could fill it for her.

Suddenly, at some sign from Violeta, Mehdi Bajri rose from the table and jumped up on to the stage. He took Violeta's double bass and only missed two or three beats before getting into the rhythm. Violeta took a microphone and shot a quick smile at Hašek as she began to sing about the stars that were aglow in the heavens, to guide you through the desert sand.

Hašek noticed Ian and Ankers exchange a look, as if the lyrics were especially significant to them. They had all lived an adventure, all seen miracles. It had been an extraordinary year.

As Violeta sang, so indeed did the cares of the day seem to vanish and the end of day bring release. The way she delivered the line about nights filled with peace prompted a look that was almost electric to pass between Ian and Gabriela. Bentinck, meanwhile, had rested the side of his head on the table top. He was still watching Violeta while she sang with a twist to her lip and a rosy glow in her eye. Throughout, she substituted 'Albania' for 'Tunisia'. The right number of syllables, a perfect fit. It was all so right.

When Violeta took over the string bass again and Mehdi Bajri sat down, Hašek launched into a solo.

Ankers kept hearing the line about the stars guiding you through the desert sand. To him and Ian it recalled the landscapes created by the painter through which they had been led by siren songs and nightmarish trains. The painter, Delvaux, was sitting at the back of the bar. The lenses of his glasses shone like newly minted coins. Even in the heat he wore a dark suit. Ankers didn't know if Hašek had seen him.

Ankers had heard Ian saying that the dead things had disappeared, and asking aloud if this meant the flux was straightening out. Did it mean, Ankers now wondered, that the Norwegian glaciers would freeze solid again, so allowing him and Inger to go home? Did it mean the end of the dreams and the condensation of time?

He had decided to see if it was now safe to play music with Hašek without them finding themselves transported across the continent. In the middle of Hašek's solo he played a note, long and mid-register, which was impossible to ignore. In fact, Hašek finished his phrase and came in a fifth above. Ian maintained a subtle rhythm and Gabriela played the occasional chord. Hašek and Ankers freewheeled together just like they had in the very beginning. Ankers thought of Norway and the people returning to Narvik as the glaciers settled back into place. But he couldn't even smell the sea.

They played in this way for three or four minutes and nothing happened. It was over. The laws of nature applied once more. It would take some getting used to. Ankers was puzzled by one thing: why hadn't Hašek returned to his own grave beneath the sea?

Was it that his death had been in some way less real than those of the dead things, the victims of Stalin and his heirs? It was Delvaux who had killed Hašek, painting him into a school of mermaids and failing to equip him properly with the means to survive. The North Sea had been rising as the ice caps and glaciers had started to melt.

Or did it go even deeper than that? Were the resonances inherent in his death – spreadeagled in the wave troughs – and his resurrection more significant than might first have been thought?

Was he now immortal? In Ankers's view he deserved to be, the way he played the saxophone.

'Night in Tunisia', or 'Night in Albania', was one of Hašek's great favourites because it finished with an ostinato, a continuously reiterated phrase, so that you never knew when the song would end. The phrase might be repeated five times or ten or twenty, and it could finish at any point. On many occasions he had sat in audiences predicting the end of the song, to be proved wrong every time. It always seemed to extend by one or two phrases beyond where he had guessed it would finish. The tension it created was of the most delicious kind.

Playing the song, however, he usually knew beforehand how many times they would repeat the phrase, or the musicians sensed the right point to finish and always managed to do so together. But this time felt different. Everyone was playing: he and Ankers and Gabriela played the phrase itself, a ten-note sequence, repeating it over and over again. Ian drove the rhythm relentlessly on, playing on and off the beat, and Violeta anchored the melody of the phrase. That Hašek didn't know when they would finish did not mean the quintet were not playing in sympathy. On the contrary, he had never known such togetherness in a group of musicians.

The fact was none of them wanted the song to end. Like life itself the song would go on and on as long as they had breath to play.

Coda

While the quintet were playing their ostinato Delvaux slipped unnoticed out of the bar. Carrying a light easel and several canvases, and his box of paints and brushes, he walked across Skanderbeg Square. The sky had darkened to blood orange. The trees were darkest green, like the deepest ocean trench barely penetrable by light. The letters PPSH glowed beaconlike above the university.

Climbing the hill to Hoxha's tomb, Delvaux had to keep stopping for breath. He was an old man but there were still pictures to paint, and more warning bells to sound. He created his world, but once the people he painted made mistakes and it started to go wrong, there was only so much he could do to save it. He couldn't undo the effects of decades of industrial pollution and waste and greed, just like he couldn't rewrite the tide tables to save his women from drowning. When it got too late the only changes he could make work were cosmetic, like painting tails to create mermaids.

His function, after a certain point, could only be to illuminate the future and allow people to act on the knowledge he showed them. In that way Ankers had saved Inger. Delvaux had merely provided a little help. He painted dreams, his own and other people's, and dreams sometimes turned out to be either premonitions or self-fulfilling prophecies.

He erected his easel by the side of Hoxha's tomb. The drunken man, Fatos, was still writhing in the grip of his dreams. Delvaux sat down on the edge of the grave and looked at the city below. Pinpricks of red and yellow light pierced the smoky, sooty blanket of dusk. It was very beautiful.

After a time, as Fatos dreamed, Delvaux began to paint. He painted what was in the man's head and he threw in his own images as well. Otherwise he would be nothing but a reporter.

He painted the spectre of evil rising once more out of the secret tunnels in Bucharest, and gangs of black-faced club-wielding miners attacking students while police looked on. He painted the plains of Kosovo awash with blood, as ethnic Albanians fell beneath the crushing blows of mighty Serbia. He painted terror on the faces of Jews throughout Europe as the death of communism brought right-wing filth crawling out of the sewers, raising their thick white arms in Nazi salutes. He painted a bull-necked white-haired Frenchman whipping up a terrifying tide of popular hatred and malice directed at his country's immigrants.

He painted pictures of widespread persecution of ethnic minorities as an empire broke up and nationalism became the dominant force there and all over the continent: Latvians and Lithuanians against Russians, Armenians against Azerbaijanis, Bulgarians against Turks, Romanians against Hungarians, Serbs against Albanians and Slovenes.

He painted the Eiffel Tower standing on a windswept, sun-baked desert plain. The Thames basin become Europe's biggest lake. The Netherlands reduced to a fraction of its original surface area. Malaria-carrying mosquitoes colonizing the Highlands of Scotland all the year round. Swarms of locusts darkening the skies over Mediterranean resorts. Armies of cockroaches marching on scorched cities long since abandoned.

He would finish his paintings later, adding his trademark, the wide-eyed women who walked in their sleep through the landscapes of his own dreams. And one or two jazz musicians; saxophone players. Maybe a drummer. Why not the whole quintet?

Down in the basement bar of the Hotel Tirana he knew they would still be playing. They wanted to play for ever and there was no reason to stop.

READ MORE IN PENGUIN

In every corner of the world, on every subject under the sun, Penguin represents quality and variety – the very best in publishing today.

For complete information about books available from Penguin – including Puffins, Penguin Classics and Arkana – and how to order them, write to us at the appropriate address below. Please note that for copyright reasons the selection of books varies from country to country.

In the United Kingdom: Please write to *Dept. EP, Penguin Books Ltd, Bath Road, Harmondsworth, West Drayton, Middlesex UB7 ODA*

In the United States: Please write to *Consumer Sales, Penguin USA, P.O. Box 999, Dept. 17109, Bergenfield, New Jersey 07621-0120*. VISA and MasterCard holders call 1-800-253-6476 to order Penguin titles

In Canada: Please write to *Penguin Books Canada Ltd, 10 Alcorn Avenue, Suite 300, Toronto, Ontario M4V 3B2*

In Australia: Please write to *Penguin Books Australia Ltd, P.O. Box 257, Ringwood, Victoria 3134*

In New Zealand: Please write to *Penguin Books (NZ) Ltd, Private Bag 102902, North Shore Mail Centre, Auckland 10*

In India: Please write to *Penguin Books India Pvt Ltd, 706 Eros Apartments, 56 Nehru Place, New Delhi 110 019*

In the Netherlands: Please write to *Penguin Books Netherlands bv, Postbus 3507, NL-1001 AH Amsterdam*

In Germany: Please write to *Penguin Books Deutschland GmbH, Metzlerstrasse 26, 60594 Frankfurt am Main*

In Spain: Please write to *Penguin Books S. A., Bravo Murillo 19, 1° B, 28015 Madrid*

In Italy: Please write to *Penguin Italia s.r.l., Via Felice Casati 20, I–20124 Milano*

In France: Please write to *Penguin France S. A., 17 rue Lejeune, F–31000 Toulouse*

In Japan: Please write to *Penguin Books Japan, Ishikiribashi Building, 2–5–4, Suido, Bunkyo-ku, Tokyo 112*

In Greece: Please write to *Penguin Hellas Ltd, Dimocritou 3, GR–106 71 Athens*

In South Africa: Please write to *Longman Penguin Southern Africa (Pty) Ltd, Private Bag X08, Bertsham 2013*

BY THE SAME AUTHOR

Counterparts

Gargan, a tightrope walker, repeats a ceremonial act of self-mutilation as he travels across Europe in pursuit of an elusive Yugoslavian waitress. Meanwhile in Paris, Adam, an impoverished actor, is gradually bullied out of his identity. Like the wire that divides Gargan's vision, both men's lives drift between fantasy and reality, a process at once drawing them together and tearing them apart.

'[Royle's] cool, steady prose sets a tone between Pinter and Derek Raymond. *Counterparts* is a uniquely uncompromising fugue on duality, and the ultimate state of loneliness' – Christopher Fowler in *Time Out*

'Enormously accomplished and ambitious ... marked by a high degree of formal sophistication, a strong and vividly conveyed sense of place' – Jonathan Coe in the *Guardian*

'Nicholas Royle writes at the very edge of genre, both at the cutting edge and at the border with something that is rather different ... A nightmarish feeling that one might be still dreaming, or, worse, one might really be awake, is crucial to the ambiguities of this excellent, odd first novel' – Roz Kaveney in *The Times Literary Supplement*